FIRST,
BECOME
ASHES

ALSO BY K. M. SZPARA

Docile

FIRST, BECOME ASHES

K. M. SZPARA

A TOM DOHERTY ASSOCIATES BOOK
NEW YORK

FIRST, BECOME ASHES

Copyright © 2021 by Kellan Szpara

Edited by Carl Engle-Laird

A Tordotcom Book
Published by Tom Doherty Associates
120 Broadway
New York, NY 10271

www.tor.com

Tor® is a registered trademark of Macmillan Publishing Group, LLC.

The Library of Congress has cataloged the hardcover edition as follows:

Names: Szpara, K. M., author.
Title: First, become ashes / K.M. Szpara.
Description: First edition. | New York : Tordotcom, 2021. | "A Tom Doherty
    Associates book."
Identifiers: LCCN 2021008748 (print) | LCCN 2021008749 (ebook) |
    ISBN 9781250216182 (hardcover) | ISBN 9781250216175 (ebook)
Subjects: GSAFD: Fantasy fiction.
Classification: LCC PS3619.Z68 F57 2021 (print) | LCC PS3619.Z68 (ebook) |
    DDC 813/.6—dc23
LC record available at https://lccn.loc.gov/2021008748
LC ebook record available at https://lccn.loc.gov/2021008749

ISBN 978-1-250-21632-8 (trade paperback)

Our books may be purchased in bulk for promotional,
educational, or business use. Please contact your local bookseller
or the Macmillan Corporate and Premium Sales Department
at 1-800-221-7945, extension 5442, or by email at
MacmillanSpecialMarkets@macmillan.com.

First Tordotcom Paperback Edition: 2022

Printed in the United States of America

0 9 8 7 6 5 4 3 2 1

We're going on a fucking quest!

AUTHOR'S NOTE

First, Become Ashes contains explicit sadomasochism and sexual content, as well as abuse and consent violations, including rape.

FIRST, BECOME ASHES

1

LARK / NOW

The fence that surrounds Druid Hill is ten feet tall and made from wrought iron. It encloses the 745 acres the Fellowship of the Anointed calls home. Along the east side of the hill, at the foot of the bridge, resides the only gate. In my twenty-four years, nine months, and three days, I have never known an Anointed One to pass through it. Until today. Until Kane.

I stand with him and the other Anointed. The toes of our boots overlap a red line painted across the road, exactly fifty feet inward from the gate—the fence's weakest spot. Across it, Fellows gather to see Kane off. *They're* allowed to cross the line. They have nothing to lose. My fingertips tingle, head feels light. We shouldn't even be this close. And Kane is going to cross the line, going to cross the threshold of the fence.

The backs of our hands bump. When I feel his fingers slide between mine, I grip them hard. I know it's an honor to go out into the world. We've trained our whole lives to slay the monsters that have corrupted and influenced those beyond the fence for generations. Kane for twenty-five years; I for twenty-four years, nine months, and three days. Isn't that close enough to go with him? He shouldn't be alone out there. Maybe Nova will allow it. We can be each other's strength.

"Coming through." A body bumps between ours, head turning. Deryn looks over their shoulder at Kane as they walk toward the gate, as if it were his fault. Their lips purse as they toss their

long, loose hair over their shoulders; it falls across their wool shawl
and soft, flowing dress.

I run my fingers over one of the three French braids that holds
mine back. Deryn doesn't wear their hair back—they don't need
to. Despite their insistence that we are siblings, Deryn and I
look nothing alike, not least because they are a Fellow and I'm
Anointed. They don't wear denim and long sleeves to protect their
limbs from sparring in the woods. Don't require a leather harness to carry weapons and potions. Don't spend hours every day
running around the lake, strengthening their muscles so they can
fight a literal monster.

Their days are spent mending and making clothes. Mine are
filled with training and the intimacy of the Anointed. With fire
and sweat and scholarship. With ritual and righteous discipline.

The Anointed are my real family and Nova is our leader. She
raised us—the Fellows who conceived us mean nothing. I don't
even like knowing their names. I wish Deryn had never told me.

"Don't," Kane says. "You can't let them fluster you, it—"

"—dilutes my magic, I know." I press my pierced tongue
against the roof of my mouth, comforted by the pressure of the
warm metal barbell that makes my words more powerful.

He deflates. Looks at his feet and purses his lips, as if to keep himself from saying more. I squeeze Kane's hand. His fingers are hot and
sweaty between mine; is he nervous?

"Before I go . . ." He turns to look me in the eye. His are so
dark brown, they're almost black. They shine in the moonlight,
just like his hair. I release my hold, reach up and run my hands
down its length one last time. Rest my palms flat on his chest.

I'm not sure I can say goodbye again—especially not in public.
"We did this last night." I try to blink away the tears before they
can erupt.

"I know." Kane covers my hand with his, curling his fingers
around mine. We slide naturally together, his arms circling my

back, mine his waist. We hold each other so tight, my body begins to tingle. "Just remember what I said." He kisses my hairline, the few strands that freed themselves during the day.

I was mostly asleep, but won't ever forget his words. To them, I add, "You love me—I love *you*. Don't forget that either."

Kane tips my chin up, and then his lips are on mine, strong and sure. As we kiss, all I can focus on is the soft stroke of his thumb over my cheek. When he pulls back, I feel the memory of his touch against my face, though my lips are cold and alone.

The murmur of voices surrounding us drops to whispers, then silence, as several Anointed step aside. Nova walks forward, resting her hand on the shoulders of those nearby, greeting them one by one until she stops in front of us. I need to ask her if I can go with him. I've earned her favor. Maybe she'll—

"Meadowlark." Nova places her hand on my right shoulder, and I do the same to her. We greet each other with a brief exchange of power. An openness. Vulnerability. For a moment, we both close our eyes, and I feel her energy probing mine, like fingers digging between the tight strands of my braids. "Good, very good," she says as we gaze upon each another.

I take a breath, open my mouth to ask—*please, I'm ready*—but her words outpace mine.

"I know it's not easy for you to say goodbye to Kane." She pauses, staring at me with such depth that I swear I can feel her inside my mind. "But your time draws near. Until then, you must remain disciplined."

I release my held breath. Nod. She's right; it was wrong of me to doubt her.

"You'll join him soon. In the meantime, I'd like you to mentor a pair of promising Anointed Ones. You have much insight to offer."

"Absolutely." I bow my head slightly to her, think of the opportunity she's giving me—and the compliment. Kane is moving on and so am I. "Thank you for your wisdom."

She squeezes my shoulder, looking down the long, pale ridge of her nose at me. A sudden wind lifts her waist-length hair up around her in a spindly brown web as we stand holding on to each other. Nova doesn't need to braid her hair or commit to chastity in order to discipline her magic. She is the original—the strongest of us. I shudder, overcome with warmth and love, reminded of why I believe in her. Of the person she's helped me become.

When her hand slips away, I know this is right. I'll leave when it's my time. Now, it is Kane's. Nova holds out her hand to him. He doesn't look at me or anyone else before taking it. He believes in his destiny—in all of our destinies. He's the best of us, and he can manage without me. I can wait two months and twenty-seven days.

Nova leads Kane across the red line—the closest any Anointed has ever been to the gate—through the throngs of our Fellows, those who've birthed and supported us. They gather around him, the youngest giving him flowers they picked during their Fellowship class, the eldest laying hands on his shoulder like Nova did. I crane my neck to follow him as he disappears into their mass.

An elbow jams into my side as I feel Maeve step into Kane's place. She brushes soft baby hairs from her face, the ones that never keep, even in Zadie's meticulous braiding. "What do you think it's like out there?"

On my left, Zadie squeezes up to the line. Instinctively, I look down at our feet, making sure none of us have crossed accidentally. I shiver to imagine the atonement such a transgression would require.

"Empty," Zadie says.

"Empty?" I look between the girls. They're the only other Anointed approaching their quarter centuries. The only others who feel the pressure of going out into the world. The curiosity. The nerves.

"Not literally," she says, rolling her eyes. "I can see their concrete towers and smell the black smoke of their cars as well as the rest of you. I meant in here." She slaps her hand against her breast. "Imagine living your whole life out there, unaware that your soul is being corrupted by damn monsters." She squirms as if one's passed right through her. Normally, I'd correct her for using outsider profanity, but words evade me.

The three of us watch through breaks in the crowd, catching sight of the big toothy key Nova hands Kane. Fellows obscure him as he turns toward the gate. I wish I could *see*. Over their heads, the tall gate swings open, and I hold my breath, as if a stampede of monsters will surge through the opening. That's not how it works, but that doesn't stop me from worrying.

I need to see. I shouldn't. I'm going to be in so much trouble, but suddenly the atonement feels worth it. I can handle the pain. Quickly, I slide away from Maeve and Zadie, and into the crowd. Over the line. I creep, stealthily, until I'm close. Obscured by a cluster of Elders but close enough to see Kane pull the key free from the gate and loop it around his neck on a chain. He tucks the key under his shirt, clutching it through the thin cotton. Knives line the bottom of his leather harness, its pockets similarly packed with potions. A Fellow hands him his quiver and sword, helping him fasten them to his back. Pride warms my chest and tears threaten my eyes once again.

Kane looks like the hero he was meant to be. Humanity's savior. Ours.

I am going to miss the stars out of him.

He looks over his shoulder, not managing to find my eye before Fellows surround him again. That's the last I see of him, the last time I'll see him until my quarter century, and I try not to care. I make out the towering gate swinging closed. Kane's gone. Kane's gone, and I am so, so proud of him.

The Fellows disperse—my cue to rejoin the Anointed on the safe side of the line. I weave my way through them, keeping my head down as their volume swells. While they break into groups and wander off into the night, I glimpse Deryn chatting with their friends. Every now and then, one looks over their shoulder toward the gate. The Fellows are taught what lies beyond it, but not the gruesome details. They know that monsters wait out there, but not that they look like us. They haven't heard about the other-worldly scales and ichor, the teeth like carving knives and eyes like holes drilled through wood, all hiding within fleshy suits. They'll never have to face the filth and wickedness that monsters emanate, burning like the sun. They're free to play and laugh and work, protected by Nova's wards, by Kane's sacrifice.

Zadie beelines toward me the second I cross the red line. "What the hell was that?"

I pull myself together. Remember what matters. "You shouldn't use outsider profanity."

"And you shouldn't cross the line! The gate was open. You're vulnerable."

"I know." Shame burns through my core, but I don't regret it. "I'll atone; I just had to see . . ."

Zadie sighs. "Let's go to bed." She takes Maeve's hand and turns away from the red line. From me.

Bed. The word hits me like the first hard blow of a paddle. I have to go to bed without Kane. Nova's going to assign me to an existing pair of Anointed to mentor, but not tonight, surely. I don't want to be alone, but, even more, I don't want to be with anyone else.

"I'll catch up with you," I tell the girls, knowing I can't put off sleep for the next two months and twenty-seven days. Fatigue doesn't wait for you. "I want to . . ." I realize I shouldn't finish my sentence. I already crossed the line to see Kane off. Let them assume I'm off to see Nova or grab a snack.

"Zadie and I can wait up for you," Maeve says in her soft, kind voice. "Hold a quick circle before bed, process what's happened."

"No," I say quickly and firmly. "We can address it tomorrow during morning ritual."

"Okay." Her tone is skeptical, but I can tell she only wants me to know she's there for me.

I wave as the two of them head down the path toward the commune, past the empty swimming pools and the track with its rusting exercise equipment. Before Nova bought Druid Hill, it was a public park, with tons of amenities. It even had a zoo. The only animals that remain are poultry and livestock.

I step up to the red line, not brave enough to cross it a second time, and align the toes of my boots with its edge. Kane can't be far, yet, and for my magic to reach him, I need to get as close as possible. I was wrong to think last night was enough, or that I was strong enough to continue on without him. Looking over my shoulder one more time, I raise my palm to my lips and whisper my goodbyes to Kane—even though I said we'd already done this—my confidences and *I love you.* Magic rushes out of me and into my words, pulled along the connection between us. I squeeze my eyes shut and my hand into a fist. Hold it over my head and, with a deep breath, release my words to him. Hopefully he's close enough to—

"Lark?" Nova's voice shocks my eyes open and wide. Each crunch of the leaves under her boots sends a chill through my spine. "What are you doing?"

I was supposed to let him go. "Noth—" What *am* I doing? Am I going to lie, as well? Kane's barely gone a minute and I'm struggling to discipline myself. Sneaking over the line. Lying. My body is suddenly prickling with warmth despite the cool air. I don't lie to Nova, and I never ignore her instructions. "Speaking to Kane." My eyes fall to the ground, head heavy.

"Mm-hmm." The sound rolls around in her mouth like a bite of red meat. "What did I tell you?"

I mumble my response. "To remain disciplined."

She pushes one thick finger against the bottom of my chin, until I'm looking square into her eyes. "What was that?"

"To remain disciplined," I repeat, clearly this time.

"First, you cross the red line—"

I open my mouth to object, but stop. A wasted breath.

"And now, despite knowing better, you're wasting your magic on mindspeech. Have you considered you're also wasting *Kane's* on receiving your words?"

"I hadn't thought of that." Her fingernail digs into the underside of my chin as I swallow.

Nova's face tightens, her eyes narrowing. They're blue like mine, but dark as storm clouds. "Remember who granted you power, Meadowlark. Who can take it away. You haven't worked this hard to lose it all worrying about Kane. I would not let an Anointed leave before they were ready, just because they reached their quarter century."

I shake my head, held in place by the tip of her finger. "I won't cross the line again. Or attempt to contact Kane."

"Good." Her lips flatten into a smile, age creasing the corners of her eyes. Nova drops her hand from my chin to my back, encouraging me to walk with her. "Why don't you take guard duty for a few nights?"

We stop momentarily as an orange cat dashes across the road. We're not supposed to pet them. Any that live on Druid Hill have snuck between the fence posts and may be tainted; monsters can influence all manner of creatures.

I don't hesitate to agree, not after having just broken two rules. I need to correct myself. I risked losing her grace, by which we are Anointed.

I force myself to look forward as we continue down the path. Not at the pool to our right—and definitely not at the lake on our left. I don't dare glance back at the fence, lest Nova think I'm searching for Kane. I close my eyes and listen to the footfalls of our boots against asphalt, to the distant shrieks of children who don't want to go to bed. The bleat of goats on the hills.

We stop at the entrance to the old zoo. Two metallic cranes top the smaller fence that surrounds the commune. Between them hangs a wooden sign crafted by one of our Fellows that reads HOME.

"When the time comes, you will want to be ready," Nova says. "Until then, take comfort in the other Anointed and focus on strengthening your abilities."

"I am ready." I don't mean to say it—to be so presumptuous after demonstrating my fragility. I hope the night hides the embarrassment I feel hot on my face. Why has losing Kane undone so much of me? "I mean—"

"It's okay, Lark. I understand." Her voice softens and I feel my body relax. "Someone you love has gone, a thing that's never happened before. I admit I've worried over the day you would leave each other, but I have faith in you. And you're going to make a wonderful mentor, in Kane's absence—think of the good deeds this situation has granted you." She rests her hand on my shoulder and I return the gesture. "Go, now. The fence won't patrol itself." She smiles and nudges me toward it.

"Thank you," I say, cherishing the warmth of her encouragement.

"I expect to see you for morning ritual!" she calls as I jog away.

I pass the last of my Fellows making their ways to bed. Outside the commune, it's dark. Trees twist their way up through sidewalks no longer used. A sheep chews a mouthful of grass with ambivalence as I rush past.

When the light from the commune no longer illuminates my path, I stop and reach into one of the chest pockets on my harness. From within, I draw a long plastic vial filled with a clear potion. One hand on either end, I snap it. Release the contained ingredients and shake them together, so a magical light glows from inside, brighter than the oil lanterns the Fellows keep in their quarters.

I take it with me to join the younger Anointed who keep watch along the fence at night. To the red line that borders the gate. To the place where Kane crossed over, and where I will soon. In two months and twenty-seven days.

•   •   •

I struggle through morning ritual the next day, and every day of the week that follows. Maeve shoots me a worried look when Nova asks me to stay behind, on the tenth day after Kane's departure. Two months and seventeen days.

"You're off guard duty," she says with a stern face.

I don't question her because it's not my place, but also because I feel the exhaustion in every muscle of my body. The ache around my eyes barely eases anymore when I close them.

"Yes, Nova."

"You're no good at half-strength, Meadowlark. You've trained for too long only to flag in your final days."

"Understood. My apologies." Shame grips me. This is the second time since Kane left that she's scolded me. That I've shown weakness. *Get it together, Lark.* "If you'll allow it, I'll go rest for a while and rejoin the group for skills training."

"I will. Eat first. I'll see you at training."

"Thank you." I don't look her in the eye when I leave, but I can feel her gaze penetrating me. I didn't think it would be this hard. That I would lose sleep, ignore hunger. Slip.

I hear Maeve catch up with me before I see her. "Are you okay?" she asks quietly, even though Nova can no longer hear us.

"Yes."

"You're trembling." Before I can stuff my hands into the pockets of my wool robe, she grabs them. "It's okay."

I go limp in the warmth of her grip. Squeeze my eyes shut.

"I miss him too."

My eyes fly open. "I don't miss him," I say. "Neither should you. Kane's following his path. We all are."

Maeve blinks, her long lashes only making her look more surprised. "I'm not Nova. You don't have to pretend around—"

"I'm not pretending!" I yank my hands from hers. "I'm fine. I've been foolish and weak, but I'm going to eat and rest. Nova's orders. I'll see you this evening." I hurry off before she can try to comfort me any more—I don't need it. I need to pull myself together before I lose everything.

Between meals, the food court is empty, but inside the kitchens, Fellows work to prepare lunch for the two hundred of us that will descend upon them in a couple of hours. I glimpse Deryn leaning against the service area, playing with their unbound hair, skirt swaying in the breeze as they laugh with a friend. All the Fellows have jobs that support the Fellowship and keep our commune running, so the Anointed can focus on training and ritual.

Quietly as I can without utilizing my powers, I slip inside a kitchen whose old sign is painted over. I'm old enough to remember when it still used to say POLAR BEAR PIZZA over the awning. Now, it says LUNCH.

I sidle up beside a Fellow I've known since early learning classes. We Anointed are acquainted with almost everyone in the Fellowship, but we don't really *know* them, nor they us. I can't remember her name, but we smile and greet each other with a hand on the shoulder. I don't feel the same exchange of power when I greet her as I do with Nova or the Anointed. I feel nothing.

"Would you mind if I made a sandwich, real quick?" I ask, inserting myself in their assembly line. "I haven't been feeling well lately, but my appetite's finally kicking in."

"No need." She puts aside the sandwich she was assembling and grabs two fresh slices of wheat bread. "I'll make it for you. Chicken, right?"

"That would be great. Thanks so much."

I'm watching her slice the meat when I hear Deryn's familiar, sneering voice: "What are you doing here?"

"None of your business." I don't have to justify myself to them.

"Shouldn't you be off practicing magic or something? I didn't think you hung out with us Fellows anymore. Don't cater to him, Emily." They step between us.

Emily—of course, she's Emily—freezes, knife halfway through the chicken. "Meadowlark is Anointed, Deryn."

"And?"

She falters. "If he's hungry, it—it's our job to—"

"No, it's not. If he's so big and powerful, he's strong enough to make his own sandwich or wait until mealtime like everyone else." They straighten up, an inch taller than me. Even though I see myself in their features—in light blue eyes, thin face, and harsh cheekbones—their attitude has long since tarnished any connection we might've had.

"It's okay, Emily," I say, deliberately looking past Deryn. "I'll finish up." I nod, and she leaves for another station. Deryn always pushes, always tries to cut me short. But I'm Anointed and they're not. I've forgotten myself and my station since Kane left, but no longer. "Nova told me to eat and rest." I face them. "Are you questioning her?"

Across the kitchen, knives stop banging against cutting boards, hands stop tossing potato salad. Everyone turns and waits for Deryn's response.

"I'm questioning *you,* Lark. Barking orders as if you're better than the rest of us. As if you're any more powerful than Nova allows you to be. As if you're above the rules."

"I'm bound to a higher set of rules than you, Deryn." Heat swells at my palms. My fingers tingle—itch for motion.

They laugh. "I bet."

"Fellows support the Anointed, Deryn," Emily says. "We're the lucky ones, safe inside the fence thanks to them and Nova."

"You don't wonder why they're 'Anointed' and we aren't?" Deryn grabs one of my braids and twirls it between their fingers. "Lark and I aren't different. We're siblings. Born of the same—"

"Enough." I swat their hand away. "Shouldn't you be at work with the other sewists? Go get a needle, or I'll report you to Nova for disrupting routine and obstructing her orders." I turn back to the sandwich ingredients, intent on ignoring their provocation. I am disciplined. I will not react.

Deryn grabs the front of my shirt and spins me around. Greens and poultry topple from their bread, spilling onto the ground. "Don't you dare tell me—"

I whisper a command I've long practiced, press my palms against Deryn's chest with a familiar motion, and thrust them across the kitchen. Their back thuds against the refrigerator. I stand braced with my feet apart and my palms up, maintaining my hold on them from across the room. My hands barely warm against the cool September breeze that flows through the open service windows. No one moves.

"The next time you want to try something, remember that this is easy for me." I don't smile. I want Deryn to know I'm not going to spend the next two months and seventeen days letting them test me. "I've been guarding our home from outsiders and monsters for the last ten nights. I'm exhausted and hungry, and the person I'm closest to in the world just left. So, I'm taking a sandwich. You can wait there, watch me make it, and then return to your work."

I bend two of my fingers and twist my hands, pinning them in place with the power I've already expended. What I said was only half true—I can't afford to waste more energy on them. I curl my fingers into fists as I turn back to the destroyed sandwich. Emily looks at me and then down at my shaking hands.

"Let me help you." She cleans up the scattered ingredients, sets out a clean plate, and begins from scratch.

"Thank you," I whisper, clasping my fingers together. I try to focus on her motions, on the slicing of fresh tomatoes and lettuce. On her mundane questions about mustard and mayonnaise. Not on the constant scratching sensation I feel from behind, where Deryn remains fixed.

Emily puts the sandwich, a bag of granola, and a water bottle into a reusable lunch bag and hands it to me. "All set." She looks over her shoulder at Deryn; her smile falters.

I snap my fingers, releasing Deryn. They slump, but don't fall. Wordlessly, we stare at each other. You'd think after two decades, they'd get it through their head that being birthed by the same Fellows does not make us family. And never will.

• • •

Nova said to eat and rest. I eat, I try to rest. Mostly, I lie awake surrounded by empty beds, staring at Kane's. Consider crawling into it. I slide my hand down my torso and wrap my fingers around the metal cage between my legs. Remember what it felt like when Kane locked it into place. The sensation remains with me, almost like he's here.

"Dinnertime." Zadie kicks the metal bed frame, jolting my hands from my body and my eyes wide. She pours water from a glass pitcher into a waiting basin and wets her face before taking soap to it. "Nova says to remind you you're supposed to be eating." She rinses herself off.

"I'm coming." I hop up, dunk my hands into the basin, and rub them over my face.

"You know that water's dirty, right?" Zadie asks as she towels off.

"Yeah."

"You're gross."

"The water has soap in it. It's fine."

She rolls her eyes and follows me out of our quarters—a big old round building with several stalls that used to house giraffes. They house us now, two beds in each room. We know what the animals look like from the few textbooks Nova keeps around, and the sun-bleached signs along the path. I used to imagine giraffes walking through the city outside the fence, but one night on guard duty, Zadie pointed out we'd probably see their necks sticking up over the roofs if they did.

When we arrive at dinner, Maeve is already sitting at our table. Strands of thick black hair spring out from the braid that crowns her head like a fuzzy halo. Zadie beckons to her with a flick of her fingers. Maeve juts her head forward, still holding a forkful of barbecued chicken, while Zadie licks the tips of her fingers and weaves the stray hairs back into her crown.

I turn away when Zadie kisses Maeve's forehead—bite my bottom lip, sending a sensation like magic shooting through my body. That's how memories of Kane feel.

Zadie bumps into me as she walks past, jolting me back to the spread of umbrella-covered tables and the shady gazebo where the younger Anointed eat with the Elders. They watch us with big eyes and untempered smiles as we walk past the winding food line—past Deryn—to a separate window where the Anointed are served. We have different dietary needs—more chicken than anyone should be forced to endure and a strength potion that tastes vaguely sweet.

I feel Deryn's anger radiating against my back as Emily prepares our trays with a smile, but I don't acknowledge them. We thank her and sit with Maeve. I eat while trying my hardest not to glance at Kane's empty seat. Why, in the company of two hundred Fellows, has the loss of one Anointed left me feeling so alone?

I try to kick the feeling. To match my friends' smiles as they joke around. We clean our plates, then clear our table, taking our potions to go. Maeve casually pops the top off her bottle as she walks, challenging us both without looking either of us in the eye. I look sideways at Zadie, who's grinning. I thumb open the wire swing on my own bottle and hear the clank of Zadie doing the same. We stop on the path and face one another.

We don't have to speak the stakes—we face the same challenge every night. The one who runs the slowest after chugging their potion has to lead evening ritual. Not that we don't like to, but the competition is our thing. The one pleasure we allow ourselves.

As he approached his quarter century, Kane won every single day last March—Nova was pissed we let a game override our responsibilities. She was right: leading evening ritual reinforces our authority within the Fellowship. And she made us wake up before sunrise all April to atone. We stopped playing for a while after that, too afraid to win. We drank our potions at the dinner table and divided leader duties evenly. But after a couple of months, the itch to play got to us. To push one another, to prod and tease—to *win*. Now, we each make sure to lose regularly enough to keep Nova's eyes off us. Not that we discussed it—we never did and never will. We just know.

"One," Maeve says slowly.

Zadie follows. "Two."

They both look at me, lips parted and hovering an inch above the glass rims of their bottles. Inside, small bubbles pop as the opaque potion settles.

I lick my lips. Look between them.

"Three!" I upend the bottle and gulp the thick drink down, barely swallowing as a drop leaks from the corner of my mouth and tickles my neck. I don't stop until I run out of air and my stomach roils with the sudden rush of liquid.

I gasp, wrestling with a hard stuck-in-my-throat swallow as Maeve takes off running. Zadie wipes her face with her sleeve—an amateur move—giving me a head start on her. I hear her belch behind me.

"Stars, I cannot run on a full stomach," she groans.

A full-bodied laugh slows me down. I'm not far behind Maeve. That girl is all thick muscle. Some of our Fellows underestimate her because she's quieter, but she spends her time training rather than studying.

With Ritual House in sight, I push myself, drawing on my power to enhance my speed. The trees blur alongside me, my feet barely touch the ground, and then—I trip. Zadie rushes past me as I fly through the air and land rolling across the cool grass. The girls run victoriously up the stone steps of the ritual house as I stand and brush leaves and dirt from my grass-stained jeans.

"You cheater." I smile as I join them.

"You used your powers too!" Zadie snaps before leaning against a nearby column.

"One of us didn't have to use magic to win." Maeve uncrosses her arms, her freckled face flushed from the sprint.

She places her palms flat on one of the glass panes between the house's double doors. Before Nova bought Druid Hill, when it was still a zoo and recreation center and disc golf course—whatever that is—this was some kind of mansion. I don't think anyone had lived here for years, though. Kane and I were kids when she and our teachers hauled everything outside—broken wooden tables and ripped leather chairs, dusty cardboard boxes and yellowing documents. After dark, they burned it. We followed the smell of smoke to the bonfire. They invited us to watch. Now, the mansion's a big empty building, warded so that only Nova and the Anointed can open it.

As the winner, Maeve does the honors. Under her touch, the wards dissolve. I watch her shake off a shiver before grabbing one of the doorknobs and opening the hall. Zadie and I leverage ourselves off the clean white columns and follow her inside, leaving the doors open behind us.

We take our boots off—Maeve carefully unlacing, Zadie prying them off by the heel—then tread with bare feet across overlapping rugs as we open the rest of the doors and windows. I pause in the middle of the room and breathe deep. Sunset filters through the windowpanes, warming the space. Invigorating me.

Ritual House is the heart of Druid Hill. Twenty-five years of magic resides within these walls. Morning and evening, the Anointed have conducted rituals here every day since Kane was born. I feel stronger here. More confident. Better.

We finish readying the space and, soon, the rest of the Fellowship trickles in. Without guidance, they sit in circles that grow out from the center of the room, leaving an aisle open from the center to the front door. Maeve and Zadie, as the reigning winners, stand beside the doors and greet the Fellows who enter, resting a hand on each of their shoulders in turn. The younger Anointed file in under the watchful eyes of their teachers, before taking their places in the closest circle.

It's my job to greet them. To exchange a small dose of power with each of them. The littlest ones barely register a spark, but I'm careful with the teenagers. I remember when my brain and body were still evolving so turbulently that I was powerless one day and blowing things up the next. There's a reason we don't go on our quests until our quarter century, until our magic has settled into its strength.

Nova is the last inside, and she greets each of us, Fellow and Anointed alike, as she walks up the aisle to the center of the circle. "I'm glad to see you at the helm tonight, Meadowlark." We rest our hands on each other's shoulders and I feel relief. Her confidence warms me along with her magic.

Her hands fall to her sides as she gives me space to lead. I raise mine, channeling the energy of the room through my body like a lightning rod. The Fellowship falls silent. Through the many-paneled windows, the last rays of sunlight blind me before the horizon swallows them.

I close my eyes. "Join me, Fellows and Anointed, in giving thanks to Nova for the home she has given us. For bringing each of us into safety. For sparing us from the corruptions of the world beyond the fence. For the gifts—"

Glass shatters. I gasp; my body floods with the heat of surprise. Heart pounding, I watch a metal canister roll down the empty aisle toward me.

Gray smoke erupts forth like I haven't seen since the bonfire. At first, all I can do is watch, but then the smoke reaches me—coughs burst from my body.

Another window breaks. A canister clangs and smoke fills the room as the youngest scream, their teachers attempting to calm them. Nova. I can't see her—or Maeve or Zadie or—*cough*. I double over. Drop to the ground. Smoke billows up around me, obscuring Anointed and Fellows; all I can see is their feet as they stumble blindly around Ritual House.

What is happening? Are these monsters, come for us? I crawl, my belly scraping over the floorboards as I try to find the door. Someone tumbles to the floor beside me—dark skin, braided hair. "Zadie!" She rolls over, clutching her head. Blood coats her fingers.

"Everyone down on the ground!"

"Hands on the back of your head!"

Human voices bark orders above us. No one I recognize. Strangers—FOEs? All I can see of them are heavy boots stomping past. I pick up a discarded canister, immediately dropping it with a scream as its heat sears my hands. They tremble with pain, wet and red with blood. *Zadie.* I force myself to absorb the pain, use it to power myself. "Come on." I grab her robe, and together, we crawl toward the side door. "Where's Maeve?"

"I don't—" She coughs.

"I'll find her." I nudge Zadie out the door, into the open air. "Go. Meet me at the—"

She screams as an armored figure grabs her out of my arms and drags her down the stairs. "Lark!" Zadie's voice cracks as she shouts through the smoke.

It stings my eyes. I blink furiously as tears blur my vision. "Zadie!" I can't see her. She's gone. I flatten myself against the interior wall, coughing as I pick up a discarded scarf and wrap it over my nose and mouth. Below the smoke line, Fellows struggle to escape, but black gloves drag them to their feet one by one. Shock paralyzes me. There are FOEs on Druid Hill. Inside the fence. Beyond the wards. This isn't supposed to happen in my home. We're safe here. We were.

My breaths come hard and heavy as smoke weaves its way around bare feet, boots, and screams. *Enough.* These are my people. My family. And I've trained almost twenty-five years to defeat monsters. I can handle *this.*

When someone grabs my arm, I throw my weight and bring them to the ground. I see a black-clad figure with bug-like goggles and enough padding to break their fall. They reach toward me again, with the same gloved hands that pulled Zadie away.

"Stay down!" I shout. Power rushes through me as I pin them, twisting my fingers to keep them in place.

They lunge at me, ripping through my magic. The surprise puts me on my back.

"I said—"

But they flip me over, wrenching my arms behind me. Plastic tightens around my wrists.

My magic won't come. It's failing me.

Below the smoke line, I catch Maeve's eyes before she's hoisted up out of view. All around me Fellows and Anointed are pulled to their feet and disappear. And then, the same happens to me.

"Let's go. Outside!" they bark, still holding tight.

I move with them—I can't *not*. And as we breach the doors, I feel their grip loosen. In the distance, surrounded by people in uniform—people with cropped hair and radios—stands Kane. My stomach drops. They have him.

With a final surge of power, I break the plastic ties that bind my wrists, slide my ritual knife from its holster, and thrust it into my captor's thigh. I feel hot blood on my hands, hear the FOE's distorted scream.

Kane, from beyond the wall of outsiders, rushes toward me, but FOEs stop him. A swarm of them push me to the ground. And I feel the spark inside of me flare before fading out.

2

LARK / NOW

We drive through the gate as if it means nothing. As if the fence and its wards aren't there. Nova cast them herself, when she bought this land. We maintain them for her weekly. Nova has to personally disarm the gate when we trade with outsiders for supplies. But these FOEs don't even notice them.

Fifteen minutes later, the car stops, my door opens, and a hundred lights flash against the darkened sky. An outsider guides me inside. Into a towering stone building with stale air and artificial light. Inside wait a dozen FOEs with pits for eyes and skin that shifts and writhes. I can barely look at them, blinking as I fight the sting of their presence.

I am in enemy territory, painfully aware of the two months and sixteen days remaining before my quarter century. How stupid of me to have thought I was ready to go with Kane. Kane and I needed every day of training we could get, but, more than that, we needed the magic to mature in us. Only the power of our quarter century could allow us to enter the poisonous realm of outsiders without being poisoned ourselves.

I look over my shoulder at the two FOEs guarding the doors, their unworldly bodies disguised with bulky uniforms and gear. Nova warned us about outsider weapons, crude, non-magical devices that shoot electricity and lead, and I spot the dull black metal waiting at their hips. They must've used one at Ritual House, some kind of smoke gun. I didn't win then and I won't win now. Not unless I learn more about what I'm facing.

They hand me off to someone they call a social worker, whose eyes look more like mine than a monster's. At that, at least, I am relieved. I glimpse some of my Fellows being ushered into rooms. Hear the cry of children taken from their teachers. The social worker does not let me stall. They lead me, hands still bound, down the hall. Outsiders stumble back against the walls as we pass, disappear behind closed doors. I frighten them. I should.

I walk with my head high, feeling Nova's finger under my chin, even when we stop. The door is impenetrably thick wood. The number 147 stares back at me, a shiny gold. So many rooms in such a small space. The walls close, halls narrow. The social worker flashes a card in front of a black plastic pad affixed beside the door handle. A bright green light flashes as a click sounds from within.

With a quiet snip, the outsider cuts my bonds. They push open the door for me. Tell me they'll bring a doctor to my "hotel room" tomorrow, that they'll explain everything in the morning. To-night, I should get some rest. When the outsider leaves, the door shuts between us with a metallic clang. I wait. Listen as their feet pad down the carpet, as another door opens and closes, as heavy silence falls.

I walk toward the door, run my fingers over a small, glass-covered hole at face height. My eyes still itch with irritation, but I press one against it, peering at the distorted hallway. No one's out there. Slowly, I press down on the handle, pull. The door opens and a tall FOE stares at me from the hallway. Outsider weapons line the holsters around their waist. I close the door. No matter; I can break the lock when I'm ready to leave.

I take a tentative step inside what the outsider called my hotel room. Number 147. Assuming there are at least 146 others, they can't possibly be unique. I reach a cautious arm out in the darkness.

There are no lanterns and I have no lightsticks with me. Outsiders use different methods to achieve what they can't without magic, like the key card. I inspect the sparse furniture. Obviously, I know what a bed is, though I've never seen one so tall or plush. Opposite, a wide black mirror hangs on the wall over a set of drawers. In the corner, a table and chair that looks like it's covered in wool. Beside it—a lamp.

I reach a hand up its shade and wrap my hand around cool glass. A bulb; there must be a knob to turn it—my fingers find plastic and twist. Warm light emanates throughout the corner of the room. Some of the buildings on Druid Hill still have bulbs, like Nova's office, but those are operated by a wall switch.

I don't like this space—don't feel at all at home, despite the furnishings. A hotel must house temporary living quarters; I certainly wouldn't want to spend more than one night here. The lifelessness unnerves me; I must stay vigilant. Search the room, find a way out. But my body aches from fighting and the bed calls to me. I sit on its edge. Allow myself to sink onto its mattress. Fall back on blankets so cool and soft, I'd swear they were clouds. Exhaustion consumes me. I close my eyes—only for a minute. I need my strength back. Need to recharge my body and my magic. Need to sleep . . .

The bed dips, I jerk—"I'm awake."—did I fall asleep?

"Shh, sleep." Lips press a familiar kiss against my forehead.

"Kane?" I push myself up onto my elbows. Blink against the quiet dark of the room, eyes straining until he materializes, lips pale and thin, eyes nearly black.

"It's late." He unbuckles my harness, emptied of potions and weapons. Lifts my shirt over my head, and I acquiesce, letting him pull the filthy clothes from my body. They smell like smoke. Not the kind that erupts from a dampened fire. Acrid. Like rotten eggs. "We can talk in the morning, when you have your strength back." Kane drags me down with his weight—it's not hard. My body aches like I've been running since the moment he crossed the red line. I curl my body against his and pretend we're home in our quarters. Maybe we are, maybe this is all a dream. Maybe he never left.

"What are you doing here?" I mumble, eyes closed. Already, I feel myself drifting back to sleep. "You're supposed to be . . ." *on your quest.*

.   .   .

I wake all at once. Eyes open, mind alert. I feel the blanket, the pillow, the unnatural softness of the bed, and the sensation of eyes on me. Kane lies on his side, watching me. "I didn't want to disturb you," he says, sitting up when I do. Light peeks around the edges of the curtains. Morning. "Let's clean you up. Come on." He takes my hand and stands, pausing when I don't follow. "You okay?"

"No." I feel deep grooves forming in my forehead. "Kane, what's going on?" I stand, but not to follow, only to look him in the eyes. To meet him on even ground. "Why are you here and—" I take his hands. They look so clean next to mine, soiled by work and battle.

"Please, let's wash first, and then I'll explain."

"Okay," I mutter.

Something is wrong. Kane doesn't look at me as he leads me into the hotel bathroom with its white tile floor and mirrored wall. He manipulates a lever until water shoots forth. I hook my thumbs into the waist of my underwear and slide them down my legs, while he undresses. I don't recognize his clothes: bright blue jeans, a white shirt—we would never wear white. It'd be ruined in an hour. I watch as Kane's reflection kisses my shoulder; I feel the soft press of his lips against my skin.

"Tell me." Our eyes meet in the mirror. We stand side by side, Kane in his underwear, me wearing only my chastity cage. Steam billows out from behind the flimsy shower curtain. "Tell me what happened after you left."

He doesn't. He guides me into the shower, under the hot spray, still wearing his underwear. He's pulling the elastics from his own hair, not waiting for my help. That's not how it's supposed to be done. We don't touch ourselves and we don't braid our own hair. We tend to one another, as part of the morning ritual that disciplines us and charges our magic. I realize when he pulls the clumsy, asymmetrical braid out that he did it himself—of *course* he did. Who would he ask for help, an outsider? I shiver at the thought of being that intimate with anyone who isn't Anointed.

Despite my wariness, I let him wash me. He works with a focus and deliberation that eases me and erases our surroundings. His fingers free my hair from its elastics, massage my scalp with gels that smell like oranges and mint. They wash the blood and dirt from the creases of my knuckles and under my fingernails. Gently, he soaps my cock and balls where they meet metal. The remains of Ritual House and Druid Hill wash down the shower drain and into outsider pipes. I know it's only dirt and grime, but it was home and I miss it.

When I reach for his underwear, Kane turns away to grab a cloth. He tells me to close my eyes, washes my face without letting me wash between his legs. My wariness turns to worry. Something is wrong—he's not letting me complete our ritual—but I don't speak up yet. I let him finish with me. See where this is going.

Kane shuts down the shower and steps out, grabbing two towels and handing me one. I watch him rub his own through his hair and down his body. Over the soaked black fabric of his underwear.

"Something is wrong." I don't mean to say it out loud, but the feeling is too strong, my worry has become panic. "Please."

Kane wraps a towel around his waist and walks into the bedroom. I follow, water dripping from my soaked hair onto the carpet. "Tell me what happened—tell me what the FOEs did to you."

"They didn't do anything to me," he says through gritted teeth.

"Then why won't you let me wash you, touch you? You're barely looking at me." I take hold of his shoulder, pushing some of myself into him and receiving nothing in return. Even when we're depleted, the echo remains because it is part of us. "Your magic feels wrong. Something happened. Let me help—"

"Nothing is wrong, Lark!"

His words fill the room, pushing me back, making space between us. My hands lose purchase and drop to my side. He's never shouted at me before.

Kane pushes his hands through the long, loose strands of his hair. Digs his fingers into his scalp. "For the first time in my life, I feel good. Safe. Like I have a real future."

"What do you mean?" I've never heard Kane talk like this before. My head buzzes with confusion, with a sudden lightness.

"I left Druid Hill, Lark."

"For your quest."

"No. I left long before that." He thumps a fist against his chest. "In here. After what Nova did to me—after what she arranged for the Elders to do to you . . . I snuck through the fence."

"What?" Kane telling me he snuck out is like someone claiming they went to the moon. It can't be done. No point in asking how.

"I couldn't stay any longer, Lark. I had to know what was on the other side of the fence, if it was all true. If it could be worth what she was doing to us."

My eyes widen, head seems to enter its own cloud of outsider smoke. Somewhere separate from Kane and the nonsense spilling from his mouth. A question forms on my lips, but I don't know if it's *what* or *why*. The premise is too senseless to interrogate.

"I met an outsider. I met their *dog*!" He smiles to himself as if at a fond memory. "They were kind to me."

"Even if I could believe that you got out, which isn't even—" I shake my head, bewildered. I can barely put my scattered thoughts together, much less words. "You talked to outsiders?"

"Yes . . . and they put me in touch with help."

I'm shaking my head so fast, the ground appears to shift under our feet. I won't think it. Want to keep the pieces from snapping together. I refuse. "No."

"I did this, Lark. I gave them the information—"

"You didn't." He couldn't.

"How else could I get you out? Get everyone out? Zadie and Maeve have been training almost as long as we have, and more Anointed were coming into their power every few months. I couldn't watch them go through what we did. It was my responsibility to stop—" He cuts himself off. "What Nova convinced us we needed to do to each other in order to build our magic—what she convinced us we needed to do to ourselves in the name of discipline, was . . ." A frustrated, *monstrous* growl rips through him.

I step back. Cross my arms in front of my chest to protect myself. That's not the Kane I know. A monster got him. He's been corrupted.

"I knew I was going to lose you when I decided to leave. You believe so deeply. Which means you're not going to believe what I'm about to tell you, but I have to anyway." He looks momentarily at the floor. "I still have trouble myself. Hopefully we can work through it together."

Together? I shouldn't even be in the same room with him in his current state. In the shower, he touched me. Last night, he kissed me. I was going to ask him to braid my hair, but now—"No, we can't—"

"Lark, listen." He reaches for me and again I step back. The backs of my knees hit the bed, and as I stumble, Kane grabs my upper arm. "Listen to me!"

I squeeze my eyes shut as if against a gust of wind so strong it pulls the air from my lungs. When I open them, he's crying. It feels like something is writhing under my skin where he touches me, but I let him hold on. If Kane has been corrupted by a monster, he needs me. It can't be too late. It can't.

He whispers, "None of it's real."

I don't know what he means and I don't ask. The monster must be deep inside him. I can barely look at him, *fuck*. The outsider profanity slips through my mind—probably because I'm in Kane's presence. Monsters corrupt you, make you do and say things you normally wouldn't.

But Kane goes on as if he's himself and I'm paying attention. "What we've learned about the world. That there are monsters for us to slay. That we are in any way special or Anointed. That we can do magic. Nova made it all up."

I'm not falling for this, obviously. It's bait. "She did, huh?" It's all I can manage while I sort through my thoughts, through my strategy. That Nova "made it all up" is a laughable idea; I can literally feel magic pulse in my flesh and blood. I've never been more sure anything was real in my whole life.

Kane's grip loosens. "You don't believe me."

You don't taunt a monster unless you're prepared to attack, and I don't want to hurt Kane. I want to save him, so I lull him. "No, I do. I'm just processing." I rub my hand across his shoulder like I'm petting one of the sheep. Nice, but devoid of human connection.

He steps back, still skeptical but otherwise calm. With him placated, I need to think. Need a plan. If a monster's gotten to Kane, then I can still save him just like I would the outsiders— after all, that's the whole point of our quests, to save humanity from the grip of corruption. That's what I need to do. Go on my quest. Start slaying monsters until Kane is free.

I'll have to get out of here. I take stock of the hotel room, placing its now-rumpled bed and woolen chair. Windows, door, bathroom . . . which is my best escape? Ideally, I'd find Zadie and Maeve, but which room are they in? This place is a maze.

Kane glances at a clock on the small table beside the bed. "I want to introduce you to Agent Miller. She helped me, and I know she can help you understand too. She works for the Federal Bureau of Investigation. F-B-I, they call it."

More like F-O-E. Stars, I cannot believe he's been speaking with one of them. On purpose! "Sounds good," I say, forcing myself to nod and look him in the eye. To stop myself from scanning the room.

We dress to the sounds of drawers sliding open and closed, hangers clanging and wet towels slapping against tile. The clothes we wear are not our own. They barely fit us. Kane has returned to the blue jeans and shirt he came in, but my clothes weren't where Kane discarded them last night, and all I could find was some kind of loungewear. Soft stretchy pants and matching sweatshirt that I pull over a plain white tee shirt. As I stuff my feet back into my boots, the disconnect hits me. These are not the clothes of a hunter. Not made to withstand journeying or battle—not even the weather. They're for someone content to get comfortable amidst monsters.

Kane nods at the door and holds out his hand to me. Oh. He wants to go now. This is my way out. I'll play along. If Miller trusts him, then she'll underestimate me. I take his hand. When he squeezes mine, I return the gesture. The affection sours my stomach. I fight not to grimace, to keep my lips relaxed.

He knocks on the door and the FOE guarding the hallway opens it. They're going to let me walk right out of here, under his supervision. My heart throbs in my chest as I follow. As he pulls the door open and leads me into the hallway.

Even though we're on the first floor, the way this space is enclosed—how insulated and winding the inside of this "hotel" is—reminds me of the belly of a beast. Our footsteps fall softly against the thick carpet. Muted voices, sniffles, and weeping bleed from behind closed doors. I'd reach out to Zadie and Maeve with mindspeech, but Kane is so close, surely he'd hear and then my plan would be ruined.

Light brightens the end of the hallway where it opens into a communal space with chairs and end tables and a FOE whose uniform reads FBI. Beyond them, an even bigger space, illuminated by sunlight through wide windows. A door. I can take one FOE. *And Kane,* I remind myself. Could I fight him if I needed to? Yes. For his own good.

"I'm going to see if she's available," he says, eyes landing on a door marked CONFERENCE ROOM A.

I nod and loosen my grip on him. Kane knocks, pressing his ear to the wood and waiting for an answer. When he doesn't get one, he grips the handle. Presses down and pushes open.

Now. Now's my best chance, while he's distracted. My hand slips easily from his grip while he leans through the open door. Walk calmly. With determination, I move toward the door, feel the warmth of a sun-filled space and the FOE's eyes on my body. I don't look at them. Don't look. Almost past.

They step in front of me with a firm "Stop. You're not authorized to—"

I feel calm—feel the last of my power welling up inside me. With a flick of my wrist, I slam the FOE at the wall, like I did Deryn. But maintaining the connection exhausts me. I'm not on Druid Hill anymore. Don't have the resources to discipline myself or recharge my magic. I relinquish my hold and break into a run. The sunlight barely touches my skin before a shock buries itself in my back and seizes my entire body. I feel the scream in my throat, but it sounds distant, feels like I am outside myself. As I lose control of my body and fall stiffly to the ground, I wonder whether this is what the last throes of magic feels like.

3

DERYN / NOW

Footfalls pound past the door of Conference Room B. Inside, I make myself tall. Thrust my shoulders back and my chest out. Hold my head up as if I'm balancing a tray on it, as if one of the FBI agents might walk in suddenly and ask me to prove my worth. What for, I don't even know. The only information I've gathered has come from the volume and tone of conversations muted by carpets and walls. The only thing I'm sure of is that I'm out. Outside the fence. Out of the Fellowship. That sends cool relief coursing through my body—

The door jolts open.

—but doesn't reassure me that these outsiders are trustworthy. I startle, quickly readjusting my posture to hide my surprise as an outsider walks in and sits opposite me. They set a folder on the table between us, then push up their already-rolled cuffs. Run a hand through their hair. It's short, the longest strands no more than six inches slicked back.

I mimic the motion, wondering what it would feel like not to carry this weight on my neck. To work and run without my hair falling in my face. Fellows aren't allowed to bind their hair like the Anointed do. It strikes me that I might be free from those rules. That out here, Anointed and Fellow mean nothing.

"Sorry I'm late," the outsider says, "I got—"

"Do you have an elastic?" I lean forward, forgetting the effort I was putting into my stance. Suddenly, this is more important.

The outsider raises their eyebrow. "For your hair?"

"Yes," I say.

"Um." They look between me and the door. "No, but I can get you one after this."

"Thanks." I sit back in my chair, feeling the confidence flood me. This outsider took my request seriously. "What's your name?"

"Agent Miller."

"Pronouns?"

"She/her."

Nova always told us outsiders have no sense of self, that their proximity to monsters erodes their ability to know themselves like we do. But Agent Miller doesn't flinch at my questions. "Agent, is that your first name, or are you a FOE? You don't look or smell like one. I expected you to smell like rotten meat—that's what Nova always told us. But you're wearing a uniform, so you must be."

She holds up her left hand and takes a pen with her right. "Back up." Her handwriting is small and cramped. "What's a foe?"

"F-O-E," I spell. "It stands for Forces of Evil. Outsiders who work in conjunction with monsters. They wear uniforms and enforce outsider law. They're supposed to look different, wrong—I don't know how. I've never met one before you."

"Well," she says, "I assure you I am not in league with any monsters. In fact, I'm trying to take one down." She rests her pen on the table and sits more casually in her chair. "Agent isn't my first name, it's my title. I work for the FBI—the social worker explained that to you, yes?"

I nod.

"You can call me Miller. What can I call you?"

"Deryn, they/them."

A flicker of recognition crosses Miller's face, as if she's heard my name before. "Do you know your surname?"

"My what?"

"Surname, also known as a family name or last name."

"I only have one name. Do outsiders have two?"

"Sometimes they have three or four."

"Well, I only have one." I suddenly feel inadequate, lacking something I never knew I needed. Naked. Like maybe I won't have a place here either.

"That's fine." Miller picks her pen up again. "Do you know who your parents are?"

"Flora and Sky."

"Are those their legal names?"

"I don't . . ." I never knew names could be illegal. Are these the kinds of outsider laws FOEs enforce? I'm not sure I like it.

"Probably not; it's fine. A legal name is what goes on official government documents, like a state identification card, driver's license, birth certificate, et cetera."

My heart beats hot and fast in my chest, pulses in my palms and the soles of my feet. I don't have any of those. What if they send me back without them?

"Do you know how old you are?"

"Of course." I latch on to the things I know, the ways I can help. "Everyone knows how old they are. The Anointed can tell you to the damn day. I'm twenty-eight years, six months, thirteen days old."

Miller cocks her head. "Did you already go on your quest? The other Anointed I've spoken to stated they were expected to go on a quest at age twenty-five."

Goodwill curdles inside me. Does she only want my help because she thinks I'm Anointed? "You can stop interviewing me." I push my chair out and grab its arms. "I'm not Anointed. I'm a Fellow."

"You are? But I—" She presses her fist over her closed mouth, as if too stumped to speak. For a full thirty seconds, she stares at me. Rethinks me. Evaluates my worth.

Why am I leaving? Giving up, when this is a chance to prove myself. "I—"

"I'm sorry," Miller says. I let her cut me off. "I just thought—you talk about FOEs and monsters, and are one of the oldest, if not—"

"I am the oldest." It comes out an accusation. "And I know plenty. Just because I'm a Fellow doesn't mean I'm stupid."

"No, I didn't mean to imply—it's been my experience while studying the Fellowship that the Anointed are taught more about the organization's structures and beliefs than its Fellows."

She's not wrong, even though I hate to agree. To tell her the only reason I know a little more than most Fellows is because I used to be Anointed. Can I trust Miller? She works with the outsider authorities that broke up the Fellowship. They're helping. And I bet Lark isn't giving them anything.

I could be the one to help. Here, outside the fence, I could be favored . . . "Who did it?" I ask. "Before I tell you more, I need to know why we're here. Which of us talked. We live behind a fence—it's not like a Fellow walked into town and—"

"You're right," Miller says. "A Fellow didn't." She pauses, puts down her pen, and crosses her arms. The way she looks at me feels familiar. Cold and powerful. I lower my eyes before she says, "An Anointed did."

I manage not to look up—not to show the shock on my face. An Anointed. They all love Nova, and Nova monitors them. If one had gone missing, she'd know immediately . . . "Kane. Kane was on his quest." Miller doesn't have to say it. "He went to you."

"He did," she says.

It doesn't make sense; Kane pranced around with the rest of the Anointed like he owned the place. He was the first of the Anointed to go on a quest. He was partnered with Nova's number one fan, Lark. *Lark.* Does he know? My lips curl into a slow smile, remembering how he fell apart over the last ten days, wandering aimlessly like an abandoned child. Kane didn't tell Lark.

I relax, lean back into the warm leather chair. Look at Agent

Miller across the conference table with new purpose. "I was Anointed. I was the first born on Druid Hill, the first Anointed by Nova's grace, and the first to have that taken away."

Miller folds her hands together, leaning on her notepad. "I didn't know that was possible. None of my research—would you mind . . ." She waves me on with her hand, unable to finish her sentence. Rapt.

Power floods my body like I haven't felt since childhood. For a moment, I'm silent, basking in her attention. "Anything is possible for Nova. We call the chosen ones Anointed—Anointed by whom? Nova. Chosen by whom? Nova. She can and does change her mind, especially when a child's parents step out of line or question her. Mine were among Nova's earliest followers, the first to bear a child within Fellowship. So, I was Anointed and, I'll admit, it was nice." Miller blurs as I stare past her, my own past seeming to materialize right in Conference Room B.

"I don't remember my Anointing ceremony; I was an infant. I have vague memories of Kane and Lark joining me—I would only have been three or four. I was alone, and then I wasn't. It was fun having other kids in Nova's special classes, training for the magical powers she said we'd develop. But the two of them were born so close together, and those few years between us made a difference growing up. They were close friends, even at six and seven, and Nova encouraged their connection. Looking back, I should've seen it coming, but I was only ten.

"Do you know what it's like to be ten years old and told you're going to save the world some day? On a very *specific* day. On your quarter century." Miller doesn't answer, and I don't expect her to—how could she? How could anyone understand? "I carried the weight of those expectations for a decade, but never got the chance to follow through. One morning, Nova showed up at our quarters for Kane and Lark and left me behind. They attended lessons and I didn't. Neither of them said anything about it to me. They moved out that night.

"Lark stopped talking to me after that—stopped everything. Sitting with me, acknowledging me. He carried on as if we were strangers rather than siblings."

The conference room comes back into focus, and I am aware of the numbness that's settled into my limbs, making them heavy and cold. I blink. Roll my shoulders and neck. Feel the warmth of life come back to me.

"You mean siblings in a figurative way," Miller says. "Like you, Kane describes the other Anointed as family." She makes a note then looks up for confirmation.

"No, I'm being literal, but I'm sure Kane and Lark consider themselves family. Lark and I are actual siblings—have the same parents. Don't remind him of it, though, unless you're ready for a fight. The day I was forsaken, I was also forgotten. Lark only cares about his quest. About his magic and his training and Nova. He loves Kane, but he might love his status more—I'm not sure how that's going to hold up against Kane's betrayal."

Agent Miller stops writing. "You implied earlier that Nova revoked your status because your parents stepped out of line. Why, when Nova forsook you, as you called it, did she not also forsake Lark?"

I've asked myself the same question a thousand times, and the real answer is *I don't know.* I've never known what Nova saw in Lark that she didn't see in me. I don't even think he remembers I was Anointed. "I don't know the exact reason, probably won't ever. I assume forsaking one of us was enough to put the pressure on, the implication that their other child could also be. I wouldn't be surprised if Lark's status was also under threat, but he never knew."

"Lark never questioned whether the same would happen to him?"

I shake my head. "Not that I'm aware of. I've never known any-one surer of themself."

"Okay." She looks at her notepad. "I'm trying to compile a list of Fellowship members, their names, ages, relationships, jobs within the Fellowship, and designation as Fellow or Anointed. If I provide you a list of what we have so far, would you be able to confirm my information and fill in anything we're missing?"

"Sure," I say, trying to muster the power I felt only a short while ago. A struggle I've grown used to over the years. "I'll help how-ever I can."

"I appreciate that," Miller says. "Most haven't been so forth-coming. Your cooperation would go a long way to show others they can trust us."

I purse my lips. "Obviously, I've decided to trust you, since I'm here talking with you, but why should the others? As far as they—we—have been taught, you're evil."

"Do I seem evil to you?"

I shrug. "No, but I've been around longer than most and have seen how things work. I'm not your average Fellow. You're the first outsider I've had a real conversation with, but I don't know you and can't vouch for you the way I would for my Fellows. I don't think you've corrupted me—I certainly don't feel any different, but . . . if you want me to put my full trust in you, to encour-age other Fellows to do the same, it would help if you disclosed your plans. What's going to happen to the Fellows? The Anointed? Nova? Will you send us back home, or are we expected to join the outside world?" I'm not sure what I want the answer to be. Druid Hill is familiar, but there are possibilities beyond the fence.

"We're not sure yet," Miller says. "Where you end up depends on what happens to Nova."

"What do you want to happen to her?" I hold my breath. Try not to hope. For once, I could determine my own future.

"Personally, I'd like to see her behind bars." She pauses. "As for the rest of you, I'd like to see families reunited and eased into society. Children enrolled in schools, adults given job training. We have social workers on staff to help get personal documents in order and arrange for financial assistance, but, even more so, mental health professionals and other community-level organizations have reached out to help. You all are big news."

I don't know if this is the answer I wanted. I don't know what outsiders mean by financial assistance, or which of their laws Nova broke. Of course, Nova ruined my life and molded the lives of dozens of others like me, but I don't hate *everything* she represents. The Fellowship was my home, despite the limitations it placed on me. But if it's no more, then I am damn well going to make sure I have a place in the outside world. One I make for myself, that can't be taken from me.

Agent Miller slides a blank notepad toward me, along with a pen. "If you would write down those names now, with any other information you can offer, it would really help. I'll bring around what we already have momentarily."

"Absolutely," I say, picking up the pen. Staring down the blank page. Wondering whether I can fill it with enough useful information to prove my worth here.

Miller pushes her chair out. Stands, hands still resting on the table. "One more question," she says, as if she's been debating whether to ask it this whole time. "Do you recall whether Nova had any children of her own?"

"I don't think . . ." The sentence dangles from my lips. It's hard to remember. Druid Hill feels timeless, like it's always existed exactly the way it does now. Did, until recently. But it hasn't. I was Anointed, and then I wasn't. "Nova had a child and then she didn't." I say it out loud to myself, unsure whether I've imagined the memory. "I can't be sure Nova *never* gave birth on Druid Hill; she could easily have done so in secret, especially since children are raised communally from birth, never knowing their parents.

Mostly. The practice wasn't fully established during the earlier years, which is why I know Lark is my brother." Think, Deryn. "But I'd swear there was already another child—older than me. I was so young, though, I wouldn't know their name or age or whether they were Anointed. I'm not even sure they existed."

"That's okay." Agent Miller pushes her sleeves up again. When she smooths her hands through her hair, loose strands fall across her face. She looks determined. Like she's neglected herself in favor of a quest.

When she reaches for the door, I draw in a breath. Even though she's asked for my help and left me with a task, I find myself wanting to give more, be more—

"I'd like you to come with me." Miller turns to look at me, gripping the doorknob. "Back to Druid Hill. I think Nova's stashed records somewhere, and I could really use the help of someone familiar with the space. Someone who grew up there, but isn't too attached."

My chest clenches. I don't want to go back, but—

"Kane has agreed to come as well. If that matters to you."

An Anointed. I roll my eyes before remembering he's the one who betrayed Nova. Does that make a difference? He never befriended me, or any other Fellows, when we were on Druid Hill. Wasn't as rude as Lark, but never tried to be kind. We were the first two Anointed. He was the first to forsake me.

"I want to help," I say. When my confidence returns, this time, it's hot and determined. "I'll go."

4

KANE / CONFIDENTIAL

The first time I felt the rush of my own power, it was cold. December, the day after the longest night of the year, and I was hungover. Us Anointed weren't supposed to give in to the temptations of sweets or games or sex or alcohol. But it had been the longest night of the year, and the Fellows in our age group had invited us to celebrate with them—Deryn had invited Lark and me to play cards and drink.

We never really hung out with the Fellows, especially not blood relations. Nova encouraged us to forget those links—actively disavow them. Nova was our caretaker, our teacher, and our mother figure. The people who gave birth to us or who shared natal parents were not our family. They were our helpers. They supported us by keeping the Fellowship working. Cooking and crafting, farming and herding. Building, fixing, cleaning. That sort of work made them almost invisible to us.

Which is why I accepted the invitation. Lark didn't want to at first, he always followed the rules. We'd never tasted alcohol before, and he had no desire, telling me what I already knew. That it would dull our senses and inhibit the magic he believed would come because Nova told us so.

I didn't even enjoy the alcohol. The first sip burned all the way down my throat, but I refused to show it. Lark was nervous; I shouldn't have pushed him, but I wanted this for us—for us to relax and have a good time together with the Fellows. Like two people who weren't carrying the future of humanity on our shoulders.

He coughed, spitting the clear liquid onto the ground, before handing the cup to Deryn. "How do you drink that?" he asked, wiping his mouth on his sleeve. I remember a hazy feeling coming over me as the night went on—from the atmosphere or the laughter or the alcohol. From Lark's glow in the dim light of the maintenance building where Deryn swore no one ever looked.

We tasted candies that Deryn's friends made in the kitchens and snuck into their pockets. Played games with a deck of outsider cards that someone had traded for—Lark didn't even want to touch them at first. As if he could absorb corruption through them. But I convinced him to play, even though I couldn't convince him to drink. Probably for the best. I got so drunk, the Fellows had to help Lark walk me back to our quarters.

When we got there, Nova was waiting. Behind her, Zadie and Maeve stood nervously, glancing up from their feet with fear in their eyes. I was only just sixteen. Lark, a few months behind. The girls were thirteen and fourteen and, when we arrived, it looked like they'd been crying. I was instantly sober.

"I'll never disobey you again," I swore as Nova tied my hands with a long rope, tossed it over the ceiling beam, and hoisted me off my feet. "Never sneak out at night, never drink alcohol, eat candy, play games."

I didn't fight when she tied the rope off or when she cut my shirt up the back or when she gave Lark the cat o' nine tails. His hands were shaking. I noticed before he disappeared behind me. I remember trying to will them still with magic I didn't have yet. Weakness wouldn't have done either of us any good in that moment.

You can suffocate hanging by your wrists. Gravity stretches you out, making it hard for your ribs to expand—most people don't know that. I didn't. Drawing breath felt like pushing a boulder uphill. I tried to focus on them, to count, but couldn't.

"You're the oldest, Kane," Nova said. "You should know better."

The cat's metal claws bounced off my back—a hesitant swing. It didn't hurt any more than a handful of pebbles. I heard Nova say, "No, like this." The moment between her words and contact felt like a century. Like I was outside of time.

I can still go there: the swing that knocked the breath out of me. When I do, a shiver ripples through me.

The snap and sting felt like thunder and lightning fusing themselves with my skin. Shooting through my veins, down my legs, sparking between my toes and the ground. I didn't scream or cry. Both required energy I needed to breathe, and besides, our punishments were not for the Fellows to see or hear, just as our lessons weren't.

I lost count of the lashes but remember hearing Nova tell Lark to keep going. She urged him on through sobs I could only hear. I was silent. Enduring. I lost track of my breaths, lost track of everything, but remember the sudden point when I could breathe again. I remember the ache of relief in my shoulders, the lift as if someone had placed a block under my feet. When I looked down, I was still a foot off the ground. When I looked up, I realized: I was flying.

Even now, I couldn't tell you if it was real. I remember the thud of the cat against the floorboards and Nova's gasp. The tickle of blood that slid down my exposed back. Her words, "It's happening."

A lightness settled into my head, my body unsure how to handle the situation. The last thing I remember before blacking out is the sensation of ropes peeling away from my wrists, strand by strand, like a braid coming undone.

After that, pain became a part of our lives, no longer a punishment.

But, after that one stroke, Nova never laid a hand on us. She was careful like that. Once we showed signs of magic, she paired us off and gave us the tools we needed. Lark was eager to catch up, and it was only a few weeks later that his powers manifested too.

He'd poured cooking oil on his arm and lit it on fire. He was always like that—always pushing harder to improve. Devouring whatever Nova gave him. He loved his magic. I only tolerated mine.

5

LARK / NOW

"It's called a Taser." The FOE Kane called Agent Miller sets a hunk of metal on the table. It looks like a gun without a handle, but heavier. "It fires an electrical—"

"I know what it does." I try to hold my breath while I talk, but it's impossible. This whole room smells like her, like carpet mold and wood rot. I know it's coming from Miller. She's hard to look at. I've never been this close to a real live FOE; the ones that abducted me from Ritual House barely count. This one is facing me, and she is grotesque.

"I know about your crude outsider weapons," I say, so she knows exactly what I think about Tasers and guns and smoke bombs.

"Of course. Forgive me . . ." She trails off, as if waiting for me to fill in the blank.

I wince, her words grinding through my brain like metal on metal. I can't stand it—I have to stand it. This is what it means to be Anointed and go out into the world. I look down at the flimsy metal cuffs that fix my wrists to the leather chair I sit on. Agent Miller sits freely on the other side of a wooden table. I'm a threat and she knows it. No table, no cuffs, and no Taser will keep me from destroying her, her kind, and the monsters that roam this land. As soon as I escape this awful hotel, where everything feels close, false, oppressive.

"Why should I give my name to the enemy?"

"We already know your first name is Meadowlark," the FOE

says. If I focus on her words, rather than her sound, I can handle it better. It almost doesn't hurt. "Your sibling Deryn was actually helpful."

"Deryn is *not*—" I'm on my feet before I realize it, tugging at the rickety metal cuffs. Don't expend more energy than necessary, Lark. Don't give this FOE what she wants. With a deep breath, I sit. "Deryn is not my sibling. They're a Fellow. They know nothing about me or Kane or Nova."

I have to close my eyes and breathe to calm myself. Every time I inhale, I grow more used to the stench. This is how monsters get you.

Stars, I wish Kane were here. That he was himself again. I miss my partner. There is a hole inside me where he used to be, and I don't know how to fill it. Why didn't Nova prepare us for this? Or perhaps she did and I can't remember. That must be it. Nova isn't to blame, so it must be my fault. Be better, Lark. Work harder. Recall your training.

"They're adamant that you are." The FOE flips through her pad of notes. "Your parents'—"

"Nova raised me." I feel rage boiling inside me. "I don't have 'parents.'"

"—names are Flora and Sky, correct?"

Overflowing, I shout, "The Anointed are my family! You're an outsider. A FOE." The creeping feeling of disgust works its way under my skin and infuses itself into my words. "What makes you think you know me?"

Silence hangs between us like a thick fog. The FOE's eyes flash black. Her skin blanches a pale white. Veins crawl like insects beneath it. I need to get out of here.

When she finally speaks, a pink warmth returns to her flesh. "I've studied the Fellowship my whole life, Meadowlark." Her pupils return to their normal size. I don't look at her veins, fighting the urge to reach for the weapons they took from me. If I happened upon this FOE in the wild, I'd split her up the seams. "And after multiple conversations with Kane and Deryn, I'm satisfied I'm more aware of its practices than you are. I, after all, was not brainwashed by a malicious cult leader." She leans forward on her bony elbows, shoulders jutting out at unnatural angles. "Who, by the way, we have arrested, along with several Elders. I will see them locked up for good, with or without your help."

I offer my bound wrists. "And am I under arrest?"

"Not yet."

"Then release me. You're holding me against my will. According to your own laws, I'm of legal age, and I want to go." Another reason we wait until our quarter century. Outsiders have no dominion over us at that age.

"You're being held as a witness. You'll remain here until you've satisfied that obligation. If you prove you won't attack anyone, we can take off the cuffs."

"I won't speak against Nova, but I will defend myself as necessary."

"You slammed one of our agents against the wall so hard, they're being treated for a concussion."

"They blocked my way."

"You *stabbed* a member of our SWAT team."

"They were abducting me." I relax back in my chair and stare at the FOE. I will not accept blame for what these outsiders have done to me, nor help them lock up Nova. That Kane and Deryn betrayed us only proves the power of monsters. The influence of FOEs. Their corruption.

She checks her watch, then says, "If you cooperate, this process will be much easier for you. I don't want to keep you in cuffs, but I do need you to answer at least some informational questions. You can decline any you're not ready to address yet. How does that sound?"

I look between her and the door. At my hands fastened to a chair with feeble metal I should be able to break with a quick spell. All I'm able to dredge up is anger. No pain. Only an empty well where magic usually resides within me. I'm going to help outsiders the only way they can be helped. The way I was born to. By taking up my quest. By slaying one monster after another until they're all dead and the people of this land are liberated. That is what Nova raised me and the other Anointed to do.

I just need to get out of this room, out of this building, and on the road. For Kane. I need to humor this FOE so they'll release me from these cuffs.

"Fine." I relax my hands on the arms of my chair as if they're not restrained. Let the outsiders remember I can throw people out of my way with almost no effort. They don't need to know I'm depleted. That my magic feels different out here, beyond Nova's wards.

"Thank you." The FOE opens a notebook. I draw in a deep breath to remind myself of her stench. If I grow used to it, she's got me. "Were you born on Druid Hill, or did you move there?"

"I was born there." I choose not to elaborate.

"I know you can't all have been born there, since Nova's only owned the land for thirty years, according to property records, but what about the others? I'm specifically interested in those under thirty. Not the Elders." I hate how she almost looks human, sitting there, writing notes. This is how she lured Kane into complacency and corrupted him. "We don't have a birth certificates on file for the majority of the Fellowship of the Anointed."

"Did Kane tell you our name?" I try not to sit up straighter— not to appear interested.

"Yes, but we already knew; everyone in Baltimore knows about you," the FOE says. "You live on a big hill in the middle of our city. Druid Hill used to be a public park—people were outraged when the government sold it."

"We work for their own good," I say. "If you know about us, then you must know our purpose is to save humanity from the corruption of monsters."

The FOE holds her pen at the ready. "And how do you intend to do that?" Her question is a challenge, but this is sacred knowledge I studied for years to grasp. No normal person could understand it after one interview, and I'm certainly not exposing our secrets to a FOE.

Even when this FOE called Miller behaves like a human, repulsion tugs at my upper lip. "With magic. And weapons."

"Can we rewind?" she says.

I don't know what rewind means, but I play along. "Sure."

"I want to talk about your powers."

"They're real." I leave space for my assertion to sink in. "In case you plan to tell me they're not."

"Is it possible," says the FOE, leaning forward, "that Nova has only convinced you they're real?"

Her voice drips with pity I neither want nor need. This is useless—this whole conversation. Nova said outsiders wouldn't believe us. Not that we were acting in their best interests, nor that we were Anointed. She warned us about their zealots and skeptics. That I could literally work magic in front of them and they wouldn't see it. Well, I know myself and I'm not going to waste time or magical energy proving their ignorance to them. I don't care if Miller believes me, I just need her to uncuff me.

"I suppose anything's possible," I say. "But why should I believe you over what I know to be true of myself? Evidence I can not only see with my own eyes, but feel—literally feel—like a muscle burning in my body?" I can humor outsiders all they want, but they'll never understand. "I'm done. Take me back to my room—leave the cuffs on if you insist." I relax my arms.

"We'll resume tomorrow, after I've gathered more testimony from your friends." To my surprise, Miller unlocks the cuffs.

"You're to stay in your hotel room. No more escape attempts, or I will put these back on. Understand?"

The FOE's sudden cooperation doesn't fool me. When she reached to uncuff me, her arms folded in ways a human's shouldn't, eyes absent, visage jumping against the static of her pose. Unlike Kane, I will not forget. I don't want to become part of this world beyond the fence. I want to go home for another two months and however-many days—I've even lost track of time—until my quarter century. I want Nova free from their outsider prison; she is not for them to judge. I want Kane back the way he was— uncorrupted, powerful, mine—and I want my fellow Anointed, my true family, around me. We were never meant to live in isolation, separated in this land of monsters.

•   •   •

I'm alone, again. I don't know where Kane is or when he's coming back—*if* he's coming back. Don't know how I feel about that either. After our last conversation—I wince as I hear *none of it's real* again and again, even when I bury my head under the pillows on my extravagantly large bed. But I miss him. Or, at least, I miss who he was.

The back of my neck prickles. I know that sensation, but my head swells with pain—I've barely any magic to receive the spell. A voice slices through me like a shard of glass, and I cry out, clenching the pillows so tight against me, I can't breathe.

<<Lark?>>

I press my fingers against my temples as the voice comes again.

<<Lark, it's Maeve.>>

"I can hear you," I say before realizing she probably can't hear me. She's using mindspeech—that's why it hurts. My depleted body is dragging up any magic it can find. "Hold on."

There's nothing in this hotel room I can use to recharge my

magic. Usually, Kane does it. Usually we're in a safe space, with clean tools that were made for this purpose.

<<Lark, if you can hear me, say something.>>

I slide open the closet door. Looks like outsiders removed the hangers, but on the top shelf rests a plastic triangular object with a metal plate and a dangling cord, and I'd bet anything that plate gets hot.

When I plug it in, a red light shines. I hold my hand an inch from the plate to make sure it's heating up, then take off my pants. If I burn myself where the FOE Miller can see, she won't let me go, I just know it. Her whole game is a play to corrupt me. She doesn't know how far I'm willing to go to complete my quest. It's the only way any of us can really be free.

<<Lark, can you hear us? It's Zadie.>>

I grind my teeth together as their voices slice through me—if I don't recharge soon, my body will use itself up. I glance around the room one last time for anything I can bite down on, but this place is ill-equipped for practicing magic, so I grab my sweatpants and stuff as much fabric in my mouth as I can.

Hand trembling, I hold the plate against my thigh until I smell my flesh burning and then I press it against the other one. Cotton muffles my moans as the pain builds, and power with it. It's more effective if you don't rest between applications. Otherwise it's too easy to tell yourself *enough*.

I stop when Maeve and Zadie's voices no longer hurt to hear. When all the pain settles and transforms into power. I yank the cord from the wall without getting up and set the device down. My hands are red and shaking. I need to get into a cool bath, but I'm not sure I can walk to the tub. I'm not used to caring for myself afterward. That's why Kane and I have each other. Why Maeve and Zadie have each other.

This time, my power comes effortlessly when I call. <<I'm here,>> I say, with my mind and my voice, too tired to split the two.

<<Thank the stars,>> Zadie says. <<We thought we'd lost you. Have you heard from Kane?>>

<<Yeah.>> I realize, as I say it, that I'll have to tell them what he said, and that hurts almost as much as my burns. I haul myself up and into the bathroom, twisting the knobs until cold water pours into the tub. I gasp between gritted teeth as I ease out of my underwear.

<<Lark, was that you?>> Maeve asks. <<Are you okay?>>

<<I'm fine. Drained, is all. I had to hurt myself. Used up most of my power during the raid.>>

<<Damn.>>

<<Don't use their profanity,>> I say. <<Especially now that we're on the outside. We have to be disciplined.>>

<<You're right,>> she says.

I pull my shirt over my head and step into the water. It's so cold, a shiver slides up my spine, but the relief outweighs any discomfort. <<Look, I have some important stuff to tell you about Kane and—have you talked to the FOE that calls herself Agent Miller yet?>>

<<Yes,>> they both say. The silence that follows tells me their conversations didn't go well either.

<<We need to talk, but I don't want to spend any more of my power.>> Mindspeech is one of the most taxing spells and, even then, often only works between us when we're close. Usually, it feels like a link. A passive connection or quiet ping, reminding one another of our presences. I can only maintain coherent speech because Maeve and Zadie are doing most of the work.

<<I bet that social worker would let us visit,>> Maeve says.

<<You do?>> I can practically hear Zadie raise one of her thick brows. <<She works alongside the FOEs. She's trying to make us like outsiders.>>

<<I know, but at least she's kind,>> Maeve says. <<I think she

wants us to be well, according to her standards, even if that means allowing us to see each other.>>

I leverage myself back up to a sitting position. <<I'll ask.>>

<<No,>> Maeve says. <<I will. You need to conserve your strength and power.>>

I nod before remembering neither of them can see me. <<Thank you.>>

<<Thank me when you see me.>>

<<See *us,*>> Zadie says.

I smile to myself, tight-lipped and worried, as I let go of my connection to the girls. The pain of being isolated cannot be healed by cold water. And it certainly isn't magic.

6

LARK / NOW

I hear the locking mechanism beep and whir a second before the door opens and feet sound on the carpet. "Call me if you need anything," says the social worker, before the door closes again.

"Lark?" It's so nice to hear Maeve's voice in person that I don't answer right away. "Where—" She stops in the bathroom doorway and smiles when she sees me.

Zadie squeezes in beside her. "I hate this place." She crosses her arms and looks around as if it's her first time inside a bathroom. Our bathhouse wasn't this—I don't know what to call it. Decorated? Mirrors span the length of the wall. The lights are so bright, I can barely look at them. No windows to let the steam out. And all this for one person?

Not me. I don't want it.

"Same," I say, tossing aside the towel I'd wrapped around my head. Damp hair falls around my face and tickles the back of my neck. When I look at the girls, I feel shame burn against the cool wet strands. It's bad enough they heard me burning myself for magic.

Maeve beckons me out of the tub, her brown eyes soft and glossy. "Come on." She takes my hand. "I'll help you with that."

After I dress, Zadie sits facing me on one of the big beds, legs crossed. We hold hands while Maeve combs my hair, dividing it into sections.

I close my eyes. "Thank you."

Zadie shushes me. She's working too, pushing her magic

through me—an exchange of our powers to refresh mine. A part of morning ritual I used to do with Kane. It hasn't been the same doing so with the mentees I was assigned.

When Zadie finishes, I feel as scrubbed as I did after my bath. Glowing. She squeezes my hands then releases them. "Feeling better?"

"For the time being." I press my tongue against the roof of my mouth, feel the comfort of the metal barbell. It's not enough. "Kane's not one of us anymore."

I feel Maeve's hands stop, the hair still taut between her fingers. Zadie's eyes flick up to meet hers.

"I think he failed his quest. I think . . ." The words make my stomach churn. "He's corrupted."

"Oh, Lark." Maeve exhales. I feel her fingers go limp against my head.

"He told me he didn't believe." My voice is almost a whisper. "In Nova, in our quests. Monsters or magic."

"Damn." Zadie leans back on her elbows as if she can no longer hold herself up under the weight of the news. "He really is gone."

"That's why I wanted to see you two." Maeve tugs at my hair, then resumes her work. "The whole reason we leave Druid Hill is to save outsiders. We're Anointed. This is what we train for a quarter century for: to go out into the world and save people. We're not meant to live behind a fence our whole lives."

"But you're not old enough," Maeve says.

"No, but I'm close . . ." I tilt my head as she ties off one of the braids. "I wish we could talk to Nova. Ask her whether we should forget about Kane or . . ."

Zadie shakes her head. "You don't need to talk to anyone." Raps her knuckles against her breast. "You know."

She's right. I can't abandon him. He's my partner. If I slay a monster and free Kane from its influence . . . Once he's free, imagine what we could do together. I know we're supposed to quest alone when our time comes, but I always dreamed of fighting monsters *with* Kane. Travelling the wilds of the outside world, saving people, caring for each other. This isn't how I pictured it.

"I have to go on my quest. For Kane."

"You're right." Zadie sits up. "We've got to get out of here."

"Before they can 'ease us into society,'" I say, rolling my eyes. Maeve yanks at my hair. "Ow!"

"Sorry," she says, though it doesn't sound like she means it.

"Don't tell me you think we should stay here." Zadie gestures around the room. "In this *hotel,* while they put Nova on trial. They're going to make us speak against her in their courts, did you hear?"

"Yeah." A shiver runs through me as I remember the creeping, oppressive feeling from the conference room. "I couldn't stand being so close to that FOE, Agent Miller."

"Me neither! Imagine being in a room full of them." Zadie's eyes widen as she rolls onto her knees. The bed wobbles under her weight, and Maeve stops moving for a moment. "Sorry."

"I felt it too," Maeve says. "But the social worker told me they were going to split us up—give the children to their birth parents, as if that's what they need. We don't even know who our parents are! I'm worried; I don't want to leave the young Anointed. They're our responsibility while Nova is indisposed. We should be training them."

"I kill monsters," Zadie says. "I don't babysit."

I feel Maeve finish my braid with a pat on my shoulder before settling beside me. "It's not babysitting. If we don't safeguard our community, there won't *be* any Anointed to kill monsters. They'll corrupt us one by one, pin us down with social security numbers and birth certificates, houses and jobs, bank accounts"—she gestures to me—"until we're mindless outsiders like the rest of them. We have to look out for our own."

"Shit." Zadie bites her thumbnail, like she always does while she's thinking.

I wait until a moment passes. Until Zadie's spitting pieces of her fingernail onto the carpet and Maeve is glaring at her. I say, "I can't, though."

They both look at me. Zadie starts, "If I have to—"

But I cut her off. "No. You have Maeve. You have your partner, but I don't. I can't go on like this. I feel ripped in half. Jagged." I dig my nails into my thigh. "And the only way to get him back is to kill monsters, and keep killing, until I defeat the one that's corrupting him. I have to go on my quest, quarter century be damned."

Slowly, Maeve nods. "Okay." She looks at Zadie then at me. "Okay. We support you."

"Thank you." I feel my hair for the first time. Maeve's plaited a crown atop my head, like she and Zadie wear. "And thank you for this."

"How's your magic?" Zadie asks. "I don't like the thought of you powering yourself up in this room." She sneers at the walls. "We can help you with that, too, before you leave."

"Good idea," Maeve says. "Let us take care of you before we break you out of here." She throws her arm around my shoulder. Zadie launches herself forward, knocking the bunch of us over. We laugh and hold one another. Maeve kisses my forehead. She and Zadie hold hands, encircling me.

I don't tell them I'm terrified to leave. To walk among the outsiders, hunt a monster on my own. I have a feeling the outside world is much bigger and more dangerous than Nova prepared us for. But I have to undertake my quest for the world and, selfishly, for Kane. If I don't, I'm just as corrupt as the rest of them.

· · ·

We set up the ritual as best we can in the cramped room. Move the dresser in front of the door. Sit on the stained carpet, backs pressed up against the beds and the wall. Zadie finds two glasses in the bathroom, and lights a magical flame in each of them. They glow in the center of our three-person circle. I focus on the back of my shoulder, on the pain—on the burns where Maeve pressed hot metal against my flesh over and over. It takes several sessions to build up a full reservoir of magic, to nurture it, but this one is all we can manage given the circumstances. I'm grateful for their help.

We hold hands. Immediately, I feel their presence like a hug. All three of us flexing the muscle we've spent years building. This ritual will camouflage me for an hour or so, long enough to sneak out of this hotel and find my path. Get a lead on the FOEs. Figure out what in the stars I'm doing.

Kane was the first of us to leave. I was counting on him returning victorious, on his regaling us with tales of victory, on hearing his tips and strategies. I don't even know what monsters look like, except *wrong*. I imagine a bigger and worse version of a FOE, but it would've been nice to know for sure. I wish I could say goodbye, but I know I can't. He's corrupt. I'm not even sure he's Kane anymore.

I focus on Zadie and Maeve, on their energy. They're more than my fellow Anointed, they're my family, and they're strong. Several years younger than me, but together, they're a powerhouse.

It makes me wonder why Nova doesn't wait until we can quest in pairs. What's the point of encouraging us to work so closely with a partner as to become inseparable, only to separate us? Why would she—

Stars, I'm questioning Nova. I can't do that—especially not now. After so many years of her commitment to us, we owe her our commitment in her time of need.

Maeve hums. When Zadie joins her, their harmony adds vibrancy to the ritual, heightens the pull. I feel it whirling out of me: three sources of power growing until they combine. The air churns like wind around us, but I know we are the force of nature moving it. My crown of hair holds fast, though the covers fly off the beds and the curtains splay open. Sunlight burns through my eyelids and I open them to see Maeve and Zadie.

They're screaming. *I'm* screaming. Three notes that sound as a single chord—as magic. The flames flare. Behind me, glass shatters and I bow my head to shield it from the shards that rain down on us.

Voices not our own shout over our song. I hear the banging of fists on metal and metal against wood as I watch the door force open into the dresser. I see Kane's face in the crack, before the FOE Miller blots him out.

"Stand back!" she shouts.

Zadie and Maeve each grab one of my hands, and I feel the circle's energy work its way through me, changing me. When I look at my body, I see only its echo, a faint form where a person might be.

"Go!" Maeve shouts. "We'll hold them."

The three of us stand as the dresser tumbles over with a loud thud. As our connection breaks, the room begins to calm, and I know this is the only chance I'll have to leave.

With quick steps, I hop through the field of broken glass and hurtle through the empty space where the window used to be. I feel a momentary surge—two pings. One from Maeve, one from Zadie. Goodbyes.

And then, against my better judgment, I send one of my own. To Kane: <<I'm doing this for you.>>

•   •   •

I race up a street lined with cars and uniformed outsiders. I'm holding my breath. I should trust the magic, but we've never performed that ritual before, and I've never moved among outsiders and I'm alone, again. Damn, damn, *damn.*

My chest heaves with a stuttering sob. I need a plan. I wipe at

the corners of my eyes as I run. I can do this. I've trained for it.
I'm Anointed.

I time my thoughts with the pattern of my feet as they fall one
in front of the other. As outsiders jump out of my way, paper bags
swinging from their elbows. First, I'll go back to Druid Hill. See
what the FOEs left behind: weapons, books, potions. I'll need a
pack for the road. I make a mental inventory now, so I won't have to
once I'm there: water filter, a tent, a change of clothes. Once I cross
the fence, I won't have time to waste. For all I know, the FOEs are
still there. They're not stupid. If anything, I'll have to assume the
monsters they serve have enhanced their abilities.

An outsider reaches for their children, gathering them against
a glass shop window as I pass. I catch their eyes and they follow
me. Follow. Can they see me? Impossible. We only performed the
camouflage ritual minutes ago.

I slow, looking at my own arms, looking at the people fleeing
as I stop in the middle of a sidewalk. Dozens of eyes trained on
me like arrows. Do they know who I am? That my quest is to save
them? The idea of talking to them repulses me—what if it dilutes
my power? I can't spare any on the road—but it could work. If I
explained my purpose, they might listen and help.

Trusting outsiders corrupted Kane.

But I'm not Kane. He said he'd abandoned us months before
he left. My heart is on the right path. I'm strong. I approach one
of the only outsiders that isn't walking swiftly away. An outsider
with a black device strapped over their head and against their ears.

"My name is Meadowlark," I say. "Don't be afraid. I'm Anointed."

They don't even look at me.

I clench my jaw. "Which way is Druid Hill?"

Suddenly, their eyes latch onto mine, wide and blue. They
stumble back, pulling the device off their head; it rests around
their neck. "Oh shit."

I follow. "Tell me the way."

They stick their hand in a leather bag and pull out a pink plastic container. Hold it toward me like a weapon. "Get away from me. Fuck!" They back up so fast, they almost fall. Then, they run.

So much for helpful outsiders. I knew Kane's story sounded off. Nova told us outsiders wouldn't understand us and wouldn't want our help. They live their whole lives beyond the fence, soaking in corruption. Like the stench of a filthy home, they don't even notice.

"Oh my god, is that . . . ?"

"Dude, it is."

Two outsiders walk toward me. These two must be brave— must want to be saved. I meet them at the corner. "My name is Meadowlark."

"Hey, I'm Optimus Prime." The outsiders look at each other and snicker.

"And I'm Thor." Their faces contort as if trying to suppress their emotions.

I don't really care what their names are, but I suppose I'm glad they trust me enough to share. Maybe they'll actually help. "I'm from the Fellowship of the Anointed and need to find my way to Druid Hill—"

Optimus Prime snorts.

"—so I can begin my quest—"

Thor bursts into a laugh. "I can't do it, dude." They clap a hand on their friend's shoulder, barely coherent. "I mean, I can't do it, Optimus!"

"Yeah, I'll tell you where to go," Optimus Prime says. They point to a nearby street. "If you wait by that sign, the Hogwarts Express will take you to Narnia."

"That's through a closet, dumbass." They consult each other.

I try to get their attention. "What's Narnia?"

"Ride it toward the second star to the right and straight on till morning." But they keep laughing at each other, giving instructions

I don't understand, names and places I don't remember from any map.

Wait.

"God, I can't believe you really think you're a wizard." Thor looks me over, shaking their head. "Do you have a wand too?"

This is a joke—outsider humor. The heat of rage burns through my body, and I whisper against my palm. I don't need a wand to make magic. Like I threw the guard from my path at the hotel, I thrust Thor against the glass wall of a shop. Inside, people shout and disperse. How naive of me to think I could trust outsiders.

From the corner of my eye, I see Optimus Prime come at me. They rear back their bony fist and swing.

I step easily out of the way. The outsider stumbles, confused. I'm not wasting any more magic on these people. Optimus doesn't see the punch coming. I leave him stupefied on the cement. Power courses through me. Even though I barely used any, I feel more Anointed than I ever have. Surer of myself and what I must do— for Kane and the Fellowship. For everyone.

I don't care that our camouflage ritual didn't work. Let them see me. I walk past onlookers with purpose. They scatter before me like birds from the sidewalk.

A siren wails in the distance. FOEs, no doubt. I move faster, but can't seem to shake the attention I've drawn. Running only makes it worse. I hear a voice crackle from a black device on a uniformed person's belt—an outsider leaning in through the window of a white car emblazoned with BALTIMORE CITY POLICE DEPARTMENT. ". . . on the lookout for . . . dangerous . . . approximately five foot eight, long blonde hair, probably braided . . . wanted as a witness . . ." The FOE doesn't respond to the report right away, and I don't chance their speed.

I dash through the crowd, looking for a way to shake them. I don't know the city from within, but if I can find privacy, I can cast a homing spell. But the streets only thicken with outsiders the farther I get from the hotel. I'm not used to this many people, and I don't like it. Don't like how close the buildings are or that the air stinks like grease.

It becomes impossible to run. Shoulders bump into mine—outsiders dressed in bright colors and masks, carrying weapons? I see swords, shields, extravagant guns. Are these FOEs? None of their eyes are blacked out like Miller's. None of them wear uniforms, exactly, and they're all going the same place. When I realize I'm being dragged along in a current of them, it's too late to escape. Then I *do* see a FOE. A thick bald outsider whose skin ripples under their black buttoned shirt. I focus my eyes forward instead of on the holes where theirs should be.

Out—I need to get out of here, away from the push and crush. Breathe, Lark. Remember your power. You escaped Miller, you can escape this crowd.

Someone bumps into me.

"Hey, isn't that the guy they're looking for?" another says.

They draw back, exposing me. I had wanted space, but not like this. Not here, not now.

"I heard he stabbed someone."

I turn, trying to figure out who's talking, but can't.

"Does he have a knife?"

Can't keep up.

"He has a knife!"

"No," I say, bumping into someone. The FOEs are going to find me.

A scream rips through the air. The crowd surges, a hundred people running a hundred different directions. The crowd swells and rushes like a powerful wind toward open doors, and I can't go inside. It's too close, too tight, too much—

I squeeze myself through the throng of hot, sweaty bodies, gasping for air, clutching the thick oversized sweatshirt from the hotel, as if I might have to rip it off at any second. As if these clothes can no longer contain my body, my chest too small for my lungs.

Then, like a gasp of fresh air, I slip into an alley alongside the building. My body hasn't burst yet. I might even survive. Stars, what did I do wrong? I duck behind a row of tall plastic bins that smell like garbage. Rest my back against the cool brick wall and close my eyes long enough to check in with my powers, give myself a moment to relax. But not so long that I miss the outsider who followed me. They make their way down the alley toward the bins that shield me. When I bring my palm to my lips, it is not to cast a homing spell. It is to attack.

7

KANE / CONFIDENTIAL

The rod was hot, even through the damp towel I'd wrapped around it. Steam hissed through my fingers. Water dripped onto my bare feet. In front of me, Lark's naked body heaved, shining with the sweat of endurance and the summer heat.

He let his head fall back for a moment, rolled his shoulders to ease the strain of the ropes that bound them to the back of the chair. Lark groaned around the thick stick he clenched between his teeth before hauling himself back up. Bracing for the pain.

I wrapped my hand around his thigh, so close to his cock, not daring to touch it. I wanted to, but Nova's warnings lived in me, and we hadn't committed to chastity yet. Pleasure was a distraction. Pleasure dulled the senses and stunted our magic. Maybe it had stunted mine. I never became aroused during our sessions, but Lark always did. We didn't speak about it, and we never told Nova.

"Only one more." I pulled the iron rod from the fire and watched the tip glow red-orange in the moonlight. "Then, bed."

Lark nodded, his eyes half closed, and I wondered whether he would like it if I pressed the rod against his balls. I was afraid he would. Not a thing I'd do without asking anyway. Instead, I placed my left hand on the inside of his calf, massaging the tired muscle. He moaned as I leaned in and pressed my lips to his knee. I'd never done that before—never kissed him—but it felt right in the moment, and Lark didn't object. His head lolled back again as I positioned the rod near the outside of his leg.

He must have felt the heat in the moment before I pressed it against his flesh. His ragged scream escaped around the gag as I dragged the glowing metal down the side of his calf. It took all my strength not to squeeze my eyes shut—to watch my work. To take care of him.

Nova would push us as hard as she needed for results, and Lark eagerly rose to her expectations. As the eldest, it was my responsibility to care for him. Make sure we never went too far, that no one hurt him irreparably. I worried every night about his future without me. About the two months and twenty-seven days he'd spend alone on Druid Hill after I left for my quest.

I stood and tossed the rod onto a leather mat, my own hand red and damp and shaking. I pulled a wet towel from the bucket and wrung it loosely before applying it to Lark's forehead. "It's over," I whispered, untying the rope that held the stick between his teeth. I tossed it into the trees then untied his arms from the chair. His fingers wiggled as I massaged his shoulders and upper arms, easing each one gently forward into a natural position. "How're you feeling?"

"Good." Lark's chest rose and fell with a deep breath. "Powerful." The word sent a feeling of unease through me. I never felt power, only responsibility. Obligation.

The next thing I knew, lips pressed against mine, a hand on the side of my face—he was kissing me. I forgot my hang-ups, my worries, everything except the warmth of Lark's mouth and rough of his fingertips. I straddled him, sitting on his lap. He was still hard, and I took him in hand, not having a damn clue what to do.

Heat radiated from his body—blood rushing, magic swelling. Lark slid his arm down my back, gliding easily through a layer of condensation and dirt. The forest wasn't the cleanest or coolest, but there was something special about working beneath the stars. Being with him in that space.

My hand glided quickly and easily over his cock, both of us slick with sweat. When he came, I knew what he meant. That's when I first felt powerful, felt the magic in my hands that could bring him to orgasm, lips that made him moan. But as Lark softened and relaxed, I watched his cheeks turn as red as the heated rod.

I came back into my body. Remembered how little it meant what I wanted when humanity was at stake. I stood and doused the fire, sending billows of smoke and steam into the air. Lark hurriedly dressed, ignoring the burns on his legs and the come on his chest. We weren't supposed to do that. I'd crossed a line. It would be the last time.

8

CALVIN / NOW

Lilian places the crown gingerly on my head, fitting the knotted branches over the fronts of my ears. She fidgets with my wig, careful not to let strands catch on the leaves, then pats my forehead. "There you go, Daddy Greenleaf." She jumps from the hotel bed onto the carpet with a thud. A move not hotel recommended.

"You do know Greenleaf isn't a family name, right?" I adjust my crown in the mirror, face already long and tense. Lips pressed and pouty. Eyes dramatic. I was never a good stage actor—though I desperately wanted to be—but the second I'm fully dressed in a cosplay, I can't help but become that character. And Thranduil is one of my favorites: stylish, powerful, old as fuck.

Lilian flips her hair, pulling her grown-out dye-job into a bun. "You know what I meant."

"He *is* Daddy, though."

She rolls her eyes, smiling out of the corner of her mouth as she snaps her elastic in place. "You wish."

"Not really my style." I shrug, piercing the illusion of confidence. "But it's fun pretending." I dig my phone out of my pocket—always sew a pocket into your costume, even if you're wearing spandex, even if you're wearing a loincloth—and snap a selfie. "Say hi if"—I read aloud as I type—"you see me on the floor today! And don't forget, if you pledge $25 per month, you can swipe up for the naughty photos, xoxo." I add a heart gif and link to my Patreon, then post it to my Instagram stories.

"Nice," Lil says, head buried in her backpack. Not the kind of backpack you're supposed to lug podcasting equipment around in—Golden Snitches patterned across stiff white leather with matching zippers and straps—but Lilian is a committed femme. She always makes it work. "Have you seen my portable battery? The lavender one. I have the cable, but . . ."

When she doesn't finish her sentence, I look over. She's stopped searching—stopped everything, really. Across the muted television, captions appear beneath a guy who looks like an elf being led away by a SWAT team. Like Modern AU Legolas wearing jeans and a Henley. His blue eyes stare through the screen as if he can see me.

"Oh, oh, oh!" Lilian whacks my arm progressively harder until I have to fend her off. "That's one of those what's-their-names! The cult people who live on Druid Hill!"

"Of course." I blink as if the idea lightbulb is going off directly in front of my face. "The Fellowship of the Anointed." I grab the remote and unmute the television.

"—stabbed a SWAT officer," says a windswept journalist. Behind her, a crowd of con-goers in cosplay and nerdy tee shirts wave at the camera as they pass. "Authorities have advised that Meadowlark does not pose a threat to the public despite conjecture that Fellowship members are being held in a hotel downtown, near the convention center."

"Yo." She turns in a circle, hands pressed to either side of her face, looking at the various piles of equipment on the floor but not approaching any of them. "Do you think he would guest on my podcast?"

"They just said he stabbed a SWAT officer." Even though I'm the one reminding her, I can't help but watch him and wish . . .

Looking at him feels like magic. Could it be real, everything I've heard about the Fellowship? This Meadowlark looks like he could relieve an orc of its head, and he's wearing denim. Something to do with his eyes and the way he holds himself, even as an armored SWAT officer leads him handcuffed into a car.

"Do you think they can really do magic?" I hold my breath, feel my heart beat with slow intent against my chest. Dare to look at Lilian.

She's cramming a handful of escaped cables back into her bag when she says, "No." Then, "Wait." She stares at me. "Do you? You don't, right?" Her eyebrows shoot up her forehead without waiting for my answer. "You do."

"I think . . ." How the fuck do I answer this? Lilian knows more about me than anyone else in the world. She invited me to sleep on her couch when I couldn't afford to stay in the dorms, so we've had more late-night conversations than a group of middle schoolers at a sleepover. She was the first person I told *out loud* that I wanted to be a professional cosplayer. Not a career goal you share with your college advisor—or your parents, it turned out. At least my advisor didn't revoke my financial support when I told him.

Even though we lived together for almost a decade—even though we still share hotel rooms at cons, when Lilian can afford her own room thanks to being a famous podcaster and having a *Grey's Anatomy*-level hot doctor girlfriend—I've never told her just how badly I want it all to be real, whichever "all" that is. Any kind of magic, any fantasy you could name. I'm not picky, only desperate. Now that I have my own (small) apartment, I can even walk around dressed like an elf or wizard or slayer, and no one will call me weird. It's socially acceptable to dress up for other people, but not for yourself, and definitely not because your deepest desire is that the costume adhere to your body, and the illusion become reality.

So, yeah, I've watched every documentary on the Fellowship

I could find. If there's any magic in this goddamn world, that's where it would be. They claim to have it, so why not believe them?

Lilian zips her bag closed, finishing the motion as if she'd been on pause. "I'm going to leave you to finish what is clearly some deep soul-searching. I've got to go." She slings her bag over her shoulders then hikes her leggings back up over her belly with a jump. Somehow, she's managed to avoid putting holes in them with her stiletto nails—hot pink, today. "If you see this Meadow-lark dude, give him my card." With a wink, she's gone.

I stand in full cosplay while the news anchors continue to discuss the Fellowship in the background. I couldn't answer Lilian, because I'm unsure what to think of all this—what to think of myself. It scares me how badly I *do* want to meet Meadowlark and also how nervous I am to. Right now, I live in a place of hope. Where magic could be real. Where this Anointed guy could go all Edward Cullen on me and open a world of blood and monsters. I want it more than anything. I also have to pee, dammit.

·   ·   ·

It takes me half an hour to get over to the convention center, despite our hotel being a block away. It's hard to piss while wearing a brocade coat and royal mantle, hard to walk without messing up my wig or losing my crown entirely. Somehow, I manage this true hardship and find the line for registration. The first day of a con is always the worst in terms of logistics and the best in terms of energy. The power of being amidst fellow nerds. Fellow believers.

I follow the long line down the sidewalk, around the corner of the building, down *that* sidewalk, across the street to the next block, and another, until I'm regretting spending my entire morning working on this crown. I have other cosplays with me, but this one is the best. It shows too. It takes me twice as long to reach the end of the line because people keep stopping me to ask for photos, which I don't mind. A number of them recognize me from social media and, who knows, maybe I'll even gain a few Patrons.

As I make my way toward the end—I can see it, finally—the crowd grows unwieldy. People push up against my costume, their fingers catch the ends of my long blonde wig, bodies threaten to topple my crown. With a hard sigh, I hold it in place. I bet Lilian's already inside. If I'd left when she did, instead of fretting about magic, I could've snuck in with her—she has a fancier tier badge than me. Sucks that I sort of have morals.

"Whoa!" I reach out to steady myself as a wave of people crashes into me, as security tries to keep us in line, keep order. I try to move, but can't. A thick black boot presses my cape to the concrete. "Excuse me." I try to get their attention, to leverage myself free, but another wave hits as security redirects us.

I hear the rip over the shouts of a thousand shoving fans. Dammit. I give up on getting into the con for now, lifting my coat in gird-your-loins fashion, as I squeeze between people in search of a way out. The alley stinks, but I stumble into it with relief and I don't stop. Looking over my shoulder to make sure the line doesn't follow, I tiptoe down the pockmarked alleyway, past a row of bins, until I am fully alone.

I let down my costume, pulling the tangles from my wig as I search for the rip and my sewing kit. This is why I have a pocket. When I bend down to inspect the hem, movement between the huge, green, city-issued trash cans catches my eye. I see someone wearing lumpy gray sweats and brown boots. With blonde hair braided around the crown of their head and otherworldly blue eyes.

I look away, even though we've seen each other—we both know it, and I know him. It's Meadowlark, from the news. The guy who escaped the Fellowship of the Anointed. Or who was escaped from it. He looks as unhappy in this alleyway as he did being led into a SWAT car. I should say something, but my heart is caught in my throat like a chunk of food.

Armed and dangerous. I remember the anger narrowing his eyes and the hard set of his jaw. What do I have on me besides a sewing needle and thread? My cell phone, a tube of superglue? None of that's going to help, if he even wants my help. If he's really from that cult, if he's Anointed, this could be it. My wardrobe door. And it's a trash can.

I glance down the alley to make sure I haven't been followed. Back on the sidewalk, the line reorganizes itself with the help of a woman in a yellow polo shirt. Event staff. It's just Meadowlark and me in this alley. I can do this. I catch his eye again.

"Are you okay?" It seems like the right thing to ask. I don't want to scare him off. The costume probably isn't helping. I hold out a hand, palm up. Open and waiting.

Meadowlark brings his own palm to his lips. The muscles in his face move slightly, like he's talking into his hand. Like it's a walkie talkie. Is he . . . talking to someone? Just as I'm about to give up and stuff my hand back into my pocket, he takes it. Eyes trained on me, he allows me to help him to his feet. I position myself between him and the cross street to block him as much from view as I can manage. The crown helps.

"I'm fine," he says, with so much confidence, I don't believe him.

We look each other over—neither of us tries to disguise it. He studies my crown and my wig, the braids Lilian added and the metallic threads in my mantle. I, like a total creep, can't stop looking at his hands. At long slender fingers, callused. Tanned by the sun and burned by fire. They've known magic. I can feel it.

"Who are you?" Meadowlark asks, as if he might've heard of me. Of course, he grew up knowing everyone around him.

"My name's Calvin."

"Do you have pronouns?" he says, as if I'm a dunce for not offering them.

I feel my face flush. Not an hour ago, I was the Elvenking. Now I'm a kid playing dress-up. "He/him."

"Calvin." He tests my name in his mouth. "Why are you dressed like that?" Despite his question, he's still looking at my hair. Er, my wig. In this cosplay, we look eerily similar.

"For the convention," I say. And then, before I can think better of it, "Why are you dressed like *that*?" I bite my tongue until it burns. Get on his bad side, why don't you, Calvin. Ruin your only real shot at magic.

But he rolls his eyes and pushes up the sleeves on his sweatshirt. "These clothes were provided by the FOEs that held me captive. I hate them." He rests his hands on his hips. A grimace tugs at his lips. "I suppose you know who I am, since you haven't asked."

I nod.

"And you haven't run away or mocked me."

"No." Please sound cool, please sound cool. "You looked like you needed help. What kind of person would I be if I didn't offer it?"

Meadowlark purses his lips. "So far outsiders have only shown me disrespect. I anticipated rejection—you have no magic to resist the monsters."

Oh my god, he just said "monsters" and meant it. Is my mouth hanging open? Look cool!

"But I had no idea how that rejection would manifest." He glances over my shoulder at the growing line. "I do need help. If one of these FOEs catches me, they'll lock me in a hotel room and try to force me to testify against Nova. I don't know how long I'll be able to resist corruption in those circumstances." His eyes fall to the ground. When he looks up, tears glimmer along his lashes. "I, uh, already lost someone." He blinks until his eyes are clear and bright again. "But I'm going to save him—I'm going to save you all."

I let his words linger. Let the chill of inspiration and power run its course through my body. Then I remember. "After you escape your foes."

"Hm? Oh. Yes." He shrugs. "I admit, I'm not used to fighting alone, so the FOEs present a challenge."

"Okay, well, I'll help you."

Meadowlark opens his mouth, pauses, and closes it. Crosses his arms over the gray sweatshirt. He's right. It does look stupid on him. "Thank you."

I have a feeling he's never spoken those words to an "outsider" before, so I don't belittle them. "You're welcome." He doesn't return my smile, but my hopes weren't high—he's already given a lot. I can't even believe we're still interacting.

I shrug off my mantle. "Do you mind if I . . ." *touch you*. I'd ask anyone first, but it feels especially important with Lark, like he's a precious artifact and I'm a less-shitty Indiana Jones. "You stand out in these clothes, but if I dress you in my costume, you'll blend in. Your foes won't be able to tell you apart from people like me in the crowd."

Meadowlark looks down the alleyway, at those who stream past. "You may," he says.

Meadowlark naturally accommodates my motions, accepting the hand-sewn garment as I drape it over his shoulders. The mantle falls into place like I made it for him. I expect the crown will look the same. I extract it from my wig, careful not to snag any hairs, then fit it on him. The braids that circle his head fight me as I try to affix it.

I reach for their ends. "If I can just take these—"

Meadowlark wrenches my arms away in a practiced motion. He holds my wrists, grip firm, staring wide-eyed at me as if he's reevaluating his decision to accept my help.

"Sorry," I say quickly. "I didn't mean to offend you. We can leave your hair up. I'll make the crown fit."

Slowly, he releases me. Straightens up to his full height. Holds his head high as if to remind me that I'm beneath him. He's Anointed and I'm an outsider. I don't want to be.

I treat his braided crown with reverence as I fix the elvish crown around it. Stand back and admire my work. Admire *him*. I've never wanted to get to know someone more. "Looks good." My voice cracks and I clear my throat. "Just cover as much of yourself with the mantle as you can, and no one'll look twice at you."

Meadowlark reaches delicately up toward the crown and runs his fingers over the branches, lets the fake leaves flip through his fingers. His eyelashes flutter and, for a moment, it's like he's somewhere else. With a deep breath he says, "Okay. Get me out of here."

We pass easily through the crowd. Everyone's going somewhere— no one sticking around long enough to notice that Meadowlark and an elf went separately into the alley, and two elves emerged. When we stop at the corner crosswalk, he grabs my upper arm. Not hard, not desperate. Like a child who is afraid to lose their mother in a crowd. I don't look at him when we cross, allowing his fear some privacy.

Meadowlark pauses on the threshold of my hotel. Looks at the automatic doors. Right. He escaped from a hotel. I really hope it was a different one.

"It's okay." I press my free hand over his for a moment, to re-mind him that I've got him, then take a step forward. He follows. Slowly, we slip through the crowd toward a packed elevator that closes right before we make it to the front. This, however, is where Meadowlark draws the line.

"Where'd they go?" he asks, peering around the sides.

"Up. It's an elevator. It moves between floors, so you don't have to take the stairs. It's safe. They're tested by the city regularly."

He watches with glazed eyes as the next batch of people cram into the small space which we, notably, are not getting into. Again. "Which floor are you on?"

"Eleven."

"We'll take the stairs."

"What?"

But he's off before I can stop him. The stairs. I did not get a hotel room so I could climb eleven stories. God knows my fifth-floor apartment is enough. I make it up six flights before I need to rest, flushed and breathing hard as I lean against the concrete wall. This costume is heavy and, unlike Meadowlark, I'm not Anointed.

I wonder if he'll show me magic.

"Come on." He nods at the next set of stairs and we continue.

I want to die by the time we reach the eleventh floor. Meadowlark matches my speed as we walk down the hallway, fiddling with the crown, inspecting the mantle, reading the numbers on doors. I'm walking too slowly for him, but my body is not built for endurance. It's built for slutty Pikachu costumes.

I unlock the room and he follows me inside. A moment later, I hear the door open and shut again. Meadowlark tests it twice, then tentatively joins me. His eyes dart into the bathroom, across the beds, over the mess of cables and microphones Lilian left sprawled across the floor in her quest to, well, to find *him*.

Lilian! I slap my pocket to make sure my phone's inside. I should tell her. Across the room, Meadowlark slides the mantle off his shoulders, extracts the crown from his braided hair. A few strands pull loose, but he tucks them in after setting his disguise down on the desk.

"Is this where you live?"

"No, just where I'm staying for the convention."

"What *is* a convention? You keep talking about it."

Right, I never explained. "It's where a bunch of nerds get together and . . ." I shrug. "Hang out? Celebrate the stories they love. Talk about books and movies. Television, video games." He probably doesn't know what those are—not video games, at least. But he doesn't ask me to explain, and I don't want to accidentally corrupt him or whatever. The way he hangs back, eyeing everyone he encounters as if they're going to fight him, it's obvious no one on this side of the fence has taken him seriously.

An old, familiar annoyance burns through me. Heaven forbid

we believe people when they tell us who they are and what they
want. My fingers glide down the front of my coat. "You don't have
to tell me what you're doing—I know I'm not part of your Fellowship. But if you need someone to talk to, I'll listen. I'll believe
you."

He reaches for the crown again, fingering one of the red plastic
leaves. "I'm on a quest." His narrowed eyes dare me to challenge
him. The silence he leaves in his wake is an invitation I don't
accept.

"I need to kill a monster—as many as possible, really." Meadowlark crosses his arms and stands straight. "You're not going to
tell me that's fake?"

"No," I say, with as much seriousness as I can muster. I mean it,
but I don't know what words or movements will set him off. He
was raised in isolation. Druid Hill might as well be Mars.

"That's . . . all right, okay." He stumbles for words, unprepared
to be unopposed. "I need to go home so I can gather supplies:
books, maps, potions . . ." Again, he trails off, waiting for my ob-
jection.

I refuse to show doubt. "And you're going to carry all that with
you?"

"I suppose."

"Alone?" My brain automatically fills in *It's dangerous to go*—
but I bury the reference. He won't get it, and this is serious to
him—if I truly believe him, it should be serious for me as well. I
want it to be.

Meadowlark doesn't answer.

"I can help—keep helping," I add to reinforce that he can trust
me. I could've turned him in or called the tip line. I haven't even
called Lilian yet; I'm dying to.

He stiffens, every muscle tense—"An outsider, help on my
quest?"—then snaps. "Why are you doing this? Do you want
magic? I'm not going to show you a party trick."

I'm suddenly aware of how hot I am, in this coat and wig, in this hotel room. Aware that I do want him to show me a trick. I want some kind of proof, even though I shouldn't. Even though I would tell off anyone who asked for it.

But this is real magic we're talking about. Imagine . . .

"I wouldn't ask you to." I try to mean it, hope I do.

"Oh. Well." Meadowlark crosses his arms as if they're giving him trouble. Toes the floor with his boot. He looks as flustered as I feel. Even though I have no idea what his life was really like growing up beyond speculation, or what he's capable of, I can tell he's lost. "What, then?" he asks, voice reaching for authority. "How can you help me?"

9

CALVIN / NOW

I don't know what to offer him. I can hear my family telling me I should've majored in something useful, gotten a *real* job—but what the hell would I have offered him as an attorney? Legal advice? Granted, he might need that if he's caught, but I'm not going to let that happen.

I feel the familiar, invisible tug of my phone, my fingers sliding toward my pocket. I want to text Lilian—she's always been my voice of reason or inspiration when parents and professors have let me down. But she's not here. I am. What do *I* have to offer Meadowlark? Most of my weapons are made from Styrofoam or wood, and my magic is limited to a sewing machine.

Think, Calvin. He wants potions and books and maps and—I close my hand around the bump in my pocket. Over my phone. My keys. That's it. I don't have to be good with weapons and magic because he already is. But he probably can't drive and definitely doesn't know anything about the world outside Druid Hill.

"A car. I have a car and a phone." I slide my hand into my pocket slowly, so he doesn't think I'm pulling a weapon on him. So he doesn't pull a weapon on *me*. I hold the device up between us, tap the screen to turn it on. "This thing does a heck of a lot more than call people."

Lark eyes it suspiciously. "Like what?"

"You said you needed maps." I open the app. "I don't know how old yours are, but this has maps that are current to the minute, and we can search anywhere in the world." It hits me when I say it that I don't know *where* he's going. "Do you have an idea where— for your quest—like a general area . . ."

"Not yet. I'll have to use magic to track the specific monster . . ." Meadowlark's voice tapers off. "By all indications, outsider, you have been kind, have demonstrated that I can rely on you. But before we continue, I do need to tell you . . ."

I hold my breath. Tense every muscle in my body.

"You've lived under the influence of monsters your whole life. Because of that, I'll never be able to fully trust you—not until I slay them and free you. That is my life's purpose. To save you and everyone else. But if the part of you that is monstrous does anything to hinder me—to threaten my greater quest—I will stop you with force."

His words stab between my ribs. All I can do is nod because I know he means it. No matter how badly I want this to be real, it already *is* real for Meadowlark. I'm only a side character in his quest. And I've read enough books to know they don't always make it.

"If you understand that, we can continue," he says.

"Yeah—yes," I manage. "Understood."

"Okay. Then, here's what you need to know." The story pours out of Meadowlark like a burst dam. He tells me about Kane, his partner who betrayed them. How he's been corrupted, and only Meadowlark can save him. He describes the SWAT team storming their home and tells me about the FOEs—Forces of Evil— holding his friends to testify against Nova, their leader. Though he doesn't say it, I can tell he's scared—for himself and the rest of the Fellowship—that they'll have to integrate themselves into the outside world. Lose everything they grew up with. I want to say I couldn't possibly know the feeling, but I sort of do. Being forced to drop out of college and live on your friend's couch isn't the same as the Fellowship being forced from Druid Hill, but starting a new life *is* scary.

"I need to shower," I say when he finally goes quiet. Not the smoothest transition, but I need some privacy or I'm going to explode. Need to text Lilian, check the panels and events I'm scheduled for—will they blacklist me if I bail?—check my bank account and every other app that has money sitting in it, available for withdrawal. Meadowlark probably doesn't even know what a credit card is.

"Need to freshen up and change," I say. "Will you be okay to wait out here?"

He assesses the room as if he can see things I can't—and, who knows, maybe he can. I hope so. "Yes."

"I've got some clean clothes somewhere in my suitcase. You should probably change if people are looking for you."

"Agent Miller," he says. "The FOE looking for me is named Agent Miller. She works with your FBI."

"Okay." It takes me a minute to remember that FBI is an acronym I know and not something made up by a cult.

Oh my god, what am I doing? Stop. The first step to believing Lark is to trash everything I learned about the Fellowship as an outsider. To not treat them like a cult. They're a Fellowship.

I make the mental adjustment. "Got it." I also get that anyone whose name begins with capital *A* "Agent" isn't someone I want on my tail. Maybe this is the worst idea. This isn't an RPG where I can kill the people pursuing me without moral or legal consequence—what if Meadowlark thinks he can do that, though? And I'm with him. "Okay, I might be a while, so . . ." I gesture in the general area of my bed while I rummage through my suitcase for a change of clothes. "Feel free to relax. Watch some TV. Red button."

He catches the remote when I toss it. Watches me pick up a pile of clothes and walk into the bathroom. I click the lock then hold my breath as I stand still. Waiting. He's got to move. I'm realizing, as I listen, that I've assumed he won't rob me and run. On the other side of the bathroom door, I hear slow footsteps over carpet. No running. No frantic rifling through drawers and pockets. Only the slow, careful silence of someone deliberating. He's not going to rob me. I think I'm all he's got.

I turn the shower on. Steam billows out around me and fogs the mirror, makes the surface of my phone slippery as I start texting, but I need the white noise to separate me from Meadowlark. Pretend I'm in this hotel room alone and that a guy who is either an Elven-king, or totally brainwashed, isn't picking through my underwear.

Calvin
You are never going to believe who's in our hotel room

I set my phone down on the counter and take out my contacts, glancing at the screen so much, I shove my right contact up under my eyelid with a "dammit."

Lilian
If you need some privacy for a few hours to fuck an aragorn cosplayer I support you

There's no use in teasing her.

Calvin
That guy from the news
Calvin
From the fellowship
Calvin
Meadowlark
Lilian
You're shitting me right??
Calvin
Nope

Lilian

Omg

Calvin

And I kind of?? Offered to drive him?? On his quest???

Lilian

Omg???

Calvin

Am I making a terrible mistake Lilian help

Lilian

OMG!!!

Calvin

THATS NOT HELPING

I set my phone down, ignoring it while I remove my prosthetic ear tips and begin to work the wig from my own hair. Even in the humid bathroom, my head feels cool as I pull the stocking cap free. Run my hands through my sweaty hair. When I glance at my phone, Lilian's still typing.

The shower feels like a pocket universe, where no one is waiting in my hotel room, where I'm not expecting a text from my best friend chiding me for how impulsive I'm being. I scrub the makeup from my face, the grease from my hair, and the grime from my body. I try not to glance at my phone until I'm as dry as I can get in this sauna of a bathroom.

When I touch the screen, I see one text, sent fifteen minutes ago.

Lilian

I'm coming over

Shit.

I struggle to pull clothes onto my damp body, barely remembering deodorant, wondering if Meadowlark even *knows* about deodorant. Because we are not sharing a car if he doesn't. Okay, who am I kidding, I wouldn't ditch him over deodorant, and, besides, he doesn't smell bad. Not that I sniffed him, but I didn't *notice*. Now, I have the urge to, though, *ugh*.

I run a hand through my hair and put my glasses on as I emerge, steam billowing out behind me, like I'm walking away from an explosion. Meadowlark sits cross-legged in the middle of my bed with the television remote limp in his hands as he watches the news. Same channel Lilian and I had on earlier.

"And what would you say to Lark if he was listening?" A journalist holds her microphone out to an East Asian guy with long braided black hair. Scars shine on his arms—from cuts and burns and who knows what else. He's the one who left. Who betrayed the Fellowship. Who betrayed Meadowlark.

"I'd tell him how much I miss him, and to please come back. That we need the strength he brings to our community. And that I lo—"

The television goes black. Meadowlark looks at me and startles. His eyes widen, body flinches back. He scans me like he's the TSA. "What happened to your hair?"

Oh. He didn't know. Oh no. Please don't think I lied. "That was a wig."

"A what?"

"A wig. It's fake hair you put over your own if you want to look different."

"And your eyes," he says, "are a different color."

"Oh, yeah." I shrug. "Thranduil's a Grey Elf, so his eyes are, well, gray, and mine aren't."

He tenses like a predator. "You can change the color of your eyes? Which monster are you in league with?"

"No! None!" I hold up my hands. "I used contacts. They're little clear lenses you put on your eyes to change their color. Some people use them to see better." I tap my glasses. "I put these on instead. I can't see very far without help, like contacts or glasses, but the contacts dry my eyes out when I've been wearing them for a while, so I changed into my glasses."

Meadowlark rises up onto his knees, braces on his toes, angling himself as if to attack. He could probably hurt me. The only look we've had into Druid Hill since the city sold it was a helicopter fly-over for a documentary. The Fellowship shot arrows at them—real arrows. Whatever happens on Druid Hill, the Fellowship members can defend themselves.

"Who are you really?" Meadowlark asks.

"Calvin?" It's more a question than I intend. Then—Oh. *Oh.* Oh my god. He thought I was an actual Elven-king, and why wouldn't he? I doubt he's ever read *The Hobbit* or any of the Lord of the Rings books, much less watched the movies—and my cos-play was spot-on. Okay, how to explain this . . . Meadowlark's expression remains the same: angled, hard, suspicious. I realize, now, that I breezed through that definition earlier, as if he knows what a video game is, when he clearly doesn't even know what a wig and contacts are.

"Remember when I told you I was staying in this hotel for a convention? That it's a bunch of nerds talking about comics and movies and video games and stuff?

"At conventions like these, people dress up like their favorite characters. They sew costumes." Surely, he understands this. "So, when you met me, I was dressed as Thranduil, the Elvenking. He's a character in a story."

Lark relaxes slightly back onto his heels, no longer prepared to leap at me.

"It's pretend—not a lie or anything! Everyone at the convention knew that wasn't my real hair. Did you see the other people dressed up in masks and capes, holding fake weapons?"

His lips are the only part of him that moves when he says, "Yes."

"I was supposed to participate in a costume ball later, where the people who dressed up show off their costumes on a stage." As I say the word "stage," I realize there are so many words he might not know. I have to tailor my vocabulary to the word bank the Fellowship provided him with. "Oh, sorry, uh—"

"I know what a stage is," he says, as if he can see the wheels spinning inside my head. "Why aren't you on it?"

A good question. "Because I met you." I'm not sure if my answer is good enough. I have roots in Baltimore. Friends who'll miss me. A costume ball to attend. *Bills.* Technically, I can take my job with me; thank god for smartphones. But quests are for people without commitments, ready to risk their lives. Just because I'd rather live in my favorite story, doesn't mean I actually could.

Lilian's *OMG* pounds in my chest so loud I could swear—

Someone's running down the hall toward us. As long as it took Lark to relax, he's braced again in an instant. "They're here," he says, rising to his feet.

I check my phone. See a text from Lilian telling me she's on her way up. "No," I say. "No, it's not the FBI; it's my friend Lilian."

"You summoned someone!" It's supposed to be a question.

"No!" I hold his gaze as I back slowly toward the door. Wow, everything is suddenly going badly. "She summoned herself, but I promise she won't hurt you or tell anyone you're here."

Meadowlark surveys the room from where he stands on my bed, as Lilian and I open the door at almost the same time. The surprise, the conjunction of our efforts, causes her to stumble ungracefully into the room.

She stops short of the bed, and, if Meadowlark is looking at her like prey, she's watching him like a zoo animal. "Holy shit, you weren't kidding."

"Lilian, this is Meadowlark. Meadowlark, Lilian."

Neither says hi. I move between them so he doesn't kill her when she inevitably reaches out to see if he's real. Then, with a shiver, Lil breaks the hold he has over her and holds out a hand. "So good to meet you. Big fan."

He looks from me to her pointy pink fingernails. Like a cat, he jumps to the floor, not registering any shock from landing. He takes her hand but doesn't move as she shakes his limp arm up and down. I suck in a nervous breath as he pulls her hand up to his face and turns it over, examining her fingernails.

"Are these weapons?"

I have a feeling he might break her arm over the wrong answer, and yet he looks genuinely interested, running his fingers over their tips, feeling the glossy gel polish. Peering underneath them as if Lilian has poison sacs hidden beneath her nail beds.

"No," she says, "they're acrylics." They catch each other's eyes. "Fake fingernails that someone shapes and paints—*oh my god,*" Lil whispers the end of her sentence to me. Meadowlark neither notices nor cares.

"My pronouns are he/him, and yours?"

"She/her." Lilian gives me an impressed nod. The number of times she's had to explain to people that nonbinary femmes are real and can use whatever fucking pronouns they want . . .

"And I go by Lark," he says, pressing the pad of his thumb against one of her stiletto tips.

"Oh, sorry," I say. "Didn't know."

"Now you do." Finally, he drops Lilian's hand. "Are you wearing a costume too?" he asks her.

"No. Are you?"

"No!" His forehead creases with offense. "I only asked because Calvin was. For all I know, you're attending this convention too."

"I am," she says. "I left a panel about zombies for this."

"What are zombies?"

"The mindless undead; they eat people."

"And they're *not* real," I say, watching Lark's eyebrows rise with horror. He's barely calm when I ask Lil, "The *Walking Dead* panel?"

"Yes! I talked my way in with my press badge, but this is way cooler." She grins, bites her lip, plants her hands on her hips. "We're going on a fucking quest!"

10

LARK / NOW

I pick through Calvin's clothes, while he and his friend Lilian pack. Nothing will be as good as the clothes made specially for the Anointed, but I find pants that have an elastic waistband and ankle hems, and are surprisingly comfortable. The shirt, well, it has some sort of animal on it—not one I've seen or even heard of. A yellow mouse-looking thing with floppy ears and a tail like lightning. Every one of Calvin's shirts is equally ridiculous, so I settle for the first and change in the bathroom. There are some things I'm not ready to share.

When I emerge, Lilian ducks past me and scoops handfuls of bottles and tubes out of the bathroom. I stand out of the way, watching the rush until the last zipper is pulled closed. Until the two of them line up behind me with bags slung over their shoulders and luggage trailing on wheels.

"Will you get the door?" Lilian nods at it expectantly.

"Sure." I hold it for them, then follow empty-handed. I consider offering to help, but then they stop in front of the doors Calvin called an elevator and I freeze. The two of them squeeze their suitcases through the open door, gesturing for me to follow. It's empty of outsiders this time, but no less dangerous looking.

Calvin holds his hand between the open doors. "We trust you," he says, "but you've got to trust us too."

"We promise you won't plummet to your death." Lilian tilts her head side to side. "Most likely."

That doesn't make me feel better. But how can they help if I constantly question them? They survive out here beyond the fence every day, and I wasn't prepared for all the cars and people and—as long as they're useful, I can accommodate them. Until they hinder me. I won't hesitate to sacrifice a couple of outsiders for my quest.

With resolve, I step into the elevator. I watch the doors close. The floor shudders, but it's smooth as it descends and none of us falls.

"Stay close," Calvin says, when the doors open once again.

I do. I follow them through a crowd that presses like it did on the street, and I close my eyes as I push through them. Don't get swept away. Please don't lose me in this crush of bodies.

They don't. Soon we're in a cool, dark catacomb of vehicles. Only a few outsiders traverse its levels. Calvin leads us to a glossy orange car covered in colorful signs. It reminds me of an insect, it's so . . . bright. How are we supposed to escape when we're this visible?

"Is this your car?"

The answer is obvious when its lights flash and he opens its backside. "Yup."

"Okay." I can figure this out. Quick. I have seconds before these outsiders simply drive us off without protection.

Lilian hauls her rolling bag onto the top of the pile then hooks a small satchel over her shoulder—a purple leather that looks so soft, I want to touch it. She slams the car's back door and steps aside.

"I'll need to cast a concealment spell." It's easier on inanimate objects. Doesn't require the whole ritual we did in the hotel. I can do it myself. It'll work.

Calvin and Lilian look at each other, communicating something I can't decipher. Not mindspeech, surely, but they seem to have a connection like I do with the Anointed. "You won't need to do anything to my car for this spell, right?" Calvin says. "Like, change it in any way . . ." He gestures nervously at it.

"No. It'll only take a moment." I whisper the spell into my palm then press it flat to one of the cold glass windows. Magic spills forth, coating the vehicle in my protection. I have to yank my hand free. Shake it out. "That should do it."

Calvin and Lilian look at each other again.

"It won't look any different to us, but to anyone who seeks to harm us, the car will adopt properties from its surroundings," I explain, because how can they understand? They wouldn't know magic unless it slammed them into a wall.

"What about the license plate?" Calvin points at a metal plate with letters and numbers printed on it. "These numbers will identify me."

"The spell will adapt," I say with confidence. Outsiders need reassuring. "No one who seeks to harm us will be able to read it. The numbers and letters will appear to shift and scramble."

"Cool," Calvin says. This time, he avoids Lilian's gaze as the two of them head for the car's side doors. As I follow, I can't help but wonder whether they believe me. In the hotel room, Calvin seemed to give me credence. But now that Lilian's here, he sounds less sure. I'll have to keep a close eye on her. Remind them that, while I appreciate their assistance, I will not be stopped. That I will push onward by whatever means necessary.

•　　•　　•

We drop Lilian at a tall, colorful building with pictures of people plastered to the side over the words: BECOME INSTA-POPULAR. I'm all the more suspicious of Lilian for living there. It shows she values visibility and influence, and is thereby vulnerable to corruption. Calvin, on the other hand, lives in a plain brown building. It has an elevator, but it does not work. I don't mind, but when he grumbles about lugging his things up the narrow staircase, I hoist two of his bags over my shoulders and begin climbing the stairs without him.

"Which floor?" I ask over my shoulder.

Behind me, the wheels of his suitcase clunk over each step, only quieting on the landings. "Fifth. Top floor."

When I reach the fourth floor, I no longer see him behind me. Presumably, he does this several times per day. How is he not used to it? I should not have to wait for him. His body appears muscled. When he comes into view again, I continue onward, stopping only when he shouts, "That's it!"

He wheels his suitcase down the hallway, panting for breath, before shoving a metal key—no cards here—into two different locks and pushing the door open. A piece of gray rubber along its bottom splinters as he forces it over a thick rug.

An overhead lamp turns on like magic. I try not to look surprised, but my heart bounces as if my chest is empty. Calvin drags his bags halfway inside before abandoning them on the floor and turning a corner, but I don't follow. Before I enter this outsider's dwelling, I want to make sure it's not a trap. That nothing is lurking around that corner or in the walls.

I whisper into my palm then press it against the doorframe. Close my eyes. Exchange energy with the building. It's older than Lilian's, has a history of use and neglect. Though its insides are bruised and scarred, it does not feel malicious. Calvin should not live here any longer than he has to, though. Down to its very bones, this place is broken.

"You can relax for a bit," he says, suddenly reappearing in a tiny hallway. "Sit on the couch, watch"—he points at the shiny black screen—"television."

I remember the device from his hotel room. Remember Kane being interviewed. How he said he wanted me back. That he loved me. I wish I could believe that was him talking and not the corruption. Not a monster's tongue luring me to my death.

"If you like books, you're welcome to pick a couple of mine to bring with us. I need to pack." He puts his hands on his hips and glares at his bulging suitcases. "Re-pack." Calvin grabs them one by one and hauls them down the hall, leaving me by myself in his living area.

I have never seen so many shelves. Only Nova's office has this many, but we're rarely invited inside, much less left alone. Glancing over my shoulder, I walk over to one that's lined with plastic cases. These can't be books, but titles show down their sides. I touch the spine of one called *Jurassic Park* and pull it slowly from the shelf. It opens with a snap and a thin disc pops out. I scramble to catch it; rainbows reflect off its underside and against the wall. It's beautiful.

I press the disc back into its case and examine the front cover—almost like a book. A scaly head with dozens of sharp yellowing teeth protrudes from the side. This is some kind of monster. "Collector's Edition, Widescreen," I read, utter nonsense. I slip the case back onto the shelf and walk over to the books. These, I've seen before.

When I was a child, there were more. I remember books with weathered spines and colorful illustrations, books with yellow pages and black text. They were gone before I could read them all. Relics from beyond the fence, Nova explained. Each one a different path to corruption.

Wait. Is that? *Jurassic Park*. I slide my finger down its spine and pull it from the shelf. A white cover with the same monster, this time coming down from the top as if eating the title. Its outline a skeleton. The monstrous cover unnerves and excites me. I open to the first page, looking over my shoulder yet again—as if Calvin didn't tell me I could touch his books. We're not allowed to touch Nova's.

I don't recognize half the words that make up the introduction: "biotechnology," "genetic engineering," "commercialize." They don't sound good, and yet . . . I look at the cover again, glide my fingers over the raised title. I will take this book of monsters with me. Learn what the outsiders make of them.

I skim the rest, seeing titles evoking magic and the sky, with pictures of flying monsters and ships. None of that is how magic works. Those are the lies outsiders imbibe, helping real monsters mislead them. I skip the rest when I notice a familiar tool on the mantel. I have a wand, crafted from a tree branch; it's thick like a rod and imbued with years of magic. We call it Spellslinger. This *thing* is long and thin and—I pick it up—plastic. Words are printed up a seam, tiny and black.

I march into the hallway and emerge into a small kitchen. No Calvin. I grab the first handle I can find and yank the door open. A bathroom, still no Calvin. Only one door left.

He turns when I open it, startled by my presence. He's wearing elastic-hemmed pants like those he loaned me, with grass-green shoes and a long-sleeved shirt. Except for my braids and his glasses, we don't look that different. I press my tongue against the roof of my mouth to remind myself of the piercing. Of what makes us different: that I can speak magic.

"This is fake." I extend the wand I found in his living room. "Thought you should know." As I hand it to him, I notice a bin full of swords, a bow, and staffs. "It's all fake."

"Yeah," Calvin says, "they're for my costumes. That"—he takes the plastic wand from me—"does actually work, but only at the theme park, so please be careful with it." Without explaining what a "theme park" is, he sets the wand on a shelf otherwise lined with small statues.

"It doesn't do magic, though," I say.

"Not like you're used to," Calvin says. "It's got a sensor—I'll explain on the road."

"Okay." I don't know what to do empty-handed. The room is hot—or I'm hot, foolishness burning me. I pull at the neck of my borrowed shirt, glance around the space. Sorry I don't know "sensors," or all the words in his books, or that his weapons are fake.

Calvin hands me a bag I can fit over my shoulders. "This is for you. I didn't want you to travel without a change of clothes or toiletries." He shrugs and looks at his feet. Is he nervous, even here in his sanctum?

I glance at Calvin's bed, smaller and less extravagant than those in the hotel room. "This is where you sleep." Of course he's nervous. I'm in his private quarters, riffling through his books and assessing his weapons. "I'm sorry, I can leave."

He draws breath as if to stop me, but I don't wait. I take the bag and wait in his living area perched on the edge of his couch, afraid to touch anything else. Needing to escape, I remember *Jurassic Park*. Flip to the first page and force myself through it, even if I don't know what's going on. The words lift me from the present, from the outside world and into another one. I don't even care that it's not my own; it's away.

"Ready?" Calvin appears framed in the hallway. He wears a similar backpack and holds another bag in his hand. He looks good. Tall, broad-shouldered, and sharp, he reminds me of Kane for a moment. But Calvin's dark hair is short and flies away from his head haphazardly, unbound. I want to run my hands through it.

Stop, I would never.

"Yes." I close my book and tuck it into my bag. "I've prepared my whole life for this." And yet my stomach flutters like there are birds inside me. I prepared with Kane, to quest in his wake. For an adventure across the countryside with proper weapons and the strength of the Fellowship behind me. Today, I leave with an outsider from his dilapidated apartment building, with nothing of my own but hope.

11

KANE / CONFIDENTIAL

Lark carried the keys—two small keys that looked like they'd break if he clenched his fist. They hung from long silver chains, nestled in the crook of his finger, shining in the light I carried. I was the eldest, and yet Nova trusted him with them. Lark, not me. A strange jealousy worked its way into my heart.

I twined my fingers through his, trying not to stare at the keys where they swayed in the thick summer air. Lark caught my eye—caught *me*. The lightstick warmed in my empty hand, and I knew he was pushing some of his magic into me. A consolation.

"Are you nervous?" I asked, the night giving me more confidence than it should. As if my words didn't count in the dark.

"No," Lark said. "Are you?"

I didn't answer. I'd hoped he'd say yes. I felt so far behind him, even walking hand in hand. Even though I was months older. Even though I was supposed to want this.

Lark squeezed my hand hard. "They'll help us focus better, make us stronger. Trust me."

"You mean, trust Nova." The words curled out of my mouth like smoke.

His head snapped in my direction. "Of course we trust Nova." He tugged on my arm until we were shoulder to shoulder. "You shouldn't talk like that." He looked beyond me, into the dark. I should've cared—that I sounded disloyal, that someone might hear me, what Lark would think—but I didn't.

He hurried us past the faded zoo signs until we were safely inside our quarters. The cement dome felt as big and open as the night sky around us. For a moment, it felt like things would be okay.

Then, Lark took both of my hands and led me into our room with a look that said *we need to talk*. He cleared his throat. "Are you with me on this?" A hint of nerves laced into the otherwise grounded timbre of his voice.

I remember feeling the chain scratch the side of my fingers where we clutched it between us. Wondering if I could take it from him in this moment of—not weakness, but need. Despite the heroic confidence instilled in us, we were only human. Nova wanted us to forget that.

"I need you," he said before I could answer. "Even though I know this is for the best, it's still hard. If we support each other—"

"I am with you," I said, instead of *no. No, this isn't what I want.* I didn't want him to give the key to his body to anyone but me. But I was too far in, I'd fallen too far for Lark.

"Okay," he said, brow creasing with uncertainty. He looked around the domed room as if Nova might pop in at any moment. She'd done it before. Lark lowered his voice. "You seem off lately. Your magic doesn't feel the same. During lessons, you're a model student—smarter than me, for sure." He laughed briefly to himself. "But during physical training?"

I had to stop him before he went too far. Before he spoke his doubt and made me face my own. I couldn't voice what had kindled inside me. It was bad enough the ideas lived in my head; they could never pass my lips.

"I'm tired is all." The easiest excuse. "Overexerted. Stressed about being the first to leave." That was true. Even though I was dying to know what waited beyond the fence, I was terrified. The Anointed had grown up on stories of monsters and FOEs. Humans turned feral and hungry by corruption.

I had to believe, for Lark. I could discipline myself, for Lark.

I could hurt Lark when he asked for it. Let him hurt me because that was how he cared for me. Because when we did magic, when he was happy, I was happy. I could forget. Lose myself in his joy and the pain and his lips and—

I pressed my lips against his with such force that he stumbled. Squeezed his bare waist, dug my fingernails hard into his flesh. Four half-moons were nothing among the dozens of other marks I'd left behind.

He moaned; his lips parted. I pressed my nails deeper, rubbed at the growing bulge between his legs, biting his lips. Reminded him that pleasure was good. That our bodies matched. That we were made for each other.

Lark drew back, bottom lip catching between my teeth. The delicate skin broke, and blood filled the crack as if from a whip. "What are you doing?" He freed himself from my grasp, breathless, lip swelling. I watched his hands curl into fists—watched him force them to his sides. I watched him walk away.

With a deep breath, he stopped and set his bag beside his bed. From within, he retrieved two clear bags. Their contents were sterilized and cleansed by Nova herself.

"Here." He held one out to me.

If I wanted to stay in good favor with Nova and Lark and the other Anointed, I needed to take it. I willed my hand out like I was willing myself to fly, again. *Take it.* Closed my fingers around the plastic seal and took it.

This was happening. And why not? I already ate what I was told, drank potions whose ingredients I didn't know. Swore off games and alcohol and friends who weren't Anointed. Hurt the person I loved and let him hurt me. What did one lock matter? Besides, if it helped me grow closer to Lark and grow stronger in my magic, maybe it would help me survive my quest.

I tore my clothes off, nearly breaking the buckle on my leather harness. The glass vials inside jangled as it hit the cement. I yanked

my boots off, kicking them past Lark. He flinched, but never broke
eye contact as I tossed my shirt and pants and underwear and socks
aside. Finally, I was naked. I stared him down—almost a dare.

Take your clothes off too. Face what you're about to do.

Lark removed his clothes with as little spectacle as possible,
dropping the pieces into a pile at his feet. "We're supposed to wash
each other first." His voice sank into the humidity.

I dropped to my knees in front of him, opened the plastic bag,
and took out the small metal contraption. *Just do it,* I told myself.
Get it over with. As I fitted it around my genitals, I remember
thinking it was warm. Of course. Lark had kept it stashed in his
bag, warm against his body, safe from me.

The lock closed with a click. I squirmed against the foreign
object, aroused, and painfully aware that I couldn't do anything
about it. Instead, I leaned into Lark's touch as he smoothed his
hands over my braids, closed his eyes, and then *gasped* as I pressed
my lips to the head of his cock. I opened my mouth and looked
into his eyes as I swallowed him.

This meant more to me than my own pleasure, than my own
body ever could. Metal clanged against the cement as I dropped
the other bag and wrapped both hands around his thighs, felt his
length between my lips for what would be the last time, at least
until we both reached our quarter century. Maybe forever.

For a cold moment I thought he'd pull away, until his fingers
found their way between the strands of my braids, pressing against
my scalp. Mine gently cupped his testicles, rolling them in my
palm. A slight squeeze wrung whimpers from his lips. He held
tighter, and I took my time, kissing and stroking, feeling every
ridge and vein, breathing the scent of his skin.

When I could tell Lark was about to burst, I engulfed him.
Dragged my fingernails hard down the backs of his thighs. His
head fell back, lips parted. A cry escaped his throat as his come
filled mine.

Lark held on as if he'd fall without me. As his body stopped bucking and his grip eased, I kissed the sensitive skin between his pelvis and thigh. Rested my forehead against his sweaty hip, stroked the length of his leg, and pressed my lips against the tip of his softened cock.

Before I could think on it any further, I picked up the metal cage, slid it around his balls, and fit his cock between the metal bars. I closed the lock. There.

We dressed ourselves in silence, only glancing at each other to make sure we were still there. I fitted my harness back into place, buckling the straps as he moved behind me to adjust them. Not missing a beat, I returned the favor. When we finished, Lark's fingers scraped the ground, catching the delicate silver chains between his fingers. He stood, looking down at the hanging keys that could unlock our bodies. With a twist of that key, he could have me whenever he wanted, but we'd sworn off pleasure in favor of discipline. In favor of belief.

12

CALVIN / NOW

Lark, despite only having ridden in a car once, is a back-seat driver. "You're going the wrong way." He holds his left arm out between us, consulting an invisible spot on his palm for directions, while my GPS gives me detailed instructions in a soothing British accent.

"We have to pick up Lilian first."

Lark shakes his head. "Druid Hill is more important."

"Don't you think we'll have better luck in the dark?" I ask, turning opposite the way he gestures.

"Can you see better in the dark?" he asks.

"Well, *no*, but . . ."

Lark glares at me. "You swore your assistance would not slow me down."

I don't change course. "It would actually take us longer to drive all the way out to Druid Hill and then come back for Lilian. She's not far. I promise I'm saving you time."

He sighs dramatically and drops his arm into his lap. "I suppose you know the outside world better than I do. I'm not . . ." He trails off, turning to look out the window. "I'm not used to being so ill-equipped. To relying on an outsider."

His voice carries a vulnerability I've rarely heard. Just because he threatened to stop me with force, doesn't mean he doesn't have feelings. The Feds ripped him from the only home he's ever known. "I would never make light of the trust you've placed in me," I tell him, because I do want him to like me. I mean, find me useful.

We pull up outside Lilian's apartment: a huge block of buildings with bright exterior walls, balconies every couple of windows, and banners proclaiming things like you can "be on top anytime" if you rent there. Clearly written by a straight person.

Lil and I used to make fun of this development before she moved in. There's nothing in the immediate area except a hospital, the court, a couple of hotels, and, admittedly, the best donuts in the city. But her girlfriend's a surgeon at Mercy; I guess some people have normal jobs. Needless to say, I don't dunk on the building slogans anymore. In front of her.

She's waiting in the lobby when we pull up. I get out, opening the hatch. "Did you bring all your podcasting stuff?" Rearranging the bags, I can't help feeling we've overpacked. Like, Lark would definitely just start walking with nothing, sleep under the stars, wash in a river. I wrinkle my nose at the thought of bathing in the Jones Falls.

"I did. You?"

"Camera, a few slutty costumes, mobile Wi-Fi hotspot."

"Dammit, Wi-Fi hotspot. I didn't think of that." She slams the hatch shut.

"You can use mine. Just pitch in for gas."

"Sounds good to me!"

•   •   •

The sun's setting as we reach the periphery of Druid Hill. I've never been inside, but have often glimpsed the hulking metal fence where it crosses old entrances. We're driving slowly up Sisson Street when Lark says, "Here!"

The bridge he points to is blocked with barricades. Didn't he say the FBI was after him? My hands tingle with nerves as I grip the steering wheel, my stomach flopping like we're on a roller coaster. We can't stop. Not here. I shake my head and keep driving. "There's nowhere for me to park the car," I say. "Isn't there another way in?"

"There's only one gate."

Lilian leans between us, squares herself with Lark. "Do you have a *key* to the gate?"

"No, and there are wards." Lark purses his lips, considering this. Finally, he says, "There's an old entrance on the north side. Should be quiet there."

I cross the light rail tracks, getting as close to the trees as I can, following the curve of the park through Remington, Hampden, and Woodberry. Neighborhoods lined with rowhouses and corner stores and hipster pizza places. Imagine living here, alongside the Fellowship. Always close, never allowed in. These neighborhoods remember; they haven't forgiven the city for selling their park.

"There." Lark points to the left, where the road crumbles from pavement into gravel. A dead end where potholes and building materials lie abandoned by the city.

The car rumbles over loose stones before I pull onto a flat patch of dirt, hoping the trees and shadows will disguise the bright orange paint. Lark is out the instant I put it in park. Lilian and I look at each other, then at Lark as he moves quickly and sure-footedly through the tree line.

"What do you think he's doing?" Lilian crosses her arms and leans close, rubbernecking.

I shrug. "Magic?" Please let it be magic.

Lilian shows no sign of hope. She watches him with lips half-parted and eyebrows raised. She's still skeptical. *Still.* Since birth—or at least by the time she got to college. That was the first time I was actually on my own, living somewhere my parents weren't constantly looking over my shoulder. Where I felt comfortable exploring my queerness and the possibility of magic. So, I ordered a deck of tarot cards with naked men on them. Some candles, even though they were "illegal" in the dorms. And a book called *Manifesting Magic.* The cover art looked like a bad nineties instructional video, but I read that thing a dozen times. Used the tarot deck so much, the edges softened and frayed.

I was still nervous to share them with anyone—thanks, Mom and Dad—but one drunken night, I offered to read Lilian's cards. She laughed. I did too, playing off how much I wanted to believe in what she called "new age bullshit." I'm not sure I ever believed *Manifesting Magic* was real or that the tarot illuminated anything except my enjoyment of naked men. But that was when I knew Lilian didn't even want to believe. Not then and not now.

Lilian is interested in Lark because he offers mystery and adventure—and she genuinely wants to help people. She believes him, but doesn't believe *in* him. I do. I need to. He's not a deck of cards; he's a person. And I don't know why the Fellowship was disbanded, but I can't help but envy him for growing up around magic, learning how to practice spells. Training with real weapons, to fight real monsters. Fuck, I am tired of being an outsider.

I close my eyes, allowing the shiver of want to pass through me, unwilling to see whether Lilian's giving me A Look. "Whatever Lark's doing, we'd better keep up."

We both get out, crunching fallen leaves underfoot. Lark stops and glares at us over his shoulder. He lets us catch up, then whispers at Lilian, "Has anyone ever told you how loud you are?"

"Yeah," she says, "but I mostly assume that's misogyny talking."

"Who's Misogyny?" he asks.

She pats him on the shoulder. "I'll tell you later. Let's get through that fence."

"It sure is a big boy." I plant my hands on my hips and trace the iron pickets with my eyes. It must be twice my height, and there are no rungs, no weak spots. How the hell did his partner get out?

"Step back while I check the wards." Lark approaches the fence, hands spread wide, palms open to it. "The invading FOEs may have disturbed them. We're supposed to perform regular maintenance on them." He shakes his head, tightens his lips into a line. Sorrow creases his forehead.

Lilian and I stand back, watching as his body expands and deflates with a deep breath. As his shoulder muscles flex and pinch against the long-sleeved Pikachu shirt he picked out from my suitcase. His head rolls forward, then back. Long, silent minutes pass, which I spend nervously looking over my shoulders. Finally, his hands clench into fists. He drops them to his sides dramatically, before addressing us.

"I found a weak spot. It's not far."

"What kind of a weak spot?" Lilian asks. "A point where the fence is broken?"

Lark looks quizzically at her, says, "No, a point where the *wards* are broken," and starts walking.

She gives me a big shrug and perplexed face once Lark's back is turned. Mutters, "I'm more worried about the fence. I'm not really the parkour type."

"Yeah, same," I lie. About the fence, not the parkour. Lark looks like he could scale a tree like a monkey.

We follow at a distance until Lark stops again and holds his hand out as if taking the fence's temperature. I keep glancing over my shoulder as if I can see the car, but it's long behind us. Already, I'm playing out excuses in my head. *Sorry, Officer, we're performance artists. The fence is a metaphor for personal boundaries.* We are definitely going to jail.

"This is it," he says. His sorrow deepens as he closes his hand around an iron bar. "Someone's come and gone through here, multiple times."

I assume he means the one who turned them in. Kane.

"When I say the word, walk through the fence."

I feel my eyebrows hit my hairline and know Lilian's are doing the same. "*Through* the fence?" As badly as I want it to be real, I also don't want a concussion. Even Harry was nervous to blast through Platform 9 ¾, and he'd been shown magic by then.

"Yes. I know it looks solid, but it's not. The wards have been bent so many times, the iron's bent with them."

I muster up as much belief as I can. "Okay." I step forward, hoping Lilian will follow. That I won't walk headfirst into the fence and knock myself out.

Lark whispers into his palm and grabs one of the iron pickets. Leaves whirl around us as a sudden breeze hits. I watch Lark as he continues whispering into the wind. Small strands of his hair free themselves from the crown of braids on his head—does the air feel warmer?

"Go," he says, lips resuming their quiet motion. His blue eyes open. "Now."

If I look at Lilian, I'll remember that this might not work. I want it to work, so I obey. *Forward,* I urge my feet. Look not *at* the fence but *through* it. Look to the park beyond, as if the iron doesn't exist. At the last minute, I close my eyes and hold my breath, tense the muscles in my shoulders and back. Be small, so small. Small enough to fit between the pickets.

I walk forward, then stop. Open my eyes. Turn.

"Holy shit." I'm on the other side of the fence. I watch as Lilian walks through, cringing as she passes through the bars like they're an illusion.

Lark passes through quickly, then stumbles and sways drunkenly. I reach out just as his dead weight slumps into my arms. Slowly, I lower him to his knees. "Are you okay?" I look for the answer in his eyes as they flutter open. He nods, and I get the sense that he couldn't speak if he wanted to.

"I'm fine," Lark mumbles as he finds the earth with his hands. Leaves crunch loudly beneath his palms.

"Are you sure? Did the wards—I don't know—hurt you or something? I don't know how magic works."

Lark pushes off the ground and rests on his heels. I let go, suddenly mindful of how long I've been holding him. I can still feel my arm around his back, fingers pressing into the soft fabric of the old tee shirt. He smells fresh, like laundry detergent.

After a slow, deep breath, he says, "I'm fine." Brushes the dirt and leaves off his borrowed jeans, off his palms. He stands without my help. "Nova set those wards up herself—they've protected us for thirty years. They're strong. I shouldn't have been able to do that."

Worry crosses his face as he passes in front of me, heading off into the woods. Lilian and I walk silently behind him, looking where he looks, pretending to understand why he chooses some paths over others, until we spill out into the crumbling remains of a parking lot. Cracked concrete slabs peek up like tombstones, memorializing where minivans full of families used to park. Grass grows between cobblestones. Tree branches rustle, the wind rushes against my ears. It is so quiet here. Eerie. If I close my eyes, I can hear the laughter of children long grown up—the only ones who might remember visiting this place when it was a zoo.

We pass between two pavilions, through gates with empty ticket windows, emerging onto concrete under dark skies. A slight breeze lifts three limp banners into the air, where they hang from tall metal poles. They look handmade, like kids crafted them in art class. The only word I catch, as we pass, is FELLOWSHIP. What did this place look like when it was full? When a couple hundred people lived here—when there was magic?

Lark doesn't stop to gawk. He storms down a long road, not waiting for me as I linger in front of a one-story mansion with busted windows and dark stains on the steps. Is this where it happened? Is this where he was taken?

"Come on!"

Lilian's hiss drags me back, pulls my feet forward. I run to catch up with her and with Lark. He waits in front of a locked gate—but not an impassable one, like the fence that surrounds Druid

Hill. Iron spikes twisted and shaped like branches in a marsh, with metal cranes perched on top, wings spread as if taking off, too beautiful to stop anyone.

The lock is shiny and new, probably attached by a federal agent or investigator. "Can you open it?" I ask.

Lark holds his hand to his mouth and whispers, then closes his fist around the lock and yanks. Nothing happens. Lil and I exchange a look, a promise not to ask if it worked. I know there's no magic inside me, but I wish with all my heart for him to open the lock. I close my eyes and push good vibes his way. As much of my yearning as my heart can pump. *Work, please work.*

Lark yanks on the lock again, but it doesn't budge. Without explanation, he says, "We'll have to climb over." He speaks slowly, as if the notion disgusts him. I want to tell him it's okay. I believe him. But I don't think he cares what I think. He doesn't need my validation. I'm an outsider. In the end, neither of us comments.

We let him help us over, one at a time, but don't watch as he scales it on his own. I don't even feel like I should be here. I'm watching him face something immense and personal, something I couldn't ever ask him to share with me. I don't want him to hold back on our account, but I'm sure he is.

As we continue, I can't help but notice the places the Fellowship built over the zoo, like exposed layers of an archaeological site. Signs that once pointed toward animal areas now designate sleeping quarters, artisan workshops, and ritual spaces. Big open pools for penguins and polar bears are now lined with chairs and rock circles. Walking past repurposed concession stands and empty exhibits, it feels apocalyptic. Like the animals, caretakers, and visitors were driven away by a zombie horde.

We follow a long winding path through an artificial marsh until it ends at a series of fake caves. Outside, faded signs describe stalactites, bats, and salamanders—but I don't see the exhibits, only vines and fallen leaves on dirt paths and boulders. Lark stops alongside one, looking over his shoulder at Lilian and me, before reaching his hand through . . . *something.* I can't see and get the impression he doesn't want me to. But I don't wonder long. Lark leans into the boulder and it *moves,* rolling aside to reveal a concealed entrance.

"This is some secret passage shit," Lilian says, as she inspects the rock.

Inside, the Fellowship has lined its walls with bows and arrows, staffs and swords. My eyes are drawn to the whips. A chill slices through me as Lark takes a sword down from its hooks and places it into a long canvas bag. Alongside it, several daggers, their handles inscribed with sigils. A bow and quiver of arrows, several wooden sticks that I swear to god are wands, and a staff that's taller than Lilian. Well, she *is* only five feet tall.

Lark zips up the bag and heads out of the cave. Lil follows. I stop, eyeing the weapons. I don't know how to wield anything that isn't made from Styrofoam or wood. It's hard to believe you're Strider when your sword weighs half a pound. When I look again, the two of them are gone and I'm left alone with the urge to touch.

I wrap my fingers around a length of wood with no apparent function, lifting it free from the hooks it lies across. I brandish it like a wand, waiting for light to flare from its tip, a sudden wind to swirl up around me, and a chorus to sing its power. None of that happens, and it hurts. I didn't really expect to feel the magic, but disappointment knocks the wind out of me.

I would give almost anything to go home for Christmas with the ability to turn my shitty cousins into toads. To cast a spell that stopped everyone from asking me when I'll get a *real* job, *marry a nice girl,* whether I've given any *thought* to *law school.* Imagine if the family's only college dropout was more powerful than any of them.

I slide the stick into my front pocket and pull my sweater over it, just as Lilian pokes her head back into the cave. "Coming," I say before she can ask what I've been up to. "Where is he?"

She leads me to another cave, a boulder already pushed aside, exposing its entrance. This one looks less like an actual cave and more like a rock archway leading into darkness—into a tunnel. Murky water surrounds us behind thick plastic walls. The last rays of daylight illuminate algae and detritus. Dead leaves fall from their trees and sink slowly to the exhibit floor, resting like corpses in the Dead Marshes. Beautiful and unsettling.

A shiver of cold slices through me when I read the sign at the end of the tunnel: ENTER HERE FOR HELLBENDERS. The only way is through a heavy black curtain that crosses the other end of the tunnel.

"I'm not going in there." Lilian backs into the shade near the entrance.

"A hellbender's just a salamander," I say, reassuring myself.

Lilian doesn't follow, as I slip past the curtain alone into total darkness. "Lark?" I hear shifting and scraping. See the ripple of a shadow in the low light as my eyes adjust. He crouches over his bag, fitting items inside—I can't make them out. Only hear the gentle clank of metal on metal. "Do you need any h—" Lark catches my eye, stopping me dead. In his hands, a length of leather with a handle and multiple tails. Gently, he fits it into the bag and pulls the zipper.

"Let's go," he says. "We have one more stop before the road." Lark marches through the curtain and down the tunnel. I stand alone in the dark, feeling the stolen wand press flat against my torso. Wondering what kind of magic I'm getting myself into.

13

LARK / NOW

I thought I'd feel wicked or rebellious when I entered Nova's office—we were rarely allowed inside, and never alone. But instead, when I press my hand to the sigil on the door, I feel righteous. Mature. She isn't here to protect this place and its power, but she trusted me. I will carry on its legacy.

Calvin and Lilian hesitate on the threshold, beyond plastic yellow tape; I hold my shoulders back and head high, defying their doubt. Press my pierced tongue against the roof of my mouth and relish the feeling of hard metal. Remind myself that discipline nurtures power, even in the unsure. I stride over to an old wooden cabinet—heart racing with hope—and pull its doors open, gripping the splintering wood as I scan the emptied desk and tables, usually cluttered with books and papers. Only a few items remain: a carved wooden paperweight, teacup, and spoon. Cool relief floods my body as I see several sets of keys hanging from dulled hooks. The last thing I want is some FOE having control over my body.

I take one of the leather harnesses from within the cabinet and slip my arms through the straps, wrapping the hanging ends around my waist and buckling it. Tightening and loosening where necessary. This one isn't mine, but it will do, and it feels good to outfit myself for the journey ahead. The worn leather stretches and slides nicely over my shoulders and across my back as I flex. I slide my fingers through the delicate key chains, where they hang, and lift them free before lowering them carefully into a small pocket along my waist.

The old floorboards creak as the braver of the outsiders approaches me—which, I'm not sure, and I don't check. Don't have time. Rapidly, I read the labels on vials and hand-drawn maps and sigils, fitting what I can into my harness.

"You need any help?" It's Calvin I see when I turn around. It was him in the cave too, watching me pack knives and scourges. His face appears calm and genuine, but I can't help wondering why he's so quick to offer help.

Across the room, Lilian's reading the few titles that remain on Nova's private bookshelf. She shouldn't be doing that. "No," I tell Calvin, trying not to sound annoyed. They don't know any better. "Not in here, anyway." I press forward with open palms, ushering the two of them out, as an undisturbed expanse of wall catches my eye. The groove ever so slightly worn into the panel where it slipped open to reveal her safe. Kane and I used to joke about what Nova might keep in there: sweets, dangerous potions, a monster. She barely let us look *at* it, much less *in* it. I shouldn't want to know—anything she locked up should stay that way. I brush my hand against my crotch in reminder of my own dedication.

Dedication to what?

The question hits me like the first swing of a paddle: hard and jarring. Throwing me off my feet. Nova's not here anymore. Those FOEs locked her up. I'm the only one left who can carry on. I am the cause. What if there's something inside this safe that could help me? That Nova would've shown me before my quarter century, anyway?

I point Calvin and Lilian down to the path before ducking back into Nova's office. My fingers slide into the groove right where hers did, prying the wood paneling back. With my hand to my lips, I speak, "Open." I press my palm to the cool metal surface. It doesn't budge. Damn. Must be advanced magic.

I fit the panel back into place, throw the canvas bag over my shoulder, and jog to catch up with Calvin and Lilian. They wait for me by the locked gate. Facing it, and the long walk back to the fence, with a bag weighed down by steel and leather, I find myself surprisingly glad for their company. Even if they are outsiders. We climb over the small gate one at a time, finagling the heavy bag up and over.

I'm the last one out, my feet slamming against the pavement. When I rise, I see him, coming up the path toward the commune gates—not fifty feet from the outsiders. Kane. Long black hair hanging loose around his arms. A sweatshirt zipped up to his neck. Lips parted as if my name is waiting on them.

I push between the outsiders and run to him—almost run *into* him. I stop short, only feet away. Rest my weight on my toes, but don't spring into his arms, not yet. My breath comes ragged and desperate. When I left Kane earlier, I was prepared to risk everything to save him, the person he was before he left us. Is that person here, now? Did he manage to throw off the bonds of corruption?

Has he come back?

"You're here," I say, daring to smile. I can't hide the note of hope in my voice, even though the emotion bleeds my magic.

"Yeah." He looks over his shoulder, worried, then at Calvin and Lilian, who stand whispering behind me. "Who're they?"

"Outsiders. They offered to help me on my quest. One of them has a car. But now that you're here . . ." Kane looks over his shoulder again, and I try to catch what he's looking for. "Are you here with someone?" He seems off. "How'd you get out?"

"Lark . . ."

He doesn't have to finish. I see them coming up the path in the distance. A FOE dressed in a black-and-white suit with short brown hair. The one that calls herself Agent Miller. I draw in a breath, but her stench invades my nostrils. The sickening scent of rot. My mouth fills with the saliva that comes before vomit, but I swallow hard. "You're here with them," I whisper.

Kane doesn't look at me directly. "Agent Miller asked for my help. She needed someone who knows the facilities, including the Anointed's and Nova's."

"You don't have to do this." I grab his forearms, forgoing caution, and pull his body against mine. He feels warm and familiar, not like a monster at all. It's cruel that I need him so much, that our connection both strengthens our magic and drains it. "Come with me. Please," I beg, squeezing his arm, pulling and hoping.

Before he can answer, a familiar voice shouts, "That's Lark! I see him over there!" It's Deryn, looking like a dull version of me. Undisciplined, their hair and clothes free-flowing. Not unlike Kane, now . . .

"Let's go." I turn and Kane's fingers slip through mine. "Come on, it's not too late!"

But Kane doesn't move. I back up, and he lets me go, unmoving as I retreat toward Calvin and Lilian, even as the FOE Miller approaches with her inhuman eyes—pits so black as to be absent.

"Run," I say to the outsiders, and they don't hesitate. Lilian takes off first, followed by Calvin. "Get to the fence, same way we came. Go!"

When Miller reaches Kane, I see it. The ripple, the unnatural shiver beneath his skin. A hint of what FOEs look like. Has it come to this? I knew he'd forgotten himself, but has he spent so much time helping evil that he's become a Force of Evil himself? He didn't feel like one, but . . .

I don't look back at Kane again. I run, because I cannot bear to see him becoming one of them. But I can't outrun the image in my head, the twitch of wrong under his skin. I feel nauseous and the smell of decay isn't helping.

Ahead, Calvin looks back for me, as he and Lilian navigate the winding path. They disappear into the trees—that means they aren't too far from the fence. They'll beat me. They can start the car. Good. I struggle to keep up my pace, to breathe without vomiting.

"Freeze!" shouts the FOE.

I can't. Can't be near her. Have to keep moving. The path veers into the trees and I follow, jumping the railing that lines the cement as it winds like a snake. I land on my feet, run to the next railing. Jump and land. Miller's footsteps grow louder behind me. Pounding faster—she's not hopping the rails, and she *stinks*.

I round the last bend and bump into Lilian. "What are you doing?"

"Running!" Lilian says, waving the shoes she now holds in her hands.

They should be in the car by now. They're not fast enough—never trained like I did. The FOE is going to catch us, unless . . .

"Keep going," I shout, not that I need to. She doesn't stop.

But Calvin does. "What are you doing?"

Together, we watch Miller as she races down the path toward us, suit rumpled, hair hanging in her eyes. "I'm going to stall her. Can you take the weapons?" But he doesn't answer; her approach paralyzes him. I push the canvas bag into his hands. "Calvin!"

"Yes! I've got it."

"Then, go!"

He struggles to find his grip on the heavy bag before jogging off. I don't have time to make sure he reaches the fence, or that Lilian is there. I can only trust them at this point. Our lives are in one another's hands.

I bring mine to my lips. Speak into them as if I am speaking directly to the FOE Miller. Through my fingers, I watch her approach. Watch Kane trying to keep up. She won't make it past me, though. None of them will. I pour my words into my palms, feeling my energy swell. Watch Miller pull her weapon from its holster.

"What are you doing?" Kane shouts, whether at her or me, I can't tell.

The FOE slows, only a few dozen feet away now. With one hand, she pushes her sweaty hair from her face. With the other, she raises her gun. I flatten one of my hands against my chest, digging my fingers into the borrowed shirt. Protective magic flows through me, coating me.

I am not afraid of her outsider weapons.

"This is your final warning." The FOE slows to a stop, catches her breath, steadies her aim. "Put down your weapons, get on the ground, and put your hands behind your head."

I do not bend to FOEs. I thrust my other hand in her direction, throwing the force of my magic with a *bang* so loud, my ears fizzle. They hurt. I hurt. I'm hit.

I wipe trembling fingers through the blood that flows down the side of my arm, look up to see the gun skittering across the path and, as the buzz in my ears quiets, the muffled shouts of Miller and Kane. I have to go.

I try to run, but stumble. Find my footing, but I'm becoming light-headed, and the blood—I loosen my hold to assess the wound, but it's too much. I stagger. Force my feet forward, one in front of the other. *Faster, Lark.* I've bled in combat before, but only in practice. Never against a true opponent. Never someone who's trying to kill me.

I fix my sight on the weak spot in the fence. Calvin stands on the other side, having already crossed through. He's waving me on, looking between me and the car, which I can barely hear Lilian start over the buzzing. The bang still echoes in my head.

I cross through the same broken wards in the fence as before, eyes closed this time, as I hold on to the iron pickets—try to hold myself together.

"Jesus, are you okay?" Before I can tell him I'm fine, Calvin slides his arm around me, taking most of my weight as I stumble over a patch of sprawling roots. "You're bleeding."

He grabs my arm, and I wince. For a fleeting second, I'm grateful for the pain. Maybe it'll recharge some of my power, after I put so much of myself into stopping the FOE. It did work—at least partially. Outsider weapons are harder to defend against than I thought.

As Calvin and I slide into the back seat—as he slams the door—I watch Miller slam into the fence, searching for a way through. Kane isn't far behind. Kane. It's almost more painful to lose him a second time. And even more important that I see my quest through.

Shouts follow us as Lilian peels away from Druid Hill. Another *bang*! I don't look—none of us looks, as the car speeds up the street and swerves onto the main road.

"What the hell happened back there?" Lilian asks. "Who was that? And why were they shooting at us?"

"That was a FOE—ow!" I gasp as pain shoots through my arm.

Calvin shifts away from me. "Sorry, sorry," he says. "What do we—I don't know what to do." He seems to be talking to himself, which is not useful. If another Anointed were here, they would heal me. Care for me.

"Oh my god, is he bleeding?" Lilian shouts.

My ears fizzle painfully again. "Can you please not be so loud? My ears hurt."

"I'm more concerned about the blood!"

"He'll be worse than bleeding if you don't look where you're going!" Calvin tells her.

The car jolts sideways, and I open my eyes. Lilian repositions her hands on the wheel, muscles tense in her fingers. "Sorry, I'm not used to driving your car, but I can do this. The nearest hospital is—"

"No," I say with as much authority as I can muster. "Outsiders can't help me. They don't know how to treat Anointed Ones. And they all wear uniforms."

"What's wrong with uniforms?" Lilian asks, half looking at me, half at the road. We swerve again. Sirens sound—close enough that we can hear them, but not so close that I'm worried. Even if the FOE chased us, she was on foot. We have the advantage as long as Lilian doesn't drive us to an outsider hospital.

"Outsiders wear uniforms to project authority—enforce outsider rules. They follow the bidding of monsters. They're FOEs." A wave of dizziness hits me; I sway between Calvin's body and the window as gray specks fall like snow across my field of vision. "I can deal with this on my own. Let's just get out of here."

The car stops, and Lilian looks at Calvin again. At me.

A surge of hot pain slices up my arm and through my shoulder. "Do you want them to catch us?" I ask through gritted teeth.

"It's a red light." She nods toward a hunk of yellow metal hanging from a thin wire over the street. On its face, two blank circles and one bright red. "That means stop."

"Do you think the FOE will stop for a red light?"

"N-no? But I can't just—" She looks left and right. Curls her pink pointed nails into the wheel.

"No one's coming, Lil, just go," Calvin says.

"But—" The siren cuts her off. It's close enough to worry now.

"You heard him." His eyes meet hers in the overhead mirror, and I feel their unspoken bond. "Please, this is important."

The car lurches forward through the intersection. Lilian drives for several minutes, hands tense, eyes forward. She doesn't look into the mirror at us again. "Where do you want us to go?" Calvin asks, when we can no longer hear the siren.

"Um." Truthfully, I've never left Druid Hill before this week. In the month leading up to his quest, Kane took one-on-one lessons with Nova, plotting his journey, but I never got that far. I have no idea how to pick a monster to hunt, or how to track it once I do. How to kill one when I reach it. All I know is I need someplace quiet and safe where I can heal and recharge my magic.

I'm going to have to ask one of them for help. The thought brings a flush to my face so hot, it feels like I was shot there too.

"West. Go west," I say, because I know we're on the East Coast. I want to get as far as possible from the FOEs that destroyed my home. Monsters are everywhere. If it were my quarter century, I wouldn't hesitate to track them across the country, but after facing only one FOE, I'm not certain I'd succeed.

I readjust my grip on my arm and a stream of dark red blood blooms down the length of the white shirt Calvin loaned me. The one with the yellow mouse-looking creature on the front, with a tail like a lightning bolt. It's kind of cute, actually, and I don't want to see it ruined. But I don't tell him that. I can't enjoy outsider artifice. That's what leads to corruption.

"I know you're going to heal yourself later, but please . . ." Calvin reaches toward my injured arm. "Let me help you with that. We can at least stop the bleeding."

I don't hesitate as long as I should. Every time I move my arm, the pain sears through me, and I doubt we're anywhere near stopping. "Okay," I say, offering my arm to him.

"I'm not, like, a medical professional or anything, but I've watched enough action movies to know that pressure helps." He sticks his arm elbow-deep into his backpack and feels around, eventually pulling out a red bandana. "Woody cosplay." He smiles sheepishly as he shrugs. Neither word means anything to me.

Gently, he pushes the sleeve up until it reaches where I've clamped my hand against the wound. "It's from an animated movie about—"

"Wood?" I grit my teeth, hold my breath, and release my grip. Instantly, blood begins flowing, my heart pounding. I hear it like a strong wind in my ears.

"No." Calvin chuckles. "Toys."

Toys are nonsense distractions, but I don't say it. Doesn't seem right to insult something that's got him smiling. I rest my head back against the seat and cede control to Calvin. I've already accepted his help, his clothes, a ride in his car, so what's a bandage count for in the grand scheme of things? It's impossible to save the world from behind a big iron fence.

"Yeah." His laugh is breathy and hot. "But really it's about chosen family and what's real." With a hard pull, he secures the bandana over my wound; I wince but manage not to yank my arm away.

Calvin keeps going on about the movie, but I can't concentrate. It's not like I can't handle pain, but this injury is outside my control. A FOE's bullet *pierced my body*. My enemy's weapon working inside me, tearing my muscle or poisoning my blood. Our blood—the blood of those Anointed—is lethal to monsters. That's why they try to kill us from afar. But as Calvin works and talks, the pain dulls. Maybe, we beat the FOE Miller's toxin.

"You'd like it," Calvin says as he ties off the bandana. "All done."

I glance down at his handiwork and cradle my arm so that it doesn't shake every time Lilian hits a bump in the road. "Maybe." I don't tell him I've never watched a movie in my life, and never plan to. Outsider propaganda beaming right into my body, corrupting me? Not if I killed every monster in the world.

"Can I ask"—Calvin lowers his voice—"was that Kane? The one on the path."

I don't answer right away. The car hugs a tight curve before emerging onto the widest stretch of road I've ever seen. Four lanes wide on each side. Dozens—no, *hundreds* of cars speeding past and alongside us. Nothing I trained for prepared me to see this.

"Yes." Really, it's none of his business, but I suppose if he's going to help, he should have at least the basic information. I rest my cheek against the cold glass window and take comfort in seeing

that the autumn leaves are just as beautiful outside the fence. "But
he made his choice."

My eyes grow heavy. And while I'm glad I'm not alone, I ache.
Kane should be beside me. Zadie and Maeve in the front seat. Four
bodies full of magic and a tank full of gas. I crack the window
and fall asleep with the breeze nipping at the hairs loosed from my
braids.

14

DERYN / NOW

I stand near the entrance to the commune like an abandoned doll. I came here to help Agent Miller, but, of course, she and Kane ran off the second she saw Lark. After a shinier toy. I shift my weight, not leaving the place they left me—I could if I wanted to. This was my home too. I know its paths and places. I'm not a prisoner; I can go. But, where?

I stuff my hands into the pockets of the coat one of the social workers gave me. It's purple and shiny and the material whirrs when I scrape my nails over it. Kane didn't want one. Too bulky, he'd said, too hot. But I thought it was nice to have options, to style myself in something besides muted earth tones.

Ten minutes pass before he appears over the hill, alone. Mouth a taut line, forehead furrowed. Hands balled into fists, he storms down the path toward me, looking into the distance at Miller's car, as if he's going to drive off on his own.

"What happened?" I ask when he's within earshot. Still, he doesn't look at me. It's odd even talking to him. Fellows and Anointed rarely cross paths, and then only during rituals and meals. Since we crossed the fence, I've had to work myself up every time I wanted to speak to him. How ridiculous. He's no better than me—even he doesn't think so anymore.

"Kane." I turn my body to follow him as he nears. "Kane, where'd Lark—"

When I use Lark's name he sees me. As if, until then, I was a tree to walk around. "She shot him."

I raise my eyebrows. "Miller *shot* him? With what?" My words are breathy with . . . hope? I feel the curl in my lips. A smile? I know Miller didn't kill Lark, or Kane wouldn't be throwing a tantrum. He'd be sobbing on the ground, inconsolable. He'd wail like the sirens that sound outside the fence.

"With a gun." Kane stops when he reaches me, as Miller comes jogging over the hill. Her suit jacket is unbuttoned, gun visible in its holster, hair falling out of its sleek hold.

"Where?" I ask, but my question is lost to Miller's arrival. It's probably for the best. I force my lips into a straight line, mimicking Kane's anger.

Miller doesn't slow. She digs her keys from her pocket and barrels toward the car. "Get in."

But Kane doesn't move, so I don't either. I stand off to the side like one of the teachers supervising recreation. I watch and wait for him to combust. For Miller to react. She holds the door open and looks between us—as if I have any stake in what just happened. I don't care about Lark. I've tried to be his sibling numerous times, and he's reminded me consistently that I am not. That he's Anointed and I'm a Fellow. He's someone and I'm no one.

"Let's get you two back to the hotel," Miller says. "I'll send out a team to pick up Lark."

Kane doesn't move. He pinches his fingers together and punctuates his words. "You *shot* him."

"Why are we still arguing over this?" Annoyance threads her voice. "I wasn't aiming for anything vital. The situation would be under control right now, if you hadn't grabbed at my gun."

An Anointed charging in to save the day and fucking things up. I roll my eyes.

"You shouldn't even have been pointing it." He scowls.

"Look," Miller says, waving him off. "We'll get Lark medical help, as soon as they bring him in."

"Absolutely not," Kane says. "You think I'm going to let you call more outsiders with guns? We need to go get him ourselves."

Miller already has her phone out. A ring emanates from its speaker. "I'm calling for backup. You can come back to the hotel with us or not."

Riiing.

Kane shrugs.

Riiing.

"I can testify or not." He stares at Miller. Challenges her.

My heart is in my damn throat, and I'm choking on it. I've only ever seen Kane prostrate himself before authority, but we can object now. Can make choices outside what's handed to us.

I take a chance. "I'll testify. Let's go back to the hotel. We don't need Kane—or Lark."

Miller doesn't even look at me. She holds Kane's gaze. "You're really going to risk Nova going free?"

"Yes," he says. "If it means Lark's safe. You just shot him! I can't imagine what a bunch of agents will do."

"They'll take him to the hospital, and then bring him back to the hotel."

Kane crosses his arms. Looks at his feet. Why is Miller even allowing this to drag out? "Lark can take care of himself," he finally mumbles. "Better than outsiders would."

"Hello?" a tinny voice says from Miller's phone. "Miller, can you hear me?"

She holds the phone in front of her face, not speaking, not looking at it. She bites her lip. "False alarm, ma'am. I'll contact you with any updates."

The person in the phone sighs. "Thank you, Agent."

Miller pockets the phone and strolls toward Kane, eyes trailing up his body, sizing him up. I can't decide who I want to win. I hate that, even on the outside, an Anointed One gets all the attention, holds all the power. But I need Miller to need us. Need me.

"You don't need Kane." I step between them. "I can testify for you. I can even help your team track down Lark—he's my brother." That doesn't feel like much. But what is real? If there was never magic, what does Kane have that I don't?

Miller looks between us. Doesn't even look at me when she says, "No. I need Kane's testimony, if not Lark's."

"But, why? I told you, I was Anointed as a child; it clearly doesn't mean anything."

Kane rolls his eyes. "It means *everything*. Just not in the way you think." He clips his words.

"He's right, Deryn." Miller's face slackens. She shakes her head and looks at me, sympathetic for the first time. "I'm sorry."

"Doubt it," I mutter.

"I won't call for backup—we can bring Lark home ourselves—if you agree to testify," she tells Kane. She's back to ignoring me, but I will stand up for myself.

Kane works himself back up. "If Lark's hurt—"

"—I will make sure he gets appropriate medical attention; I would still like him to testify." Miller smooths her loosed hairs back into place, then opens the car door. "Ride in the front with me, Deryn."

I perk up at the sound of my name. At the scowl that crosses Kane's face, when he's denied special treatment. Being Anointed doesn't mean what it used to. They're not special anymore. They can be wrong. They can be hurt. And I don't feel one bit sorry that the thought warms me inside.

•   •   •

We drive in the big car-truck that Miller calls a sport-utility vehicle. Not that we're playing sports. But it's shiny, black, and fast, and from the front seat I can see everything. Over other cars, through traffic. I wish I could enjoy the advantage, but my stomach tightens as I try to dredge up any knowledge about Lark and the Anointed. I don't want Kane to be right—I don't want Miller to need him. The Anointed were and are in no way better than me. If I can help her, she'll see that.

I count the things I know about him. Lark rejects family—both me and the parents we share. He thinks he's invincible, better than everyone else. He believes he needs to slay a monster that isn't actually real. Probably. I scan the trees that line the highway, trees that could hide anything. If the outsiders are wrong, I'll be glad Kane's with us. They're not wrong, but they could be. Anyone *could* be.

I bounce my knees up and down. Try to flush everything I was taught from my brain. The world is different now. It doesn't matter if Kane could kill a monster, because monsters aren't real.

Lark is hurt. That's real. He's on the run with two outsiders. Where would they go? Not back to the city. He had a bag of supplies from Druid Hill. He was wearing one of those harnesses. His mind is on one thing only: monsters. Nova didn't teach us Fellows any of the details, but I know monsters are the reason the outside is corrupt.

"So, where is he?" Miller asks, her eyes on the road. "Where would Lark have gone?"

I feel Kane look at me, consulting. Only fifteen minutes ago, he said being Anointed was everything.

"Well, he's hunting a monster," I say.

Kane shakes his head. "No—I mean, yes. He is, but he's hurt. He'll—"

"He'll need to heal himself," I finish, face burning. I don't look at Kane, but I know he's still watching me. Miller isn't, thank goodness. Her eyes remain on the road, her jaw set.

"Can he do that in a car?"

I'm not sure, but I say, "No," before Kane can. He wouldn't have brought it up if it wasn't relevant to Lark's journey. I remember the ritual spaces we Fellows weren't allowed to visit, the secluded outdoor clearings. "He'll need to stop."

"Okay, good." Miller nods, relaxing her grip on the steering wheel. "I only grazed his arm, so the injury isn't urgent, but he might not know that. Hm."

I can tell she's thinking, and I don't have anything else to offer. Quick, Deryn. What can I—

"He'll also need to . . ." Kane trails off. What's he going to say? I try not to look at him. To focus forward as if Miller and I are on the same level. "He'll need to recharge his magic."

I can't help but snort. "You know that's not real, right?"

"It is to him." Kane leans forward so that he's practically in the front seat with us. I grip the armrests to resist pushing him back. "That's what matters."

"So, how does he 'recharge his magic'?" I ask. "Does he need to sleep? Eat? Plug into an outlet?"

"No." But Kane doesn't elaborate. I hate that I want him to. "He'll need to stop and he'll need . . ." He pulls back slowly. I don't even notice until he's not there.

"He'll need what?" I ask.

"Help. From someone else, probably one of those outsiders." Does Kane sound *sad*? I glance in the mirror above the glass front of the car. He is sad. What in the hell is going on with him?

"So, he'll be stopping soon for various reasons. No surprise," Miller says. "I'm more concerned about which direction he's going. We're currently going north because that's the nearest highway out of Baltimore, but I'm going to have to choose soon. Do I continue north? Turn west? South?"

Neither of us answer—I don't know how we would. Could Kane track the monster Lark's chasing? I sure can't. When I look his way, he's staring gloomily out the window.

"Kane?" Miller looks at him in the overhead mirror.

It takes him another moment to meet her eyes. "What?"

"You're the one who demanded we go after Lark. Is there anything you can do to help?"

"What do you mean?" I don't intend to say it aloud, but there's an edge in Miller's voice, like she's hinting something forbidden.

Kane's face creases with suspicion. "I know as much about where he went as you do—and you're the one who chased him off. What do you expect out of me?"

"Magic," I whisper.

"I'm sorry, what?" Kane blinks as if surfacing from underwater. "Magic? You want me to do magic, which you told me isn't actually real. I've spent months sharing the intimate details of my life, trying to get over that—over all the lies Nova taught me. The hurt she caused. And now you want me to do magic."

Miller shrugs. "I didn't say that."

Kane folds his arms. "You meant it."

Until the last few days, I've believed in magic my entire life, but I can't do it. My Anointed status was revoked long before my powers could manifest. When Lark's did, it confirmed everything he ever thought—that he was better than me and everyone else. Magic became his identity. If it isn't real, is he even Anointed?

"What about mindspeech?" Miller says.

I've never heard of mindspeech before—have the Anointed been able to communicate silently all this time? No, because it's not real, I remind myself. Kane doesn't comment.

"You could reach out," Miller continues. "Ping him, as you call it."

"Why are you asking me to do this?" His voice wobbles. "You don't even believe."

I watch Miller consider the accusation. Kane has poked something. What is it?

"I thought you wanted us to find Lark. Without backup. If

you're not willing to help, we can set up a dragnet and close all the roads out of Baltimore. I don't need you to find Lark, but I am trying to work with you, because I value your testimony."

Kane sniffs. He catches me looking and holds my gaze for the first time, as if he needs me. He's looking for my company, my sympathy, my support. I snap my head forward to the road and readjust the uncomfortable belt that crosses my chest. How am I supposed to respond to Kane's need? After all these years, he wants something from me. I'm just as surprised to hear Miller suggest magic; I have no help to offer him. She didn't bring it up during our interview, but I assumed . . . it's what all the social workers and other outsiders were telling us.

I wait. Listen to the hum of the road beneath us and the *thump-thump* every time we hit a bump or dip. Miller looks sideways at me. Nods toward the back before returning her eyes to the road. She wants me to check on him. She consulted *me* to make sure the Anointed One is doing his part.

I glance over my shoulder. Kane's eyes are closed, his cheeks wet. He blinks rapidly. He looks at me when he says, "West. I feel him moving west."

"Thank you." Miller switches lanes, glancing up at the big green signs that cross the highway.

Kane wipes his tears on his sleeve, and I have to look away. I force myself to read the signs rather than watch him cry. It isn't my fault . . . is it? He's the one who said being Anointed meant "everything." He said he'd help Miller. He agreed to this. I still can't help wondering why she asked, though. Why she would bring up magic after everything.

• • •

Eventually, Miller presses a button and voices fill the car. I hear two people talking about current events. They mention Lark. Neither Miller nor Kane reacts as I listen to the outsiders describe him as armed and dangerous. Delusional. I hear them laughing at him—at us.

It's dark for a long time before Miller says, "We're stopping. Do either of you know how to use the maps app on a smartphone?"

I shake my head. Kane doesn't answer out loud, and I don't look back to check on him.

"That's fine," she says. "We'll do it the old-fashioned way." She scans the signs as we pass them, eventually pulling off an exit and into a small, half-empty parking lot of something called a Night Inn.

"This is a motel," Miller says, getting out of the car. I do the same, but when Kane doesn't, she opens the back door for him. "Can you two share a room?"

Kane's feet hit the ground. The door slams behind him. He shrugs.

"Fine with me," I say, and Miller nods. Not ten minutes later, she hands me a white plastic card with NIGHT INN printed on one side. I remember how to use this thing from the hotel in the city, and I'm pleased to unlock the door without having to ask Miller for help. I can handle myself out here, beyond the fence.

The door clicks quietly shut behind us. It's odd, closing ourselves off from the outdoors. It's not that we slept outside on Druid Hill all the time, but I'm not used to sleeping behind a door that locks. A few weeks ago, the whole Fellowship moved into their winter quarters, and I moved with a dozen other Fellows into a big glass building that used to house giant apes. When I was younger—when I was Anointed—I used to imagine that's what monsters looked like.

"Was that true?" I ask Kane, now that we're alone. "Is Lark really going west?"

He flops down on one of the beds. It creaks under his weight. "Maybe."

"You'd better not be lying." I unlace my boots, wishing we'd thought to grab some clothes before chasing Lark. Surely, *he* did. The room is warm enough and so dry I feel an itch creep across my arms. "You heard Miller; she can send a team of agents to—"

"To what? To shoot at him again?" Anger sears hot across his cheeks.

"She didn't kill him or anything," I say. "Sheesh."

"Didn't kill him? That's your standard." Kane stands and walks toward me slowly.

Even though I feel like his prey, I don't move. I'm not a Fellow out here. Kane's not Anointed. We're the same. "Yeah, well, he's attacked multiple outsiders. Besides, it's not like he couldn't stand to be reminded he's human like the rest of us—that he bleeds too."

"Of course he bleeds!" Kane hisses. "I know. I've seen it."

My heart pounds in my ears; I'm afraid of the Anointed, even though I shouldn't be. I can still feel the bruise on my chest. "Then see this." I hook a finger in the collar of my dress and drag it down. Expose the yellowing edges of the mark Lark left when he slammed me across the kitchen. I take it back. We are different. "See what you Anointed do to us. Look what I went through."

"What you went through?" Kane pulls his shirt over his head as if he's fighting his way out of it. Strands of black hair fall in a halo around his face and land on his shoulders, breaking the line of a thick scar. "What about what I went through?" Dozens of thin shiny lines trace down his arms. Divots mark the left side of his torso. "Consider yourself lucky."

Kane turns and walks into the bathroom, exposing a web of scars on his back. He slams the door so loud, I'm sure Miller heard it. I sit on my bed, hand still against my chest. As I listen to the shower water blast, I press my palm against the fading bruise. Feel the residual pain.

I take it back. We are different.

15

CALVIN / NOW

"Is he still breathing?" Lilian glances into the back seat before returning her eyes to the dark of the road. A car pulls up alongside us and she watches them longer than a driving instructor would recommend. I do too. Even though I believe Lark cast a spell to disguise the car, I need to believe it worked—believe *him*.

"Yeah," I say, watching the slow rise and fall of his chest. "He's still breathing. Been out for a while, though. What time is it?" I yawn.

"Almost ten." She adjusts her grip on the wheel and watches the car beside us pull slowly ahead. Too slowly. "Do we keep driving?"

"I have no idea." But I was wondering the same. This isn't really our trip. We've never hunted monsters before. Didn't even know they existed until today. "Probably? He said he wanted to heal."

"What happened to him?"

Normally, Lil and I would've dished as soon as Lark fell asleep, but for some reason it felt like he was still watching us. Like he'd know if we said the wrong thing. Catch on that we have no idea what he's doing. Three hours is a long time to sit in silence.

"Bullet grazed him, I think. Didn't get a great look. He told me to take his bag and go. It looked like he was going to fight her, but I didn't stay to watch." Should I have helped? I would only have gotten in the way. I'm no use against a gun.

Lilian sighs and looks at me in the rearview mirror. "You gave me a goddamn heart attack when you got back out of the car and went to meet him at the fence, Cal. Promise me you won't do anything stupid like that again. This isn't a fantasy novel."

I shift, adjusting my shirt over the stolen wand that's still jammed into my pocket. Its length presses hard against my abdomen. Lilian would laugh at me for taking it, and Lark . . . I'd probably lose his trust.

"I promise." But my gaze drifts to Lark, curled up against the window, and I can't help but want to hold him. Protect him from people who would rather shoot than help him. If I could do magic, things would be different.

"Okay, good. Everything's going to be fine." Lilian grips the wheel so tight, her hands tremble.

"Let's stop," I say, taking the burden of decision from her and opening the maps app on my phone. "We all need to rest. I'll check if there are any motels in the area. Any *cheap* motels."

Lilian nods, her limbs relaxing. The car that was driving beside us finally pulls far enough ahead that my suspicion eases.

"There's a Motel 9 twenty-three minutes away. Only fifty dollars a night."

"Sold." She holds her hand out, and I press Go before giving her my phone.

Our silence resumes for exactly twenty-three minutes until we pull into an empty space at the Motel 9. The parking lot looks like a mouth with missing teeth, so few cars dot its spaces. Fluorescent light beams from behind an expanse of sliding doors.

"If you want to get us a room, I'll wake him." I nod at Lark. He never buckled his seat belt.

"Do we—" Lilian lowers her voice and leans closer. "Do we want to sleep in the same room as him? What if he . . ." She shrugs dramatically as her lips thin.

"What if he what?" Lark hasn't given us any reason not to trust him. He's the one making the leap of faith. He can't drive, doesn't have any money, doesn't know what *Toy Story* is. And he's hurt. I wonder if he'll let me watch him heal. Wonder what it'll look like. As polite as I'm trying to be, I'm desperate to watch more magic. To do some.

"He's got a bag full of weapons."

"I'll . . ." I can't find an argument against that. "I'll tell him to leave them in the car if he tries to bring them. It's probably against hotel policy, anyway."

Lilian nods, shuts the door, and walks off to the lobby. I sit beside Lark, watching him sleep. Something glitters around his neck, disappears down below his collar, and ends in several small bumps between his chest and shirt.

What is he keeping so close to him? So hidden. He's been asleep for hours; he won't notice if . . .

Gently, I lift a silver chain from his collarbone. It slides effortlessly through the crook of my finger as I pull it from under his shirt. The bumps rise toward his collar, and I'm sure I'm about to discover a magical medallion or sigil or potion vial, when—

Lark gasps.

I drop the chain and press my fingers against his shoulder as if I were nudging him awake. My body burns with embarrassment as he looks at me, at the empty driver's seat, at the length of chain hanging over his shirt.

"We stopped." It's all I can think to say.

His eyes flick to the lobby as he straightens up. "Stopped where?"

"A motel," I say, unbuckling my seat belt. "You said you needed to heal, and it's late. Lilian needs a break after driving so long."

"How far have we gone?"

"Three-ish hours west. We didn't know where to go, so we kept driving the direction you told us before you fell asleep."

"Good," Lark says. "West is good." He looks at the various buttons and handles on the car door before pulling the correct one.

When I get out, I feel the press of the wand against me, reminding me of what I've done. Lark doesn't seem too alert, though. He stands beside the car, blinking the sleep from his eyes before look-ing around the parking lot, as I open the hatch. "Here's yours." I hand him the duffel I packed him, then move to close the hatch. I unzip my bag. Make sure to stand between it and him, before quickly slipping the wand inside.

"Wait, my . . ."

I freeze. He can't have seen.

"My other bag."

Relief floods me. "Sorry, we're not actually allowed to bring weapons into the motel."

"Oh." He ponders this for a moment before saying, "I suppose that's fine. I'll ward the hotel room as a precaution."

I lock the car just as Lil's exiting the lobby. She looks both ways before crossing the extremely dead parking lot and trades me a key card for her suitcase. "Room 216."

Lark and I follow her around the back of the L-shaped motel, past a rusty playground, up an elevator with an expired certificate—I don't tell Lark—and down a long row of doors. Whenever I stay at a motel, I'm glad to be on the second floor. It feels safer for some reason. I hate the idea of opening my bedroom door onto the street.

Jeopardy shines so brightly through our neighbor's window, I have to shield my eyes while Lilian unlocks the door. She opens it for me and I hold it for Lark, but he doesn't follow. His grip on his bag slackens before he drops it on the concrete walkway and steps up to our neighbor's window. He stares, face alight from the glow of their television.

I know *Jeopardy* isn't *The Fellowship of the Ring.* It isn't even *The Hobbit* (though I refuse to hate those movies). But when I watch Lark watching Alex Trebek, I remember how I felt when Orlando Bloom dismounted his horse at the Council of Elrond. I saw that movie eleven times in theaters, just for that moment. I told my mom I needed the money for a field trip. When she found out what I spent it on, she stopped giving me allowance. A prelude to when she stopped paying for my education.

"What're you watching?" I ask quietly, stepping closer. I'm afraid that asking will ruin this moment.

Lark blinks and turns to look at me. "Nothing." His eyes linger on the screen for a second—long enough that he could play it off if he wanted. Long enough to notice. "I don't watch television. I'm Anointed, and outsider media corrupts us." He picks up his bag and brushes past me as he walks into our room.

I know that's not true because he was watching Kane on the news in our convention hotel room. Shut that off the instant I caught him, though. I wish he didn't feel like he had to deny himself joy. It's hard to give yourself that permission when you're expected otherwise.

Lil pokes her head outside. "I'm okay," I tell her before she can ask, and bring my things inside. In the time since Lark and I were staring at Alex Trebek together, he's claimed the bed closest to the window and is untucking the meticulously folded sheets.

I drop my suitcase beside the other bed. Lil's already hovering over the sink, taking her makeup off. Every now and then, she sneaks a glance at Lark in the mirror, while rubbing a cream or serum over her face. She doesn't trust him. I really want to, but he's sure as hell not making it easy. Maybe I'm going about this wrong. I should just talk to him. Explain that it's fine if he's interested in outsider media; it won't make him less magic. It might even make him happier.

We walked through that fence. It was solid and then it wasn't. Lark did that, and Alex Trebek can't take that away from him.

"Uhh, Lark," Lilian says, pressing a sheet mask onto her face. She points into the mirror. "Lark, where are you—"

I turn in time to watch him slip out the door and onto the walkway. "Dammit."

"Real talk time," she says, before I can go after him.

I know where she's going with this. "No."

"No, *you* no. Listen to me. That guy just got shot. What if we're doing more harm than good here? What if he doesn't want to be with us?" She trains her eyes on the open door and says, "What if this isn't real, and you just want it to be?"

I purse my lips.

"I'm sorry; I had to say it in case it's true—I don't want it to be!"

I feel my brain form the words, *Even if it is,* but refuse to finish the sentence. Even thinking it feels traitorous. Sure, I've barely met the guy, but I know belief when I see it. Know the deep longing of needing something to be true. "You know what sucks?" I don't wait for an answer. "When no one believes you—when the person you're *closest to* doesn't believe you." I rush out into the cool night air, unsure whether I meant Lark or myself. I don't dare speak either into existence.

"Calvin, come back!" I hear Lilian call out, but I don't stop and she doesn't run after me. Probably finishing her face mask or whatever, and that's fine.

I need to find Lark. Part of me expected to bump into him watching *Jeopardy* through our neighbor's window, but I look both ways and only see an expanse of orange doors and a concrete walkway. A dozen rooms to my right, a woman leans over the railing, a cloud of smoke hovering around her head. To my left, a soaking wet kid walks up the steps, holding an inner tube around his waist. Behind him, his parents laugh and say, "I told you it would be cold!"

Maybe Lark went back out to the car to get his weapons. Maybe Lil was right, I feel myself think. The words barely graze the surface of my mind. No. I decided to trust him. His magic is real. He's real.

I accidentally brush the inner tube as I walk past the kid who thought a pool in October would be a good idea. The plastic seam grazes my elbow, and I shiver, wiping the cold wet spot off my arm.

I check the parking lot as I make my way down to the ground floor. Two salt-and-pepper bears split around me, carrying laundry baskets and arguing over whether it's worth separating whites and colors. One is proclaiming that mixing everything saves time and water, when they stop. Not like the conversation ended or their gruff voices faded into a hotel room, but like their voices were snuffed out.

I turn on my heel, forgetting the car. I forget everything else, when I see what they see. On the other side of the pool, Lark pushes yellowing lounge chairs aside before removing a small vial from his harness. He opens it and pours a thick liquid in a circle on the concrete. When he brings one of his hands to his lips, my heart races with anticipation. I don't know what's coming, but I know it's magic.

Lark speaks a hushed word against his palm, then points at the circle. Flames flicker up from the cement around him—not golden and raging like a bonfire, but blue and tame, like a gas stove turned on low.

I push past the two bears and walk with quiet purpose around the edge of the pool, with no fucking clue what I'm going to say when I get to the other side. The sound of squeaky hinges and muttered conversation rises around me like a mantra—my skin prickles. I don't believe in God, but something about this motel patio feels sacred. Otherworldly.

Everyone is watching Lark, but he's not watching anyone. His lips move quietly and quickly, like hummingbird wings—almost a blur. I feel my phone buzz in my pocket and slide it half out to glimpse a panicked text from Lilian: What are you doing??? Get him inside everyone's staring

I don't answer. When I look up at the balcony, she's standing in her robe, motioning unsubtly for me to bring Lark back upstairs. Maybe I should. Only a few yards away now, I watch as he sits inside the circle and unties the bandana from his arm, peeling the sticky fabric from his bloodstained skin. My ears pop.

My phone buzzes incessantly against my thigh. I don't try to ignore it, really. The sensation becomes a part of it all: the whispers and stares, the disorienting pressure as I step slowly closer.

"It's that guy from the news."

Two housekeepers abandon their cart to watch.

"What'd he pour on the cement?"

The night manager leans half out of the lobby.

"Should we call someone?"

Lark's eyes meet mine like tractor beams. Wide pupils nearly black out his blue-gray irises. His lips continue moving, a soft faint chant spilling forth. I suck in a breath. My phone unleashes a stream of vibrations. My mouth hangs open for what feels like an eternity as I struggle for the right words—words that will earn his trust and, maybe, an invitation to participate.

"Do you need help?" The words tumble out. Not the elegance I intended, but exactly what I meant.

Lark's lips still, but the air is thick with whispers—his or everyone else's. He considers me. Glances down at his arm. At the bloody handkerchief. "Yes."

"Am I—" *Please say yes. Please say yes.* "—allowed to help? Would you be breaking any rules?"

He huffs a laugh deep in his chest. "I'm breaking the most important one by sitting here and speaking to you. By wearing your clothes and getting into your car. I'm tainted."

It doesn't sound like the end of a sentence, and I have no clue what to say, so I wait. Listen to a door swing shut in the distance. Feet slapping down steps. What if they've already called 911? We should be running. I should drag him out of the circle and lock him in the back seat of the car. We should go, but . . .

His skin looks clammy and pallid. His left arm trembles as it rests against his leg. "But that doesn't matter now. Come on. Come inside the circle." He holds out his uninjured arm. "It won't hurt you."

Taking Lark's hand feels like touching a plasma globe. A low, warm hum like electricity vibrates across my palm. I follow as he leads me to sit across from him.

"Whatever's in your pocket—"

"That's my phone. Sorry." My skin cools the instant I let go and dig around my pocket. Thirty-nine texts from Lilian telling me to get him out of there. The last one reads: I'm serious!!

I look over my shoulder at the balcony where Lilian stands, gesturing toward a woman in khakis, a button-down shirt, and striped tie, then stuff my phone back into my pants. I meet Lark's eyes. This close, they look even darker. They're electric—supernatural, as if he's transformed into a god or demon. "Lark—"

He doesn't have to shush me to silence me; I feel the impulse as if he's sent it through my nerves. My mouth dries, suddenly sticky. Lark takes my other hand and our fingers slide together, hot and slick, as if they're fitting back into place. Blood gathers at the edge of his exposed wound, forms a fat drop, and slides slowly down his bicep and the inside of his elbow, coming to rest above his wrist. The overwhelming urge to wipe it away comes from within me, not from him, so I know I can ignore it.

I hear the footsteps of the manager as she comes up alongside us, feel the heat of the circle that surrounds us. If my heart's beating, I can't tell. My whole body feels like it's pulsing—with adrenaline, with fear. This has to be what magic feels like.

The manager clears her throat. "Excuse me, gentlemen, but I'm going to have to ask you to extinguish—"

A sudden breeze cools the air. I glance at the ground and see only a damp circle on the concrete where the flame used to be.

"Oh, um. I suppose that's all." She turns but immediately spins on her heel. "I don't suppose you're the one on the news. Who escaped from that cult, the—"

"The Fellowship is not a cult," Lark says. "And I didn't escape; we were torn apart."

"Right, I'm so sorry." She clasps her hands so hard that her brown knuckles turn pale. "Do you need me to call a doctor?" She looks at the long stripe of blood on Lark's arm.

"No, but thank you. I can heal myself, if you would kindly allow my friend and me some space and quiet." From anyone else, the words would sound passive-aggressive, but it's clear Lark is choosing them carefully. Genuinely.

"Okay." The two housekeepers sidle up beside her and whisper something in another language. The manager responds to them, then says to us, "We don't call the cops here, but please be safe and don't light any more fires, or I'll have to ask you to leave."

"Reasonable," Lark says. A hint of smile shows in the dark. "Thank you."

The three of them leave, still whispering and glancing at us. I watch them enter the lobby, but linger against the glass. Watching. Everyone is watching, but no one is moving. No cops are coming.

Another drop of blood glides between the light hairs on Lark's arm. Concern lines his face. "I used too much of my power today."

I don't know how to respond, so I listen.

"I'll need to deal with that soon, but not tonight. Tonight, I need to heal." He closes his eyes while he sighs, deeply. "And rest."

Whispers rise around us again, as his lips begin to move. The sounds come faster than his lips—as if there are others here with us, chanting. I feel like I should close my eyes, but I can't. I want to see. I watch as he heals the angry line left by the bullet. Every time I blink his wound is smaller and yet I can't exactly see it shrink. Like stop motion, the cut is there, less there, faded, and then gone. A red smudge stains the spot where the bullet grazed him. Only the two blood trails down his arm give evidence there was a hole in his body.

Lark squeezes my hand and sways. When he opens his eyes, it's as if he's been roused from sleep too early. "I did it," he says, voice breathy and singular, the whispers gone. "Thank you."

"You're welcome," I say, unsure what I've done to help. All I did was sit here. I couldn't even speak up when the manager came over. "Do you need—" Lark wavers as he stands, and I quickly duck under his arm, so he can rest his weight on me. "—help? Lark, are you sure you don't need a doctor?"

He shakes his head. "Your doctors can't help me. I'm just low on magic. We can deal with it tomorrow."

We. Earlier it was *I.*

"Okay. Let's get you to bed." I become aware, as we make our way back to the stairs, how many people were watching us. Not a hundred, by any means, but dozens. Enough that any one of them could've turned Lark—and us—in, but they didn't. They part for us, still holding laundry baskets and suitcases and smoldering cigarettes. Looking into their eyes as we pass, I see bewilderment. A teenager stares, unmoving except for her thumbs flying over her phone. I try not to think about what she's typing, as Lilian meets us at the bottom of the steps. She secures her robe and helps me carry Lark up to our room.

We sit him on the edge of the bed, and I bolt the door behind us. Lilian draws the curtains closed. We look at each other and then at the exhausted, beautiful man sitting on the edge of the bed. I imagine how it would feel to press my lips against his temple. Along the messy crown of blonde hair on his head.

Lilian goes to the bathroom and returns with a wet face cloth— thin and white until she takes his left arm and wipes the blood away. Together, we unlace his boots and pull them free from his feet.

"I can do it," he says. "Thank you, though." Lark disappears into the bathroom.

"What the hell did you two do down there?" Lilian asks, still watching the bathroom door, in case he comes back out.

"No clue. I didn't mean to join; it just sort of . . ."

"Did he heal himself? Did you see it?"

"Yes and no." I scrape my nails along the insides of my palms, remembering the current that passed between us. "It didn't happen while I watched. It just sort of . . . *happened*."

"Okay." Lilian nods as if she's working through the math in her head. As if there's a scientific explanation for all this. I've seen it. I know there's not.

Lark emerges all at once, carrying his clothes in one hand. Well, not all his clothes. I try real hard not to stare at the bulge in his boxer briefs. *My* boxer briefs, technically.

The silver chain still hangs from his neck, and now I can see the small key that dangles from the end. I don't ask what it's for, but I'm dying to know. Watching him walk toward me is like watching a character walk out of a fantasy novel. I want to know everything about him. Want to learn his secrets. To absorb his magic.

Lark hangs his harness in the closet and rolls up his dirty laundry, packing it away. Then, he climbs into bed, pulls the covers up to his neck, and closes his eyes. Seconds pass but I'd swear he was unconscious already. The thin ratty blanket drapes his body as he breathes slowly and methodically.

When he doesn't move, Lilian and I take opposite sides of the other bed, sliding under the white sheets and rearranging the under-stuffed pillows until we're buried, back to back, beneath the covers. I'm closest to the nightstand, so I reach out and click off the lamp. The room is silent.

As fast as Lark fell asleep, I lie awake in the dark. Beside me, Lilian begins to snore quietly. The soundtrack as my eyes adjust and I watch Lark. In our motel room, there's nothing remarkable about him. By now, hundreds of strands of yellow hair stick out from his braids. Shadows fall under his eyes. And yet, I can't forget the electricity of his touch or his whispers filling the air. I fall asleep with them echoing in my dreams.

16

KANE / CONFIDENTIAL

None of the other Anointed were present in Ritual House. I was the first to turn twenty, Nova had explained. My powers were maturing in ways the others' had not yet. But when I arrived alone, I knew something was wrong.

Inside, it was dark and warm. Sweat blossomed on my shirt where my leather harness pressed against it. "You can remove that," Nova said.

I did without thinking—as if her words were magic that willed my fingers to move. I heard my feet scuff on wood; I hadn't noticed when I entered that the carpets that usually covered the floor had been removed. As my eyes adjusted to the dim light of the room, I made out the sigil drawn on the floorboards. Moonlight illuminated circles and lines painted stark white on the old wood.

Was all this for me? I looked around desperately, as if Lark or Maeve or Zadie might come running up the steps shouting, "Sorry I'm late!" But no one else came. It was only me and Nova.

She stood at a table littered with glass bottles and ceramic pots. Creams and oils and herbs. Ingredients. We were going to work a ritual. I could handle that. My magic did feel stronger the older I got. And she was right, without my cock to distract me, I was left only with my studies, my training.

"Remove your clothes," she said, not looking up.

Again, I did as told, folding my clothes and setting them on a chair against the wall. I wasn't ashamed to be naked. Our chastity cages and vows meant sex was never on the table. When we bared our flesh, it was for magic or discipline or ritual, not pleasure.

Nova looked up only to see if I was ready, then nodded at the sigil on the floor. "Lie down, limbs over the markings."

I studied the lines and curves, determined where my arms and legs should go, and fit myself into place like a puzzle piece. The position was strange, but not uncomfortable. Nova continued her work while I stared at the ceiling, eventually closing my eyes. The floorboards creaked and shifted under my body as she walked around the house.

Cool metal pressed my wrist against the rough floor, and I opened my eyes at the terrifying whir of a drill. Nova hovered over me, her long hair dangling around her determined face and tickling my chest as she drilled the other side of a metal half-cuff into the wood.

"Hold still," she said, not that I was moving. I was too stunned to even think about moving. What would she need to do to me that she didn't trust me to manage without restraint? I hadn't disobeyed her since my powers manifested, no matter how much it hurt.

She bolted down my wrists and ankles. The pressure forced my limbs into unnatural angles. A splinter poked against my ass as I shifted, and I heard Nova sigh.

"It's not that I don't trust you, Kane." Nova approached me with a bottle filled to the top with a dark liquid. Not our usual grayish strength potion. She sat beside me and cradled my head in her hand, tilting me to an angle where I could latch onto the spout and drink. "Your magic is more powerful than it's ever been, and I can't have you casting any spells by accident. You could hurt me, or another Anointed, or yourself, and you're far too important for that."

The drink tasted foul. Herbacious and bitter. I struggled to breathe, but she urged the bottle between my lips. Chug, I told myself. Just get this down. It spilled down the sides of my mouth as she squeezed the sides of the bottle. I coughed at the end, as she set my head gently back down onto the floor. Gasped as I watched her walk back to her workstation.

Warmth stirred inside me. I found myself squirming, my hips bucking, and the cage around my cock growing tight as I hardened against its metal bars. "What's happening to me?"

She didn't answer.

I tried to ask again, but the words wouldn't come.

Nova set a bucket beside my head and withdrew a thick wad of wet cloth. I heard the liquid splash back into the bucket as she wrung it out and felt her hands open my jaw wide. She crammed the wet, stinking cloth into my mouth, and I gagged, the taste sharp and medicinal.

"This will protect us," she said, winding another long strip of damp fabric over my mouth and behind my head, tying it off and sealing the wad inside. I tried to hold my breath, but couldn't last long, the putrid scent directly below my nose, the liquid dripping down my throat as my jaw worked hard to close.

Nova began to chant, her words lost on me as I tried not to gag. To breathe normally. My arms warmed under her touch as she rubbed them with oil, then my legs. Then, with gloved fingers, she unlocked my chastity cage and set it aside. Took my growing cock into her hand and stroked me rhythmically. Not like I would've touched myself. Nothing like someone trying to bring pleasure.

As she drove me toward orgasm, I felt something cool press against the tip of my cock. Light glinted off glass and I realized Nova was preparing a vial for—I came, *hard*. It had been so long and she'd wrested my body from my control.

Her hands sought utility, driving me to orgasm over and over. Whatever I'd drunk swirled hot in my belly, muddled my thoughts, and strengthened my erection—even when I tried to resist. When I couldn't get hard again, she drizzled more of the foul-smelling liquid onto the cloth that stoppered my mouth. It burned the back of my throat as I moaned, as pleasure swelled again in my groin and I thrust my hips up, again, seeking contact.

I don't know how much time passed. How many times I came

or when I adjusted to the stink of my gag. Once, I closed my eyes and awoke to the pressure of her gloved hand, orgasm jolting my body from one dream state into another.

I drifted, my head like a leaf floating on the lake, eventually dragged under. I surfaced with a headache, and no idea how much time had passed. Sunlight streamed in through the many panes of glass that lined the walls of Ritual House. I could move my limbs again, and despite the acrid taste in my mouth, the gag was gone. My chastity cage locked back into place.

"You should rest," Nova said. No explanation of what she'd given me to drink, rubbed into my body, or taken from it. I lifted my right arm to my nose and sniffed. Mint. Rose.

"Okay," I said, dressing.

"I'll have you back on the next full moon for another extraction." She gathered a dozen glass bottles into a wooden box. "Your seed is powerful, Kane. It'll prove a potent infusion for our wards and weapons. For our magical herbs and potions." I swallowed, my spit thick and sticky. Lips still tasting of medicine.

The next day at dinner, I sniffed my potion before drinking it, watching as the other Anointed chugged without thought. Lark turned twenty in three months and eight days. I wondered if Nova would ask the same of him—if she'd also take from Zadie and Maeve in a few years. The idea unnerved me. It felt wrong that we weren't allowed to bring each other pleasure, but that Nova could "extract" our fluids for magic. Wasn't it the same result, either way? Didn't my body undergo the same reflexes, same motions? What was so undisciplined about experiencing pleasure with our partners? I would never forgive her.

And yet, I went. I went because it was expected of me. Because that was my destiny. Because I was Anointed.

Eventually, I grew used to the taste of the potion.

17

LARK / NOW

I wake before dawn, long before Calvin and Lilian, but know the exhaustion that plagues me is not from lack of sleep. The Anointed do not require as much sleep as normal humans. We do, however, require pain and—I scratch my head—care.

I trust Lilian enough to sleep in the same room and ride in the same car as her, but not with this. Calvin . . . he's different. He sleeps with one leg over the sheets. It's shaved smooth, showing the strong curve of his calf. I trace it up to where his thigh disappears beneath the covers. Would it be awful of me to wake him? He looks peaceful, almost Anointed the way his hair crowns his head. Last night, I invited him into a ritual space. A circle. My magic flowed through his body and I know he felt it. Think so, anyway. He believed even before I offered him proof. And, especially now while I feel so alone, that means something.

I stand on the balls of my feet and walk quietly to the edge of the other bed. Bend down and lean on the mattress. I'm careful with my weight, shifting the bed enough that Calvin stretches but Lilian doesn't. She snores—a welcome sound. I'm not used to sleeping in silence.

"Calvin," I whisper. He doesn't move. I rest a hand gently on his exposed arm—the one not twisted behind his head like a wild root—and speak closer to his ear. "Calvin."

His eyes open. Come to rest on me. Stay wide. He untangles his arms from the bedding and sits up on his elbows. "What time is it? Is it morning?" He squints at the clock.

"No, but I need . . ." Even though I've decided to trust him, it's still hard to ask. I need to open myself up to someone else the way I did Kane—and Kane and I knew each other for years before we became real partners. "I need your help again."

"Okay." Calvin sits fully up and wipes at the corners of his eyes before putting on his glasses. I watch him check on Lilian, who is sleeping facedown on a pillow, hair tangled around her. The position looks uncomfortable, but what do I know about how outsiders sleep? Their beds are extravagant enough to produce all manner of strange habits.

Calvin slides out of bed slowly and follows me into the bathroom. He yawns and scratches along the band of his underwear. I look away as three of his fingers disappear below the hem. Maybe I should have asked Lilian. I might not trust her as much, but at least she doesn't remind me of Kane. Stars, this is going to be harder than I thought.

I close the door. "You trust me, right?"

"Of course," he says, still blinking the sleep from his eyes. "If I didn't, I wouldn't be here."

"Yeah." I cross my arms over my chest and look at my feet. Our feet, really. The room is so small, we're almost touching. "But you might still leave, or call the outsider authorities, or—"

"Lark."

I feel the heat of his hand on my shoulder. It feels like home.

"I'm not going to leave you, but I am very tired, so why don't you just tell me what has you up before the sun."

I nod, working up the courage to look him in the eye. "In the Fellowship, those of us who're Anointed have partners. We are paired with someone around our own age that we bond with when we're young and grow up training with. Kane was mine."

Calvin squeezes my shoulder, then lets his hand slide from my body. "I'm sorry."

"It's not his fault. He was the first to quest and, well . . ." Tension grips my jaw. "I owe it to him to undertake mine. I know I can do it—can save him. But I can't do it alone."

"You need a partner."

"No!" I say it so fervently, Calvin's eyes fly open. "Sorry. I only mean that, as an outsider, you couldn't fulfill that role. But you can help me maintain my abilities."

"Okay." He draws the word slowly out. Looks at our feet as he asks, "What do you need help with?"

I bite my lip until I feel heat swell between my teeth. "My hair, for one. We used to wash and braid each other's hair. I don't know if you know how."

Calvin looks up and smiles. "Oh, I can braid hair. Pretty standard skill in my field."

I sigh, my smile matching his. "I can't tell you what a relief that is." Even though it was the easier ask of an outsider, it requires the most skill. I worried he wouldn't be able to help me. "Thank you."

"No problem, what else?"

"Um." The heat spreads from my lip, across my entire face, and throughout my chest—my heart pounds so fast, I lose my balance. "Promise you won't leave?"

"I promise I won't leave." Calvin reaches back and presses a small button on the door handle. The lock clicks. He could open it, of course, but I appreciate the symbolism.

"Part of our dedication to training is avoiding distractions. No games or drinking, sweets or s—" Say it. "Sex."

Calvin's expression doesn't change. His face doesn't blossom with judgment or disgust. It remains still, almost determinedly so.

"That's another thing Kane and I helped each other with."

"Your partner helped you . . . *not* have sex?" Calvin's forehead wrinkles in confusion.

My body is still so hot, I can barely look at him. "Can I just show you?"

"I, um, yeah. I guess—I mean, of course."

I hook my thumbs under my waistband and push my borrowed underwear down to my ankles, stepping out of them. Otherwise I'd feel like a child.

I risk looking at Calvin; his eyes dart around the small tiled room. "This. This is what we do for each other." I finger the key around my neck, drawing his attention. "We use these keys to unlock and care for each other. Make sure we're not bruised or raw." I slide my other hand over my cage, not because I don't want him to see it, just . . . I don't know. To remind myself it's there. Of why I wear it. How much I miss Kane.

"I can do that," Calvin says, quietly but sure, and I'm so surprised, I go cold.

"You will?"

"Yeah." He scratches the back of his neck, clearly trying to look everywhere except at my cock. "I'm not exactly shy about my body either. And, I mean"—he shrugs—"I'm sexually active. I know how to handle a dick."

The forthrightness of his words evaporates mine.

"I promise I won't do anything you don't want. I can keep it clinical."

"Clinical?"

"Yeah, like a doctor or esthetician. Even though they might touch you, it's not sexual. It's professional."

"That's good." I nod even though the reference means nothing to me. "Then there's one more thing I'll need from you. We can't do it here, but we will need to soon, before I'm completely drained of magic."

"What is it?" His words barely make a sound. I'm lured in by the interest I hear in his voice. By how he cares and wants to support me on my own terms.

"Pain." There, I've said it. "Our magic comes from pain—and I don't want to break an arm or get shot again. We have specific tools we learn to use on each other's bodies. We know how to invoke pain without breaking each other."

When I finish, Calvin's eyes have drifted slightly to the left of my head. I can't parse the expression on his face, but it's not good. I don't know if I've lost him.

"I promise it's safe. I know what I'm doing." My words pull him back to me like a magnet. "I can teach you how to hurt me."

His Adam's apple bobs as he swallows. Except for the mess of brown hair sticking up from his head, Calvin looks fully awake. Fully attentive. "Okay. I trust you. And you clearly trust me." He doesn't hide where he's looking now. No point, is there.

"You can take yours off too, if you want." I wet my lips, mouth suddenly as hot and sticky as a summer afternoon. "Usually, it's mutual—I mean, you don't have to, but I would wash you too. I mean, I could. If you wanted."

I feel more exposed fumbling over my words than I do standing naked before this outsider. I haven't had to ask someone to touch me, to invite them into my intimate space, in almost a decade. I've *never* asked an outsider.

I wonder if he'll feel different.

"Okay. If you want to." Calvin slides his underwear off and tosses them on top of mine. Seeing our worn briefs piled together makes me feel as if we've done something. We are very explicitly not doing anything. A moment of pressure inside my cage reminds me that I can't, anyway. The same cage that I'm about to unlock, to let Calvin clean and care for me. I have to remain disciplined.

"Okay." I don't look between Calvin's thighs. I don't, I don't, I *don't*. I turn around and sit on the toilet lid. This is supposed to be a special exchange. It's supposed to happen under the warmth of the sun on the lawn or swaddled in blankets during winter. It's a moment of closeness, calm relaxation—I tense when Calvin's fingers brush the back of my neck.

"Sorry," he says, as if he's accidentally nicked me with a razor.

"It's okay." I shake my shoulders out, sit up straight. I was never as tall as Kane, but this outsider and I are more evenly matched. I feel the heat of his presence, and all I can think as he begins fumbling with my braids is that his uncaged cock is right behind me.

I gasp, closing my eyes, trying to disguise the memory that shudders through me. The memory of Kane's mouth and fingers, the slick of sweat and saliva.

Arousal floods my body, confusion my head, as Calvin's fingers dance through my hair, separating strands, unweaving Maeve's work. I breathe deeply, hoping to draw enough oxygen into my body to clear my mind. I focus on this cold, decrepit, mundane motel bathroom. Tell myself this is simply a job that needs to be done, rather than a profound and intimate exchange between two people.

Calvin ruffles my unbound hair, massaging the tension from my scalp. Only when his hands slide down the full length do I realize I've been rising to meet his touch.

"Thank you." I stand, his fingers still tangled in the ends, and reach to turn on the shower.

"No problem. Happy to help."

I take the key from around my neck and fit it into its lock. *Happy to help,* he said. This is *helping.* I remove the lock, then the cage. Set both on the back of the toilet. Take a long slow breath as my body adjusts to the freedom. The lightness.

I do not look at Calvin. I no longer have solid steel to keep my arousal in check. I step into the shower and close my eyes immediately, letting hot water soak my hair. Feet thud on the tub behind me. Another body in my space—I asked for this, because I need this.

I revolve under the showerhead, soaking my whole body. When I wipe the water from my eyes, he's there. He's taller than I'd thought, and paler. His muscles are like nothing I've seen, sculpted as if for show. His hair styled even in the humidity of the room, sides shaved close. He pushes the top back and out of his eyes, no longer wearing glasses. Looks with his dark eyes, as if through me. Moves closer.

"Is this okay?" He's popping the cap on a small plastic bottle, pouring its contents into his hand. I don't have time to wonder what it is before he reaches slowly for my head. A subtle tilt of his head asks permission, and I nod.

"Do you want to turn around?"

I answer by doing, not speaking. This is happening. My heart pounds like a drum in my ears. A strange man is washing my hair. An outsider. And it doesn't feel bad. It feels different. The pads of his fingers are soft, their pressure gentle. They make small circles on my scalp before sliding down the length of my hair.

Minutes pass—full minutes. Finally, I feel an absence.

"If you stand under the water, I'll . . ." He doesn't have to finish. I don't care what he's going to do; I'm already moving under the spray, tipping my head back while he rinses the suds away. He tends to the nape of my neck, shoulder blades, lower back. Then he disappears again, leaving me waiting.

Calvin returns with a cold cream, which he massages into my hair along the same patterns he just washed. "What is that?" I ask, though I don't really care. I'd let him attend to me any way he wanted, with any outsider product.

"Conditioner," he says. "I'm surprised you haven't used it before. Your hair's so soft."

"I don't wash it very frequently." We only change our braids when they become unmanageable, which varies depending on our hair type—I wash mine every week or so.

"That explains it." He pats my side. The outsider casually

touching the skin of my torso, as if he has washed my body before. "We'll want to let it sit for a few minutes before rinsing it out."

"Okay. Would—" I clip my offer. It's one thing to ask an outsider to help with basic maintenance, so I can keep myself in shape for my quest. It's another to put my hands on him. To wash him. He must be used to caring for himself, he has no need for me to do so.

But I want to.

"Would you like me to wash your hair too?" I face Calvin, and he blushes—or the steam from the shower has warmed his cheeks.

"I mean, I can—but this is supposed to be a together thing, right?" He trips over hurried words, settling on, "Yeah, okay. Sure."

Calvin's hair is short, so much shorter than Kane's. It takes me a minute to lather his hair, but only because I spend so long rubbing his scalp. It's so short, I could grab it in my fists. But I don't grab it, no. I rinse and release.

"Thanks." He turns to face me again. "Want me to—" He points at my conditioning hair.

"Oh, yes, thank you." I turn and let him work on me again, until his fingers no longer slip over the strands of my hair. This is it. I glance down between my legs, where my foreskin has begun to pull back around my hardening cock. That's normal and fine, I remind myself. Discipline means not acting on my body's impulses, means controlling myself when this happens naturally. I think of training with Kane on the grassy knolls of Druid Hill, of the empty eyes of FOEs, and of the monster I will rend throat to gut.

I rinse the conditioner from Calvin's hair with the determination my quest demands, ignoring my cock. I can do this.

"Okay, what now?" Calvin asks.

When I face him, his eyes are on mine as if looking elsewhere will turn him to stone. He fidgets with his hands, in front of his pelvis. *I know how to handle a dick.*

"Um." I don't know how to instruct him. Don't want to say the words even "clinically." "I need you to clean me, look for bruises, discoloration, chafing, abrasions." I step closer and take my own cock, as if I can hand it to him. "There shouldn't be any. I've worn the cage for years; I know how not to hurt myself."

He takes me. I wasn't ready, even though I should've expected it. One hand supporting my cock, the other cupping my balls. "I'm not supposed to be able to see from up here, through the water, am I?" He smiles, laughs awkwardly. His whole body is flushed, from the steam or his words or my closeness—I don't know.

"You can do whatever you need." I clasp my hands behind my back so I won't be tempted to touch him. That would be too far, too intimate. Washing each other's hair was reciprocal; this can't be. *He* doesn't wear a cage. I don't have to care for his cock.

Calvin drops to his knees, and I draw in a deep breath. Hold it and close my eyes. I feel off-balance, and can't rest my hands on his shoulders. I try to think of anything else, so my brain settles on Kane's mouth around my cock, his nails digging into my thigh, fingers gently fondling my balls.

I feel Calvin's fingers gently press my foreskin back before lifting my cock. His fingers run smooth up my length, and I try to imagine myself flaccid in his hands rather than swelling with arousal. Try not to imagine his mouth closing around me like Kane did, *fuck*. I open my eyes as the forbidden profanity flickers through my thoughts.

"I don't see anything unusual." Calvin cranes his neck like he is treating this with the utmost seriousness, and I struggle to breathe. To keep my head above the current of pleasure that threatens to suck me under. I am *hard*. Heavy and pulsing in his hand, the head of my cock red and exposed.

I lean against the wall, unable to hold myself up anymore. Thrust into the hands holding me, touching me. I want—*no*. His mouth is so close. He bites one plump lip, looking closely. I shudder as his fingers slide featherlight over the ridges of my foreskin.

He can't pull it back because all the blood in my body is flowing toward my groin and I am hot, *so hot.*

"It's—" I fumble for the shower handle. Make it cool, I can't— my hips buck forward, out of control.

Calvin stills, not persisting but not letting go either. "Um, is this okay?"

I'm *so* hard, and I want him to—like Kane did. I can't, I can't, I *can't.*

"No," I say. My voice sounds like it belongs to someone else, throaty and thick with pleasure. "Stop!"

"Okay, I'm not touching you!" Calvin stands, and that's almost worse, his body parallel to mine. Warm and wet. Hands out to prove their innocence. He looks at my cock, then my lips. I don't know if he's hard—if I look at his cock, I'll die. "I'm sorry, I didn't mean to—" His fingers curl into fists as he steps back. "I did what I promised, I swear. I was being as clinical as I could."

"I know. It's fine, I just—this was my mistake." I turn to face the wall, lock my eyes on the discolored grout between the white tiles. "Please leave."

"Okay." Calvin trips over the shower curtain as he steps out of the tub, knocking the shampoo bottle onto the floor with a high-pitched hollow *thunk,* then a thud as he catches himself against the wall.

I take my cock in my hand as if it's a wound I need to keep pressure on, but no magic can heal this. *Go down,* I think, half-considering a spell. A few words whispered against my palm. A shameful use of the last of my magic.

From the other side of the curtain, I can hear Calvin sliding a towel from a rickety metal bar and rubbing the rough fabric over his body. The curtain's not enough. What is this thin sheet of plastic when his hands massaged my hair and caressed my side and stroked my cock. Nothing. As I rub my thumb over the head of my cock, around the ridge. As my unoccupied fingers drift to the inside of my thigh and press half-moons into my skin. As I rest my forehead against the slippery tile, my hand might as will be his.

Might as well be . . .

His.

I come without a sound, a buzzing in my ears and black spots before my eyes.

18

CALVIN / NOW

Lilian's awake when I stumble out of the bathroom, still dripping wet. She looks up from her computer, the monitor lighting the front of her face as if she were gazing into a Pensieve. With both hands, she removes chunky pink headphones from her head, looks between Lark's empty bed and me, raises her eyebrows.

"Someone had a good morning."

Normally I'd laugh it off, but I don't feel good. "I tell you pretty much everything about myself, so believe me when I say it wasn't like that." I slide a second towel off the rack and rub it roughly through my hair while I tiptoe onto the rug.

"What was it like?"

I wrap the towel around my waist and sit opposite the nest of pillows and blankets Lilian's constructed for herself. "He asked me to help him with something—I'm not sure it's mine to share."

"Ooooookay," she says with skepticism. "But like, I'm dying to know, now."

I glance at the bathroom door. "I know, and I'm sorry, but—" It swings open with a loud whine. I hear Lark take a towel before disappearing into the bathroom again. He doesn't close the door.

I clear my throat and peer at Lilian's laptop. "What're you working on?"

"Editing the podcast we recorded at the con. Want to have it in case I can't break from our road trip to record a normal episode."

"When's that supposed to be?"

"Wednesday at 3:00 p.m." She glances at the bathroom door. Lowers her voice. "Think we'll have slayed a monster by then?"

Lark walks out of the bathroom, towel wrapped around his waist, key hanging from his neck again. "It takes a while for my hair to dry," he says to Lilian, then picks up the toothbrush and paste I packed for him. At least he knows how to use them—his teeth look cared for. "I apologize for the delay."

"No worries. Checkout isn't for a couple hours, and I need to shower too." Lilian hops off the bed. "Might as well." She trains her eyes on me and whispers, "Who knows when we'll have running water next."

Learning from our mistakes, Lilian grabs two towels on her way into the bathroom. The one Lark grabbed barely makes it around his waist, leaving open an unintentional slit up his right thigh. I should take the opportunity to get some work done, like Lilian was. I shouldn't look.

I slide my laptop from my backpack and pull up some old photoshoot sets. Lil had the right idea; we have to keep our fans fed. I pull together a couple of sets of outtakes for my supporters, at varying stages of undress. They like those. Makes them feel like they're seeing inside my life, as if all I do is bop around in cosplay.

I look around the hotel room, at the scattered laundry, backpacks, and bags. The unmade beds and stained carpet. This is not how Calvin Morris lives. He travels to conventions, has glowing skin, and lives in an adorable historic apartment building that isn't totally infested with mice.

What I mean to do is check my notifications, but instead, I open my phone's camera and switch to the forward-facing lens. Stare at my face in the dimly lit hotel room. I snap a few photos before leaning back against the headboard. I rearrange the towel around my waist, showing *just* enough V, and hold the phone over my head. *Snap.*

That's good for now. I put it on my locked story and caption,

Who's up for a road trip? with a car gif and sparkling stars. Replies come in immediately from followers who want to know where I am and where I'm going. I coyly tell them it would ruin the surprise.

The bathroom door opens and Lilian emerges dry, wearing a sports bra and rainbow cat underwear. She nudges Lark aside from the sink where he's slowly towel-drying his hair and begins lining up her skin care routine along the counter. He doesn't even pretend not to watch, rapt with fascination as she explains what's in each of the bottles, allowing him to try some of the less expensive ones.

I give them space—especially Lark. He hasn't so much as looked at me since he kicked me out of the shower. I glance up from my laptop every now and then to see Lilian putting on eyeliner or Lark getting dressed. The cheap hotel hair dryer roars to life, and I see Lark jump back into my field of vision.

"What is that?" His forehead scrunches with suspicion.

"You've never heard of a hair dryer?" Lil says. "No wonder it takes hours for your hair to dry. Here. Turn around." She aims it at him and reaches for his hair.

But he holds up his hands between them. "No. Thank you, but please don't touch my hair."

"Okay, well, you're welcome to use it when I'm finished."

As promised, she hands the dryer to him, and this time, I can't look away. The "man out of time" trope is so cute in real life. He lifts up his hair in chunks, as if it's not attached to his head, drying it slowly. After a minute he accepts some kind of serum from Lilian, which he holds like a baby bird in his palm.

That's when he looks at me.

I set my laptop aside and stand, remembering I'm still only wearing a towel. Lark is wearing another pair of my underwear, yellow trunks, and a long-sleeved scarlet shirt that says MUGGLE, PLEASE.

"Do you need my help again?" I ask.

He walks over and sits on the bed in front of me. "Yes, thank you," he says, tilting his hand over mine. I warm the oily substance between my palms then rub my fingers over his scalp.

"Can I get some more of that?" I ask, and Lilian brings the bottle over.

"Don't use all of it," she says. "Who knows when we'll see a Sephora."

"Thanks." I massage the serum through Lark's hair, roots to tips. Dry and cared for, his blonde hair shines. "Would you like me to braid it too?"

"Yes, please."

He sits still and quiet while I separate it into sections. While I twist and pull and fasten. I can't manage the crown I assume Kane gave him, but I'm not Kane. I'm not the person he grew up bonding with, who helped maintain his cock in that chastity device they wear, who washed and braided his hair. The man who sold out him and his friends to the authorities. I'm an outsider. And I only really know how to braid like we're at a Renaissance festival.

That's what he looks like when I finish. A dozen long, tiny braids that I incorporate with the remaining loose strands into one thick Dutch braid. They always look fancy, but they're dead easy.

Lark pats his head and examines my work with his hands. "Thank you."

"You're welcome," I say, suddenly very aware of how naked I am. Of how incredible his hair feels between my fingers, and how cute he looks in that Harry Potter shirt. I remember that, later, he's going to ask me to hurt him, and I've already said yes.

•   •   •

We leave housekeeping a twenty-dollar tip, pack our bags into the hatch, and get on the road. West, again, with no further directions. Healed, clean, and freshly braided, Lark sits in the back seat alone, taking stock of what he brought from Druid Hill. I can feel Lilian's tension as she stares out the window—we decided to take shifts driving, but I wonder if she wasn't better off with something to focus on. I grip the wheel, glad for something to hold on to.

"We're going to get pulled over," she mutters, peering out the window. She really doesn't like having weapons in the car, much less spread out in the open. "And then they're going to see the swords, and then we're going to get arrested, or shot."

"We are not going to get pulled over, because I'm a good driver," I say, even though her fear has slowly worked its way under my skin. I also look out my window, trying not to be obvious about it.

"You're a good driver," she says, followed by a deep breath.

"Sometime in the next hour, we'll need to stop somewhere without people," Lark says, without prompting. "Somewhere outdoors. Peaceful."

"I think that's, like, everywhere in West Virginia," Lilian says.

"Yeah, but if we don't want to stop in someone's backyard, we'll have to google a park or something," I say.

"Google a park?" Lark narrows his eyes. "Is that some kind of spell?"

"No, it's an internet search," Lilian responds.

"What's an internet search?" we say at the same time. I smirk as Lark startles, taken aback that I knew what he was going to say.

"Oh my god, you don't know what the internet is?" Lilian looks in the rearview mirror.

"No," Lark says, slowly as if to make sure we understand him. "Even if I did, I probably wouldn't use it. Outsider distractions sap and taint my powers. Speaking of which, Calvin, are you still willing to help with my magic?"

"Of course." I feel Lilian's eyes on me and a blush rising in my cheeks. "Lil, shouldn't you be googling a park?"

"He said in the next few hours!" She smiles and toys with her cell. "Don't worry about me; you drive. And don't get us pulled over."

•   •   •

That *is* it for four more hours. At Lilian's insistence, we put so much distance between ourselves and the Motel 9, we pass a sign that says WELCOME TO KENTUCKY! Every now and then, she and I sing along to her "Girl Power" playlist, but I'm terrible with lyrics and she can't carry a tune. The most we achieve is a pained complaint from our captive audience of one. For the past four songs, he's just been sitting back there, in the middle seat, back straight, legs comfortably spread, eyes closed.

"Do you mind if I put the windows down? Get some fresh air?" I ask, now that I know he's awake. I ignore Lilian's multiple glances.

"Not at all," he says, opening one eye to watch as I maneuver the windows from the front seat, before closing it again. "Though, we'll be stopping soon."

"For what?"

"We just will be," he says.

"I can feel it in my bones," Lilian says dramatically.

I try not to laugh.

"Because we can't continue without a tracking spell, and I can't perform one of those without my magic." Lark's face tenses with frustration. He releases it with a long, deep breath, then looks out the window at the trees. "So we'll be stopping soon."

His blue eyes are duller than they were last night, beside the pool. His skin looks, not paler, but lackluster. His hair thin and greasy, even though I just washed it this morning. He looks like he's fading. I don't know if that's possible, or if I'm imagining things.

"Here," he says.

I keep driving, his words catching me off guard.

"Please pull over."

"Just on the side of the road?" I ask.

"Yes." He sounds tired.

Lilian and I both look for cars as I pull into the right lane, then onto the shoulder and roll to a stop.

"Calvin?" His voice is a plea.

I fumble with the windows. "Do you still want my help?"

"Yes, please." His politeness unnerves me. Yesterday, he would've thought nothing of telling us what to do, and now he's minding his p's and q's?

I toss the keys to Lilian, hop out of the car, and open the back door, sliding in beside him. "Are you okay?"

He shakes his head but otherwise doesn't move. "No. I don't think I've ever been this drained."

"Okay, I got you." I unfasten his seat belt, and he grabs on to me as if I'm extracting him from a wreck. "Lil, would you—"

Lark shakes his head again. "No. Only you."

"It's fine," she says. "You go, uh, *help* Lark with his magic." She winks at me. "Besides." She turns the car into accessory mode and cranks up the Spice Girls. "Someone has to guard the car."

Lark heaves his legs over the seat, trembling as I help him to his feet. "Can you walk?"

"Yeah." He takes a few steps before leaning against the hatch. "But I'd appreciate if you carried my stuff." He points to the canvas bag we left in the car overnight. The one with swords and arrows—and leather and knives. I'm dying to know what they're for.

"Sure, I got it." He steps aside and waits while I grab the bag.

We walk slowly, side by side, stepping over the metal railing that lines the road and onto a dirt path that leads into a forest. I reach for my phone to make sure we aren't trespassing before realizing I left it in the cup holder, charging. Great. The only thing

I prefer about reality to epic fantasy is that I can solve most of my problems with a smartphone. I look over my shoulder as my orange car grows smaller behind us.

The forest creeps up on us. The few trees lining the road thicken and grow as we walk among them. Lark has his hand on my shoulder. I barely notice his weight until it's fully resting on me and the canopy overhead blots out the sun. I've never been to Kentucky before, but I didn't expect it to look like this. Pinpoint lights twinkling from within the trees. Air so still, it's like we're wading through it rather than walking.

"Is this place real?" I don't mean to ask out loud—didn't even realize it was a question I had until I spoke it.

Is this place real? Is Kentucky this magical or did we cross into an enchanted forest? Lark is real. I've touched him, run my hands through the thick of his hair and felt his power run through me. I believe him, and I believe this. "Here," Lark says, voice barely audible. "Stop."

I stop. Lark stumbles. I hold him tighter.

"I'm okay." He pries himself from my grip and leans against a thick gray tree with wrinkled bark. "There's rope. In my bag," he says, kicking off his boots and pants.

I set it down on the mossy forest floor in a clearing that's opened up around us. Reach my hand into the bag and feel around for the rope, but feel a sharp prick. What else is in here?

I spread the bag open and feel my breath catch in my throat. A set of knives, metal clamps with teeth, a small whip—and more. This is a toy bag. Maybe to Lark it's a bag of tools, but I have one of these in my apartment and the contents have never made any of my partners cast a spell.

When he said *hurt* him, did he mean—

I pick up a cat o' nine tails.

Does he want me to—

"Did you find it?" Lark asks.

I bury the cat in the bag; return with the rope in my hands and a sour feeling in my gut. I look down the length of his body. The messy, wilting braid, dull eyes, and sallow skin. He wears my clothes like drag.

"Yeah." I offer the hank half-heartedly.

"Good." He reaches for the hem of his shirt. "Now if you'll—"

"Lark."

He pulls the scarlet shirt over his head, moving with jerky determination. Wisps of his hair stand on end from the static.

"Lark, stop."

He does, shirt in hand. I blink. His skin ripples as if I've been walking through the desert for too long and am only imagining him. As if there's something true beneath his flesh. Something I can't see or he's hiding. If I focus, I can barely make out a web of lines twisting around his torso, looping his shoulder and arms. I shiver, unnerved.

"What are you doing?" Lark grabs a low-hanging branch to steady himself, and the lines that mapped his body disappear or fade or were never there at all. "I need your help," he says, drawing my attention. "You promised."

"I did." But I can't shake the disquieting feeling growing louder inside me. "I'll do it." I can do this. I believe Lark and he knows himself best. What he needs. "I know how to handle most of the tools in your bag." *Most.*

A deep breath wracks his exhausted body. "Thank you."

"I assume the rope is meant to restrain you."

"Yes." He looks at his soft, scuffed boots. "I'll understand if—"

"I said I'll do it." A lump forms in my throat. A knot in my stomach. I'm no stranger to pick-up play, and I've undressed my fair share of cosplayers, relished living out my fantasies about our respective characters fucking and hurting each other. But this feels different—not at all playful. Serious and sacred, like a holy ritual. I suppose, for Lark, it's similar.

If he's as low on magic as he says, he won't want a light touch. I see a single-tail whip that sends a ripple of memory through my whole body. I know the first sting and the twentieth. What it feels like when *you can no longer count*—when you begin genuinely struggling to avoid the pain, rather than leaning coyly into it. When your cries turn into crying. When your skin splits open.

"The cat," he says, voice small and strained.

For a moment, I don't know what he's talking about until—I remember the cat o' nine tails. Pick up the sturdy leather handle and brush my thumb over one of the metal barbs. This is what he wants, *pain*. I've never handled one of these before, not with barbs. I feel sick. I'm going to do this. My saliva tastes like bile.

"Please."

I swallow it down and tuck the cat into my back pocket.

Lark offers me his wrists, but I push them gently aside. On the other side of the tree, I find a strong limb only a few feet overhead. That'll do. I tie his wrists together, making sure the rope is tight and safely arranged, then loop the rest of the rope up and over the tree limb. There's more than enough length to finish off, no knots required.

I walk around Lark and the tree, checking my work. "Are you comfortable?" I ask.

"Comfort's not the point," he replies.

It is for me. He won't appreciate it later if I cause nerve damage. Can he heal that like he healed his bullet wound? When I try to remember the healing, the image blurs as if my brain is censoring the memory. The same way I can only remember the webbing on Lark's upper body—there moments ago, visible at the right angle.

I blink and lines crack across his skin like faults in the earth.

I blink again and they smooth over.

He's right in front of me. A real person, who is *telling me what he needs*. I run my hand down the length of his braid, over each bump and strand, before tossing it over the front of his shoulder.

Lark turns his head but is unable to see me. "Hurt me, already."
He doesn't have to ask twice.

I retrieve the cat from my back pocket, pull its tails lightly
through my fingers, and strike.

The scourge is light in my hand. Its leather handle soft and supple, nothing like the marks its claws leave in Lark's back. I strike
again, trying to focus—to remember where to avoid and where to
aim, how to hurt someone the *right* way—but my vision fisheyes.
Lark's muscles tense where I hit him, bones push against his skin
as he squirms. I strike, and strike, and strike again. At no point
does he moan. All the masochists I've played with have gasped and
whimpered and mewed. They gave feedback, checked in. Lark is
silent, until he screams.

My grip falters at the ripping sound. Do Anointed have safewords? He didn't give me one. How hard do I go? How long? I
should've asked, but he's been so clear and I am no longer certain.

"More," he whispers into the stillness. Nothing moves in the
clearing. Not the leaves, the air, not the birds or critters.

"Lark—"

"More, please, *more*," he cries. He's begging me. I find new expanses of skin to break. More tanned flesh to uproot. Nine tiny
hooks, nine fresh marks. I strike him until my hand is shaking
and sweat drips into my eyes. Until the sobs release their grip on
Lark's body, and he sags silently against the rope.

I drop the cat and stare at the mess I've made of his back. At
the blood dripping down his legs and the pattern that reemerges
on his back—did I do that? Sprawling lines I can't quite focus on,
that blur in and out. Nausea and light-headedness envelop me. My
ears ring—I can't hear. I lose sight of his back through the fog of
my glasses. *What have I done?*

This was what he wanted. Lark can do magic. He can heal himself. I didn't do anything he hasn't experienced a hundred times.

Oh my god, has he experienced this a hundred times?

I stumble toward his bag and fish out a knife. With the last of my strength, I slide through the rope that holds Lark. It's a bad idea—he can't possibly support himself. But I can't either. I lower myself to the ground, so I don't hurt myself when I fall. Like water swirling down the drain, I waver then pass out.

• • •

A blurry shape towers over me, loud whisper rushes past like the wind. Am I in bed? Everything is green. I'm in a forest that may or may not really be in Kentucky. The moss is soft. My joints are stiff.

I brace my arm against the ground and a reassuring voice says, "No, no. Let me." He's warm when he takes my hand and helps me to my knees. When his face is close, I see blue eyes and strands of blonde liberated from a single chunky braid. Lark looks nothing like I left him: broken and bleeding. He's dressed and packed the canvas bag—as if the rope and cat were never there. As if I never wielded them against his bare flesh.

The forest blurs behind him. I'm woozy from passing out or—

"Your glasses."

Oh.

I close my eyes while he slides them onto my face, their arms catching my hair at unusual angles as they settle behind my ears. When I can see again, all I see is his face—free from tears, from blood, from bruises.

The sight of his raw back flashes before me, and I squeeze my eyes shut, as if I can wring the memory out. When I blink, he's still there. Unmarked. Dressed. The canvas bag slung over his shoulder.

My body fights me as I stand, but I manage, unsure how Lark did. "Are you okay?" I don't want to say the wrong thing. He's acting as if all this is normal for me—has assumed I'm fine because, I realize, I haven't told him otherwise.

"My magic is recharged," he says. "That's enough for now."

"But your . . ." I gesture at his back, as we walk back the way we came, and the memory of wielding the cat echoes in my muscles. "Your skin was—I should really take a look at—"

"I'm fine." A thing people usually say when they're not. "I performed a healing spell. Usually Kane and I would care for each other afterwards, but . . ." We both know the end of his sentence.

Communicate. "I would've cared for you." When Lark doesn't respond, I push myself to continue. To be honest. "I actually could've used some care as well."

Lark stops and stares at me, brow furrowed with confusion. "You? Did you hurt yourself?"

"Not like I hurt you, but I've never done that before. It's a lot to process." I leave it there, hoping he'll bite. Unlike Lark, I don't feel recharged. I feel drained.

"Oh. I—" It's as if the rest of his thoughts fly away. "You're right. I should've checked in with you." He adjusts the bag on his back; a smile lights his face. "How fruitful can my quest be if my companions are unwell?"

He holds out his hand to me. When I take it, he continues walking and I follow by his side. We don't discuss it further—I get the feeling the chance to exchange care has passed. But we acknowledged it, and for now that's enough.

Lark glances at a black mark that stains his palm like an old tattoo. "I know the way now," he says, showing me the mark. Its lines and curves intersect like crop circles. "Tracking spell."

When we get back to the car, Lilian's video chatting with her co-hosts and charging her phone. I knock on the window and beckon her to get out of the car as Lark gets in. She eyes traffic before hopping out and meeting me behind the hatch. The roadside feels like a different planet, where human beings drive cars and listen to pop music and video chat, rather than strike flesh until it bleeds, in an ethereal wood.

"Everything okay?" she asks.

"Yeah—*no*," I say before I can try to sugarcoat what just happened. "Please don't tell Lark I'm telling you—I'm still processing."

Lilian's forehead creases, leaving a thin line in her foundation. "What did you guys do? I assumed more naked stuff."

"He asked me to hurt him." I'm blunt because I need to be. Because Lark didn't make space for me to talk about it and I need to. "Like, with a whip."

"A *whip*?"

"Yeah, a fucking cat o' nine tails with real metal barbs. I've never even held one before . . ."

"Holy shit, Cal, you're shaking." And she's right, I feel as weak as Lark looked before I hurt him.

I run my hands through my hair, leaving cold sweat in their path. "That's how he powers his magic, I guess? I fainted. Couldn't handle the blood—there was *so much blood* and he was screaming and—" I swallow bile, feel my mouth thick with saliva.

"What the fuck?" I can hear the question marks continue even after Lilian pulls my hoodie tight around my body and brings me close. "That's not okay, Calvin. It's not. We should talk to him."

"No!" My eyes widen, head shakes so fast it feels like it might come off. "We can't. We had a nice little conversation afterwards where—"

"A 'nice little conversation'?" She sounds unimpressed. It *sounds* unimpressive now. Only a few minutes ago, it felt like progress. "What about medical care and physical comfort and verbal—"

"I know." I cut her off, shaking my head. Feeling weak for not having asserted myself. Lying to myself as if holding hands and smiling was enough. I'm going to sound pathetic, but I have no choice. I close my eyes as the words spill out. "Lil, I need this to be real."

She lets out a deep breath and glances through the windshield at Lark. "I know." She finds my hand with hers and squeezes. The feeling is warm and familiar. Comforting. "One of us has to be the dreamer, and it's always been you. Just make sure you're also taking care of *yourself*, Daddy Greenleaf."

My laugh is involuntary and welcome.

She nods. Rocks on her heel. "Let's get you something to eat; I'll drive. We could all use a stop that doesn't involve magic. We're in Kentucky. Didn't they invent fried chicken?"

I feel the color return to my cheeks as I huff a laugh. "I don't think that's exactly how it happened."

We walk back to opposite sides of the front. "Oh yeah?" She opens the driver's door. "What's your source."

"I cosplayed slutty Colonel Sanders at SDCC once."

As the smiles spread across our faces, Lark clears his throat. "Do you mind if we get going?" His expression is calm. Determined. He unfolds a yellowing paper map. "We've got a monster to hunt."

19

DERYN / NOW

I watch the server take orders and deliver them to a kitchen while another brings wrapped meals on a strange red tray. Back home, not even the Anointed ate like this. Kane stares at the first page of the menu, its pages covered in a hard, clear plastic. Miller barely glances at it as she stares at her phone. Has she eaten here before? She taps at the screen, sliding her finger over it, not unlike the way I've seen the Anointed inscribe sigils. I'm four pages deep into the menu when our server asks what we want for breakfast, pulling long, paper-wrapped tubes from their apron and placing them beside plastic cups of water.

I get something called French toast, because I read about France once in a book, before Nova got rid of most of them. I like thinking there are outsiders so far away that they eat totally different breakfasts. Eggs or oats: that's how it was for twenty-eight years. This morning, I'm going to eat two thick pieces of bread, toasted and dipped in eggs, then fried and drizzled with a maple syrup.

Kane gets eggs. Miller, oats. Neither of them speaks while we wait.

"So." I dress my coffee with cream from little plastic cups and sugar from paper packets, piling the trash beside my plate. Wild that outsiders create so much only to throw it away. "Any updates today? Still heading west?"

Kane shoots me a sideways glance, his eyes falling on my cup. The Anointed don't drink caffeine. Or didn't. Maybe I went too hard on Kane last night. He does know more about Lark than me, as much as I hate it. They practiced magic together, whether it's real or not. But, most of all, Miller needs him. I can't let them ally against me, decide I'm useless.

Our server returns before either of them can answer. They easily balance multiple steaming plates, setting them before each of us in turn.

"Thank you," Kane says. "Um." He looks at Miller, as if asking permission. "Can I get a cup of coffee?"

"Sure, sweetie." Our server smiles, turning on their heel in a set of white sneakers. They bring the carafe and more cream cups, pouring dark brown liquid into his mug.

I can't believe he's going to drink that. So many things I previously thought impossible are happening right before me. Nova overthrown. Kane wearing his hair loose. Lark rejecting him.

Miller slides her phone across the table, drawing my attention. "Want to be the navigator?" Her hand is steady, eyes focused on mine. For a moment, I feel the way I used to as a child, when Nova told me I would someday cross the fence and save the world.

"Yeah, sure." I take the phone, acting casual. Miller isn't Nova. I'm not Anointed. The world doesn't need saving. Judging by my French toast, it's been doing pretty well without us.

She slides in beside me and shows me how to use it while we eat—how to use the maps and search the internet, read her messages and missed calls while she's driving. She even tells me the password. Kane looks over every couple of minutes, but doesn't say anything, slowly sipping his coffee. He grimaces every time, like he's forcing it down.

"Got a read on Lark?" Miller asks him, accepting a refill of her own small mug. She drinks it black. The thought makes my tongue curl.

Kane clasps his hands. He shouldn't. He should be whispering some magic bullshit into his palms and tracking Lark, or whatever it is Miller asked him to do yesterday. Mindspeech. I watch her watching him. Watch him staring back, hands folded firmly together. When he closes his eyes and sighs, I know he isn't doing a damn thing. "Still heading west." Kane opens his eyes then begins prying a rectangle of cold butter out of a foil packet with his knife.

Miller nods. I can't tell if she believes him, or why she's even asking in the first place. Kane's been talking with her for months, she said. Surely, she's the one who convinced him that magic and monsters aren't real. Now that we're sitting still, it strikes me: What does Miller want us to testify about? The outsider government must have better things to do with their time than tell people they've been living a lie. They're not altruists.

I open the maps app and pinch the screen like Miller taught me. Our location grows and pops with detail. It's wild being able to see everything around us, to see in an instant how far we've come, and how long it would take to drive to the ocean on the other side. The *ocean.* I only know the word from faded zoo signs. I wonder if we're near the polar bears.

"Before we continue *west,*" I say, trying not to betray my skepticism. "Can I ask . . ."

Miller raises an eyebrow in wait.

"Why?"

"Why," she says, deadpan, as if she does not understand.

"Yeah, why are we doing all this? Not," I add quickly, "that I'm not happy to help, but you didn't exactly tell me much back at the hotel. Why did you free us from the Fellowship? It can't be against outsider law to believe something that's not true. You *arrested* Nova. I didn't like her, but what did she do to deserve imprisonment?"

Kane drags his cold block of butter across his toast so hard that it tears. Last night he ripped his shirt off to show me his scars, but today he'll barely look at me.

"Nova, as you call her, has been charged with multiple counts of abduction, assault, battery, and child abuse."

"Hurting people," I say, because those are outsider words, not ours. I've heard them, but they seem to have a deeper meaning for Miller.

She doesn't look at Kane's body, but I do. Are those scars Nova's fault? She never hurt me when I was Anointed, and I've never seen her be anything but gentle. Strict, but kind. They couldn't be.

"Yes. She's also facing extensive charges of fraud and truancy. Her lies deprived you of choices and opportunities." Miller leans forward over her half-eaten oats, elbows on the table. Her shirt is wrinkled. Loosely buttoned. "There are laws requiring children to be enrolled in school, from ages five to eighteen. At first, she submitted homeschooling requests, but as more of you were born within the fence, she stopped. We had no records of your existence, and she didn't want us to. She wanted total control over your lives."

My fingers tense around her phone. Records are how outsiders put down roots. How FOEs keep tabs on them, and how monsters plant their influence. But monsters aren't real—and shouldn't Miller look like a FOE? Her eyes are brown, not black pits; her skin is pale and clear, not shifting. If we have records, though—*once* we have records—there's no going back. We become outsiders. They won't forget about us or let us go home, even without Nova.

She kept us out of school. Taught us lies.

"We're still investigating the extent of her control over members of the Fellowship. Many of the adults have reported children taken from them, despite their protests. Others accused her of neglect. The Anointed . . ." She glances at Kane, but he's still fussing with his toast. Either he doesn't want to hear this, or he's heard it all before.

"You started your investigation when Kane escaped—months before his quarter century." I open the internet and search for "Fellowship of the Anointed." It's not hard; I'm a quick learner, and the device is tempting. So many possibilities in my hand, access to any kind of information I want. Maybe, when this is over, I'll go to school.

"Well." She sighs. "I suppose there's no point in keeping this from you."

At that, Kane looks up, then over. His knife stalls, and suddenly it looks like a weapon in his hand.

"Nova's legal name is Leah Miller."

Kane relaxes. What did he think she was going to reveal?

I set the phone down in front of my plate as results populate the tiny screen. Photos of us being taken from Druid Hill. Of Lark beside a pool with two outsiders. It's hard not to look at the phone, to make myself care what Miller has to say.

Miller leans her elbows on the table and stares into her oats as she says, "She's my mother. At least, she gave birth to me."

That gets my attention—and Kane's. We both sit up. I forget the phone. "You asked me if Nova had any children, but you already knew the answer."

"I knew she had me," she says. "But I escaped twenty-three years ago." She shrugs, raises her eyebrows as if she couldn't care less. "For all I know, Nova had a dozen children after me."

"We were her children," Kane says. "The Anointed."

"I know," Miller says. "That's why I left." She picks up her spoon as if she's going to keep eating, but sets it down with a clank on the side of her yellow-rimmed bowl. It sticks in the thick goop. "I remember you, Deryn, though I'm sure neither of you remembers me. I'm seven years older than you, ten older than Kane—and it makes such a difference when you're that young. I remember the day my parents bought Druid Hill from the city. They were so excited, and I was thrilled. A whole park just for me." For a moment, her eyes glimmer. "They withdrew me from school, and we set to work building. My parents had been planning for years, but I didn't notice. I was a child. All I cared about was running over the hills and playing on the swings. There were no more animals in the zoo—hadn't been for a couple of years, the place was in decline—but Dad bought goats. And then there were sheep and chickens.

"It wasn't long before we started taking in people: single mothers or pregnant couples who were low on resources, people dealing with unplanned pregnancies. Nova told them their children were gifts. That they were special."

"Anointed," Kane says dreamily.

Miller nods. "You were the first," she says to me. "That's why I thought, when I saw you again, that you were one of them, like Kane and Lark still were."

"First Anointed, first forsaken." Decades-old bitterness infuses my voice. "Nova wanted our parents, mine and Lark's, to stop seeing us, after he was Anointed. We were taking special classes with her already, as kids. She wanted more control over our upbringing—for us to love her. But our parents weren't willing to give us up. After all, they came to Druid Hill so I'd have a better life. And then Nova took it away. Forsook me. That was enough to send the message: comply or risk your children's future. They didn't care about the rules when mine was at stake, but clearly drew the line at Lark's."

"If you can identify them for me, when we return, I'll look into what happened," Miller says. "I have so many questions for you all. I didn't start investigating when Kane escaped; I've been investigating my whole life." She pauses. Looks at her coffee but doesn't drink any. "By the time Lark was anointed, it was clear that Nova no longer cared about me as her daughter, or about my father as her husband. She considered her Anointed her only family. So we left. Dad woke me up, with no warning, in the middle of the night. We stole the key to the gate, and we snuck out."

"How'd you get past the patrol?" Kane asks. "We monitor the gate and the fence."

"She didn't back then. You think it's to keep monsters out?"

Kane's face twists as he realizes he'd been working to keep the Fellowship in. "I should've known. It makes sense—I think I knew it in the back of my mind."

Anger wells up inside me, for myself, for Agent Miller—even for Kane. And it's all Lark's fault. His zeal is the reason Nova neglected her own child and husband. Why our parents were willing to sacrifice me but not him. And now he's abandoned Kane for questioning his faith. "So, why are we going after Lark, then? Why do you need Kane's testimony? Is mine not enough?"

"Because you're not Anointed," Miller says. "Sorry."

"Not anymore, but I—"

"It's not the same," Kane says. "Your powers never manifested. You've never worked magic. You never . . ."

"I never what?" I am closer to Kane than I've ever been, and he's still holding back. Why won't he just talk to me? None of them ever talk to me.

He growls in frustration, slamming his knife onto the table. "You're so dense, Deryn! How do you think I got all those scars?"

"Training? Fighting?" I feel myself about to say, *Nova?* but stop. "She didn't . . ." My stomach turns as I remember the charges Miller arrested Nova for. As I remember what Kane's body looks like under that shirt. He didn't get those scars from one incident, but dozens. Dozens and dozens and dozens of wounds. Is that what I escaped?

"No." Kane picks back up his knife and other butter packet. His fingers are shaking too hard to open its delicate flaps. "Nova never . . ." he says, not looking up. "Lark did."

"What the fuck?" Outsider profanity flies between my lips without thought. "Why?"

"Because that's how you build up magic." His lips tighten into a toothless smile. A long thin line that wilts as he tries to hold it. "Through discipline. Through pain."

"Did the others—" Oh no. "Did you?"

"Yes," he hisses. "I had no choice."

"Of course you had a choice," I shout.

Miller shushes me, gesturing apologetically at our server as they pass by with armfuls of someone else's breakfast.

I'm not placated. "You didn't have to hurt people, especially not the ones you love."

"He *asked me to.*" Kane leans forward, slinging his words at me. "He begged for every lash. *That* is why I won't testify unless Lark is back here, safe with me. Because Lark *believes.* Because he is the most swept up in Nova's lies, he is also the one who has been the most hurt by her, inside and out. The more he continues on a quest she gave him, to charge nonexistent magic, and fight people in the name of righteousness—the harder it will be for him to deprogram."

"But if you all went through the same . . ." I don't know what happened to them—don't want to imagine how those marks were made, those divots and lines—so I don't speak for him. "I mean, you can all do magic, or, you know what I mean." Blood warms my cheeks. I'm still not sure what Miller expects us to believe. Kane clearly doesn't want to tap into his magic, and she told him it wasn't real—so why would she ask him to use it? "What about Zadie and Maeve? Why does Miller even need your testimony, much less Lark's?"

"Their testimonies will help," Kane says. "But they won't mean the same as mine or Lark's."

"Why?" I'm loud. Louder than I should be. Again.

"Is it not enough for you to *believe* me?" Kane grits his teeth. "Stars, I do not want to talk about this at breakfast." He slams his elbows down on the table and his head into his hands.

"You don't have to," Miller says, as if she cares how he feels all of a sudden.

"I know." Kane is quiet for a second. Two seconds. Three, five, ten, twenty—it feels like eternity. "Nova knew he believed, so she put faith in him," he says finally. "I was the oldest Anointed, it should've been me. I should've faked it better, but I couldn't. I doubted her teachings when Lark never did. The way he took his pain, he—I don't think he'd even call it suffering. He loved what we did. For Lark, pain was the way, and the way was magic. He welcomed pain as his way to save the world. It's why he's run off to do exactly that."

I glance back down at the phone, remembering my search results. It's gone to sleep, but I enter the password to wake it back up. Miller and Kane don't seem to notice. The former must be so used to outsiders on devices, and the latter has his head in his hands. The screen flicks on, and there Lark is, sitting beside a pool in the dark. Features illuminated from below by a blurred source of light. The image captioned, "Ex-Cultist on the Run." Beside that, "Magic: Is It Real?" And, "Dangerous or Delusional?"

I touch the first one, not interested in what outsiders think about the others. Why do they feel qualified to speculate? If Nova was right, they're the corrupt ones. Though I'm beginning to see why Miller doubted her, why she and her father left. Why Kane left, in the end. If I'd known, would I have run too? Would I have stopped Lark from hurting Kane and dragged them along with me? I couldn't have, even if I'd wanted to. He's too strong and too set in his ways. Kane is right. Lark believes, and his belief is powerful.

"Last spotted in a West Virginia Motel 9," I read, pushing the words up to make room for new ones.

Miller cranes her neck to look, before remembering she can simply take the phone from me. It is hers, and she reaches out. I give it freely. "Fuck." That word sounds lighter on her lips than on mine, but still, this must be bad news. "I'm glad one of us is paying attention. We need to go." She thrusts the phone back into my hand. "You're in charge of this. Keep searching. Come on, Kane."

He scrambles to untangle himself from napkins and dinner-
ware, plastic cream cups and paper packets—the detritus of morning coffee. I follow briskly, fixing my borrowed sweater so that it
hangs straight over my dress. It's the only thing I still have from
home, wrinkled from sleep.

I surge after Miller with purpose. We have to find Lark, whatever it takes. He's the one Nova trusted, because he believes in
her. The one who asked to be tortured, who eagerly did the same
to Kane. Who liked hurting, and being hurt. As far as I'm concerned, he's as guilty as Nova. And when we find him, I'm going
to tell Miller so.

What if he didn't know any better? tugs at my chest. *You didn't,
and he's your brother.* I hold the thought down and drown it. We
have always been different. And, now, it's my time to be better.

20

LARK / NOW

Red lights glare from the backs of the cars ahead of us, in the quiet of late evening. All we've done since Calvin recharged my magic is drive. My legs ache, stiff and cramped. The last sign I saw read WELCOME TO TENNESSEE or MISSOURI or ARKANSAS—I can't keep outsider boundaries straight. Only one car flies past in the left lane, its siren screaming, while others crawl to a stop. Something is wrong. I lean between the front seats. Lilian is gripping the wheel, peering around vehicles. Calvin is on his phone, rubbing his finger up its screen while he reads. I should know what's going on and where we are; this is my quest. Why won't he tell me?

The evening light dims around us as the air grows heavy. Lilian slows the car. I roll down the window and breathe in the dampness. Fog: a cover for FOEs and monsters. Not a good omen. I sit up straighter and position myself between Calvin and Lilian. "What's happening? Why is everyone stopping?"

"Traffic." She pushes a button on the front of the car and a screen lights up with numbers.

A voice spills out of it. "—reports of a major accident in the middle lane on—"

"An accident?" Doubtful. Vile creatures know how to disguise themselves from those who would destroy them. But I am Anointed. I know their tricks.

"Yeah, we might be stuck here for a while." She presses another button and music starts to play quietly in the front row.

My veins sing as adrenaline rushes through my body. We are vulnerable in the open, packed into rows—every one of us. Calvin, Lilian, hundreds of unsuspecting outsiders, on their phones, listening to music, talking to friends. If a FOE finds me here, strapped into this back seat, it will be hard to escape and impossible to drive away. If a monster shows itself . . . I don't dare imagine the carnage our battle would bring.

The car lurches to a stop. Vehicles bunch up in lines on either side of us, blocking any chance of escape. We're stuck here, exposed. My heart thrums in my chest. I unfasten the belt that's supposed to hold me in place and protect me. As if this flimsy thing can protect anyone from what's coming. Only I can.

The fog thickens and swirls as I press my face against the glass. Two figures—one tall and one short—get out of a blue car and run into the surrounding trees. I twist my neck, trying to follow their trajectory. Where are they going? Who would get out of their vehicle in the middle of the road, even if they're all stopped? I've never been on a highway before this quest, and even I know that's dangerous. The cars could begin moving again at any moment. Another "accident" could happen.

There goes another! I rise onto my knees so I can see better, track the flash of pale skin and dark clothes that dashes from the front seat of a car, to the back. They open its back end, looking for something, before returning safely inside. That's not a monster, it can't be. It looks too human—and yet . . . Another figure approaches, like a feral cat stalking a field mouse. It stops, two rows of cars away.

Pits where eyes should be. Blackened veins under skin that refuses to settle. The FOE looks directly at me. My breath hitches in my throat.

I have to go out there. If Lilian can't move the car, then I need to make sure she and Calvin are safe. There could be more than one. If they converge on us, Calvin and Lilian can't protect themselves.

I take inventory. What do I have? My weapons are in the back, but I can reach them over the seats. Patting my harness, I feel the vials I know are stuffed into its leather pockets. I need something for my face, something to keep myself from breathing the fog—if a FOE has deployed it, I risk breathing whatever corruption it carries. What did Calvin pack me in his little bag? Probably nothing sufficient.

I lean over the back seats and scan the bags that fill what the outsiders call the "hatch." I unzip the bag Calvin packed for me and dig through clothes, looking for anything I can tie around my face—a scarf, bandana. He wrapped a bandana around my injured arm last night. I remember it hanging on the towel rack at the hotel, the brown stains of blood still spotting its bright red and white pattern.

"What are you doing?" Lilian asks, but I ignore her. "Calvin, figure out what he's—"

"Got it."

I pull the handkerchief from a plastic bag, still damp. It must not have had time to dry. All the better for filtering the air. I rest it over my shoulder before shoving their bags out of the way and pulling mine to the surface.

"Lark, do you need help finding something?" Calvin asks. I hear the click of his seat belt.

"No." I draw the long zipper down the length of my bag. The one with my tools and weapons inside. My knives. Spellslinger, still charged and ready.

Arrows. That's what I need.

"Lark." I hear him climb between the seats, but the space is narrow and his body is thick, shoulders and thighs wider than mine. Torso a brick. He wasn't made to crawl through small spaces, climb trees, and run swiftly over great distances. "I can help—"

I pull my bow free and set it in the back seat. Grab a fistful of arrows and fasten my bracer.

His eyes widen, body frozen in the space between the front seats. "What are you doing?"

Lilian's eyes find mine in the overhead mirror. "What the fuck!"

"I'm going out there."

"Uh, no you're not," Lilian says.

"I am, and you're not going to stop me. That was the deal we made. You drive, I kill monsters." I look into Calvin's eyes. Now he knows what I meant when I said I would pursue my quest at any cost. That I wouldn't let him hold me back. That I would use my skills whenever and however necessary.

I push my braids out of the way and tie the damp handkerchief around my face. Pack my arrows into their quiver and slide my hand through its strap. "Stay in the car." I don't bother addressing Lilian; she doesn't understand like Calvin does. "If I'm not back in half an hour, go home. No, not home," I think aloud. "FOEs have probably found where you live already. Go to a motel and wait. Check the news on your phones—I'm sure outsiders will report if I'm successful. A monster is hard to miss."

"So is your death, if you get hit by a car," Lilian interjects.

But Calvin doesn't object. He nods ever so slightly, lips parted as if he wants to say something. Wish me well, or ask to come along. He can't come with me. He stayed with me while I healed, he washed and braided my hair, he hurt me when I needed it, but he's not Kane. I trust him more than I ever thought I'd trust an outsider, but that doesn't qualify him for battle. Not against FOEs, and especially not against a monster. Only I can save us.

I duck out of the car swiftly, closing the door as quietly and quickly as possible. It's a fine line. I don't want the fog leaking in to infect Calvin and Lilian, and I don't want to attract the FOEs I've seen lurking between cars. Feeding off this evil fog. Hunting me.

I speak a quick locking spell into my palm and press it against the front door. I don't want Lilian to follow me to her death. There may be outsider casualties—I'm at peace with that—but I am still doing this to save them. In the end, they're victims of the monsters around them. I will do my best to protect them, even if they don't understand it's for their own good.

Movement behind me. I turn on my heels, keeping low against the car, quietly making my way to the next one. Outsiders look out their windows at me as I pass. Some roll them down. Others hold up their phones to fingerprint-covered panes. They vanish as I make distance, only their lights following me through the fog: a yellowish white as I walk against the direction of traffic, red if I turn back. I pause only long enough to memorize Calvin's license plate numbers, so I can return.

If I survive.

It's only some FOEs. I fought one off yesterday, and I can do it again. I've trained for this. I pull an arrow from my quiver and nock it, waiting. A blur of flesh passes between lanes of cars. A form like a person and yet very much not. Its skin squirms, unable to contain the evil within.

I draw my arrow back, in time with my breath, and flatten against a big silver truck. Muted conversation rises inside the vehicle. Fingers tap on the windows until someone shouts for them to stop. I hold my breath as I wait for the distant figure to move again. To show itself.

There.

"Don't!"

I hear Calvin behind me, and try not to look. Already, I've breathed out. Lost my tension and focus.

I hear Lilian's protest: "No, this is too far."

The FOE steps onto the white dotted line, the one that separates traffic and leads right to me. The holes where its eyes should be face my direction. Then, it calls my name: "Lark!"

I loosen my hold on the bow. If it knows my name, it must know me. It knows I'm after the monster that gives it power. That I won't hesitate to strike it down in the middle of the highway, surrounded by outsiders. They roll down their windows, chatter and music spilling from their cars as they watch.

"Lark, put the weapon down. I only want to talk. You can trust me." It's Agent Miller. Despite her request, she doesn't lower her gun—I recognize the black metal. I remember what it did to me. My arm aches just from gripping my weapons.

An outsider shrieks through their open window; another rolls theirs up, cursing. A door pops open. The FOE's head swivels left and right, gauging the situation. "FBI," she shouts. "Everyone remain calm and lock your doors. Do not leave your vehicles."

She is distracted. Now is my chance. I plant my feet firmly, draw the arrow back again, and hold my breath.

"Lark, it's me!" Another figure darts in front of her. "I'm here!" I look. The arrow looses crooked.

I hear it hit—hear the point lodge in flesh. But I haven't hit the FOE Miller. The second, familiar figure lumbers in front of her. Its eyes aren't pits—they aren't black at all. As they come closer, I see their eyes are brown and their skin only twitches, rather than squirms. Only hints at unnatural movement—or is that because they're injured? It's not a FOE; it's not even an outsider. It's Kane.

The arrow's buried itself in his thigh, stopped by his thick muscle. A cry slips from between his lips, as his mouth hangs open. Fog whispers around the edges of his body—as whole and beautiful as I remember. Did he manage to free himself from the monster's grasp?

The FOE Miller holsters her weapon. "Everyone stay in your cars!" she shouts, rushing forward toward Kane. I won't let her have him.

"Away from him!" It only takes a moment for me to loose another arrow—this time with her head in my sights.

She ducks, rolling out of the way and disappearing behind a wide black vehicle. I close my eyes, attuning myself with the vibrations of her footfalls, trying to track her escape—do I stop her or help Kane?—but a pounding overtakes my senses.

I feel Lilian and Calvin run past me—wind rushing in their wakes as if they are cars, themselves, driving against traffic. They disappear into a cloud of thick fog that descends on Kane's staggering figure. Cold realization floods my body, that he's not a FOE. That he came for me and I shot him. I should follow them, help them help him. Calvin has rudimentary supplies and a helpful touch, but only I can heal—

Someone grabs my shoulder. "Lark! You need to come with us."

I wrest myself free. Turn and look at—"Deryn? What are you—no!" I stumble back, draw another arrow from my quiver; Miller is still out there. I sweep the area, but too many outsiders have disobeyed her, have begun running away from us. I can't make out her silhouette in the fog. "I'm not going back."

"We came for you." They hold out their hand. "Kane told me what happened and, please, we can help you."

I narrow my eyes. "We? You mean Miller. You're working with Miller. She's a FOE! I won't—"

"No, she's not. She's a person—a person who the Fellowship hurt, just like me and you and Kane." Deryn keeps their hand out, waiting. I'm not taking it. I won't go back to the city with them, won't trust their word on Miller. They don't know what they're talking about. They're not Anointed.

Cars awaken like beasts around us, as the traffic ahead begins to move. An engine roars to life. Wheels creep slowly over asphalt. Horns blare at the abandoned vehicles in front of them. The FOE reemerges from the fog, gun in hand. Tires screech. An outsider screams and this time Miller doesn't reassure them. She walks slowly forward, avoiding car doors as they fling open, sidestepping the people who run for the trees.

"Please, Lark. I want to help," Deryn says. Concern furrows

their brow, but I don't believe it. They've been jealously poking at me for years. Why should I think they've changed, after they set the FOE on me back at Druid Hill? I nock another arrow, and I see fear on their face. Desperation as they search mine for sympathy. "Look, I'm sorry for the way I've treated you." But their jaw is tight and the words come out as if forced. "If I'd known . . ." They shake their head. "We're family."

"Thank god, you're still here." Calvin approaches from the side of the road, gasping for breath. Where has he been? He was with—"Lilian's bringing Kane to the car. I came back for you, let's—Holy shit!" He grabs onto me when he sees Miller.

"Put the weapon down, Lark!" Her voice is loud but steady. Clear. "I don't want to shoot you, but I—"

Before she can finish her sentence, I let a second arrow fly. She ducks behind a car and the arrow lodges itself in metal. A translucent yellow fluid spurts from the car's side.

"Please, Lark." Deryn takes a step, their hand trembling. "She doesn't want to hurt you."

"Who is this?" Calvin asks, looking suspiciously at Deryn.

Another group of outsiders runs from their car, the adults scooping children up into their arms. Shouts of "Gun! She's got a gun!" and "A fucking bow and arrows!" echo around us.

"Lark, we've got to go!" Calvin pulls me back as the FOE's form becomes clearer amidst the fog.

I lower my bow and accept Calvin's hand. Look Deryn directly in the eyes, so they know I'm not simply choosing Kane. I am making this decision. "I will not abandon my quest for you or anyone else. And if you've allied yourself with a FOE, then we are enemies." I don't wait for Deryn's response. I turn my back on them and go with Calvin. At least he wants to help. He doesn't lie to me or cut me down or ally with FOEs.

We run through traffic as it starts and stops, screeches and squeals. As horns blare and people shout and a siren draws nearer.

I almost want to see the thing that makes that sound; I've heard it for so long but never seen one.

Calvin's car is still stopped in the middle of the road, doors wide open. As we near, I see Lilian in the back seat with Kane. I stop in shock. Blood stains his blue jeans black.

"Get in the front." Calvin pushes me toward the passenger side then asks Lilian, "You good to go?"

"Yeah," she says, and he slams the back doors closed, blocking my view of them.

That gets me going. I run around the car and into the front seat as Miller shouts over the panic that surrounds us. I can't make out her words over the screams, and don't stop to listen. Cars swerve past us, trying to squeeze around empty vehicles. Calvin and I close our doors at the same time, and he doesn't wait for me to buckle up. With a twist of the keys, the car starts and he thrusts his foot on the pedal.

"Can you get us out of here?" Lilian shouts from the back.

"Think so," Calvin answers, but his eyes are on the road, fingers white from gripping the wheel. "We'll find out . . ."

A shot bangs over the commotion. I feel its force in my bones and a ringing in my ears. Look over my shoulder in time to see the FOE Miller, gun braced, with Deryn at her side. As the fog thickens around them, I see Deryn's form twitch. Their eyes darken and then—they're gone. As we speed away, I wonder whether I've left them for now, or for good.

21

KANE / CONFIDENTIAL

Lark showed up at dinner bouncing with excitement. I should've known something was wrong; he only ever got excited by magic, discipline, or ritual.

"Can I tell you a secret?" He moved closer, lowering his voice even though we were alone in the line for food. Zadie and Maeve went to wash up after sparring. The Fellow at the service window beckoned us forward, and Lark followed as if he were attached to me. I didn't mind the closeness but worried what it meant.

I grabbed trays for both of us, thanking the Fellow and handing one to Lark. He took it without acknowledging them, and hurried to keep up with me, a smile gracing his lips. We passed the Anointed children, and I remember thinking how, when I was young, almost every child was chosen. Anointing was becoming rarer as our population grew. Anointment had always been a big deal, but it was becoming a week-long celebration. The children were treated like heroes before they could even walk, much less wield a sword.

I pried my eyes off them, trying not to think of the day their magic would manifest and the discipline would begin. Their tongues pierced, fluids harvested, bodies kept under lock and key.

Zadie and Maeve were just arriving when we sat down. They waved, getting into line. Lark sat beside me and leaned so close our thighs and shoulders touched. Flyaways from his long fishtail braid tickled my neck as he pressed his lips to my ear.

"Nova invited me to participate in a special ritual tonight." His words played over and over again in my head as he stabbed a forkful of roasted vegetables.

"Oh?" was all I could muster, not close to matching the excitement that coursed through his body. He was practically jittering beside me.

"Mm-hm," he said, mouth full. "I'm supposed to meet her at sunset for further instructions. I think it's a ritual. Advanced, obviously." He pushed his food around his plate, clearly distracted. Over at the service window, a Fellow handed Zadie her tray.

"Do you want me to come with you?" I asked, not daring to look up from my plate lest he react badly.

He did. I heard his dish rattle as he pushed back from the table. "No. I'm supposed to go alone."

"Yeah, but I'm sure Nova wouldn't mind. She's invited me to private rituals before."

That got him. His blue eyes lit up. "She has? Why didn't you tell me? Were you not allowed?" Lark looked around, in case anyone was within earshot. At a distance, the Fellow handed Maeve her tray.

"I don't know," I answered. "She didn't say explicitly."

She had, of course. She ordered me to tell no one about the secret ritual, including the other Anointed, and I hadn't. I was too afraid of what they'd think of me. I couldn't share the fact that Nova had removed my chastity and collected my fluids—even my tears—as if she were picking herbs. She was planning to do the same to Lark, I just knew it. The thought made my stomach turn. I stabbed my fork into my chicken and left it there, unable to fathom eating.

"Well, she called this one a blessing. Is that what you did?"

"I don't know." It felt like someone was pinching the top of my nose, pressing their fingers against my bones. If they kept pushing, I'd fracture, and their whole hand would press into my skull. "I'll come with you and we can try it together."

"No!" Lark pulled back, a sudden distance opening between us. A few of the children looked over their shoulders before their teacher pointed them back to their food and scowled at us. We were supposed to know better. Any emotional outburst was like springing a magical leak. He was setting a bad example.

"Sorry," I said, not nearly loud enough for others to hear. I didn't want to draw any more attention.

"What's gotten into you?" Lark poked at his food again, thinking about eating or thinking about the ritual or thinking about me. "You know jealousy will drain your magic."

I blinked, stunned. "Jealous? Lark, I'm just looking out for you. I've done this before. Nova, she . . ." I bit my lip. Maeve and Zadie drew closer. Too close to finish my sentence. I swallowed my warning with a sigh. If I'd been brave enough to tell him, maybe he wouldn't have gone.

He didn't speak to me for the rest of dinner. That was Lark, always doing as he was told, practicing discipline and enforcing it in others, holding Nova's words closer to his heart than he did mine. He got up from the table first, leaving food on his plate, despite the diet Nova mandated for us. That was the only rule he broke that night.

I knew he was angry—angry that I would be concerned for him. I assumed he would be a lot angrier if he found out I followed him to this blessing ritual.

• • •

Ritual House was dark, though, when I arrived, Lark nowhere to be seen. The sunset only a red smear on the horizon. I kept walking—away from the gates of the commune, toward the old zoo ticket booths. No way Nova would perform a private ritual where others might happen upon them.

I did, though. The two of them stood in one of the wooden gazebos that surrounded the commune's entrance. Nova's hand slipped from Lark's shoulder, and, as they murmured goodbyes, I ducked behind a tree. They couldn't be finished already; where was she going? I held my breath as she walked back the way I'd just come—back to the commune.

I was about to leave my hiding spot and go to him when someone stepped into Nova's place. An Elder. It was too risky to move closer while they were walking toward me, so I cast a spell that would help me see in the dark. Magic and fear burned through my blood.

They both wore long woolen robes—ritual robes. The sleeves bunched slightly at Lark's wrists. I dug my fingers into the bark as they lowered their hoods and greeted each other. It was Elder Zephyr, who taught the younger Anointed children about herbs. I watched him lay a hand on Lark's shoulder to exchange energy, but Lark didn't return the gesture. Something was wrong with Lark's wrists: they looked bandaged. Was he hurt? I moved closer for a better look.

Zerphyr's hand lingered on Lark's shoulder, sliding down the length of his arm, taking the robe with it. Exposing his bare shoulder; it glowed in the moonlight. That's when I noticed the pillows and blankets that covered the gazebo. The floor looked soft, like a sacred grove covered in moss and pillowy foliage. That should be me in there with Lark, sharing the beautiful moonlit space, holding each other.

Zephyr took one of Lark's hands to his lips. They weren't bandaged from injury, they were blunted. Fat white gauze wrapped around his wrists and wound around his balled fists. Nova had bound them so he couldn't perform magic. Zephyr kissed each in turn, before pushing the robe off Lark's other shoulder. It slid away smoothly, falling into a pile at his feet and exposing his naked body to the starlit sky.

I wasn't near enough. Just one tree closer couldn't hurt. There was one ten feet ahead, and they were so focused on each other, they never noticed me as I moved. I wanted to do something—to stop whatever was about to happen. Chase Zephyr off. Tell him Nova sent word that the blessing was canceled.

I wanted to hurt him. The way I felt, I could have killed him and not lost sleep over it. I didn't, because I'm a coward. I didn't care about Zephyr, but Lark would report back to Nova, and then . . . then I'd lose him for sure.

A shiver rippled through my body at the sight of Zephyr unfastening his pants and pushing Lark to his knees. I imagined his hard cock bouncing between his legs as he steered it into Lark's mouth. I couldn't see from that angle and I didn't want to. It was too much watching like this, unable to *do* anything about it, and despite the sick fury, my own erection strained against the metal bars of my chastity.

I wanted to feel what Zephyr felt. Wanted to be with Lark on a bed of soft blankets, making love under the moonlight. Alone, without anyone telling us how to behave.

I turned my back, but the sounds—the *sounds*. Gagging and heaving. Loud gasping breaths and moans. When I dared to look again, when it was finally quiet, I could see Zephyr's fingers threading through Lark's hair. He was ruining the braids I had woven that morning, splaying the strands as he forced his fingers between them. And then he grabbed one of Lark's thick braids in his fist and yanked his head back.

I took the chance to move to the next tree. The closest one—I was so close.

"Turn around," Zephyr said.

I was so caught up in what they were saying, I didn't stop to think that I was near enough that Lark might see me. He turned, and I saw his face. Gasped, pressing my hand over my mouth. There were straps on his cheeks. The same brown leather our harnesses were made from. I hadn't noticed before because they buckled beneath his hair, but now I could see what had been done to him.

The straps held a black plastic circle in his mouth, behind his teeth. It was a gag—a gag that kept his mouth wide open while Zephyr stuffed his cock down Lark's throat.

My scream lodged itself in my throat as I peeked again. I watched Lark position himself on all fours while Zephyr *fucked* my partner. He was trying not to feel it, I could tell from how his eyes closed in concentration. His body swayed back and forth with Zephyr's thrusting. Saliva dripping in a thin line from his open mouth.

Why had Nova done that to him? Turned him into a glorified hole for an Elder's pleasure? This was not a blessing. It was cruel, whether or not Lark thought so. He should have thought so, but I have no doubt he enjoyed serving her purpose.

Then I heard Zephyr ask, "Can you come in this thing?" Zephyr sat back on his heels and pulled Lark's body against his, sat Lark on his cock. He bounced Lark's cock in his hand, heavy in its metal cage, and pulled a small plastic-looking object from somewhere beside him.

"What is that?" I whispered, before clapping my hand over my mouth.

Zephyr turned his head, and I flattened myself behind the tree, not daring to move. Barely daring to breathe. "Thought I heard something," he said. A goat bleated in the distance.

I waited for him to come barging over and haul me from my hiding place. I counted the seconds—got to one hundred twenty-six before I heard the loud vibration of plastic against metal, two materials not meant to bang rapidly against each other.

"Must've been an animal," Zephyr said.

Lark moaned, and I risked peeking again as he leaned his head back on Zephyr's shoulder. Squirmed on his lap. I remember watching his hands, still wrapped in white bandages, two solid white balls vainly seeking purchase. I thought about how perfect the bonds wrapping his fingers into fists would be for punching Zephyr in his face.

"See, I brought my own magic wand." Zephyr spoke his words loud and rough against Lark's ear. Rolled his balls gently in his free hand. Maneuvered the wand up and down the caged length of his cock.

It didn't take much. We only removed our cages once a week for cleaning, and did so as chastely as possible, never touching our own genitals. Sometimes we even used the ropes to ensure discipline. Nothing we did could have prepared Lark for Zephyr, who dropped the wand and wrapped his fist around Lark's cock, pressing the bulging skin back into its place. He rubbed, and Lark thrust. He pressed his entire mouth against Lark's neck and sucked.

White seed leaked from Lark's cock as he cried out. An open-mouthed cry, ugly and warbling. Round. His wrapped hands pressed against Zephyr's thighs as he relaxed, seating himself fully on the Elder's cock.

I couldn't watch the rest, but I heard Zephyr moan a few minutes later as he came deep inside Lark. Inside my partner. A *blessing*.

"I can feel it," I heard him say. "Thank you, Meadowlark, for blessing me. I trust you won't discuss the details of our ritual with Nova. It was too beautiful for words, do you understand?"

Lark didn't answer.

"I'll let her know we've finished, after I'm cleaned up."

I waited, listening to the shuffle of bodies and robes, of feet over blankets and then earth. I listened until the only sound was the low, raspy breathing of an exhausted man. I should've left then. Gone back to bed. For Lark's sake, I should've pretended I never saw anything. But I couldn't leave him like that.

With a deep breath, I stepped out from behind the tree and scanned the silent hills for any sign of Zephyr or Nova. Finding none, I hurried into the gazebo. Lark looked up at me, blinking as if I'd woken him from a deep sleep.

"Shh," I said, finding the buckle behind his head and releasing the gag. He cried out as he closed his mouth for the first time in—I didn't know how long it lasted, and didn't want to. "Quiet," I whispered as I sat him up. He placed his hands in mine and I unraveled the wrappings one at a time. My hands were shaking; I tried to still them.

"I told you not to come with me," he said, but the anger from earlier was gone. "Nova will be here soon."

"I was on guard duty, anyway," I lied. "So she sent me instead." We both knew I was only there because of him, but he must not have minded, because he just nodded and rested his head against my shoulder as I finished.

Lark held his hands out and flexed his fingers. "They were wrapped for his protection," he said. "So I didn't accidentally cast a spell. I could have hurt him—or myself."

"Yeah." I helped him stand, no other words to offer. It was hard not to tell him how much I wanted to kill Zephyr.

Lark looked down his naked body before I slung the robe back over his shoulders. "I came," he said, as if it were his fault.

"It's okay," I said.

"No!" He looked at me with the same shock as when I asked to accompany him. "It's not okay. The Elder was only supposed to deposit his seed inside me. That was the blessing, not me coming. We were selected for a beautiful ritual and he ruined it." Anger creased Lark's face as he pulled the robe tight around him. "And he trusts I won't discuss this with Nova." He rolled his eyes.

It wasn't my place to tell him how to feel—what version of hurt or anger to carry. I hated every second of that, even if he didn't. Even if Lark was so wrapped up in magic and monsters that he couldn't name what Nova was doing to him. The abuse. The result for Zephyr was the same either way.

The next morning, Lark told Nova what happened and gathered the Anointed whose powers had manifested. Together, we performed a ritual binding Elder Zephyr. Not an hour later, Nova opened the gate and put him out with nothing but a robe. Lark was deadly serious about the rules. No one broke them if he had anything to say about it. No one messed with the Anointed.

I don't know what happened to Elder Zephyr after that—I never saw Nova kick anyone else out. It wasn't even talked about. He was written out of our rituals. Forgotten. That was when I decided to leave—to end to her dominion over us. It was the only real way to help, and I was the only one who could do it.

22

CALVIN / NOW

Oh my god oh my god oh my *god*. I can hear every breath in my ears, hear the blood rushing through my veins. Adrenaline surges through my body, which is not great considering I'm sitting in the driver's seat of a car. The only outlet for my panic is to step on the gas.

I race down the shoulder, the wailing of sirens behind me—are they fading? I think they are—maybe they aren't after us. There was an accident, after all. When I check my mirrors, I no longer see flashes of blue and red. Don't hear a second gunshot. My ears are still ringing. Was it really that loud? I never heard a gunshot at close range before meeting Lark, let alone one aimed in my direction. I pull back into the right lane, not trying to look any more suspicious than we already do.

The FBI shot at us, oh god *oh god oh god*. We're wanted. I'm an accomplice. Lark warned me before we started. Why didn't I take him seriously? It feels so fucking real now.

I glance into the back seat. It's quiet. How is it so quiet? Lark bumps against me, squeezed half-between the front seats, bent over Kane's leg. A Honda Fit is very little like an ambulance; it was never built to accommodate a surgery. Lilian leans up against the door, holding Kane against her, on her lap. He's huge. Way too long to lie in this car, and so thick with muscle. I imagine he's crushing Lilian, but she doesn't seem to mind. They're all focused on Kane's wound, and no one is buckled up.

I almost ask them to, as if that could make this whole thing safe. But I can't ask Lark to leave Kane like that. I turn back to the road, blocking out their conversation while I try to remember how to read. I can't focus, can't make out the company logos on the green exit signs. I can't do this, I can't keep going.

"We need to stop," Lark says, but I hear his words as if they were my own, projected into his mouth. "I can't heal you in this damn car."

Okay, that wasn't *exactly* what I was thinking.

I hear Lark whispering, unsure if he's resuming a spell or starting something new. I can't watch while I'm driving. I can only feel my seat move as he leans against it, hear his urgent, "Come on!" and then, "Dammit." He sighs.

"He's bleeding pretty bad," Lilian says.

"I know." Lark sits on the console between our seats and wipes his hands on his shirt. Blood glistens wet on the scarlet fabric. "I can stop the bleeding, but I need space. We have to take him outside, lay him flat."

I swallow a mouthful of air, trying to keep down the nausea that threatens me. I don't think of myself as squeamish, but there's so much more blood than I expected. What *did* I expect? There's an arrow lodged in Kane's thigh.

"How about a hospital?" I can tell Lil is suggesting it with as much kindness as she can manage. Her eyes are on mine in the mirror, but I can't look up the nearest hospital on my phone. If I let go of the wheel, I'll see even more blood on my hands.

"No," two voices say. Lark and Kane in unison.

There are two Anointed in my car, right now. It hits me all at once. There's two of them, and two of us, and if we needed the numbers advantage, we don't have it anymore. Even though he's injured, Kane is Lark's partner, and I have no idea what they could do together. Seeing their relationship overwhelms me with memories. I touched Lark in the shower and flogged him in the woods. I sat with him while he healed himself, helped him work magic. It felt intimate to me, but to him?

Lark and Kane's intimacy radiates throughout the cramped car, in a way I didn't expect. Before, Lark talked about Kane almost as if he were dead. I thought they'd both changed too much for them to fit together again. But they do; they fit together as well as any couple I've met. You can't erase a dynamic like they've built together, especially not in two days.

But Kane betrayed the Fellowship. Left Lark to go on his quest alone—except he's not alone. I'm here. Lilian's here, even though she has doubts; she's still helping. What's Kane doing?

"Aren't you the one who left the Fellowship?" I can tell, after I ask, that I shouldn't have. Even the shuffling in the back seat stops.

Ten slow seconds pass. Kane says, "Yes."

I ask, "Why?" on autopilot. My brain wants to know, and my mouth reacts as if this is a normal conversation. As if Lilian and I aren't two fugitives chauffeuring a couple of renegade wizards cross-country.

None of the fantasy I've read has prepared me for this. For real danger and magic and blood—so much blood. For tangling with people and their histories. Reading is not the same as experiencing. Cosplaying a warrior is not the same as going into battle. Writing smutty fanfic is not the same as negotiating real intimacy. Lark and Kane are not characters in one of my books. They have roots, friends, family, regardless of whether those words mean the same thing to them as they do to us. We can really get hurt on this quest. By weapons and words.

"We need to stop," Lark says, sparing us Kane's answer. "Get this arrow out."

"We aren't taking the arrow out," Lilian says, and Kane looks at her, away from me. I'm relieved. Even though I'm part of this, I'm not sure it's my place to have that conversation. "If we take it out, he'll bleed more. Look, I made my surgeon girlfriend watch

fourteen seasons of *Grey's Anatomy* with me, and I've heard like a
hundred hours of doctorly complaints about the inaccuracies of
medical TV shows. There are a lot of veins in the leg that, if you
nick them, will one hundred percent kill you. Now, Kane is obviously not dead, but—"

"That 'but' doesn't sound good," he says.

"—well, you could die still. I just want to throw out how very
real that possibility is. The human body only contains so much
blood. Hospitals have more. They can take care of you."

"No!" Lark shouts. "We're not going to a hospital. Those doctors are outsiders. They'll open Kane's body, put their hands inside
him, expose him to all kinds of corruption. It's not safe. Only I
can help him. I know how."

Lilian pleads with me wordlessly in the mirror, but I don't
have the answer. All this time, I thought I believed in Lark. I
realize I've been practicing my belief, trying to believe. Lark's
belief is unconditional. Mine's not. When he got us through the
fence to Druid Hill, I was surprised. When he healed himself in
front of me, I was in awe. From the start, I wanted magic to be
real, and I still do. I wanted to be the person Lark needed, who
would take him seriously, the way I needed to be taken seriously
once. But what if Kane dies? Can I weigh Lark's need against
Kane's life, when we could choose the option that I know will
definitely save him? Can I risk Lark's partner's life to protect
Lark's feelings?

"Look," Lark says. "If my healing spell doesn't work, we can
discuss other steps. But I know I can do this. I already lost you
once," he says, and I hear his voice change for the man who kept
his chastity and flogged him bloody. Is that a healthy relationship?
Should I even encourage it? What right do I have to judge Kane,
when I stepped right into his place?

"How did you even find us?" Lark asks him.

Kane forces a smile through his pain. "Magic."

"I'm stopping," I say, because someone needs to make a decision and I'm the one at the wheel. I take the most boring-looking exit. One without any logos splashed on its sign. No fast-food chains or motels. No scenic spots to draw Instagrammers, I hope.

"Where are we going, Cal?" I hear what Lilian is implying. That there'd better be a hospital nearby.

"I don't know. I'll have to check my phone when we stop."

She sighs. "Okay. You're going to be okay." That was for Kane. The way she's talking to him worries me. I was her roommate, so I've *also* watched fourteen seasons of *Grey's Anatomy,* and she sounds like a doctor calming their dying patient.

Kane doesn't respond—at least not out loud. Lark slumps back into the front seat, beside me. I glimpse his bloody hands before fixing my eyes on the exit. I follow the narrowing road to an empty intersection and pick a direction without asking anyone's opinion. I turn right, taking us off the main road, and pull onto one of those winding country roads that go for miles without anything to see.

I slow to a stop on the side of the road. No other cars pass. We're not too far off the main drag but enough that I can breathe and assess the situation. *What now, Calvin?*

Lark climbs halfway into the back seat, never having buckled up. "I'm going to clear a space and find some herbs to make a salve." He has a plan, even if I don't.

I watch Kane nod. "Okay."

Lilian tightens her grip on him and looks at me. Her bun is destroyed, hair falling loose across her shoulders. Her makeup is still perfect. Whichever setting spray she uses should offer her an endorsement deal.

Lark takes Kane's hand and presses his lips against it. Then, he kisses him as if Lilian and I aren't there, as if he and Kane are alone in the world. "I started this quest for you," he says. "I'm going to kill whichever monster got its claws in you."

"Lark . . ." Kane tenses, sucking breath through his teeth. He's in pain.

"We're going to finish it together, okay? I'm going to heal you, and we're going to finish our quest together." He squeezes Kane's hand and kisses him again. "I'll be right back. I love you."

"I love you too."

Then, Lark is gone. His hand slips through Kane's and he jumps out of the car, pulling on his borrowed hoodie as he runs into the trees. I watch until I can't see him anymore.

"Calvin, look up the nearest hospital," Lil says.

I unplug my phone from the cup holder, where it's been charging since before the traffic jam. Open the maps app. The road appears pixelated—service must be terrible out here.

I need to know. "You never answered my question." I turn to look at Kane. He really is tall. If he were in better condition, I probably wouldn't confront him, but the question has been weighing on me since before we met. If you can call it meeting; he never introduced himself.

Lilian smooths her hand through the length of his unbraided hair. "Find it yet?" she asks, looking urgently at my cell. I know this isn't the time, but it's not loading and I want to know.

"You left him, and I don't know if you realize how much that hurt him," I continue. "Why are you here now? Why come after him?"

"You want to know why you should trust me," Kane says. "That's your real question."

I shrug. I suppose, underneath it all, that's what I'm asking, but the "why" is much more complicated. I wouldn't dare tell Kane, after watching them together, how much I wish I were in his place. How I want to learn magic with Lark—maybe not with the chastity and cat o' nine tails, but we could find healthier methods. If I were his partner. I stare at the makeshift bandage stemming the flow of blood on Kane's leg rather than at his face; I can feel my own face burning.

"You have no reason to," he says, voice quiet. "But I don't need you to trust me—I don't expect Lark to trust me either. I know that's not what you want to hear."

"Not really." I glance out the window. Still no sign of Lark.

"I love him unconditionally."

"But you didn't support him unconditionally."

Kane huffs a small laugh that turns into a whine.

I hear a slapping sound, and Lilian snap, "Don't touch it! Cal?" She nods at my phone again, and I make a show of restarting it. It's not my fault there's no signal out here.

Kane continues: "I did, for years. I don't know how much he's told you about our lives, what it was like living as an Anointed member of the Fellowship, but it wasn't all magic tricks and archery. Nova used us. She hurt us."

"I thought that was your job." I clamp my hand on the console to stop it trembling, to banish the memory of worn leather in my fist and the feeling of impact when barbs lodged themselves in flesh.

"It was," he says. "And it was his job to return the favor, not that it's any of your business. I hated it, but I knew Lark loved it. I didn't leave because I didn't support him. I supported him by leaving. I left because Nova was abusing us, and Lark couldn't see that. I left him even knowing that once I did, he might not love me anymore. Believe me, I wish I could've told him beforehand. I wanted to so badly, but I couldn't. He would've told Nova, and who knows what would've happened—I certainly wouldn't have been allowed to leave. Feel free to imagine what that would've looked like for me." His chest heaves as he grasps for a breath.

Lilian tightens her hold on Kane and looks desperately at my phone. It's on again, and the signal isn't any better. I try the map one more time, unsure what I'm hoping for. That I'll find a hospital close by and we'll save Kane? That Lark will return and heal him? That he'll die . . .

I bury the thought, never having felt more ashamed. Of course I don't want Kane to die; I just don't want him here, pushing me further from a life full of magic with Lark.

"Maybe it was selfish," Kane says. "Maybe I should've just gone on my quest and waited for Lark on the outside. Maybe I should have trusted him—I don't know. The only thing I regret is that you two are on this quest with him now. Should've been me. Once we were both on the outside, I should've gone with him. He'd have been safer with me. I don't have money for food or a hotel, and I don't know how to drive or use your phones, but I know him. That would have been enough." Kane's eyes flutter shut.

"Calvin," Lilian says quietly. She mouths, "He needs a doctor."

I look at him for a long minute. Am I qualified to judge how he's treated Lark? Does my opinion matter? I promised Lark I wouldn't get in the way of his quest. Is that still the support he needs? Do I trust that he can heal Kane? Do I need to believe in him? Or should I do what's best for him, even if it hurts?

"Okay. I'm going to check on Lark," I say. "I'll be back."

I stuff my phone in my hoodie and hop out of the car, not bothering to close the door. I find him quickly, clearing a small circle in the middle of the trees. He's gathered wood into one pile and various plants in another. I don't know what they are and don't ask.

"Oh, good, you're here," he says. Relief rises through his body. I watch the tension release his muscles, leave his face. Lark means it, he's glad to see me.

"How's it going?" I ask.

"Fine." No one's ever meant that, and I suspect that doesn't exclude the Anointed.

"Did you find everything you need for the salve?" I crouch to examine the plants as if I have anything to contribute.

"Not exactly, but I made some substitutions I think will work. It'll just take more magic on my part."

I nod. I refuse to ask him what he'll do if his magic isn't real, even if I'm thinking it. How can I? Whether or not I think he made the right choice, Kane's life is at stake.

"Okay." I slap my hands against my thighs. "How can I help?"

That's when the door slams. Lark and I look over at the car and watch as Lilian starts the engine and backs onto the grass.

My "what the fuck?" fills the brief pause as she changes gears, and then she's off.

Lark doesn't hesitate. He drops the purple flowers in his hand and runs. I follow, chasing him as he chases them down the road.

"Lilian!" I shout, feet pounding so hard against the pavement they hurt. "What the fuck!"

Lark's feet barely touch the ground. He runs as if he's flying, and as Lilian slows down for a series of potholes, I realize he could catch her. She's heading back to the main road, the direction I didn't choose after we took the exit. A road with lights and two-way traffic and a shared turn lane in the middle, with businesses lining its sides and busy parking lots. She slows—I could pick that orange hatchback out of traffic, anywhere—but doesn't stop.

Cars keep coming as Lark runs into the intersection—keep turning and speeding around him. I keep running after him, holding out a hand to stop oncoming traffic, just fucking hoping they see me in the dark.

When I was fourteen, my parents took me with them to visit some family friends who'd moved to Utah. We went for a picnic alongside a canyon with a shallow side, and of course, us kids went climbing. I climbed too far—shallow became steep—and the ground slipped under me. That was the only other time in my life I thought I was going to die. I imagined falling down the side of the canyon. Would it hurt when I hit the ground? I wondered. For a moment, I made peace with death.

Standing in an intersection between two strip malls in Arkansas, holding my hands out as if they have the power to stop traffic, I'm at peace again. Cars going opposite directions pull out to make their left-hand turns as I stand in the midst of blaring horns, coming toward me before curving away. I stand as confidently as Edward Cullen, as if my hand will put a dent in any car that dares approach. None of them slow, only swerve around me.

I hear tires screech and close my eyes. Brace for impact.

It doesn't come. When I open my eyes, the cars are stopped. Drivers lean out of rolled-down windows, asking me if everything's okay. I don't know—where's Lark? I scour the ground for his mangled body, before I spot him weaving his way through the sudden standstill. He's the only thing moving on a road full of cars. My orange Fit is nowhere in sight.

"Sorry," I say, weaving through them. "So sorry." Behind me, they move again slowly, horns honking. Oh god, Lilian left us, she left *me*.

Panic threatens to consume me, but—I can do this. I have Lark and my phone, thank fuck. Ahead, Lark runs onto the shoulder, slowing to a walk. I do the same, apologizing the whole way. Digging my phone out of my pocket, I find one missed call: Lilian.

I call her back, catching my breath while the phone rings and rings and—

"Hey," she answers.

"Hey, I was just wondering if you've seen my car. Someone stole it."

"Ha-ha."

"Seriously, though, come back."

"I will, once I know Kane's safe. I'm taking him to the hospital."

"He doesn't have insurance, Lil. He doesn't have literally any money."

"He could *die*, Calvin. I can't believe you carried on humoring Lark as long as you did."

"I wasn't humoring him."

"I—" She cuts herself off. "Look, you should stop this. Go sit in a coffee shop somewhere and text me your location. I'll pick you up once Kane's admitted. Bring Lark. This whole thing is a stupid mess, but he's good for Kane."

"It's not stupid." I worry I'm lying.

"Supporting him is one thing," she says. "When your parents stopped paying your tuition, I let you sleep on my couch to save money. That's support. When you told me to leave Ariana, helped me see how shitty she was to me, *that* was support, even if it didn't feel great at the time. But what you're doing isn't that. You're enabling Lark, Calvin. Thanks to Kane, he was liberated from a *cult*. They hurt him, and they brainwashed him, and you're following along on his deluded quest because, why, you want magic to be real? What Kane did for Lark was magic. He didn't betray the Fellowship; he saved them. So, stop this. Give up this quest. It's not real, and it is hurting Lark. I hope I can show you that by taking Kane to the hospital. You figure things out with Lark, Cal. I'll talk to you later."

She hangs up without another word from me. Hers hang around me like fog as I walk. As I close the distance to Lark, I feel a drop. Another. I put my hood up, wishing I'd taken my luggage with me when I'd gotten out of the car. I had an umbrella in there. My hoodie absorbs the rain as it begins to fall harder.

Lark's walking when I reach him. He doesn't look at me and doesn't stop, not that we're moving fast. He breathes normally and looks determined. I'm no stranger to exercise but all the chasing-after-cars has taken its toll on my legs. The rain comes harder, but Lark doesn't even put the hood of his sweatshirt up. He tilts his head back, lets the fat drops splatter his face and roll down his cheeks like tears.

"Stop," I say when my socks are so wet they squelch inside my high-tops.

He does. I'm a little surprised. We're under a streetlamp on the side of the road. Its bright light flickers on above us, as if we activated it with our presences. Reality is, it's dark. It's raining and chilly, and I'm worried Lilian's right. I'm worried I'm going to have to betray Lark. I don't want to; I want him to be right with every fiber of my being. But I don't know how to help him.

Lark turns, leans against the tall metal pole, and looks at me with those electric blue eyes. He still looks straight out of Middle Earth, and it's easy to forget he's human. But in this moment, I see the person he is, and I know it's not just rain running down his face.

"I don't know what to do, Calvin." Lark presses his hands hard against his face before wiping them away. The rain and tears keep coming, and I can't do anything to stop either. "I already left Kane once. Can I do it again? Should I keep going on my quest, or run after him? I don't . . ." He drops his hands to his sides. "I don't even know where I'm going anymore." He hunches his shoulders. "When I saw Kane in that fog, I thought he was a FOE."

"What does that mean?"

Lark gestures to his face. "He had no eyes, his skin moved like there was something underneath it. FOEs are hard to look at because they're agents of monsters. Miller is a FOE."

Miller looked like a regular person to me, eyes, skin, and all. But I believe that Lark sees her like that. That he saw Kane like that for a moment.

"Kane's time outside the fence may have changed him, but it couldn't have made him a FOE. He would never work for a monster. If they're even real," he mumbles, looking down at his hands.

This is my chance. To take Lilian's advice and support Lark by steering him in the right direction. I could do it now.

"The outside world isn't anything like I thought." His cheeks redden. "I believed everything Nova taught us. I feel stupid."

"You're not stupid." *Say something, Calvin.* Tell him maybe it's all in his head.

"I should've run into a monster by now, with all these FOEs around. I should know where I'm going, or what to do." Lark takes my hands. Slides our fingers together and holds them tight. "I haven't told you how much it meant that you came with me. I gave you no reason to trust me."

I hazard a smile. "You threatened me, actually."

Lark returns it, looking between his feet and our hands and my lips. I try not to look at *his* lips. Not to think about how much I want to kiss him. Press my body against his and feel his warmth against this rain. How can I tell Lark something that isn't in my heart? The words are simple, and yet . . .

"I did, didn't I?" he says.

"Yeah."

"I wouldn't really have hurt you. I don't think," he adds, smile fading.

"You wouldn't have," I say confidently. "I came with you because I believe in you. I can see that you know yourself, and I trust in that."

"But what if I don't?"

You're enabling Lark, Calvin.

Give up this quest.

It is hurting Lark.

I sigh. Suck it up and say something actually helpful. "Then, that's okay. You have time now, and people who will help you figure yourself out. I know I'm one of them."

Lark kisses me, and I forget Lilian's words. His lips are warm, hands strong and rough, even when wet. When he pulls me against him, I go, pressing his body against the lamppost while cars *whoosh* by, spraying us with water. I reach for that same feeling he gave me beside the pool, while he was healing himself. That wild magic. I don't know if it's the same thing, but I feel a flutter in my chest. The tug of want and the heat of need. Excitement I felt when we first met—was that only a day ago? It feels like ages. I find myself wishing we'd grown up together on Druid Hill. That I was Anointed, that we could make magic together.

I don't want him to give up and go home. I want to finish this quest with him.

The rain surges. Drops hit my skin like a thousand pinpricks, and when I open my eyes, I can barely see him. "Do you want to get out of this rain?" I raise my voice over its roar.

Lark nods. "We need to find shelter. Follow me."

I take his hand and let him lead me off the side of the road and into the trees—away from the shopping centers and whatever coffeehouse Lilian imagined me waiting in. Far from anywhere a Lyft might pick us up to meet her at the hospital. *Find shelter,* Lark said, as if we weren't running through the edges of a rural town in the middle of America. As if there are caves and ruins to hide in, as if we're in a land of fantasy.

That's the quest I was looking for, but this is the one I got—and isn't that how quests work? When I take his hand, I make my decision. It's cheesy as fuck, but I've always followed my heart, even when it meant turning down family support or living off ramen for five years. So, I'm not going to start faking it now. If Lark wants to turn back, I'll support his decision. But until then, I'm not giving up. I grip his hand tighter, follow more closely, and wipe Lilian's words from my memory.

23

LARK / NOW

Calvin's hand warms mine as we run through the rain. My boots stick and slide in the mud, splash through puddles. I have no idea where we're going, and I love it. I love being soaked to the bone, surrounded by trees, heading west. This is what my quest was supposed to feel like all along. A journey of freedom and determination. No cars, no guns.

No Kane. Don't think about him. He's going to be fine. Calvin reassured me that Lilian drove him to a hospital, and they would take care of him. I suppress my fear that their doctors will corrupt him. Kane's been going outside the fence for months. He's survived this long among outsiders, and I do trust Lilian to look out for him.

All along, she doubted me, but she took my partner to safety when he needed it most. When my magic failed me. I try not to think about it. Back in the car, with healing words on my lips and my hands on Kane's leg, I couldn't help him. No matter what I tried, the bleeding wouldn't stop. I think he wanted to go to the hospital, anyway. I was the one who wouldn't let him. I'd have killed him if I'd stopped her.

Kane may be safe at the hospital, but I wouldn't be. After all I've done, someone would call the outsider authorities, my FOEs. I'm not ready for that yet. Even though I'm not sure what's right or real anymore, I know I need to find out on my own.

Well, I don't mind Calvin's company.

We reach another road. With no cars coming, we decide to follow it, hoping it'll lead to some kind of shelter. It doesn't, and it's so dark out now that I can see the stars. Calvin and I walk hand in hand. Eventually, a single car slides up the road from behind us, slowing as it nears. Soon, we are going the same speed. Calvin stares resolutely forward. Says, "Don't look at them."

"Why?" I ask. "Are they evil? Are they FOEs?"

"No." He shakes his head. "I doubt it. But strangers don't usually approach you without a reason. People get killed accepting free rides."

"They do?" I can't help looking.

The front passenger window rolls down and an outsider leans out the window. They have big curly red hair, dark skin, and black lips. I hope it's lipstick—that stuff Lilian showed me. Otherwise, it's some kind of necrosis or evil infection.

"You're that guy," they say. I roll my eyes. Nothing like an outsider who thinks they know you well enough to guess your gender.

They snap their fingers and point at me. "Meadowlark!"

"Yeah, that's it!" says the driver: a person with skin my color, hair shaved to the scalp, and a face full of freckles. "The Fellowship guy."

The passenger smiles and rests their chin on their hand, gently poking long red nails into their cheek. Nails like Lilian's. "Do you two need a ride?"

"No, thanks!" Calvin waves and keeps walking.

The passenger raises their angular eyebrows. "It's raining and there's nothing around for miles. We're not going to hurt you."

"I believe that," Calvin mutters.

"Why not accept?" I ask quietly. "When you offered me a ride, I trusted you."

"And I trusted you," he says, giving my hand a squeeze. "But I don't trust strangers who pick people up on the side of the road."

"How about this." I stop and face him. Face away from the car and hold both of Calvin's hands. "We accept their offer. Get a ride, get out of this torturous drizzling rain. If they try anything, I'll kill them." I add a smile to the deal. As much as I love the adventure, it's dark and cold. If I were on my own and the weather were better, I'd have set up camp for the night already, but I haven't found anywhere warm enough to protect Calvin.

"Okay, fine," Calvin says. "But don't kill them. Maybe just intimidate them."

I pat the various pockets and sheaths on my harness. "I have two knives, a dozen offensive potions, and Spellslinger."

"Isn't that like a magic wand?" Calvin asks.

"Of a sort," I say.

"Then, that'll do it," he says.

"Oh, and I'm trained in hand-to-hand combat."

"I get it." But he's smiling.

"We'll take the ride, thanks." I wave at the passenger and hear the click I now recognize as doors unlocking. Calvin and I get into the back, and it's not long before I watch his eyelids droop and his body go limp. "I'll take first watch," I say as his eyelashes flutter, struggling to stay awake.

He mumbles, "Mmkay." Calvin may be brave and trustworthy, but he hasn't trained for this quest. Doesn't have my stamina and endurance. Can't survive on as little sleep, food, and water as I can.

I watch the countryside fly past the windows, as the driver and passenger ask me questions. I answer them as broadly as possible, telling them what they want to hear. That yes, I can do magic, and wow, isn't the outside world so great. All partial or exaggerated truths. I don't tell them how frequently my magic has failed me lately. How much I miss home, even though sitting in this car beside Calvin isn't so bad.

After an hour or so, the driver turns the radio on, and I pretend to ignore that the disembodied voice is talking about me. Well, Nova and the Fellowship and Kane and me.

"Reports are coming in that one of the members of the cult known as the Fellowship of the Anointed has arrived at a hospital in Arkansas, of all places, with a non-member named Lilian Walker-Park. They'd been on the road with another member, who attacked several law enforcement agents before running away with a non-member identified as Calvin Morris."

It was inevitable the outsider authorities would learn his name—and I did warn him. Yet, I feel guilty.

"They were last spotted running through an intersection near Jonesboro, Arkansas, and are believed to be on foot. If anyone has any information on their whereabouts, they should call the tip line at 1-800-555-3927. There's a reward for information that leads to their location."

The outsiders look at each other, and I look at Calvin.

He's still asleep—I glance at the clock—8:37 p.m. I place a hand over one of my knives, reminding myself that I can stop the outsiders in the front seat if they try anything. But they don't. Another hour passes before we pass a sign that says:

OZARK NATIONAL FOREST
WELCOME CENTER
1 MILE

The passenger leans over their seat. "You mind if we stop here? We can grab some snacks. Hit the can."

"That's fine," I say, unsure which "can" they mean. Doesn't sound very restful, but using all this energy has made me hungry. Experiencing all these emotions has probably drained my magic, if I ever had any.

I nudge Calvin awake as we pull into the welcome center parking lot. He stirs, stretching and checking his surroundings out the window.

"We're in the Ozarks," he says, reading another sign.

"Yeah." I watch the outsiders, remembering Calvin's warnings.

They pull the car into a space and stop, but don't get out right away. It's awkward, so I say, "Okay, we're going to go hit the can."

Calvin looks suspiciously at me as he follows my lead. He's never heard me say that before. He knows something is wrong.

"You want some cash for snacks?" the driver asks. They open a small leather holder and remove several green rectangles.

"That's really generous, are you sure?" Calvin asks.

"It's only a few bucks," the driver says, their smile so big and toothy it covers half their face. "We're happy to help."

"Well, thanks." Calvin takes the cash, mimicking the driver's smile. He makes a show of putting it in his pocket before taking my hand and leading me toward one of the buildings. "What's going on?"

I glance back to see the two of them lingering beside their car, the driver talking into their phone. "While you were asleep, the radio announced a tip line outsiders could call to report our whereabouts to FOEs."

"Figured it was something like that," Calvin mutters.

"There's a reward."

"We should go."

"Agreed."

By now, we don't need to consult each other. We don't look behind us and barely look ahead. We break our hold and run. Calvin gets off to a slow start, but he's better rested than I am after his nap, and soon we're both running fast. We never hear the outsiders call after us. Never hear the squeal of tires or blare of their horn. Nothing. We run until we reach the first exit, ducking off the highway and into the trees. Past another sign:

OZARK NATIONAL FOREST
—No camping—

"How do you feel about breaking outsider law, Calvin?" I ask.

He laughs so hard, he slows. "Seeing as I'm already a fugitive . . ."

I drop my pace to match his, catching our breaths as we wander deeper into the shadows of the forest. I feel more at home here than I have at any other point on my quest. If the ground weren't soaked, I would suggest we camp. Sleep outside under the stars with each other's bodies for warmth. I blush, grateful for the cover of darkness.

"What are you thinking?" Calvin says. "I'm hoping you have a plan. Because I don't."

"Don't worry." Through low-hanging branches, I spot a wooden structure on a hill. Either a small house or some kind of way station. Doesn't matter which. "I do now." I nod in its direction, and Calvin sighs in relief.

"Do you think anyone's home?" he asks.

"I hope not."

My thighs burn as we hike up the hill. Even by Anointed standards, it's been a taxing day—not just physically, but mentally and emotionally. I long to relax somewhere that FOEs and outsiders can't find us. I knock on the door and hold my breath, resisting the urge to ready my knives.

No one answers.

"I'm going to check the perimeter, look through the windows," I say. Calvin just nods and leans against the outer wall. I give in and pull a knife from its sheath on my hip, just in case anything's lurking. I can't feel a hint of presence inside, so I'm not too worried.

The building is a small rectangle with a window on each side except the back, where a chimney sticks out of the roof. When I return, Calvin stands straight as if he had been the whole time. I don't care if he relaxes. He deserves to.

"All clear," I say. "Stand back." I whisper an unlocking spell against my palm and press my hand against the door's lock. Time seems to slow as I realize I'm casting a spell that I'm sure is going to work. When I take the knob in hand, it turns easily. It occurs to me as I push that it could've been open the whole time.

Doesn't matter; we're safe here. Calvin and I unzip our wet sweatshirts and hang them on hooks beside the door. It's cold inside, but no surprise there.

Calvin nods at the fireplace. "Think we can risk the smoke?"

"I don't think anyone knows we're here. For all the FOEs know, the owners of this cabin are home and warm."

He nods, then heads to the hearth. Puts a log into the metal basket and fiddles with some kind of lever. I know what a chimney is and how to start a fire, but I've never worked one with a lever before. Leave that to the outsider.

It's cold, my clothes are soaked, and I want to dry them by the fire, so I begin to pull my shirt over my head before remembering I'm not at home. I don't know what outsiders are used to. At the motel, Calvin and Lilian slept with some of their clothes on. Sure, Calvin and I showered together, but that was maintenance. It doesn't mean he wants to see me naked. I should ask again.

"Do you mind?" I tug up the bottom of my shirt. "It's just . . ." I shrug.

"Not at all," he says. A fire glows in the hearth as he steps back. "I'd like to do the same."

I nod and watch as he pulls his shirt off. For a moment, our eyes meet, then drop, then meet again. We both smile as we undress, mirroring each other's actions. Unfastening belts and harnesses, jeans and shoes. We drape our clothes over the sofa that's in front of the fire. Lay out our socks over the arms. Line our shoes up in front of the flames.

"Um." Calvin looks down at his own underwear, then at the pair he lent me. They're identical, and they're both soaked.

I smile, then break into a laugh. "What are these?" I point at the shapes that pattern the cloth, then read the waistband aloud. "That's how I roll?"

"Those are dice!" Calvin says, his smile as big as mine. He moves closer, pointing to one of the tiny shapes. "That's a d20—means it has twenty sides."

"A twenty-sided die?" I crane my neck, turn it so I can see the tiny shape better. "I know what dice are; I played with them and cards once. We weren't supposed to, though, so I never really learned."

"I can teach you when this is all over."

When this is all over. What does that mean? Do I have to find a monster and kill it? Even then, what's *over* mean? Is this over when I return to Baltimore City? To the hotel where the rest of the Fellowship is waiting Nova's trial? Is it only over if I testify? I don't want to go back to that. I want to go home with Kane and Calvin, wherever that might be. Somewhere safe.

I bite my lip. Touch one of the d20s on Calvin's thigh. Drag my finger slowly upward, and rest it in the elastic of his waistband. "Teach me, now."

He knows what I mean—what I want. "But your . . ." His eyes drop to my crotch, to the outline of metal bars against the thin fabric of my underwear. Then to the key that hangs around my neck, and finally back to my own eyes.

I hold his gaze as I wrap my hand around the small key and yank. The chain snaps easily, its ends dangling from my fist. Calvin holds out his hands, and I press the key into them. I hook my fingers in the elastic of my borrowed underwear and push it down over my thighs and calves. Kick it up into my hand and toss it onto the couch.

Calvin struggles to do the same with one hand, not breaking eye contact, holding the key tight—as if dropping it would kill us both. When we're naked, Calvin opens his fist slowly, palm up. He picks up the key carefully between two of his nimble fingers.

"Are you sure about this?" he asks.

I nod. "I feel magic inside me—I have my whole life. If that feeling is real, if I'm Anointed, if monsters exist, then this shouldn't matter. Nova taught us to discipline our bodies and emotions in order to power us; she taught me that pleasure would weaken me, but . . . have I not loved Kane my whole life? Have we not lain together before? I've touched and been touched. I've blessed members of our Fellowship and loved my Anointed family. If letting myself feel means losing my magic, then I should have lost it long ago. So, please, I'm asking you." I close my hand over the cage for what could be the last time. Its familiar bars press into my palm.

Calvin falls to his knees in front of me. He presses his lips against my thigh, against my hip. This time, I rest my hand in his hair as he fits the key into the lock and turns it. I swell as he removes the cage gingerly from around my cock and pulls it free of my testicles.

He slides his hands up the sides of my thighs, grabbing my hips, standing, lifting me off the floor. I gasp and smile, wrapping my legs around his waist as he carries me to the modest bed and lays me down. My back hits the cool cover and Calvin descends on me. Our lips meet and meet again. We kiss hard. Desperately. When he bites my lip, I moan. Arch my back and feel my cock harden, unfettered.

And then I'm cold, alone—no. Calvin's straddling me. He's looking down at my body as if something's wrong. He reaches for a spot on my torso, brushes a finger over the skin. It feels—it doesn't feel like anything. "Lark, what is—what happened . . ."

When I look to his finger, I see an expanse of shiny skin, raised and thick and pink like the last rays of light before the sun sets. I remember the slick feeling of oil, the burn of flame, and pain that kept me awake all night. I remember Kane by my side with an ice pack, soothing me, despite my refusal. Burns are particularly effective for recharging magic—they hurt long past the point of injury. But I don't remember this scar.

Calvin's finger traces a pattern of lines down my left arm—my nondominant arm, just in case. We were careful to protect our sword arms, but we always healed. We were Anointed.

"I've seen these lines once before," he says. "When you asked me to strike you with the cat o' nine tails in the forest. I thought it was some kind of magic or that I was imagining things; I don't know."

He pulls my marked body against his and slides his hands up my back. I shiver, his touch so light it sends a tingle through my nerves.

"I don't understand," I say. I wince when his fingers glide over fragile scabs.

Calvin kisses a spot on my shoulder, then another, and I follow the trail of scars left in the wake of his lips. I don't remember those either. I feel the thick ropey scars on my back through the path of his fingers, as if for the first time.

"We were naked together in the shower," I say. "Before the forest—and you've seen my body since then. We undressed together in the firelight. I've . . ."

I stare past Calvin, over the curve of his neck and swell of his shoulder. Through the cabin window and into the fuzzy dark of night.

"I've always had them." Saying it feels true. One by one, I did this to myself, or made Kane do this to me.

Could Kane always see the scars? Did he know?

Calvin presses harder, presses our bodies flush against each other. "Lie down," he whispers against my neck. His words tickle.

I do as he says, not because I think I have to, but because I feel safe in his hands. That he feels the valleys and mountains formed in my flesh and cares for them and for me. My lips part as he kisses his way down my bare chest, stopping to flick his tongue over my nipple and curl around the curve of my navel. He pays attention to every part of me I haven't.

He sits gently on my thighs, resting his hands on my hips. "What can I do to make you feel good?"

I don't know how to answer—apparently I don't know my own body at all. What would make me feel good? I feel his hands massage the soft skin around my cock and moan softly as my erection grows stiffer. I reach down. Close my eyes for a moment and touch myself like I haven't in ages, running my hand slowly down my shaft, feeling every vein and ridge as it hardens in my hand. Skin against my own skin. Not Kane's practiced fingers, cleaning and checking. Not hard rough strokes that I'll hate myself for later.

I let go, suddenly so hard, I'm worried I'll push myself over the edge before Calvin can join. When I look at him, he's smiling softly.

"You don't have to wait for me," he says. "I'm not mad about watching."

I almost protest. Tell him that of course I want him to penetrate me—find out if he feels whatever power the Elders felt when they did the same. I miss bestowing blessings, miss sleeping with another person, pleasuring each other. But . . .

"You won't mind if I touch myself?"

Calvin rests back on his heels and shakes his head. "It's not like I'll explode if I don't fuck you. I mean"—he shrugs—"I want to, of course. I really like you." He bites his lip and looks down at my splayed body. Casually strokes his own cock. "But I've also really enjoyed getting to know you, and I'd love to learn even more."

"Prepare to be disappointed. I don't know what's true anymore. It only took an outsider a couple of days to corrupt me." I smile, but Calvin doesn't. "I didn't mean anything by it. Well, I did, but not in a bad—"

"It's okay." He presses a smile onto his face. "I have tried very hard to *not* corrupt you, though. To be respectful."

I take his face between my hands and kiss him. Reassure him that I'm grateful for the care he's shown me, even if I didn't always express that.

"Let me do something else for you." Calvin's breath is hot against my lips. Before I can respond, he positions the pillows against the headboard and settles against them, spreading his legs. Beckons me over. "Turn around and come here."

I fill the space, resting my back against his chest and the sides of our heads together. He pulls my braid from between us and drapes it over the front of my shoulder.

"Just relax." He kisses my shoulder, then my neck. "Take care of yourself; I'll be here." Calvin plants his heels on the mattress and I relax my legs against them.

I feel the hard length of his cock pressing against my back—against the haphazard pattern of scars—as I take my own in hand. I'm under no illusion that I'll last long, but I want to. I want to live in this moment when I'm touching myself, and giving my body the pleasure I denied it for so long.

I close my eyes, let my head fall back on Calvin's shoulder, and let myself feel. The weight of his left hand on my knee, fingers brushing through the hairs on my leg. The small slow circles he traces on the right side of my chest, pausing to rub a finger back and forth over my nipple until it hardens. The rhythm of his chest as it rises and falls.

I stroke myself almost lazily, allowing the glow of pleasure to rise like the sun within me. But it's not long before I feel orgasm dawning. I shift and stiffen, press back harder against Calvin, who runs his hand over my hair and kisses my neck. The feel of his lips shoots down my arm to my hand, which picks up speed on its own. When he slides his right hand down my inner thigh and presses his fingernails into my flesh, I come. My body pulses against his, within his arms and beneath his lips. I lose control—all bodily discipline—and yet I've never felt more powerful.

As my orgasm dims, I collapse against Calvin with a deep sigh. I don't want to move—not now, not in the morning, never again. But I know I have to.

Tomorrow, before Calvin wakes up, before the sun rises or anyone has a chance to find me, I am going to dress and lace up my boots, take my weapons, and go find out if there's a monster waiting in the west. Whether I've ruined my magic by caring for myself. If my quest was ever real to begin with.

24

KANE / CONFIDENTIAL

I'd had my eye on the outside world for a while. As a child, stories of monsters and FOEs made me curious. When my powers manifested, and I started taking guard duty, I became fixated on the outsiders who walked past. After I turned twenty, when Nova started extracting my fluids for potions and rituals, I yearned for the other side. But it was her setting up Elder Zephyr's "blessing" that drove me there.

There was a portion of the fence along the northern side of the hill that was obscured by trees and prickle bushes, even when the leaves fell. I liked to stand there and watch the outside. Used to imagine that's what movies were like. It wasn't a busy area. There was one wide road, mottled with potholes and rusting construction equipment, that traced the perimeter before ending at the fence. One of the old park entrances. From there, I could see rows of houses. The only outsiders who paused to stare seemed to be passing through; the ones who lived nearby ignored us. I'd guess they thought we were good neighbors. Never made any noise. Kept the land in shape.

I didn't do anything heroic or on purpose. All I did was lean against the pickets and feel the iron shift. The fence shouldn't shift. It was driven deep into the ground, sturdy enough to withstand a car crashing into it and warded with Nova's own magic.

I glanced around the forest and listened for footsteps, making sure I was alone before looking more closely at the metal. It had rusted along a seam—and why not? It was an old fence, and this section was choked in thorns, hard to reach for maintenance. When you think your fence is protected by magic, what impetus do you have to reinforce it?

What would Nova even have told us? That the wards we strengthen with rituals and herbs and a line of our own seed weren't enough? That she needed to hire outsider contractors to fix what we couldn't? Suspicious at best, horrifying and corrupt at worst. Lark and the others probably would've excused it, somehow. Maybe I was always a lost cause, because I yanked on the bar, and it broke off. I remember looking at the iron picket in my hands like a rib I'd ripped from my own chest. Immediately, I fitted it back into the hole in the ground and returned to the commune.

But I went back the next day. I removed the picket and held it in my hand. The weight of it balanced in my fingers was all the proof I needed to know what I'd done was real. That the fence was vulnerable.

The day after, I stepped through, taking the picket with me, like I was still within the fence's boundaries if I brought a piece with me.

The fourth time I visited the weak spot, I left the picket behind. As soon as I let go and my foot touched ground outside the fence, my body lit up. Exhilaration flowed through me like magic—at first, I thought that's what it was! But magic never felt that good. Magic was work, like lifting a heavy weight. This new feeling was effortless, made me feel light as a leaf in the wind.

Quietly, I made my way down to the wide road with its crumbling gravel and piles of old metal. I hurried up it, worried a patrol might see me if I lingered. I didn't get very far. Across the street, I found a small grassy area with stone steps and benches where outsiders walked their dogs—it took me a minute to place the furry beasts.

We'd learned about them accompanying FOEs, though these

were playful. They jumped on me and wagged their tails. When I leaned close, they licked me with their big fat tongues, slobbering all over my face. I didn't know how to talk to outsiders or even how to act, but somehow my body knew how to play with the dogs. I went to that park every day for a week straight, until the outsiders got used to me. They started to say hi, to teach me the names of all their dogs. I even told one of them my name and pronouns and they reciprocated. Their name was Ashir and they had short blue-and-green hair. Their dog's name was Marley, and she was a miniature poodle.

It was going fine until they asked the question I'd been dreading: "Do you live around here?"

I bent down to scratch behind Marley's ears, putting off the answer. I had to answer. Should I lie? I could hear my heart beating like it was in my ears. If I lied, they might ask where I'd come from, and I didn't know anywhere else. I could think of no reason why I would be hanging out in a faraway park, playing with other people's dogs.

"Yes," I said, hoping the answer would suffice.

"Cool, I'm on Keystone, near Rockrose. You'd be welcome to come over whenever. We just got a grill and my partner is hankering to use it."

Partner. Longing coursed through me. I wished Lark was with me—wanted him by my side. To bring him to Ashir's house to meet their partner and dog.

"That sounds great," I said. As if I could make plans! But it felt good to say, even if it was only pretend. Ashir and I weren't friends; they were an outsider. We weren't even supposed to be talking, much less grilling together.

I looked over my shoulder at the fence, as if making sure it was still there. "I've got to go."

"Okay," they said. "Feel free to knock on my door and say hi." They smiled and tugged on Marley's leash. I watched them turn a corner and disappear, making note of the way to Keystone. Ashir had their own home with their partner, where no one told them what to do.

I didn't return to the park for a week. I was scared that the next time I went I wouldn't come back, that I'd never see Lark again. My chest ached thinking about it, the pain worse than the knife, worse than the brand or the cat. When I was tempted to run to the broken picket, I ran to Lark instead. I pulled him away from lunch and down the path toward the cave where we stored our tools. Dropped to my knees and rested my forehead against his jeans.

"I need you to hurt me."

Lark ran his fingers over my hair, tracing my braids. "Okay," he whispered, then kissed the top of my head. "Okay."

I chose the flogger because I knew it would bruise. I wanted to feel too sore tomorrow to venture outside the fence. Lark wasn't brutal by nature, but he took magic seriously, and his swing was strong. I let him hit me until my groans became cries, became screams, became sobs. Until even the smooth touch of his palm against my skin felt like fire.

He offered to carry me back to our quarters, but there was no-where he could put pressure that didn't hurt. So, he walked slowly, letting me lean on him as we made our way to bed. It was only afternoon still. Zadie and Maeve were training, and I'm sure they'd noticed our absence. But Lark unbuckled my harness and peeled my clothes away, the layers like flower petals. He kissed each of my bruises, unwound my braids, and washed my hair.

This was why I had to stay. I had to stay for Lark. I didn't want to think what it would do to him if I left, let alone how Nova would punish him for my transgression. As we lay together, afterwards, hair still damp, bruises blossoming across my shoulders and thighs, I imagined us at Ashir's house, struggling to conjure an image that contained both Lark and a grill. Imagined what Lark would make of Marley, the dog that was very much not a monster.

We'd accomplished what I set out for, though. After that discipline, I couldn't move for days. I was excused from most training sessions because every shifting muscle hurt. But as the weeks passed, and the bruises faded from purple to muddy gray, I felt the pull again. The temptation.

Lark returned one evening from performing a blessing—we never spoke about these private rituals, but Nova continued them with me, so I assumed Lark continued them with the Elders—and slid into bed beside me. He had his own, but neglected it more often than not. After the blessing, he usually passed out, exhausted, while I lay awake unable to shake the memories of Elder Zephyr fucking him. I couldn't sleep—couldn't live with myself any longer while Nova put Lark through that over and over.

When I was sure Lark was asleep, I carefully extricated myself from his arms and dressed in the dark. I left behind my harness and snuck out of the commune, down the path to the woods. Patrols were easier to spot at night because of the glowing potion we used to light our paths. I made sure to locate each of them before heading for the weak spot. Before pulling up the pike, slipping through, and sliding it home as if it were still rooted firmly in the ground.

The other side of the fence was quiet. No dogs were barking and only one car drove down the road. I waited until it passed to cross, then walked east, the way I'd seen Ashir leave the park. Walked until I reached a sign that read KEYSTONE and another at the top of the road that read ROCKROSE. But there were a dozen houses lining the street on both sides and most of them looked the same. How was I supposed to know which one?

The grill. Ashir's partner had a new grill, and grills were kept outside. I ran around to the alley and looked for grills. I found three. Which house, which house? I bit down on my fist and screamed, the frustration like a knife in my side. I pressed my back against the weak wire fence around one of the houses, unable to bear the thought that it might not be Ashir's. That I'd never find it. That I'd return alone and hopeless, unable to help the person I loved the most.

That's when the back door flew open and a sharp voice shouted, "Hey!" A dog barked—a familiar bark. A well-known tiny monster. I jumped to my feet to find Ashir brandishing a wooden club, their partner standing on the porch holding a shiny metal rectangle.

Ashir stopped when they saw me. Rubbed their eyes. "Kane? What are you . . ."

I braced myself on their fence as they lowered their weapon and approached. Marley darted out of the house and toward me, wagging her tail. Ashir's partner relaxed and called out, "You okay?"

Ashir nodded and opened both the gate and their arms, which I fell into without words. As I sobbed, they invited me inside and made me a disposable cup full of noodles with salty broth. Steeped tea for me. Waited and listened while I explained that I'd come from Druid Park, that I was a member of the Fellowship of the Anointed. They weren't surprised. They helped me contact the FBI, even though they didn't normally like to call their outsider authorities. Said an agent had given out their business card to those in the surrounding neighborhoods in case anyone saw anything. Ashir said they'd suspected something about me, but hadn't been sure. That I was welcome to stay until help came, but I declined. I couldn't spend a whole night away. Lark would notice. He would tell Nova.

You know the rest. That's why I had to wait until my quest—I couldn't risk it. But it won't be long now. I'm going to lose Lark when the FBI shows up. He's going to hate me; I already hate myself. But it's for the best. For all of us.

25

DERYN / NOW

It feels weird being alone in the car with Miller—and yet good. I feel like her partner, like we're on a quest together. She's only a few years older than me, and we were both children under Nova's care. That's a kind of family tie, regardless of blood. Unlike anyone else in that position, I respect Miller. She knows herself, understands how her mother hurt her and her family and the Fellowship, and I respect that she's making it right. And Miller seems to trust me in return, trust me with her phone and the power that goes with that. For the first time in a while, I feel like I'm helping for real—helping because I want to. Not to prove I'm useful or to show off. I like it.

"Any updates?" she asks.

I refresh the search results in the browser. "Nothing new online." Review her emails. A red dot pops up beside her texts. "Wait, here's a message from your supervisor; looks like someone called in a tip."

Her head turns so quickly, I'm afraid she'll steer us off the road. "What is it?"

I tap the message to bring it up. "Lark and Calvin were spotted at a welcome center near the Ozarks. Here, along the eastern side." I angle a photo so she can glance at it while driving.

"Can you put that into the map? The Ozarks are huge."

"Yes." I can. I know how to use outsider technology, and it feels like magic in my hands. It feels like helping. I tap Go and the phone begins speaking directions. "Looks like they caught a ride with some outsiders but ran off at the welcome center and went ahead on foot."

"Good," Miller says. "It's dark. Hopefully, they stopped to rest nearby. Now that Kane's gone and ditched us, we could call for backup."

"We could . . ." The *or* lingers on the edge of my voice. I'm an equal part of this team now. Miller would listen if I said it. "Or we could just keep going by ourselves." I look between her and the road. See her do the same, out of the corner of my eye.

"We could keep going by ourselves. No one back at the agency really understands the Fellowship like we do, and I think . . ." She adjusts her grip on the wheel. Smiles. "I think we make a good team."

"Same," I say. "Besides, if a bunch of FOEs descended on Lark, he'd probably attack them, get himself hurt, maybe take Calvin down with him. You'll want him alive to testify."

"That is true," she says.

"Outsiders don't understand, really. Don't know how to interact with the Fellowship."

"What about me?" Miller says. "Lark thinks *I'm* a FOE."

The word no longer sits right with me—actually makes me angry. Miller is Nova's daughter. Why should she be labeled a Force of Evil when she's trying to help free the Fellowship from her mother's grip?

"Well, he's wrong. You were raised on Druid Hill while the Fellowship was forming and that makes us family, or at least Fellows. Whichever feels right to you."

For a minute, the only sound is the occasional *whoosh* of passing cars. "When we first set up on Druid Hill, we were all 'Fellows.' Nova invented 'Anointed' to attract new members. She bestowed it upon their children after birth, but . . ." Miller's voice wavers before tapering off. She clears her throat. "Nova never used it to describe me, her own child. Which is baffling, since I'm the reason she bought the land and started the Fellowship in the first place." Miller takes her hands off the wheel and holds her palms up in the air. "I'm the reason she believes in magic."

I find myself holding my breath. No way—it can't be. "You can do magic," I say slowly.

"I don't know—I certainly can't anymore. Wouldn't even if I could." Miller grabs the wheel before we drift into the other lane. "Even if it is real, it's tainted. Just ask Kane. I've spent over two decades working through the seven long years I lived on Druid Hill. What it felt like to be pushed aside by my own mother so she could attract new members, call their children Anointed, favor and love them.

"When I opened my investigation, I told my supervisor the Fellowship's belief system was a lie invented to control people and abuse children—how could I say otherwise? The abuse was real, though I needed an insider source. Things were rapidly evolving when my father and I escaped. My supervisor believed me, but she wouldn't have if I'd told her my whole story. If I told her about magic. Outsiders never believe."

My head spins so fast, I have to roll down the window to alleviate my sudden dizziness. A cool breeze whips inside the car, and I breathe the fresh air into my lungs.

"You asked Kane to use magic to help us find Lark." I feel the weight of his anguish, when she asked him. The guilt of denying him a lifeline.

She sniffs and clears her throat again. Stares resolutely at the road. "I did. I was desperate, and angry that Lark would so selfishly run away when his testimony could help so many. Angry with Kane for not being more helpful."

"Do you think it worked?" I asked.

"I don't know, not sure I want to. What does it matter now?"

"You don't think it matters if magic is real?" It's all I've been able to think about for days. It's the crux of Kane and Lark's world—what holds their reality together or blows it apart.

"I don't really want to think about it, Deryn. I'm sorry. I know you used to be Anointed, that this affects you personally, but it hurts me too much, and I've worked too hard to let that into my life again."

"Okay," I say. "I respect that." But my mind is racing with possibilities—that I could still have it all: a family and magic. "But you are one of us. And Lark is my brother—even though he called me his enemy. He was wrong. You're not a FOE, so I can't be allied with one. He only said that because he believes Nova's lies. Even if he doesn't think so, we're family. And you don't turn your brother in. You try to bring him home."

26

CALVIN / NOW

I didn't expect to wake up alone, but I'm also not surprised. I'm not even really angry. It's sadness that tugs at my heart as I roll out of bed and see one set of clothes lying over the couch by the fire. When I touch my high-tops, they're still wet. Great. I dress, scouring the cabinets for anything to eat, while I pull on yesterday's pants. Lark took my shirt—technically, they're both my shirts, but he took the green Ninja Turtles one I was wearing. I pull on the one he left behind, glad to have a part of him close to me. It's stiff from air-drying after the rain soaked it through—washed away any blood that might've stained its scarlet. God, I'm a terrible adventurer. *Stiff fabric.* Who cares? Not Lark.

I pull on my hoodie and find a box of granola bars in the cabinet that only expired six months ago—no shame in that—and stuff several in my pocket. This little crime doesn't register: I'm already definitely getting arrested, or at least heavily interrogated by FOEs.

Damn, I'm thinking like Lark now. I miss him.

On the floor, in the middle of the rug, lies the abandoned chain, key, and cage. I shouldn't leave them for the owners of this cabin to find, but doubt Lark wants to see them again. I decide to bury them. It's weird, but I can't think of a better way to dispose of them. At least burial has a sense of ceremony.

I pick my phone up off the night stand and check my notifications. Too many for me to even think about. They feel so trivial compared to Lark's quest. I could be fighting a monster right now; there's no way I can go from that to scrolling my newsfeed. Sixty-seven percent battery in power-save mode. Wish I'd grabbed a charger, but I won't need nearly that much to call Lilian and get a Lyft. A really expensive Lyft.

I'm tapping through my texts to ask Lilian for the hospital's address, when I grab the front doorknob and realize it won't open. I try twisting the knob the other direction. Pulling and pushing, even though I know that's not right. What the hell? If the door is stuck, how did Lark get out? Or . . . did he lock the door behind him? I jam my phone into my pocket and jiggle the knob with both hands. Nothing.

My phone vibrates in my pocket. Lilian? I dig it out. No, it's a message sent to my Patreon account. I almost ignore it—usually they're guys trying to pay me for sex—but the preview stops me.

Deryn
If this is the same Calvin who took Lark on a quest to kill a monster, please write back. My name is Deryn (they/them) and I'm Lark's sibling.

Deryn. I remember seeing them on the highway, pleading for Lark to join them. Lark chose me instead. Well, Kane too. The point is, he *didn't* choose to go with his sibling. Why should I trust them now?

I open the message. Deryn found my Patreon? They had to donate five dollars to send that message, so they must be serious. Where did they get a credit card? I type, making sure to use complete sentences. Fellowship members can't be well versed in texting.

Calvin
I got your message. What's up?

My response hangs in limbo while the internet thinks about sending my message. Almost no signal out here. I check available Wi-Fi and there's only one, appropriately named "BnB OZRK1," password protected—as if anyone is going to steal their internet all the way out here.

Okay, *I'm* stealing their internet. I find the password on a laminated piece of paper in the kitchen, alongside information about where the cleaning supplies are and the closest restaurants.

The second I connect to BnB OZRK1, I get another notification.

Deryn

I'm with Agent Miller. She's NOT a FOE. Lark only sees her that way because he was raised to. You saw her. You know she looks normal.

He's right. I did see her, and she did look normal, even though she was shooting at my car.

Calvin

Does she still have her gun?

Deryn

Yes, but she isn't going to use it.

Yeah, right.

Deryn

I'm messaging you because some outsiders called in a tip on your location. We haven't called for backup but are worried they might show up anyway, and we don't want Lark to get hurt. Or hurt anyone else.

Calvin

You're out of luck. He ditched me.

They don't respond for several minutes. I try the knob again in case it was simply stuck and I'm a moron—I'm not. It still won't open.

Deryn

   Where'd he go?

Calvin

   I don't know. I'm stuck in a cabin in the Ozarks. The door
   won't open. I'm guessing Lark locked it behind him, but I'm
   not sure how.

More waiting. I sigh. Tap my foot. Why isn't the competent outsider handling the phone?

Deryn

   Miller and I are coming to get you. She says to send her your
   location.

Do I want them coming here? The people chasing Lark? The woman who shot at us? So much has changed since then, in so little time. It feels like an age. Fuck it, I'll never get this door open on its own and—I jiggle the window locks—unless I want to physically break out, I'll need help.

Calvin

   Okay, I'll send you my location. Get here as fast as you can. I
   think Lark went to kill a monster on his own.

It feels bizarre for me to worry about him, the epic hero I've fallen in with, but I do. Even if monsters aren't real—and I'm not even sure he believes in them anymore—the FBI is. And they're definitely going after him, with force. If Deryn cares even a little about their brother, they won't want that to happen.

I copy my location from the maps app and paste it into my message with Deryn. A few minutes later, they respond with theirs. They aren't too far away. Maybe two hours, depending on traffic? Not that I know the area. I kindle the fire on the hearth and move my damp clothes closer.

Why did Lark leave me? He trusted me, and I gave up everything for him, even when others told me not to. I thought we were in this together. I hate that this hurts. Hate that I don't know whether Lark is okay. He's powerful, but he's not immortal, and I can't think of anything I could do to help him.

I look from Deryn's messages to my subscriber count. I haven't been on social media much since I ran into Lark in that alley. How could I? I literally haven't had time. My screen time report for this week is going to be great. But I have 25,000 followers on Twitter and another 58,000 on Instagram. I have people. They could help. Will they?

I draft a tweet. Stare at it for ten minutes, tweaking the wording before I hit Send. Then I open a new Instagram story and look into the camera. Sixty-two percent battery *and* I look terrible. For a moment, I consider using a filter, but . . . I want this to look real. People need to know I'm laying myself bare to them. I sit on the couch, curl up in the corner, and hold my finger down to record.

"Hi, friends." I put on my best smile. "I know I haven't been around as much as usual the past couple of days, but some wild, unexpected stuff has been going on . . ."

I tell them about meeting Lark. Tell them how much he's been through—intimate details exempted—and how important his quest is to him. It takes twelve stories to tell everything—will anyone even watch all of these? God, I hope so. "What I need—what Lark needs—is your support. I've never asked for anything like this before, but he's a good person who's risking himself to help all of us. It's important that if you see him, you don't call the tip line or the cops or anything. He won't hurt anyone, but they might hurt him, and . . ." I say it before I can stop myself. "I care about him. More than I should care for someone I only met a few days ago. Sorry, I didn't mean to—well . . ." Tears burn at the corner of my eyes. I dab at them with the sleeves of my sweatshirt. "I guess that's all. Thanks."

I release the record button and tap Next, then Share, without rewatching or overthinking. Send it out. It's all I can do.

Or can I do more?

A thought grabs me and refuses to let go, no matter how ridiculous it feels. What if it wasn't all a lie? What if Nova only concocted some of her teachings to control the Fellowship? The idea that some people are Anointed and others are not. That magic comes from pain, and that chastity and discipline maintain it. Kane doesn't believe, but I've seen Lark's spells work—I know I didn't imagine all of it, so the magic must come from somewhere. Maybe it's not just the Anointed who can access it. Maybe I can too.

I'm glad I'm alone. If Lilian could see me gathering emergency candles and twigs from the pile of kindling, she would never let me live it down. The shame of this moment might keep me up at night for years to come, but what if it works?

I arrange my supplies in a circle, with no particular logic behind their positions except that I like the way they look. Then I grab the long lighter off the mantel and sit in the middle of the circle. Light the four candles I set at the compass points thanks to my phone's GPS. Take my phone out of its case, close all my apps except Twitter and Instagram, and lay it flat on the floor in front of me.

What does Lark say when he whispers a spell? I've never been able to hear. Maybe he just asks nicely. I don't know any other, more magical-sounding languages like Ancient Greek or Latin, so I use the only one I have.

I hold my palm to my lips and whisper: "Please, let everyone who sees and hears my messages take them to heart. Give them empathy, so they can see Lark for who he is." I almost say, "Amen," even though I'm not religious. Instead, I say, "Thank you," because it seems only right. I'm new here.

I press my palm—still warm with my own breath—against my phone. The screen lights up automatically at my touch, but I take it as a sign. I have to. I have to believe that magic is real. I make myself believe, with everything in me, that Lark will succeed.

My ears pop and my vision blurs. Light-headedness nearly topples me as I stand, it hits me so hard. I blow out the candles and stumble toward the bed, eating an expired granola bar on the way. My last thought before I pass out is of Lark.

•   •   •

Three hours and nine percent battery life pass before Deryn and Miller arrive. They knock—I'm not sure which one—and call for me. I wouldn't recognize either of their voices, and certainly not muffled by a cabin door.

"I'm in here! I still can't get out."

"I'm going to break down the door." That has to be Miller. Isn't that what Feds do? Bust people's doors down? "Stand back."

I get clear and wait.

A kick slams against the solid wood, but the door doesn't budge. Three more follow with no change.

"Okay, I'm going to try something else. There's a fireplace inside, right? I see the chimney."

"Yeah."

"Go crouch down beside it."

"Why?" I shout back.

"Because I'm going to shoot the lock off."

That's enough to get me moving. "Going!"

"I'm going to count down from five," she says. "Five, four, three"—I flatten myself against the fireplace and clamp my hands over my ears—"two, one!"

Bang, bang, bang!

I wait for the sound to clear the air. It buzzes still in my ears. "Are you finished? Can I move?"

"Yes," Miller says.

"Did it work?" Another voice. Deryn, I assume.

The handle jiggles but the door doesn't open.

"And you tried the windows?" Miller asks.

"Yeah, but you're welcome to make a second go at them," I say. She does. Even shoots at the glass. It doesn't break. In fact, I think I hear the bullet ricochet. No one screams in pain, so I assume they're both fine.

"Fuck," Miller says, returning to the front door. "Calvin, I don't . . ." She trails off. If they're speaking, I can't make it out.

"Don't what?" I shout through the door. "Miller?"

The two of them talk in hushed tones, speaking over one another. "I can't," one of them says loudly. "It's stupid; I shouldn't even have brought it up."

"It's not . . ." the voice quiets to a murmur.

"Deryn!" I knock on the door, trying to get their attention.

Outside, someone's crying.

They move closer, their voices becoming clearer. Now, I am sure it's Deryn who says, "I'll go through the motions with you, at least. We can try it together."

"Calvin, stand back," Miller says, her voice wobbly. "We've got one last trick up our sleeves."

At this point, I doubt anything will work. If only I hadn't eaten so many granola bars. If I get stuck here, I'm going to wish I had some food. "Okay." I stand beside the fireplace, its flame long extinguished. "Ready!"

I wait. Watch the door, then the windows. I don't hear any kicks or bangs. No shouts. Nothing before the knob turns and the door swings easily open. I stare at the two of them, mouth hanging wide. Deryn pushes the door as far open as it'll go, examining it. Miller stares at the spot where the handle was, now only air. Tears glisten on her cheeks.

"How the hell did you do that?" I ask.

"I didn't think I had it in me." She shakes her head.

"Neither did I," says Deryn.

Would one of them tell me what's going on? "Had what?"

"Magic," Miller says, explaining her childhood and escape from the Fellowship. Anger and exhaustion are embedded in her face by the time she finishes. Strands of greasy brown hair hang in her eyes.

"And you?" I ask Deryn.

They stare at their own hands with disbelief. "I—I was just being supportive, but . . ." Then, they stuff their hands into their sweatshirt pocket and look at Miller. This is clearly sensitive between them. "Who knows. It might have just been stuck. We got the door open, one or both of us, and that's enough for now." They brush the topic aside.

I don't tell them about my social media experiment—I feel guilty even calling it a spell after what the two of them just did to the door. "Okay, well, let's get going. I'm sure Lark isn't waiting for us."

"Right," Miller says. "I have to make this *right*. She hurt all those kids because of me—and I left them. I won't leave them again. Let's go save Lark."

27

LARK / NOW

At first, I walk. I carry Spellslinger, a handful of potions, and two knives. Their metal has long been imbued with my own blood—toxic to monsters. My body feels light, though. I miss the weight of my bow and arrows, of two heavy swords strapped to my back.

When I reach a highway entrance, I jog. A car honks at me, but I ignore it, picking up speed. I glimpse at the palm of my hand, where the tracking spell was. I guide myself now, trusting the instincts I've honed over nearly twenty-five years.

I can't run as fast as a car, but they inspire me, hurtling toward their destinations and I toward mine. Sweat permeates the shirt I took from Calvin—a green long-sleeved thing with four buff turtles, walking unnaturally on two legs like people. I don't think all outsiders dress like this; Calvin is weird. When we met, he was dressed like a different being. An elf.

I smile to myself, remembering the feeling of rain sliding down my face as he kissed me. Calvin is definitely weird, and I like that—so much that I traded my shirt for his. It feels like he's here with me, and I like that too. If that makes me corrupt, well, I'll find out soon.

A big green sign across the highway announces a rest stop, with a Burger King, Starbucks, and—Kentucky Fried Chicken. I can already smell the grease, and I haven't eaten all day. Anticipation sours in my gut as I realize I don't have any money. I'd never steal from Calvin, who's done nothing but help me. I'll have to take the food. My quest is important. The outsiders will understand eventually.

I slow as I enter the parking lot, packed with cars. Outsider family units, the children running around or screaming. Teens and adults alike focused on their phones.

They look up when I pass. I find myself wishing I had a phone to bury my face in—something to look at that isn't forward. I'm conscious of how focused I might seem, of how my appearance would scare outsiders. As one stumbles back out of my way, they drop their phone right on the concrete in front of me. They don't move, pinned in place. I pick it up—it fell practically underfoot—and offer it back to them.

"Thanks," they say, more breath than words.

Pull yourself together, Lark. It doesn't matter what these outsiders think. They've lived under the influence of the monster you're tracking for decades. They've been corrupted. You're here to free them.

I straighten my neck and shoulders as I reach the door to the rest stop. A large uniformed outsider steps in front of me. "I'm sorry, sir."

I clench my jaw, remembering how outsiders presumptively gender one another. "Sir" is an honorific. Breathe.

"I can't let you inside with . . ." They gesture at the knives hanging from my hips. "That many weapons."

I cross my arms. "How many weapons *can* I bring inside?"

"Well." They scratch the layer of dark stubble on their neck. "None."

My face slackens. *"None?"*

"You can leave them in your car; you just can't take them inside." They shuffle awkwardly in their shoes, as if they're too big, and I realize that even though they're wearing a uniform, they don't look like a FOE. Their eyes are golden brown, their skin firm and unmoving.

My body itches to draw a knife. This is what I expected when I fantasized about my quest: fighting off uniformed outsiders attempting to enforce corrupt rules. But the housekeepers at the Motel 9 wore uniforms and they were kind. No one called the outsider authorities or tried to hurt me. None of them were FOEs.

My fingers twitch. I'm running out of time to decide. If I draw, I could have my knife on this guard before they realized. I probably wouldn't even need to harm them. They look like they've never engaged in real combat in their life.

"Excuse me." An outsider in an oversized yellow sweater slowly approaches my space.

I keep my arms crossed. It's the only way to keep myself from attacking. "Yes?"

"Hey there," they say. "I'm Gina. I don't mean to intrude, but you can put your things in my car, if you want. I've got a truck, so there's plenty of room."

I look between Gina and the guard. Consider the two paths that lay before me: fighting an outsider or accepting one's help.

"I'll even buy you a burger." They look between me and the guard, unbothered. "What do you say?"

I release every instinct pushing me to fight. Send the tension right down through my feet into the ground. "Okay. Thank you," I add, before following Gina to their truck.

It has eight tires and its body raises at least a foot above each of them. I have to climb it like a tree in order to put my things in the back. Gina covers and locks the truck bed with my knives inside. At least I'm not totally defenseless. Spellslinger looks like a carved branch to outsiders, and they don't know enough about my potions to forbid them. Besides, I saw Lilian's bag. Femme outsiders carry around enough vials to support themselves for months in the wild.

"You ever had a burger before?" Gina asks as we stride right past the guard. Do they know who I am? I remember the announcement I overheard on the radio. The outsiders know I'm in the area.

"Only a couple of times, and not since I was a child," I say, eyeing the sign for Kentucky Fried Chicken. The protein I grew up with in its most glorious incarnation.

Gina notices. "Oh, you want chicken? That's cool too." They head over without making me choose, for which I feel oddly grateful. Calvin, though I never gave him enough credit, was my guide through the outsider world. He and Lilian knew how to get a motel room, and where to buy food at a window while remaining in the car.

After Gina explains the options, I select a three-piece chicken and biscuit with mashed potatoes, macaroni and cheese, and a large drink. "If you're going to be doing a lot of walking, there's this red one called Gatorade that has vitamins and electrolytes in it, but I think it tastes like salt."

"What are you getting?" I ask.

"A Coke." I watch them fill their cup with ice, followed by a brown fizzy liquid. It looks unappetizing. "Loaded with caffeine. If you're trying to stay awake, that'll do it."

I choose the red drink. I remember caffeine from the list of things I was never allowed to drink. Then, I remember not putting my chastity cage back on this morning. Either it'll matter or it won't.

Gina and I sit at a table in the middle of the room, doing our best to ignore the people staring at me. I try to focus on my food. On how much damn flavor I've missed out on all these years, eating boiled chicken and drinking Nova's potions. The food on the outside is much better. I even find myself watching Gina drink their Coke. It's got to be good; almost everyone in here has the same cup.

"I have a confession," they say, chomping on a biscuit. "I know who you are."

I swallow a glob of macaroni and cheese. "I suspected as much."

"Yeah, well, you're all over the news. They were talking about you on NPR before I pulled in, saying how you were armed and dangerous." They bite their nail, an unpainted nub with nothing on Lilian's. "I was nervous when I saw those knives. And yeah, you're armed, but dangerous? Hope you don't mind me saying, you looked . . . in need of a friend."

"Thank you," I say. "I did. Need a friend." I smile.

Gina leans forward. "I guarantee I'm not the only one here who knows who you are and what you're going to do. I heard your crew aren't keen on law enforcement, and I don't blame you. But don't be afraid to ask us regular folks for help, you hear?"

When I say that I won't, I know that I mean it.

Gina refills my Gatorade and buys me a bag with peanuts, raisins, and chocolates inside. Even though my stomach feels like it's going to burst, I find myself salivating at the colorful chocolate discs. I tuck the treat into one of my harness pockets as we head back to her truck.

"You want a ride, sweetie? Wherever you're headed, I can drop you closer." They hand me my knives.

"No, thank you." I slide them into their sheaths and straighten the straps of my harness. "A friend helped me as far as he could. The rest's up to me now."

•   •   •

Less time passes before I notice traffic slowing down around me. An hour? Two? I never wore a watch back at Druid Hill, but time seems more important out here. The sun's harder to see, the sky hazier.

I'm sucking down the last of my red drink when I realize I'm walking faster than the cars on the highway. For some reason, traffic has come to a stop. I set my empty cup on the trunk of one as I walk between them, making my way to the middle lane. I can see better from here. See that cars are backed up from some sort of line in the distance. A line of cars with colorful lights on top. If I squint, I can make out uniforms.

"Hey, that's him!" says a kid, rolling down the window of the car beside me. An adult scolds them as they point at me.

I remember the chaos as I fought Miller amidst traffic, chasing Lilian through intersections of turning vehicles and raging horns and screaming outsiders. I should've been stealthier. Should've stayed along the tree line—but I'm not used to being so identifiable. Not every outsider knows about me, but enough do that I'm in danger. They can't all be as helpful as the one who bought me lunch.

I back away from the lane, stumbling as a car rolls slowly forward—and then lurches to a stop, when they see me. "Sorry," I say, steading myself on the front of their car. Looking for a way through. I need to go.

"Hey!" The voice comes from a window, slowly rolling down. "Come here—yeah, you." An outsider calls me from their car, beckoning me over. I look between them and the congestion. Something is wrong. This many cars don't simply stop on a highway. I've spent days driving down them now, and we only slowed when the fog descended and that didn't turn out well.

I gauge my surroundings—eyeing nearby drivers for blackened eyes, sniffing the air for the scent of rot—before deciding all is clear. Still, I approach the car gripping the handle of my knife.

"Sorry, I didn't mean to startle you," the person says. They lean an entire arm out the window, slapping the side of the car. "You're that Meadowlark fellow, right?"

"Yes," I say tentatively.

"You might want to find another way around. They're looking for you. Set up a checkpoint ahead."

I turn my head slowly to where the wall of cars presses the most tightly together, before diffusing. One by one, cars are let through. "Who?" I ask.

"The cops up there. News is, the FBI put out some kind of call for help."

I stand up to my full height, glaring down the rows of cars. "Thank you," I say.

Before I leave, they shout, "We got your back!" A cheer sounds from their back seat. I smile against all instincts. I'm going to have to fight these cops, if I can't evade them; that's not fun or funny, and yet . . .

Energy surges through me. I'm filled with a confidence that doesn't come from pain, or from the magic stored within me, but from the outsiders cheering me forward. They roll down their windows and hold their fists up, hold their hands out to me. At first, I think they want me to shake them, perform their greeting, but one shows me how to slap palms. A "high five." They don't hurt, but they reverberate hot through my arm in the cold.

"I've got to go," I say. "Thank you for the information and support."

"Be safe," they say. "Not everyone's on your side."

"I know." I assess the rows of cars, slowly rolling to a stop as they approach the checkpoint. If I can make my way into the trees, I can go around. I'm not bound by a car.

Quickly, I weave through traffic, staying low and quiet. My training serves me well until a loud wailing stops my advance. I press my hands against my ears and look for the source. Cop cars speed up the shoulder, screeching as they slide to a stop. A wall of them, blocking my escape. All at once, FOEs erupt from their cars, shouting for me to get on the ground. Their skin ripples, eyes form deep pits. The rest stop guard wasn't my enemy, but these cops are. I don't let them reach for the guns I know they have. I've fought against those before and lost.

I run back into traffic, the cars no longer moving. The checkpoint closes as cops surge between the cars toward me, and I run. Without my bow and arrow, all I have is hand-to-hand combat, and I don't really want to use my knives. I want to see Kane healthy again. Want to watch movies with Calvin.

I want to go home after this, and not to outsider prison, like Nova.

"He's over here!" an outsider shouts through their open window. They open their door, jabbing a finger in my direction until— their body thuds to the ground.

Another outsider stands over them, shaking their fist. "Go!" they shout. "Get out of—" They're cut off by another outsider approaching with fists raised.

I can't be a part of this, I have to move. I run between cars as outsiders leap out and converge on one another, shouting. The cops slow as the throng swells and I duck down out of sight.

"Freeze!" a cop shouts as they run out from a car ahead of me, wobbling on their feet.

For a moment, I do.

The cop takes a careful step, looking at their own feet, before training their gun on me.

I need my magic to work. To be real. *Be real.*

I hold my hands open and empty at my sides, breathe deep as I close my eyes.

"Hands in the air!"

I feel the sting of the cat o' nine tails against my back, as if it were striking me now, by Calvin's hand.

"I said hands in the air!"

Calvin's hands. Sliding warm over my bare skin. Over my scars.

Boots pound against the road.

I cross my arms in front of my chest, fists closed, holding the memories close.

"He's armed!"

I open my palms to my lips and whisper the words. When I open my eyes on the cop, I see them through a haze. They blur as if on the other side of clouded glass. Their voice muffles and I know I'm safe.

I pick a path forward. Several outsiders open their car doors and fall in behind me, beside me. They move with me, keeping the cops away. Human defensive shields, blending with my magic.

The checkpoint is only a few cars away. On the other side, black-and-white cars light up their red-and-blue lights. A row of cops stand in line, waiting, but I don't stop. Power surges through me and those around me. With every brush of shoulder against shoulder, I feel Calvin's kind touch, and I know I'm invincible.

A bang pierces the air. A loud shot and a commotion of voices. The outsiders beside me duck, and I am left standing alone amidst the maze of vehicles, tilted into and out of lines, blocking the paths forward.

I look down at my body, check my arms and legs. Uninjured. Ahead, a cop lowers their gun, hands shaking as they drop it. The FOEs scramble into their cars as I walk through the checkpoint, unhindered. The other side is like a different world—a vast field of concrete that travels to meet the horizon and keeps going.

I look left and right at the cars ready to follow me. Those inside too afraid to confront me face-to-face. I don't know how I'll escape these FOEs, but when I take my first step, a row of outsiders races in front of them. They form a line, hand in hand, blocking the cop cars' path.

Taking the opportunity, I leap onto the hood of a black-and-white car, over its whirling lights, onto the other side.

An outsider shouts, "Go get that monster, Meadowlark!" They raise their hand in the air, holding tight to their neighbor's. My feet pound the pavement fast and hard, in sync with the beat of my heart, as they cheer me forward. Fast and hard. Alive. Still going.

• • •

I run down the center of the road. Only every few minutes does a car enter the highway and speed past me—and even that becomes less frequent as the sun crosses the sky. My stomach rumbles, and I slow down to dig the trail mix from my pocket. I pour a handful out and stare at the tiny specks of salt that cover the nuts and the colorful shells that coat the chocolates. I tip them into my mouth, licking a piece of salt from my palm before chewing.

The flavor is like nothing I've ever eaten. Salty, sweet, crunchy— words never used to describe food at Druid Hill. Certainly not for the Anointed. I eat another handful, and another, and soon I'm scraping the bottom of the bag. I don't want to finish it. I want to share these treasures with my friends. With Zadie and Maeve. With Kane.

I seal the bag and bury it back in my pocket. The highway is quiet. Sirens no longer loud behind me. Tires don't screech. Trucks don't rumble. The road is still, except for me.

Movement catches my eye. An outsider, standing in front of a trio of parked cars, waving. They and two other outsiders have blocked the entire exit. I wave tentatively, unsure whether these outsiders are as supportive as Gina and the people who protected me hours ago. As I continue, I find the next entrance blocked, and the exit after that. I pick up speed, running again as I realize outsiders have blocked every entrance and exit onto this highway— both on this side and in the opposite direction.

I run until hunger and thirst catch up to me. Until my mouth is sticky and my throat hot. Until I consider eating the rest of the trail mix even though I wanted to save it for my friends. The buzzing energy in my legs diffuses as I slow, as I stop slamming my feet against the unforgiving pavement.

By now, I'm used to outsiders waving from the deep rows of cars that fill the entrances and exits, but I don't expect one to approach. They hold up their hands so I can see they don't have a weapon. They have a bag in one and a bottle in another.

"I'm not going to hurt you," they say.

I fight against the urge to walk away from them. To put the

barrier between us and draw my knife. I stay on my path, watching the white lines disappear under my feet.

"You're Meadowlark, right?"

"Yes," I say, not looking up.

"My name's Micah. He/him," he adds, as if reminding himself to share his pronouns. That kindness gives me pause.

"He/him," I respond. "Is there something—"

"Oh right, sorry, I should've led with that. Um." He holds out the bag and bottle. "I saw a video online posted by a friend of yours. Calvin Morris?"

I stop walking. "Yeah." I didn't know his last name, the concept new to me, but what other Calvin would call himself my friend? I only know the one. "We're friends, but I don't know what video you're talking about. I don't have a phone."

"Right, sorry." Micah smiles. "It's all over social media. He told us about your quest. Asked us to look out for you."

"He did? I didn't know." I left him, but I guess he never left me.

"Yeah, I brought you something to eat. You've got to be hungry. I didn't hear that you were a vegetarian or anything—"

No idea what that is.

"—so I've got one sandwich with meat and one without."

Oh. "Thank you. That was kind."

"And this is a Gatorade." He shakes the purple liquid inside its bottle. "I saw you like that."

I cock my head as he hands it to me. "Saw? Where would you see that?" I crack the seal and take a sip of the now-familiar drink. This color tastes like salt and fruit, but not a fruit I can name. Not one that we ate.

"You're trending on Twitter." Micah holds up his phone; his nails are long like Lilian's, and sparkle despite the setting sun.

I don't know what Twitter is, but it looks like a bunch of people talking to each other in short sentences. Moving pictures fly past as he pushes his finger up the screen.

"So, where am I?" I glance past Micah as another outsider walks up and stands so close behind him, they're almost touching. The new outsider smiles at me, giggles, and then looks over Micah's shoulder at the phone. A friend or lover, I assume.

"Here, under the search tab." Micah taps a sigil that looks like a circle with a line extending from the side, like a Q. Information populates the screen. At the top, a photograph of the ritual house on Druid Hill. Below, my name. "Meadowlark."

When he touches my name, the screen changes again. I look up at Micah's friend, who's still watching, and at the growing crowd of outsiders along the highway entrance. None of them wear uniforms or have pits for eyes. No more of them approach, but some of them wave.

Standing still this long still makes me nervous. I scan the other side of the highway and the sky overhead. Clouds ripple like water toward the reddened sun.

"Everyone's rooting for you," Micah says. "On Facebook and Instagram too. On the radio. We're listening and we're here for you."

On his phone, a video plays without sound. Video of Calvin, sitting on the couch where we laid our clothes to dry by the fire. His skin is oily, hair unkempt. But he's speaking to the outsiders for me. And they're listening.

"Thank you for sharing." I tear my eyes from Calvin's video and look to the road ahead. "I should be getting on my way." I turn and begin to leave, but stop at the sound of Micah's boots over the road.

"Wait! Is there anything you want to say before you go? You don't have to, but . . ." He angles his phone in my direction.

We're listening.

"Can I talk to anyone?"

"Like your friends?" Micah smiles. "Anything you say will go live and then upload, so if they're listening for you, I bet they'll hear it."

"I don't know what that means."

"Like, it'll get saved as a video. People will be able to watch it whenever they want."

I decide I don't need to understand how it works. I only need to trust him. And he's given me so many reasons to trust him, helping block the FOEs from entering the highway, bringing me something to eat and drink, showing me information on his phone. "Okay," I say, for myself. I'm brave enough to face a monster, and I'm brave enough to speak to my friends. To those I've hurt. "I'm ready."

28

KANE / CONFIDENTIAL

I knew, when we lay down, that I wasn't going to be able to fall asleep. But that was okay. I didn't want to. I wanted to share Lark's love for one last night—wanted to wrap myself in the comfortable fiction of the Fellowship.

Our quarters weren't usually so quiet. Usually, I could hear Zadie snoring and Maeve kicking her under the covers. The jangle of Zadie's cage as she wandered back to her own bed and the creak as they settled in, separately, and fell back asleep. They'd offered to sleep elsewhere that night. Give us privacy.

We took the offer, leaving the bonfire early to be alone on our last night together for what Lark thought would be two months and twenty-seven days. He, of course, was already counting the days until he joined me. Knowing he was wrong felt like bleeding out.

Lark stopped in the middle of the big domed room and turned, facing me. Damn, he was beautiful—scars and all. His suntanned skin marked by my own hand. A quilt sewn together with metal and leather and fire. Dark blonde hair threaded with strands bleached by the sun and twisted into a long fishtail down his back. The next morning, we would wash and braid each other's hair one final time. That night, I wanted to run my hands through it, pull the locks loose until the elastics barely held it together.

Carefully, he unfastened his leather harness and hung it on a metal hook, knives and vials still holstered. Lark slid his hands under the hem of his shirt, keeping his sky-blue eyes on mine. Walked backward toward my bed as he pulled it over his head and tossed it onto the floor. I mimicked his motion, in no rush to reach him. I knew, when I finally touched him, he'd be the realest thing inside the fence.

We unbuckled our belts in sync, unbuttoned and unzipped. Slid our pants over our asses and down our thighs, letting them bunch around our ankles. Boots, dammit. Always forgot the boots. I chuckled and sat on the floor to untie my laces. Lark was near enough the bed that he could sit on its edge, unlace, kick off.

When we were both finally naked, I went to him, crawling on top of him as he settled onto the old mattress. My two thick French braids fell on either side of my neck, framing his face. Lark reached up and cupped my face with his hands, drawing me down to kiss him. Our bodies flush. Our chastity cages clanking against each other as our hips rolled and crashed like waves.

It hurt. Not like the cat or the knives or fire. Like wanting something so bad, your whole body ached, inside and out. My need for him was a wound that would never heal. My hand gripped his cage out of habit, wanting to feel him harden in my hand, but he couldn't. I didn't want to tease him. I wanted him to feel good, not taunted.

So, I slid my hand down around his balls and rolled them gently between my fingers. Lark moaned, arching his back beneath me. When your genitals are taken from you, you learn to pleasure each other in different ways. Ways that didn't result in orgasm, but still expressed our love.

What difference did it make where we touched each other? Control. That was the difference. Nova handed us our keys once a week for maintenance, and unlocked us to collect our fluids. We didn't have that privilege. But I didn't need her permission to make Lark feel good. To run my fingers through the sensitive hairs on his legs and over his nipple. When I pinched it between my fingers, Lark moaned. I knew he loved the pain, so I bent down and sucked the thin skin of his neck between my teeth.

I bit down. His voice cracked. "Kane! Kane, what are you—let me. It's your—"

"Last night," I said against his ear, before pulling the cartilage between my teeth. I could almost feel my teeth meet through the malleable skin. When I released him, he shuddered. "And this is how I want to spend it."

I collapsed onto the mattress beside him. The narrow bed was not really intended for two people. No problem. I sidled up behind him, until my cage pressed against the crack of his ass. My cock swelled as far as the metal bars allowed and I took myself into hand, rubbing against him. Dry humping, the Fellows called it. Didn't do anything but tease me, but I knew Lark liked it.

He pressed his ass back against me, while I dotted kisses across the scars on his shoulders and back. Could he even feel my lips through all the dead tissue? With the nerve endings I'd destroyed with my own hands?

"What do you think it's like out there?" Lark asked.

If I could've gotten hard, I'd have gone flaccid then. My words caught in my throat and I cleared them. Pressed his right shoulder, until he tipped onto his chest. I straddled his thighs, gave him a moment to adjust the pillow. He hugged it and rested his head sideways, looking off at the far wall, as if the answers might play out across it.

"Do you think there are many people left, or have the monsters gotten them all?" he asked. "They're certainly corrupted by now, but are they warped? Monstrous? I've heard them wailing at night. Barking and howling."

Then, so that I wouldn't imagine Ashir's little black poodle, I spread his ass wide and pressed my mouth against his hole.

Lark's hips bucked back. I lifted him up to meet my mouth, holding him still as I took my time: breathing in the ripe scent of his body, circling the tight muscle with my tongue, kissing the pucker before sliding my tongue past its ring.

"Stars, Kane . . ." He stopped asking questions after that. Succumbed as I licked the length of his crack. As I sunk my fingernails into his thighs. Kissed the crease where the globes of his ass met the thick of his thighs.

Lark moaned and rolled over, inviting me into his arms. He shouldn't have wanted to kiss me, but he did, mouth strong and wanting. There were so many more things I wanted to do to his body, so many ways I wanted to touch him and make him feel pleasure. But I could only do so much on this side of the fence, so it was my turn to succumb.

Still, I cupped his ass and pulled his groin against mine. Ground our hips together and buried my nose in his shoulder. I knew I wouldn't be able to appreciate his scent until I left. We become used to how spaces and loved ones smell, so much that they become normal.

I knew the other side of the fence didn't smell like fire. Didn't smell like sulfur or hot metal or herbs. The air was open, unbound by trees and grasses and sheep. Nova told us it was polluted, but I only smelled perfumes and flowers. Even the scent of cars was welcome. Ashir's dog smelled like peanut butter.

"Hey." Lark rested his hands on mine, stilling them. He looked right into my eyes. "I know you turn twenty-five tomorrow, and that you've trained your whole life for this. But I want you to be careful out there, okay?"

I barely nod. I'm afraid that if I give, I'll give too much.

"None of us really knows what it's like. Sure, outsiders come and trade with us sometimes, and we can tell they're alive out there, doing . . . whatever it is they do. But what if they're feral, like the animals? You could take two steps outside the fence and be attacked by FOEs. Kane, I don't know if I could live with myself, if—"

"That won't happen," I said.

"You don't know that."

I knew it wouldn't because I'd taken more than two steps outside the fence and met only wonderful animals and kind outsiders. I knew because my plan involved stepping right into the open arms of a FOE. I clenched my teeth.

He closed his eyes for a moment, shaking his head. "Sorry. I shouldn't talk like that. You're going out into the world tomorrow, the first of us to face it. And you're going to be incredible." Lark smiled. I memorized it. His thin pink lips, the dimple in his left cheek. The barely visible stubble that grew on his jaw beneath the sharp line of his cheekbones. The length of his nose and how it turned up right at the end.

I kissed it. "Thank you."

Incredible.

I was going to turn the Fellowship—my family—in to the outsider authorities. Ashir had connected me to an agent, and there was no going back. Lark was right; I had trained for my entire life, but that training was for nothing. I was done suffering for Nova's lies.

Lark thought we were meant for something more. We weren't. But I was something worse than a liar; I was a coward. How could I look in his eyes and tell him he wasn't special? He loved having a purpose, loved performing rituals, loved being magic. Nova made a mistake Anointing me.

Lark nestled his head against my chest and closed his eyes. Twined his legs between mine. Took a deep breath and released it warm against my skin. I kissed the top of his head and closed my eyes. We lay together, quiet and still, for I don't know how long— long enough that we should've been asleep.

"Lark?" I whispered, not expecting an answer.

"Yeah?" he asked groggily, clearly drifting in and out.

"No matter what happens tomorrow, please be safe. And know that I love you."

He snuggled closer against me and licked his lips, still half asleep. "I love you too, you know that," he mumbled.

"No matter what happens," I repeated.

His voice was barely audible. "No matter what."

"Because I'm doing this for you, Meadowlark," I whispered, my words no more than a breath against the small hairs liberated from his braid. "It's all for you."

29

LARK / NOW

By the time night falls, the soles of my feet throb and I glance at the highway exits with want. I ache for a big hotel bed or a couple of blankets in the back of Calvin's car. For an end.

So many outsiders are watching, common and uniformed alike, all waiting for me to fight a monster I'm not sure is coming.

I roll my shoulders, flex my back against the ache of the weight I carry. I wish Kane were with me. Wish I had my partner to feed my flame. The only lights with me are those from lamps arched tall over the side of the highway. I hear the whir of a helicopter not far off. They used to fly over Druid Hill occasionally, and Nova instructed us to shoot arrows to drive them away. Now, I let it be. The company is nice.

After another hour, the unbearable creep of pain infects every inch of my body. I stop and remove my harness, stretch against the concrete barrier separating the roads. I check Spellslinger, closing my fist around the wooden rod. I can still feel the power Kane and I imbued it with over years and years, waiting for the right opportunity to use it. I fasten my harness back on over Calvin's turtle shirt. Check my knives. Count my potions. Holster Spellslinger. Hope I have some magic left inside me. I close my eyes as I walk. Don't need to see. Only forward exists—only the open road.

I stop to remove my boots. To pry my socks carefully from my swollen feet, exposing blisters to the cold open air. Then, I place my bare feet on the road, one by one, one in front of the other, again and again. Forward.

As I walk, I wonder whether Kane is okay in the outsider hospital with Lilian. I wonder if Calvin is still holed up in the cabin where we slept last night—his video may have saved me. Even Deryn crosses my mind, tugging at me to go with them, to go home. The pleading in their eyes as I called them my enemy. Zadie and Maeve watching over the Anointed I left behind in the hotel.

I need you, I think, unsure whether I can link to their minds so far away. Not sure whether Kane is capable of hearing me anymore. *I need you and miss you. I miss your touch. I miss our magic.* Hot tears roll down my face. I didn't expect a response, but I wanted one. *I think I'm finished.*

I stop with a shuddering sigh.

The ground underfoot sighs with me. It rumbles, rises and falls. I drop to one knee, steadying myself as the earth quakes and shifts beneath me. In the distance, the highway rips open as easily as torn cotton, and a gargantuan shadow rises from the depths. Overhead, the streetlights flicker.

I shudder, no longer cold, but burning.

<<Meadowlark.>> The syllables of my name reverberate through the pavement, through the air, through my flesh and bones. It is a sound without voice. <<Anointed One.>>

I can barely breathe, and yet I stand. I straddle the long crack in the road, clenching my fists. I feel every scar on my body, naming them one by one: brand, knife, oil, cat. Pulling the pain from each metal claw, each lick of flame. From my back and my feet, and from my heart.

The monster's gray carapace smolders, showing fiery veins in its limbs. Deep pits whorl on its face where eyes should be; teeth protrude like knives from every angle, from mouth to throat. It rises, and rises further—it is so tall. Its formidable weight shakes the ground with every step, feet charring the pavement and rattling the trees as it walks toward me.

It roars an inhuman sound like grinding metal and helicopter blades and a wind so fast you can't breathe. The sound wraps around me, crushing and hot. A thousand swords buried to their hilts in my body, pinning skin to muscle to bone. I scream, overwhelmed. The vibrations in my throat, my own. The cocoon of pain on pain on pain.

<<Meadowlark, you are no match for me.>>

My body hits the asphalt with a crack. Yes, I am. I have to be. I fumble through the pockets of my harness for a healing potion and drink the whole thing. I drink another, and still everything hurts. But I have to stand.

My groan erupts into a scream as I push myself up. The monster towers over me, barely visible against the blackened sky. Eyes like pits stare down at me. Mouth shining with sharp silvery edges.

I muster the pain that lives inside me and take hold of Spellslinger, feel my power erupt from its length like the blade of a sword—forged and sharpened by my efforts, and Kane's. This is for him. With a wild cry, I thrust the beam into the monster's foot. Lightning crackles up its leg, splitting its skin. It wails and wriggles against my power as chunks of gray flesh fall from its body. I see its fiery insides, pulsing and raw.

On blistered feet, I climb. I grit my teeth and move with the pain, scaling the monstrous leg. Its fiery flesh burns the soles of my feet. They throb as I find footholds in the shifting plates of the monster's body, driving my knives in like pitons. Rot works its way up my nostrils as I settle onto its hip. I hold my breath and plunge one of my knives into its exposed insides. The blood-forged blade slides in to the hilt, and the monster thrashes. It roars until I feel like my own flesh is peeling away. I roar back, plunging the knife in again and again, unsheathing the other and stabbing it into the monster's joint.

Before it can grab me, I jump. Jolts of pain shoot through my legs as I slam into the ground, barely landing on my feet. <<Is this what you want?>> I can't help but think it with magic. <<To break me?>>

The monster bends onto one crumbling gray knee. Lowers its face until its lifeless eyes are feet from mine. I can feel the corruption that pumps through it flowing past me.

"I did this for you." My voice is weak. Hoarse. Raw like the monster's body where my magic flayed it and my knives poisoned it. They drop to the road before me with metallic clangs, but I don't pick them up. "Because I believed you. Because I believed *in* you."

I close my eyes. Feel the pulse of blood under my skin, the burn of my muscles. A thousand wounds scarred over.

"But not anymore," I whisper, bringing my palms to my face. My lips brush them with the gentleness of a kiss. I don't need to look to know that the monster is closing in on me. My ears pop as it bellows. Skin blisters from its heat as it looms closer. "You can't hurt me now."

The last spell I have the power to speak: protection, peace, hope. A faint glow emanates from my mouth and fingers and braid and my blistered feet, cradling my destroyed body. Keeping it safe.

As the monster falls upon me, I push my magic into it. It reaches for me, and I give it my pain. The world flickers, and I feel peace. The calm of the road. Gentle swaying trees alongside it. A caressing breeze. In that moment, I know I've made a world without monsters, even if my spell fails and I do not survive to see it.

30

CALVIN / NOW

We're too late.

This isn't how our quest was supposed to end. Lark lies in a rumpled pile on the ground, in a crater of destruction—as if he were a superhero flung down from outer space. Streetlamps spark, concrete barriers lay overturned. Black SUVs and cop cars litter the highway, their lights flashing. Several ambulances crowd the space, their EMTs idling nearby. Why aren't they doing anything? Why aren't they—

"Lark!" Deryn dashes past us, through the police line.

I run and Miller follows, digging in her pocket and pulling out her badge. She waves it in the air like a beacon as we run toward the circle of yellow caution tape, shouting "FBI! FBI."

Deryn reaches it first, but I'm only seconds behind, and then Miller. We toe the edge of the crater. Look at one another. What's going on? Why is no one . . .

"Don't!" An officer steps close—but not too close. "Our first arrivals are being treated by EMTs. There's some kind of . . ." She wavers. Shrugs. Sighs. "Shield. I don't know; it's some science fiction shit. Don't ask me. I'm only a traffic cop."

"What do you think happened?" Deryn asks me.

"I don't know." I focus on the air a few feet ahead of us. If I look closely, I can see the air ripple and shift. "Just like *Star Trek*." I chuckle. "It's some kind of force field." I hold my hand perpendicular to the ground.

"What are you doing?" Miller shrieks. "You heard what the officer said. Don't hurt yourself."

"That's the thing," I say. Slowly, I press my hand forward. "I don't think I will." And I push my hand through. My arm and shoulder. I step inside the shield and, moments later, Deryn and Miller follow.

"It wasn't for us," I say. "It was to keep out FOEs."

Deryn looks at Miller. "I told you," they say. "You may look the part, but you're not. You're family."

Together, we walk over the cracked asphalt toward Lark—or what is left of his scarred and battered body. Burns score his feet. Blood rises to the surface of bruises, patterning blue and purple with scratches of red. The ends of his braids fray, undone, the elastics missing. I know you're not supposed to move an injured person, but we can't leave him here, so I cradle his limp weight in my arms and lift him up.

"Careful," Miller says.

"I've got it," I say. "I've got him." I hold my breath as we cross the barrier, hoping it doesn't punish me for carrying him out of it. I release my breath when we pass through safely. With the help of EMTs, I lay him on a waiting gurney. He's wheeled away before I can consider kissing him awake like a sleeping prince. Deryn runs off after them and climbs into the ambulance—I guess that's a sibling's privilege, despite their differences. I stand still as a group of Feds descend upon Miller, shooting questions at her like arrows. No one so much as looks at me. There's no role to fill for the outsider who went along for the ride because he hoped magic might be real.

I dig my phone from my pocket: thirty-eight percent battery and dozens of notifications. Only one from the person I'm interested in.

Lilian
Kane's okay. Call me when you have a chance.

And I do, right away. Standing on the broken ground where Lark fought a monster—where he killed it—I apologize to Lilian for not trusting her. I thank her for seeing clearly when I couldn't. I warn her that when we next see each other, I have something to tell her about magic.

31

LARK / NOW

I wake, not in the peace of my protective spell, but in a room full of beeping machines and outsiders dressed in some kind of plain blue uniform with no identifiers, who adjust tubes and wires. I feel them press different areas of my body and stick me with needles.

I survived. I think.

Even though I don't speak, the outsiders do. They tell me they're doctors and nurses. They promise I'm going to be okay, as if they can know that. When I ask for Kane, they tell me, "Soon. After you've rested. Once your vitals are steadier."

A nurse asks if I want more pain medication, and I say yes. She presses a button that floods my body with some kind of potion. Medicine, I think outsiders call it. Whatever the name, I don't care. I am finished with pain. I sleep. It's the easiest way to pass the time and hurts the least.

When I next open my eyes, Kane is sitting beside me on a metal chair with wheels. A bandage is wrapped around his thigh where I shot him. The arrow gone. "Thank the stars you're awake." He takes my hand in his and kisses it gently. I squeeze his in return.

"So, did you do it?" he asks, leaning on the side of my bed. "Did you . . ." His voice trails off. He can't say it.

"Kill a monster?" I finish, taking his burden. I can still see its towering figure, gray and thick. I still smell its overwhelming rot, as if the stink sank into my skin. My hands feel its pulsing hot insides as I thrust my blade into it.

But I can also feel the breeze picking up escaped strands of my hair and the rough asphalt beneath my bare feet. Hear a song of crickets and leaves.

"I think I did," I say finally. "I think I used all my magic up. I think . . ." I feel different. When that used to happen before, I'd feel empty and shaky and sick. Now, the absence inside me is joined by a calm, like my body has settled. And yet. "I think there's one more monster we need to deal with." I take his hand. "I'll need you for this one."

"I'm sorry." His body shudders as tears well in his eyes. "I'm sorry I hurt you, and that I didn't stop when I saw the damage I was causing. I'm sorry I didn't tell you to stop when you hurt me. I'm sorry I put on that damn chastity cage and let you do the same, when all my instincts were screaming not to."

"Kane—"

"No." He sobs. "I need to finish."

"Okay." I squeeze his hand again.

"I'm sorry that I didn't bring you with me the first time I snuck out—even after Nova started giving you to the Elders and extracting my fluids. I should've taken you with me, but I thought you'd turn me in to her. I was sure you believed."

"I did," I say, the past tense more final than I mean.

"I'm sorry that I didn't warn you before the SWAT team came and that I didn't explain what I'd done. I should've been there for you. I doubted alone. I never gave you the time or space to doubt with me. I should have. And even though I doubted, I should have gone with you on your quest."

Kane hauls himself onto the bed and curls up against me. When his breathing slows and tears stop flowing—when the last sob wracks his body—I kiss his forehead.

"It's okay. You're here with me now. And, honestly?" I pull back just far enough that I can look into his dark brown eyes. "You became an inextricable part of me decades ago. I have never been alone."

Kane blinks as another wave of tears slides down his cheeks. "Thank you."

We hold each other until I fall asleep. When we wake, I drag the details out of him, of what happened while I was on my quest. Whether Calvin and Lilian are okay. Whether Agent Miller is still after us. Whether Deryn hates me for the way I talked to them.

The next time we fall asleep, I do so reassured. That Calvin and Lilian aren't angry with me or each other. That Miller has finally reconnected with her family. That Deryn and Kane still want to be part of mine.

32

LARK / LATER

Druid Hill looks the same as it did when we left, and yet it feels completely different. As if the whole thing has become a zoo again, we walk from exhibit to exhibit, looking at the enclosures in which we were kept. Those places used to feel meaningful, heavy with Fellowship and tradition. With pain but also with magic. Void of Fellows, void of meaning, what is left but a collection of abandoned buildings?

The doors of Ritual House hang open still. I haven't worked myself up to going inside yet with the other Fellowship members—Maeve and Zadie, Kane and Deryn. I dally on the grass, watching Calvin and Lilian pick up metal canisters and drop them into the trash cans that still line the path. Miller unwinds the yellow tape that ties it off.

It feels like I haven't gone through the motions of a group ritual in ages, but it can't have been more than a couple of weeks. We need this. Even if this ritual doesn't *do* anything, it still means something. This place might be hollow, but we are not.

Calvin catches my eye and he stops working. Meets me under a naked tree. "Thanks for coming," I say, tucking my hands into my pockets. Even after everything, he still makes me feel good-nervous. Makes me blush.

"Of course." He smooths his hand through the length of his hair. "Anytime. I, uh, have something for you. Actually, I'm returning it."

"Oh?" I hope it's not one of his terrible shirts, as much as they grew on me.

Calvin slides a small bag off his back and unzips it. Withdraws a long, slender piece of carved wood. A wand. From our weapons arsenal. "I may have stolen this," he says, turning it over in his hands. "I mean, I *definitely* stole this—I just wanted to know what it felt like to wield magic; I didn't use it—and I shouldn't have taken it, or should've told you, but I'm giving it back now. It's only right."

When he offers it to me, I press the wood back into his hand, fold his fingers around it. "You keep it," I say. The wand means nothing to me—one of a dozen carved for various uses. If it feels special to Calvin, he should have it. "Maybe I'll show you how to use it one day." I play with the end of my braid. I'd meant to take it out, but didn't feel right doing so myself. "Would you take my hair out?" Dammit. That's not what I mean to ask.

A confused look crosses Calvin's face. "Sure?"

I turn around. Kane looks down at us from the steps. When he smiles, I feel his warmth inside me. His support as Calvin pulls the elastic band free before picking his fingers through the strands, pulling them carefully apart. It feels nice, but I can't let my real question slip away unspoken.

"Would you like to go out sometime?" I ask in one long breath, grateful my back is turned to him. He doesn't have to see how red my face is. I can feel it. "Lilian told me that outsiders—I mean—sorry, I'm trying not to use that word anymore—"

"It's okay." His fingers reach the base of my scalp, untwisting and pulling. With every pluck, I feel more free. "I know what you mean."

"Well, Lilian said you sometimes do activities with people, while you get to know them. Make dates with them. I wondered if you wanted to make a date with me."

Calvin's hands disappear and my head feels cold and I worry

I've messed up. That he'll leave before the ritual has even begun, and won't want to see me again, much less date me.

Then, he appears in front of me. Calvin threads his fingers through my hair, massaging my scalp and shaking my hair free. It falls in blonde waves in front of my face. For the first time in ages, I run my own fingers through my hair. With Calvin's help, again, I learn how to touch myself. Care for myself. Love myself.

He takes both of my hands in his and steps close—oh, so close. "I would love to go on a date with you, Lark."

I laugh, a silly, airy laugh. "Really?"

"I assume you're still with Kane?"

"Yes," I say. "We're partners. I don't think that will ever change. But I'd like to be with you too. Lilian said it isn't common for outsiders—I mean, for people to have multiple partners—but that some do. Kane and I have discussed it. It's okay with him if it's okay with you."

Calvin smiles, then presses his lips against mine. Holds me against him, bodies warm against the cold air.

When I can breathe, I say, "I guess that's a yes."

Calvin laughs against my lips. "Oh, you think I would pass up a chance to date a wizard?"

"A what?" My face must look funny because Calvin laughs again.

"I'll explain after the ritual. I've got plans for our date—you've got to read the Lord of the Rings series, or at least watch it. I really want us to dress up as elves together. I'll add it to the list." He takes me by the hand and leads me toward Ritual House.

We stop at the base of the steps. Lilian meets us, and I hand Calvin off to her. "Thank you," I say to her. "For being a good friend to Calvin. We wouldn't be here without you."

"Damn right you wouldn't." She throws an arm around Calvin and winks at me.

Miller stuffs a handful of police tape into the trash then joins them, no longer wearing her uniform. She doesn't seem monstrous at all in jeans and a flannel shirt. I can't believe I ever considered her a FOE. Well, I can. Nova planted the idea in my head, and belief is powerful.

I believe I fought a monster on the highway—can still smell its rot and feel the pulse of its molten flesh burning my feet. Miller told me the FBI never found its remains, but Calvin said their agency covers up stuff like that all the time. It doesn't matter to me. I now know monsters are of this world—that they smile at us with human faces and spread corruption from beneath the earth.

"We're ready for the ritual," Kane says from the steps of Ritual House.

I walk up them for the first time since the SWAT team dragged me out, bound and fighting. I stop. Glance at Miller. "Are you coming?"

"Me?" She pokes her chest as if making sure she's solid.

"Yes, you. You're one of us."

She steps closer, stuffing her hands in her pockets as she kicks a yellow leaf. "I'm not Anointed."

"Neither is Deryn, but Nova hurt them too. Like she hurt you." I hold out my hand, waiting. Sometimes, I've learned, you have to bring someone in.

Miller blinks rapidly, sniffs, and rolls her sleeves up. "Okay," she says to herself. "Okay," she says to me, taking my hand. Joining us.

Only six of us are in Ritual House today, but it feels full. Inside, the wooden floorboards are bare—evidence of violence scrubbed clean, detritus taken by the FBI. Unlit candles form a circle in the center of the room. In their middle, a heavy iron safe. The one Nova kept in her office. When I join the others, Kane hands us each a robe. They're already wearing them: long sleeves fitted at the wrists and buttoned down the front. A floral pattern embroidered with bright thread into their dark gray wool. Each one different, like a garden.

Miller slides her flannel shirt off, shivering in a tee shirt before pulling the robe on. It takes her a minute to find the sleeves, to fumble with the buttons. "My mother used to wear these. I always wanted one." She smiles at the others.

"You can keep it," Zadie says. "Unless it's still evidence."

Miller shakes her head. "We have your testimonies. I think those matter more to a jury than some woolen robes. We'll be fine."

"So." Deryn twirls in their robe. "What do we do?"

"Well, who wants to lead?" I ask.

We all look at one another, no one stepping forward. There's no potion to chug today. No race to determine who leads the ritual. I don't feel the pull. In fact, I've resolved to draw less attention to myself. To make space for others to rise, and to offer help where needed.

I think of Deryn and Miller, a Fellow and an outsider. A former Anointed and Nova's daughter. I'm glad we included them, but neither volunteer, and they have no reason to. Ritual is new to them. We should allow them to acclimate without pressure.

Zadie or Maeve could do it. They hold hands, but don't step forward. When I returned home, they were the first to welcome me, their hair unbraided. Maeve's in long thick waves, Zadie's a soft puff around her head. The social worker had put them in touch with a therapist. Together, they'd started to process the pain. They invited me and Kane to a group session with them. I think they felt ashamed to tell me, like I'd accuse them of betrayal. But we accepted their offer.

"Kane," Miller says. It hadn't even crossed my mind that he would volunteer. Kane was finished with magic long ago.

Zadie and Maeve look at Miller, surprised at such surety from someone who could barely figure out the robe, who didn't even know she was invited—never participated even once before leaving the Fellowship and donning an outsider uniform.

"No." Kane shakes his head. "I'm the one who caused all this.

It's my fault Ritual House was destroyed. Lark should do it. He's the one who was driven away."

"No, Miller's right," Deryn says. "We wouldn't be here, free from Nova's grip, if you hadn't exposed her. You're the only one who had the courage to leave."

"I waited to leave until I was supposed to," Kane says, reluctance lining his face. "Even though I had a way out. I should've gone sooner."

The damaged spot in the fence, where Calvin, Lilian, and I snuck in. Was that my magic or was it only weak? Maybe Kane had come and gone enough times by then that the fence opened itself to us.

It doesn't matter now.

"You did what you needed to do," I say. "What you believed was right. We all did. But we definitely wouldn't be here if it weren't for you." I walk toward him, take his hands in mine. Razor-thin scars peek out from his woolen sleeves, over the backs of his hands. Marks I made. "Please. We haven't worked magic together in so long." My voice dissolves to a whisper.

"Is this some kind of sex ritual?" Deryn asks. "Because I did not sign up for that."

"No!" Kane and I say at the same time, perhaps too fervently.

"Okay, then, Kane?" They gesture to the center of the room.

"Fine," he says. "But I want it on the record that this is purely a formality. I don't believe that I can do magic any more than I believe in monsters."

"We're not really doing magic," Maeve says, shrugging at Zadie. "We're performing a ritual. Even people who grew up outside the fence perform those."

Kane lights a candle in a tall glass jar. He lights another and another, each strike of the match releasing the scent of sulfur into the air. We're different, all of us. I'm still working through my beliefs. I know I traveled for days across the country in a hatchback with two strangers who became my friends. That I trusted one to help with my discipline and magic. I have the scabs on my back to prove it.

Throughout the quest, my powers didn't work the way I thought they would—didn't always come when I called. But they were there when I really needed them. I haven't used any magic since I fought the monster. I don't have my cage anymore, or my bag of tools. I miss feeling magical, but I'm not sure I want power I have to kill myself for.

These days, I'm trying to focus more on healing than hurting myself. When we got back to Baltimore, I actually asked the social worker if I could see a doctor. It's not that I hate my scars. They exist on a body that's been through a lot. Exertion and discipline. Restriction and touch. Caresses and lips and fire and leather. Power. Loss. I would like to feel some of those again. See if I can't awaken those feelings.

Kane bends over the safe in the center of the circle, turning the dial. Nova never mentioned its existence to the FBI, but I remembered. I might have run from those who tried to help me, but I dragged this safe from its hiding place, today. For this.

It opens easily. The safe was never magic. The door hangs open, propped on its metal side. Heavy, fireproof, it took all four of us Anointed to carry it up here. Kane reaches inside and retrieves a box. Rests it on the lip of the safe and removes the top. Inside, I can see beige folders thick with papers and a pile of worn notebooks. Kane flips through some of the folders before finding something plastic and rectangular, the size of his palm. He looks up at Miller.

She walks quickly toward him, taking the offered card. "This was my father's driver's license." She scrambles through the folder, pulling out papers and photos, tears spilling down her cheeks and into the open box. "His birth certificate and mine. The deed to Druid Hill, title to our car, social security cards—family photos."

She holds the stack to her chest and looks at the ceiling, as if the tears will slide back into their ducts. "It took him years to get us back on the grid after we left, to prove our identities."

"They're yours now." Kane rests a hand on her back. "Like they should've always been."

Miller walks back to her place in the circle and Kane sets the rest of the box aside. When we finish, she'll take it to the FBI for use at trial. For now, we stand around the empty safe.

Kane looks at each of us in turn as he speaks. "We gather to bind Leah 'Nova' Miller. We gather because she cannot keep us apart. She cannot turn us against one another, or separate us from our families. She cannot keep us from our autonomy and future. Leah Miller is a monster who hurt hundreds of people, and today we will make sure that never happens again." He pauses. "You each brought something."

We all nod, picking up the canvas bags at our feet. Kane gestures to the safe. Zadie is the first to step forward. From her bag, she removes a wooden paddle with tiny nails sticking like teeth from the end. It drops into the open safe with a thud. "This is how my partner was forced to show her love. Never again." Zadie bends over and spits on it.

Maeve follows with a rope, rough and thin. As she coils it around her hand, I can see where reddish-brown blood stains the coconut fibers. Can smell the mint it was coated with before digging painfully into sensitive skin. "I was wearing this when they liberated us. Didn't untie it for days after Lark left. Not until I saw the doctor." She drops it and spits into the safe.

Deryn is next. They look sheepish as they offer not a tool, but a deck of cards. I recognize it; a slight gasp escapes me as Deryn opens their box and tips the cards over the safe. They slide out, most falling with a thump onto the growing pile in the safe. A few flutter down.

"I should've known better than to invite you to play cards and drink with us," they say. "I think, on some level, I wanted to know that you weren't the perfect heroes Nova—Leah—always treated you as. And I wanted you to get in trouble. I'm sorry I let anger and jealousy keep me from seeing what was really happening." They drop the cardboard box into the safe and spit on it.

Miller takes Deryn's place. She holds out a large toothy key on an old leather thong—the same shape as the one Nova gave Kane when he left. But the leather on this one is stiff and thin, almost falling apart. "I kept this because I thought I might need to go home someday." It clangs against the safe. She spits on it and returns to her place.

I'm next. The worn branch feels familiar in my hand. Comfortable. I carry it as easily as outsiders carry their phones. Unlike those, Spellslinger is dead—served its purpose. To think, we spent all those years charging it with pain. Magic doesn't have to hurt. In my hand now, it feels like an old piece of wood, soft and dry. Useless.

I drop it. Spit. Rub my hands over Kane's shoulder to signal his turn. He doesn't speak either. Doesn't have to. We all know what the small metal cage in his hand was used for. The keys never went in the safe—they hung in the open of Nova's office, as if we were free to take them anytime. We knew that we would be punished if we dared.

A key used only by others, under supervision. Never by ourselves. I remember the day I convinced Kane it was a good idea to wear the cages, and close my eyes. Listen for the sound of metal against metal. Hear Kane spit. Feel his body press almost flush against mine.

We relax against each other for a moment—not forgetting the ritual, but giving ourselves to it. Embracing because that's what matters. He kisses me with lips that are chapped but gentle. Then Kane picks up a candle from the floor and hands it to me. The black wax liquefies and pools at its top when Kane lights the wick. One by one, he hands us each a black candle, and though I know I'm not using magic, it feels powerful in my hand. Slowly, wax spills down the sides, meeting my fingers.

I close my eyes and breathe deep as more wax drips, gluing my hand to the candle, searing my skin where it hits, but not too hot. Nothing like the burns I carry on my thighs and back. This is warm. Welcome.

"Leah Miller, we bind you." Kane tips his candle, dripping wax into the safe. Normally, this ritual calls for blood—Nova had us cut ourselves when we bound Elder Zephyr before casting him out—but we refuse to spill any more for her. "With these artifacts of our pain, we bind you."

I tip my own candle over the safe, joined by the others. Together, the flames jump and dance, and I feel it again—whatever it is surrounding us. It could be magic, if not the way I'm used to.

"With pieces of ourselves, we bind you." Kane drops his candle. Black wax stains his thumb and forefinger.

Zadie drops hers, then Maeve. Inside, the wooden paddle catches fire.

"With fire, we bind you."

Deryn and Miller drop their candles. The flames catch the oiled rope, climbing the sides of the safe. The cards crinkle and blacken. I drop mine in, before the fire can escape. We take one another's hands, pressing warm wax into the others' palms.

"Leah Miller, we bind you," Kane says, louder. "With these artifacts of our pain, we bind you."

"With pieces of ourselves," I say, joining him, "we bind you."

All of us speak in unison as the flames rise. "With fire, we bind you."

"Leah Miller, we bind you! With these artifacts of our pain—"

I gasp as the others go on. Catching my breath.

"With pieces of ourselves, we bind you!"

Kane and Miller squeeze my hands, hot and sweaty.

"With fire—"

I feel the flames as if they're burning through my chest. Spreading.

"Leah Miller—"

A multitude of emotions surges through us—grief and love and anger and determination—as if we are all connected.

"—we bind you!"

The edges of the room blur.

"—pieces of ourselves, we—"

Zadie screams like I've only seen someone do while giving birth. She doubles over, not letting go, her words continuing as if she has two mouths. Tears stain Miller's face as she chants through them.

"With fire, we bind you!"

"Leah Miller—"

I inhale as if the air is diving down my throat. Our words ringing in my ears.

"—we bind you!"

Kane breaks the circle and kicks the door of the safe closed, smothering the flames. He spins the dial. Looks up at me wide-eyed. I want to ask if he felt that—whatever it was. Not pain magic, but something different. I turn my hand over and examine my palm. A familiar itch tickles its center.

Together, silently, we wrap our robes around the safe and haul it outside to where Calvin and Lilian have dug a hole. We lower Nova deep into the earth and bury her memory, ready to face Leah Miller in court. To bind her.

I stuff my hands in my pockets and help clean up. Zadie and Maeve look fine. Miller, refreshed. I make me way to Deryn, who still stares at the ground where we buried the safe.

"Are you okay?" I ask quietly, helping them out of their robe.

They nod, looking at their hands. "I think so. But did you—? No."

I purse my lips. Give them a knowing look. "Yes, I did."

"What was that?" Their eyes light up—somewhere between wonder and terror. They exhale. A tremor of fear or excitement. I know that feeling.

"I'm not sure," I mutter. "But don't say anything to Kane. He

doesn't want it. Whatever"—I hesitate before using the word—
"power we experienced was not the magic we're used to. It felt—"

"Good?" Deryn smiles. "It felt good, Lark."

"Yeah." I return their smile. "It did, but it wasn't like the magic
I'm used to—I gave all my pain to the monster. According to Nova's teachings, I should need more pain to recharge my powers, but
whatever I felt during the ritual didn't come from my body, my
flesh. It came from inside? Somewhere deep. Less like I was flexing
a muscle and more like I was experiencing an emotion. Grief and
anger. Peace."

"I felt that too," they say quickly, as if the feelings might escape.
"I didn't really know what to do with it, though. It sort of flowed
through me, and I let it."

I nod, catching Calvin's eye across the way. I want to talk to him
again before we leave, want to plan our date. But not before sewing
this up with Deryn. I'm giving this siblings thing a better try.

"I think, maybe, we've been doing magic wrong—especially by
limiting it to those of us Nova deemed worthy. Once we're more
settled in—after the trial—I want to try a few new things. Get a
feel for it. If I can figure it out, I'd like to teach you. That is, if you
want to learn."

"Absolutely," they say eagerly, then bite their lip. "I mean, that
would be cool. I've always wanted to learn."

"Good." I smile and rest my hand on their shoulder. Deryn
does the same in return and the same new feeling flows between
us. An even exchange.

33

CALVIN / MUCH LATER

Lark walks with me into the convention center. The ConCom wasn't happy that I reneged on my panels and the cosplay ball, but offered me the chance to make it up to them at their sister event in DC. If I brought Lark.

I think they wanted him to dress up. He didn't want to, but he still looks like an Elven-king, even in jeans and a tee shirt. Another one of mine; this one says:

No arsenal strapped to his back or leather harness to hold his potions and supplies, but damn if he doesn't look beautiful. His hair hangs long over his shoulders, golden and shiny, a slight wave taking hold in the strands now that they're not woven into place.

He flips all of it over the left side of his head, constantly changing the part and playing with it now that he can. "People are looking at us," he says quietly, and he's right. Usually, they're only looking at me, but I'm happy to share the spotlight.

Except for our clothes, we look almost the same. Of course, I'm wearing Thranduil's wig. His long shimmering robe and crown. "They are," I say. "But we don't have to stop for them. Want to walk the floor?" I nod at the rows of vendors.

"Sure," Lark says, moving toward a booth that's enclosed by tall metal racks. Clothes emblazoned with fan art and humor hang from them. He finds his exact shirt and points to it with a smile. Says, "It's a shame they don't allow weapons inside. Would've made my outfit."

I'm about to tell him it's for everyone's safety when he gasps and dashes to another stall. He's found a hoodie with a dozen pockets, inside and out. Lark holds it in front of him, admiring its utility and warmth.

"Isn't this what you call dressing up? Cosplay."

I nearly choke when I see what the sweatshirt says on the back. "Cosplay handler, huh?"

"Someone needs to support you." He tries it on, stuffing his hands into the front pocket.

I step closer and slide my hands into the same pocket, clasping his. "We're in the outside world now, Lark. Do you think you can handle me without magic?"

He bites his lip. Closes his eyes. Kisses me right in the middle of this vendor's booth while I'm dressed like the Elvenking. My hands warm in his. Tingle. A feeling that's born where we touch and spreads through my body like stepping into a heated building from the snow.

He pulls back, and I watch him take the hoodie to the counter and pay, using his new bank card with the assistance of the vendor. They're patient with him—everyone here knows who Lark is. He thanks the person, then walks off, looking over his shoulder as if to say, "Catch me if you can."

I hurry along after him, chasing whatever he just did to me. Whatever *feeling*. Desire, care, lust, love—I can't put my finger on it. "Lark!" I call, looking for him. He has a cell phone now but is terrible at using it. If I lose him, it could take hours to find him, for him to find his way back to me, the car, his new home. He, Kane, and Deryn moved into one of the houses in Woodberry; apparently, there's a park nearby where people walk their dogs. And now that Druid Hill is a park again, the surrounding neighborhoods are flourishing.

I stand still. Straighten up as tall as I can manage. I'm easy to spot on the convention floor because of the number of people who stop and ask to take my picture. I don't answer them, turning in place. Looking, my heart beating faster and faster until—

He stands square across from me, a single hand pressed against his lips. I tilt my head and the people around us blur as if I'm looking through a lens focused only on Lark. Then, he blows me a kiss, and I feel it. I feel a breeze where there should be none. The lights in the convention center dim and I light up. People gasp as my robes flutter and move, as if taken by a wind machine. They sparkle under the unnatural bubbles of light that swirl around me.

Cameras raise into the air as dozens of people rush to film the event and, like that, it stops. The overhead lights flicker on and the air around me stills. My costume falls back into place. Through the rush of people, I glimpse Lark smiling. He winks, watching as I lap up the attention.

"Is there some kind of rig—"

"Was it planned with the—"

"Can I—"

"How did you do that?"

The answer is that I didn't. I took a chance on my wildest dreams, chased Lark's magic, and discovered it was cruel and harmful. That I wanted so badly for it to be real, that I enabled him, hurt him. Ignored Lilian and almost got Kane killed. Lark says he gave all his magic up during the fight. That he left it on the road, and that he wasn't willing to hurt himself to see if it would come back to him. But as I hold his eyes across the crowd, I can tell he's found a new magic. Something that lives inside him. Something that doesn't hurt.

ACKNOWLEDGMENTS

Second books are weird. Like Meadowlark, I had help and support on this quest, even though it often felt like I was pushing ahead on my own. My deepest thanks to those who supported me with their words and love, time and energy.

To the places that opened their doors to me. To the Enoch Pratt Library's Central Branch, for its beautiful ceilings and long wooden writing tables. To The Bun Shop for spicy hot cocoa and being open until 3:00 a.m. Not to my apartment building, which inspired Feelings about walk-ups.

To the friends who kept me company. To Suzanne, who is a huge Tolkien nerd. To Aleksandra, who is a prolific reader. To Faith, who always encourages me to write my id. To Marianne, for her vibrancy. To Alyssa, for you-know-what. To Sarah, my co-conspirator.

To those who make me whole. To my family for their unconditional love. To my friends, for their lights in even the darkest times. To the experienced authors who were welcoming and honest. To my communities, for reminding me I am not writing into the void.

To those who had their hands all over this thing. To my agent, Jennifer Udden, for her smarts and reassurance. To the whole New Leaf Literary crew for their insight. To my editor, Carl Engle-Laird, who never told me this novel was too horny. To the wonderful folks at Tordotcom Publishing, without whom this book wouldn't exist: Oliver Dougherty, Mordicai Knode, Lauren Anesta, Amanda Melfi, Jamie Stafford-Hill, Christine Foltzer, Melanie Sanders, and Irene Gallo.

To the stories that inspired this one—but mostly to the transformative works and communities surrounding them. To Drarry but not to JKR. To Aragorn/Legolas and long-haired blond mean Daddy Thranduil but not to JRRT. Thank you.